Marvellously untouched by twelve years of formal education, Sylvian Hamilton has been, at different times, a secretary, mother, lexicographer, journalist, farmer, second-hand bookseller and antiques dealer. She is a devoted *Star Trek* fan. Since arthritis clipped her wings, she spends much of her time at home, a tiny cottage in the Scottish border country, with a very patient husband, two cats and about five thousand books. *The Bone-Pedlar* is the first in a series of novels.

By Sylvian Hamilton

The Bone-Pedlar
The Pendragon Banner

THE
BONE-PEDLAR

Sylvian Hamilton

ORION

An Orion paperback

First published in Great Britain in 2000
by Orion
This paperback edition published in 2001
by Orion Books Ltd,
Orion House, 5 Upper St Martin's Lane,
London WC2H 9EA

A CIP catalogue record for this
book is available from the British Library.

ISBN 0 75284 423 7

Printed and bound in Great Britain by
Clays Ltd, St Ives plc

With love to Patrick, prop-and-stay; to Deborah, beloved daughter and world's greatest hypnotherapist; and to my dear son Steven, Cathie his wife, and their children.

With thanks to John, for his help and encouragement; and to Jane and Cass, for nudging me in the right direction. Thanks also to the staff of Duns Library, who manage against hard odds to get many of the books I need.

And with affection and gratitude to Christine Green, best agent in the world!

Chapter 1

In the crypt of the abbey church at Hallowdene, the monks were boiling their bishop.

He had been a man of exemplary piety, whose eventual canonisation was a certainty, or at least a strong probability, and they were taking no chances. Over the bishop's deathbed, the calculating eyes of the sacristan and the almoner had accurately weighed up the advantages of a splendidly profitable set of skeletal relics, and Bishop Alain was barely cold before he was eviscerated, dismembered, and simmering in the largest pot the monastery kitchen could furnish.

'Isn't it a bit, – well, sort of *hasty*?' the kitchener protested, when ordered to hack his bishop limb from limb. 'You sure e's dead?'

'Of course he is,' snapped the almoner.

'Only I thought I eard im sigh.'

There was a flurry of panicky activity as the almoner laid his ear to the unmoving episcopal bosom, and the sacristan peered uneasily at the dulled eyes and fallen jaw of the revered corpse.

'Get on with it,' said the sacristan impatiently. The kitchener went to work with his knives and a cleaver borrowed from the butcher.

'In the Holy Land,' said old Brother Maurice, who had been there and never let anyone forget it, 'it was the custom to boil crusaders, them as wanted their bones shipped home for burial. But in the case of a *holy* body, we'd put it in an anthill. The ants'd pick the bones to a pearly whiteness. Truly beautiful. When you have to boil them,' he stared critically at the reeking cauldron, 'they go all brown.'

The youngest novice, who had been a favourite of the bishop, blew his nose on his sleeve and dabbed his eyes with the hem. 'It doesn't seem respectful,' he said.

'Who asked you?' demanded the sacristan. 'You can clear off out of this. Go and bang the dormitory mats outside!'

The boy mustered a flimsy courage to protest that a lay brother had banged the mats only that morning, but all that got him was a clip round the ear from the jittery sacristan, and he scurried off, snivelling.

'All the same,' said Brother Maurice, 'we probably shouldn't be doing this, not right away. We ought to wait a while. The new bishop . . .'

The others looked shiftily at one another. There was no new bishop yet, nor likely to be for a long time, what with the Interdict, and His Grace King John so intransigent. But eventually there would be another bishop, who might very well take a dim view of them turning his predecessor into relics so precipitately. As it was, they'd get plenty of stick from the other religious houses in the diocese. It was sheer luck that the bishop had dropped dead at Hallowdene. He could have done it anywhere during his visitations, and those crafty Austin buggers, next on the road at Carderford, would have had him parcelled out among their fellow canons before you could say knife, with not even a knuckle-bone for the Benedictines.

'Well, it's too late now,' said the almoner briskly, peering into the greasy steam. 'How long does it usually take?'

'Hours,' said Brother Maurice. 'All day. And all night to cool off, if you don't want to burn your fingers.'

The almoner's high-bridged Norman nose flared with distaste, though whether at the greasy kitchen reek in the crypt or the thought of the grisly task still to come was not evident. But the abbey felt hard-done-by in the matter of relics, having lost its chief treasure, the priceless girdle of the Blessed Virgin Mary, to thieves as long ago as the year 1160 almost fifty years before.

*

In his private chamber, the abbot, who was keeping a discreet distance from the goings-on in the crypt in case at some future date it might be politic to assert his disapproval, was closeted with his secretary, discussing that very matter – the pilfered Holy Girdle.

'*I* think,' the abbot's secretary said, 'that there's no hope of getting it back now, My Lord. That man of yours has failed.'

The abbot sighed. 'If he has failed, Petronius,' he said, in his weak whistly old man's voice, 'he would have reported back to us.'

'Why should he, My Lord? He was paid in advance, half his fee, and a very shocking sum it was, too. I think he simply pouched our gold and went off laughing at us. He never intended even to try and steal our relic back.'

'He was very strongly recommended,' the abbot said wearily. He had been fielding his secretary's arguments all afternoon and had just about had enough. 'My Brother in Christ, the Archbishop of York himself, spoke highly of him. He is no trickster. He was employed on a similar commission a few years ago, for the nuns of Sheppey, when a wicked Greek priest stole their Holy Foreskin. This man Straccan got it back for them.' So *there*, he thought with satisfaction. His secretary's opinions were too often exercised, the abbot was heartily sick of them; sick too of the man's dirty bitten fingernails and the coarse black hairs sprouting from his nostrils and ears.

'It has been almost a year, My Lord,' sniffed his secretary. '*I* think hope is lost, along with the relic and our gold.'

'I don't believe so,' said the abbot stubbornly. He shifted his thin old feet in the silver bowl of warm rose-scented water. Petronius, seizing a gold-fringed towel from where it warmed beside the fire, knelt and patted the abbatical feet dry, easing them into lambswool socks. The old man sighed with pleasure, eyeing his secretary with more tolerance. 'It is no simple task,' he said patiently, accepting the cup of spiced Rhenish which Petronius offered. 'The thieves of Winchester guard the Holy Girdle with tenacious devotion, all the more so because they stole it and know they have no right to it. It is kept under lock and key. All these years they have feared our regaining it. Straccan cannot just walk in, pick it up and walk out again with it.'

'I wonder our Blessed Lady has not smitten them,' muttered the secretary pettishly, hanging the damp towel by the fire again.

'She has eternal patience,' said the abbot.

'*She* may, My Lord, but we who are only human would be glad of an end to this affair. *I* think we should send to enquire for this Straccan. Where does he come from?'

'I don't know. York bade him, and so he came to us.'

'Then we should send to His Grace of York to ask where we may find the fellow.'

'Not now,' said the abbot. 'The weather is treacherous. There will be snow. Look at the sky.'

It was an unpleasant sky, the massed low slate-coloured clouds hazed with a dirty threatening yellow.

'A swift rider could reach York before the snow,' Petronius suggested.

'And be snowed in until spring thaw, running up bills at our charges for food and drink,' said the abbot. 'No. We will give Straccan more time.'

'As you say, My Lord. But *I* think—'

'To the devil with what you think,' snapped the abbot. 'I've heard enough of what you think! We will wait.'

Petronius shrugged. 'Of course, My Lord.' He picked up the footbowl and carried it carefully to the window, tossing the water out in a gleaming arc. A squawk of surprise came from below, where a gardener was working. Petronius leaned out and gazed down. The gardener had been tying up plants and fragile branches against the coming storm.

'*I* think,' said Petronius, without thinking, 'we should have put in more pear trees this autumn. Twelve was not enough. Two or even three dozen would have been better.'

The abbot glared at his secretary's back with loathing.

The subject of their discussion was at that moment slinking – there was no other word for it – down a slushy back alley which led to one of Winchester's quieter brothels. The Two Bells was not the sort of place rowdier young men frequented. It was almost respectable, in its way, patronised by merchants and burgesses, and the occasional shamefaced monk. The abbey was just round the corner, its back wall easy to nip over, and after all a monk was a man like any other.

Snow had been falling all day, and kept all but the loneliest or most ardent at home. There was little chance of anyone noticing him but Richard Straccan was relieved to reach the Two Bells without meeting anybody. He pushed the door open and stepped into the warm dimly lit comforting fug. His entry caused a few grins and some raised eyebrows, but men had better things to do than stare at the newcomer. The bitter wind had whipped tears from his eyes and he wiped them on his sleeve as he glanced round, spotting his servant, Hawkan Bane, in the corner by the fire, a cheerful plump girl on his knee and a leather mug in his free hand. Seeing Straccan, Bane whispered something in his wench's ear before gently tipping her off his lap. Laughing, she sauntered into the kitchen with a fine rolling sway of hips that drew all eyes.

Straccan sat down. Bane's girl returned with another mug of ale and two bowls of steaming pottage which she set on the board before them, giggling as she looked curiously at Straccan.

'Good lass,' said Bane, patting her ample bottom. 'Put it on my slate, eh? I'll see you later.'

'Put that on the slate too, will you?' Straccan asked. 'It's all right for you! I don't even get enough to eat in that bloody place!' He fished his spoon from its case on his belt and set to hungrily.

'How's it going?' Bane asked.

'Badly. It's been a sod of a job all along. Ten months we've been here and no chance of getting anywhere near the girdle. They guard it day and night. And now, would you believe it, just when I'd got something worked out, nice and neat, it all goes to hell in a handcart.'

'What d'you mean?'

Straccan drained his mug. 'They've sold it,' he said bitterly. 'The abbot has sold the relic to the King of France.'

'Shit,' said Bane. 'You mean it's gone?'

'Not yet. King Philip's man's at the abbey, he can't get away in this snowstorm. But they're supposed to hand the relic over to him at midnight.'

'That's torn it,' said Bane. 'Now what do we do?'

Straccan leaned across the table so that only Bane could hear him. 'Can you be ready tonight? It'll be a bugger travelling in this. Still, they won't be able to get after us for a while.'

'We're leaving tonight?'

'If you can have the horses at the stream two hours before midnight,' Straccan said.

Bane grinned wickedly. 'Course I can. All's not lost, then?' His face changed suddenly. 'We ain't going to ambush the French king's agent, I hope?'

'Not unless we have to,' Straccan said. 'No, touch wood.' He slapped the palm of his right hand hard on the oak table. 'I've got an idea.'

Chapter 2

The haggling was over, the bargain struck, the gold and silver counted (twice), bagged and tied, and locked in the abbot's strongbox. The two old men, the abbot and King Philip's agent, sipped wine, talking of this and that: the affairs of the world, their kings and lords, acquaintances in common, current scandal – mild and not so mild – and, more importantly, the blizzard that had raged for the past two days with considerable loss of life and, worse, destruction of property.

'Bring us wine, Brother,' the abbot had said, 'and some of those little savoury pastries.' Then, to his guest, as the kitchener hurried off, 'The chapel is in use until midnight. We cannot take the girdle from the altar until then.'

The visitor sniffed at his medicinal pomander. Half the community was down with a vicious winter cold, fourteen monks ill enough to be tucked up in the infirmary, full now to overflowing, with pallets having to be set up in the adjoining still-room and storerooms. The infirmarian himself was sick unto death and his very junior assistant in charge, while the rest of the brethren coughed and sneezed all over the place.

The abbot's parlour was small and cosy. An elegant brazier glowed, warming the room. Heavy hangings at the door and a snug shutter at the window kept out the November wind complaining and shrieking outside. The abbot's feet, in warm knitted socks, were toasting on a foot warmer tucked under his fur-lined over-robe. Pink plump and contented, he sat quietly, occasionally eyeing his visitor with an expression of smug satisfaction. Both men were pleased, the visitor because he'd paid less for the Girdle of the Blessed Virgin than he'd expected, the abbot because he'd got more than he'd thought he would. The hangings stirred slightly as gusts of draught raced down the passage outside but failed to penetrate this sanctum. Drowsy, they soaked up the warmth. King Philip's man like a dark and wrinkled basking lizard, Abbot William a cosseted, overfed lapdog.

A shaggy Saxon head, its tonsure much overgrown, appeared round the side of the curtain at the infirmary door.

'Is he dead yet?'

'Not quite.'

'Right then, shove over. Let the dog see the rabbit.'

Brother Sylvestris, elbowed roughly aside by Brother Witleof, permitted his annoyance to show.

'Oh, sorry,' said Brother Witleof. 'Did I hurt you?' His tone and cheerful grin made it clear that he couldn't care less, and Brother Sylvestris made a visible effort to appear unconcerned.

'It's nothing,' he said. 'Hurry up, do! There isn't much time.'

Brother Witleof looked undersized and almost lost in the voluminous habit hastily borrowed (against the rule) from a snoring, oblivious but much larger fellow monk in the dormitory. His own habit was saturated with blood from the pig-killing earlier that day, when he fell over a bucket of the stuff. He fumbled in the breast of the robe and took out what looked like a piece of old rope and placed it reverently on the breast of the dying man.

'Do you want to pray, or something? he asked.

Brother Sylvestris, about to do just that, thought better of it, shook his head and tucked his cold hands up his sleeves.

'No? Oh well, please yourself,' Witleof said. 'I'll say a few words, then, shall I? Does it matter what?'

Encouraged by another shake of the junior infirmarian's head, he clapped his palms together, gazed upward and prayed. 'Holy Blessed Virgin, see us here below! This is Brother Alfred who's dying! And we've borrowed your holy relic, your blessed girdle, before it's taken away from here. We know it can restore our brother to vigour—'

'She won't listen to you,' snapped Sylvestris.

'Why not?'

'You're not praying in Latin!'

'That doesn't matter,' said Witleof irritably. 'Surely God's Mother understands English?'

'The language of pigs,' hissed the Norman Sylvestris, out of patience. 'It's disrespectful.'

'Bollocks,' retorted the Saxon Witleof. The two glowered unmonastically at each other over the body of the wheezing infirmarian, and Norman fist was on its way to Saxon nose when the dying man suddenly sneezed and his eyes snapped open.

'Brother Alfred!' Sylvestris grasped the sick man's hand fiercely. 'Alfred, it's me. Sylvestris! Are you cured?'

Brother Alfred blinked, sneezed again, and stared fixedly at Brother Sylvestris. A gush of blood erupted from his mouth. The eyes lost their shine, the jaw sagged.

'Oh, bugger,' said Brother Witleof miserably. 'It didn't work. He's dead.'

'Typical,' muttered Sylvestris. 'Just like a bloody Saxon! After all we've done for him.' He swung round in alarm as the hanging over the doorway was jerked aside and someone entered. Sylvestris relaxed when he saw the newcomer was only a lay brother.

Brother Arnold, whose face and grubby torn habit were bloodstained and from whose nose blood ran freely, shrugged apologetically, dabbing at the flow with a sodden handful of tow.

'What happened to you?' Witleof asked.

'A bit of a disagreebet,' mumbled Arnold. 'It wote stop bleedig.'

'Lie down,' snapped Sylvestris. 'There's a pallet over in the corner.'

'No,' said Witleof. 'You should put a cold key down his back.'

'Or a horseshoe,' offered Arnold helpfully. 'By old bub used to use a horseshoe.'

'Wait a minute,' said Sylvestris. 'I'll get the medicine cupboard key. Brother,' he whispered urgently to Witleof, 'take the – that – the thing. Take it back, now, at once!'

'Righto.' Witleof took the girdle from the still breast of the infirmarian, and at that moment Brother Arnold fainted clean away, falling against Witleof who dropped the girdle and tried to support him, but the larger man was too heavy and slid relentlessly to the flagstones.

'Help me get him on the bed,' Witleof gasped.

Sylvestris took the shoulders, Witleof the ankles, and between them they heaved their unconscious brother on to the straw mattress.

'*Will* you get back to the chapel before they come for the girdle?' Sylvestris straightened his habit and brushed at its skirts. 'Take it, and *hurry*!'

'I am hurrying,' Witleof scowled. He groped on the floor where the candlelight cast deep shadows until his hand closed on the relic. Thrusting it into the bosom of his borrowed habit he disappeared behind the door curtain. Sylvestris listened to his sandalled feet clapping along the stone passage until the opening and closing of a distant door cut off the sound.

Brother Arnold groaned and tried to sit up. Sylvestris pushed him down. 'Keep still, do,' he said. 'I'll get the key.' Blood from Arnold's nose splashed on to the junior Infirmarian's sleeve and he pulled his arm away, annoyed.

'I cart lie dowd like this,' Arnold objected, struggling up. 'I'll drowd id by ode blood!'

'Well, sit up, then, tilt your head back and breathe through your mouth. I'll get some ice, that'll stop the bleeding. And some water to clean you up. You look like a battlefield.'

Outside in the stable yard he broke the ice in the horse trough and put some pieces in a small sack. On his way back he filled a jug with water from the butt in the passage outside the infirmary door, where the water was doing its best to freeze and would succeed before long, the surface pleating and wrinkling inwards from the edge.

Sylvestris pushed through the curtain again and surveyed his domain. There was Brother Alfred's corpse, staring straight at him. With an exclamation Sylvestris set the jug down and with icy aching fingers closed the dead man's eyes. They popped open again as soon as he took his hand away, '*Merde*,' he muttered and closed the lids again, holding them shut for some moments before letting go. This time they stayed shut. Sylvestris turned from the bloody dead to the bleeding living, only to find the pallet empty. Brother Arnold had gone. Turning back to the corpse, Sylvestris saw that one eye had opened again, and Brother Alfred appeared to be winking at him.

Bells chimed. Sandalled feet slapped on stone floors. A quiet rap at the door was followed by a billowing gust of chill and the sacristan, Brother Euphemius, wiping his red and swollen nose on his sleeve. 'Midnight, Abbot,' he croaked.

'So it is,' said the abbot with a reproving scowl. 'Fetch the girdle.'

King Philip's man stood up and stretched and yawned. 'I did not look to spend another night here. This damned storm!'

'Men will be out at first light,' said the abbot, 'to cut and haul away the fallen trees and start clearing the snow. The gale is dropping. As soon as the road is clear you will be able to leave. You will be able to sail tomorrow, if the wind's fair.'

A tap at the door and the sacristan entered, holding a silver casket. Through the opened door the perishing cold leaped into their well of warmth, and the two old men shivered.

'There you are,' said the abbot, taking the casket and placing it in the Frenchman's hands. 'The Blessed Virgin's Girdle is yours, My Lord de Mortai. Or rather, King Philip's.'

The Frenchman turned the key and opened the casket, taking out what looked like a piece of old rope. 'It doesn't look like much,' he said. 'What's it made of, horsehair?'

'Camel hair, we believe, My Lord,' said the abbot. 'Ah, may I see it, just once more, before you close the casket? You understand, we would not sell so great a treasure except that our need was great.'

De Mortai nodded. He knew of the ruinous lawsuit Winchester had lost to a neighbouring nunnery after a long and vicious fight, and the massive damages the abbey must now pay, forfeiting lands and treasure to do so. He held the casket out and the abbot lifted the girdle from its silken bed. As he did so, an odd expression crossed his face and was swiftly gone. He touched the relic to his lips, put it quickly down again, closed the lid and handed the box back to the Frenchman.

'If you wish, you can leave it locked in my strongbox here, overnight,' he offered.

De Mortai grinned. Not likely, he thought, but coughed politely, saying, 'Thank you, My Lord, but no. I shall sleep with it under my pillow tonight and every night until I place it in King Philip's hands. I must ask you to tell no one about the sale until I am safely back in Paris. Were it known that I carried such a treasure, robbers would try to take it.'

'Of course,' said the abbot. 'Then I will summon your servants and bid you goodnight.'

When the count had gone to his bedchamber, Abbot William rounded on the sacristan. 'What have you done with it? You can't think we can get away with it! Whatever possessed you to do such a thing?'

'What, My Lord?' The sacristan looked astonished and, the Abbot realised, perfectly innocent.

'Oh, never mind. I am weary and,' he sneezed, 'I think I've caught a cold.'

The sacristan was all concern, the odd little outburst quite forgotten as he ran for hot stones for the abbot's bed and hot wine with a sleeping potion to get him through the night. It would never do if he wasn't well enough to see the Count of Mortai off tomorrow. It would look like sulking.

Sweating in his bed, rising fever making him light-headed, the abbot remembered the feel of the girdle in his hands, rougher than it should be, almost prickly, heavier than before and not quite the right colour – a brighter *younger*-looking brown. Someone had stolen the real one and the King of France was getting a forgery.

Still, thought the abbot as the first thick soft veils of sleep began to cover him, he's never handled the real girdle, so it's very unlikely he will suspect. Blessed Mother of God, don't let anyone find out!

'It was a clumsy job,' Straccan said. 'I had no time at all at the end, such a rush, the damned thing sold out from under me. It was the only thing I could think of on the spur of the moment, when I heard Sylvestris and Witleof planning to borrow the relic before it was handed over to the Frenchman. Oh, God!' He knelt by a stream, bare to the waist, splashing icy water over his bloody face and chest. He had discarded the bloodstained habit and donned breeches and boots.

'Is all this blood yours?' Bane rolled up the soiled robe, weighing it down with stones in the stream.

'Some of it. The rest is pig's blood. They killed a pig yesterday.' Straccan was shivering hard. 'I had little bladders of blood to use in case my nose stopped bleeding.'

'How'd you make it bleed?'

'I had to pick a quarrel with poor silly Brother Odo. He swung at me and got my nose and I kicked him in the balls. I think he was still crawling towards the infirmary when I left. I fell over something soft.'

'Here. Put this on.' Bane produced a crumpled rolled-up shirt and a thick knitted jerkin. Straccan pulled the clothes on, carefully tucking the relic in a leather pouch between the woolly and the hide jacket he put on over all.

'We'll go along in the stream as far as we can,' he said. 'Then out and back south past the abbey. If they're looking for us, they won't be looking that way, and if they use dogs, the stream'll throw them off. They might not even realise I've switched the girdles; not for a while anyway, if we're lucky. It would be a help if it snowed some more. Cover our tracks.' His teeth were chattering.

Bane silently offered an unstoppered bottle.

Straccan drank, gasped, shuddered and drank again. 'Have you got any food?'

Bane produced bread and cold meat, shouldered his pack, and they set off, splashing along in the stream while Straccan chewed and swallowed. His throat felt sore. 'This will give me belly ache,' he said. Ice at the stream's edge crackled and clattered. He clenched his chattering teeth. 'How far to the horses?'

'More than a mile. Can you make it?'

'I'd better. I doubt you could carry me.' He sneezed violently several times. 'Bugger! I've got their sodding cold!'

It began to snow.

Chapter 3

The wicket shot aside with a sharp crack and through the aperture two pairs of eyes fixed upon each other. The man outside the gate saw a round pink velvety face with big brown eyes and a small pursed mouth framed in a starched white wimple and black veil. Dame Laurencia saw a lean face, still tinged a faded bronze from long-ago foreign suns, with flint-coloured eyes round which fans of pale creases showed sharp against the tan. The man had a wide thin mouth, square chin, straight nose and cropped sunbleached hair beneath a russet cap which he now tugged off. They stared at each other until Straccan held up a lead disc, no bigger than a penny, on which was stamped Prioress Hermengarde's seal.

The nun smiled and nodded. 'Wait,' she said.

The wicket snapped shut and Straccan heard her footsteps receding. He stuffed his bonnet down the front of his dusty jacket, rubbed a hand over the stubble on top of his head then turned and stroked the nose and neck of his horse. Presently he heard feet again. Bolts were pulled back and the gate creaked open.

'Come in.' Two nuns now: the rabbity gatekeeper and another, tall thin and pale like a scraped bone. Also a servingman, a groom by the look and smell of him.

The pale nun said, 'Martin will take your horse. You have Mother's token?' He held it up again. She looked at it suspiciously. 'Mother Hermengarde died last autumn,' she said. 'Mother Rohese is prioress now. She will see you.'

Inside the gate they scattered in different directions; the gatekeeper to her tiny room over the gate, the horse led one way, the man another, across the cobbled yard where three lay sisters laboured at washtubs, bony red elbows going up and down as they laughed and chattered, openly staring at the man, splashes flying and their sacking aprons soaked.

Through a door, along a dark flagged passage. Straccan sniffed at the unpleasantly familiar smells of damp, incense, candlewax and cooking fish. The nunnery, he noticed, was much cleaner than any house of monks – everything washed and scoured, including the ladies, to within an inch of their lives. Monks cleaned what showed, dusted what could be seen, leaving festering corners full of grease and dirt, cobwebs behind curtains, dead rats under furniture, scummy residue between flagstones. And they smelled of stale sweat. Nuns smelled of nothing, a sterile sanctity. There was a distant thin musical thread of women's voices chanting, piercingly pure. Black-clad nuns flitted purposefully along the passages like enthusiastic bats.

Another door. The nun knocked, a voice responded within and they entered the small bright room, early afternoon sun spilling golden through two lancet windows behind the Prioress's chair. Prioress Rohese was short and sturdy with ginger eyebrows and instantly recognisable Angevin features. Straccan sighed. Another of the old king's bastards. Old Henry had done his best for them, those he knew about, and now they popped up everywhere, always secure in positions of authority and influence. Straccan supposed they had to start somewhere further down their various ladders, but whenever he encountered any of them, there they were at the top.

'I am Mother Rohese.'

He bent one knee and kissed the ring on the small square practical hand held out to him, feeling the battery of eyes on his bared head and the stubble filling the still-obvious tonsure.

'I am Straccan,' he said. 'May I see my daughter?

'Certainly, Sir Richard. Dame Januaria will fetch her. Please, sit down.'

The tall nun left the room and another slipped in to take her place.

'Wine,' said the prioress. The nun opened a small wall-cupboard and brought out a pewter jug and two clay beakers.

'Is she well?' Straccan asked.

'She is, praise God.'

The door opened and Dame Januaria ushered in a child, small for her ten years, a little bundle of plain bunchy wadmal gown with bright hair escaping from a grey hood. Very dark blue eyes under gull-wing eyebrows. She slid a quick sideways look at Straccan as she bowed to the prioress.

'Gilla,' said her father taking a deep breath, longing to pick her up and hug her, 'have you forgotten me?'

They sat together in the guest parlour, sharing a sticky handful of marchpane from Straccan's pocket. Gilla's legs swung; one hand held the sweet, the other, small and warm and dry, held her father's hand tightly.

'Where have you been?' she asked.

'Oh, to Winchester and Hallowdene and home again.'

'I thought you were coming weeks ago.'

'I know, sweetheart, I thought so too. But I was ill, stuck in bed in a wretched little village.'

'Are you well now?' The blue eyes examined him anxiously.

'Oh yes. It was just a bad cold.'

'Will you stay at home now?'

'For a while. Would you like to come home to Stirrup with me for a few weeks?'

'Yes please!' The small face was transfigured by a brilliant smile, for a moment so like her dead mother that Straccan felt an unbearable stab of pain and remembered loss.

'I will arrange it with Mother Rohese,' he said.

'Father?'

'What, sweetheart?'

'You didn't really think I'd forgotten you, did you?'

'No, not really.'

'I prayed for you all the time. I told Our Lady all about you. I

bent a penny to her for you. Well, Dame Mahaut bent it for me
but it was my own penny.'

'It worked.'

'Not properly,' the child said severely, 'or you wouldn't have
caught a cold. Father . . .'

'What, love?'

'Do you think it might have been a bad penny?'

In the Prioress's parlour once more, after Gilla had gone to supper
too full of marchpane and excitement to eat it, Straccan and
Mother Rohese met each other's steady assessing gaze. The
prioress made up her mind quickly. No fool, she thought. A
careful man – intelligent, discreet – he'll do.

'First, as to Devorgilla,' Mother Rohese said, 'she is well, as you
have seen. She is happy here. She is not alone; we have three other
little girls. They play and laugh and get up to the usual sorts of
mischief. Have you decided whether she is to stay here, become a
novice and take her vows in this house?'

'No,' said Straccan. 'She is only ten years old. I won't commit
her to religion yet. Later on, she can choose whether to stay or
leave.'

The prioress's arched eyebrows might have indicated disapproval, or might not. 'At what age do you consider she will have
the good sense and experience to make this judgement for herself,
Sir Richard?'

'My contract with Prioress Hermengarde stipulates that Gilla
stays here until she is twelve. Paid for,' he added pointedly, 'in full
with the jawbone of Saint Luke on your altar, an authenticated
relic of great price.'

'Of course, I am not disputing that, Sir Richard; you misunder-
stand. I only wish you to consider Devorgilla's future, the future
she would have in our community. Security and the prospect of
high office are not to be discounted. Her companions, you see,
have their futures settled. Two will join the community here. The
third is betrothed and will leave us next year to be married.

18

Devorgilla is neither one thing nor the other. I believe she is aware of this ... limbo.'

He had misjudged her, thought she wanted Gilla for her house – a well-endowed novice who mustn't be let slip through those capable fingers. But she cared about the child. Had observed. Had considered. It merited his respect.

'Thank you,' he said. 'I will think about it. I'm coming again next month. I want to take her home for Easter. I hardly know her.'

'She is growing up,' the prioress said. 'She would be welcome among us, she is loved here. But now, Sir, there is another matter on which I should value your advice.'

It was a strange story. One night at the end of January a group of woodcutters had brought a dying man to the priory, dragging the great long body on a woodsled, beating and shouting at the wicket after dark, frightening the whole community. Badly injured by robbers, no identification, not even a saint's medal round his neck. Just a dying man, ambushed, stabbed, bleeding, grey and past speech. The woodcutters had come upon him on their way home: two skinny starveling thieves had thought better of facing four well-fed peasants with axes, and fled with their victim's purse which they cut from his belt with the knife they'd stuck in his liver.

The prioress ordered him put in the infirmary – there was no one ill there at the time – and though some of the nuns protested, she overruled them.

'You would turn away the wounded Christ Himself for being a man,' she snapped. He died. There was time for the last rites, thank God, but he was unable to confess, barely breathing, too far gone. When he was washed and prepared for burial the infirmarian found ...

'This,' said the prioress.

Straccan turned it over in his hands. An old, very old, reliquary – cylindrical, bronze, green with age. A spiral ribbon of worn symbols in no language he recognised was engraved round it and on the lid was a device somewhat like a starfish.

'Do you know what it is?' she asked.

'It's very old.'

'Look inside,' she said.

He tugged off the close-fitting cap. Inside was another cylinder, this one of stiff rolled cloth tied with a cord threaded through a lead seal. He slid the cord down and gently unrolled the material. Colour sprang up from the surface, not cloth as on the outside, but long narrow strips of ivory pierced and stitched side by side to make a smooth surface from which the intense colour seemed to bleed into the air. A painted face, a woman's, not young, not beautiful but utterly compelling. Dark, unmistakably eastern, with great black eyes full of such grief that it made him uneasy. Full lips, compressed. A red veil hiding all hair, fastened under the chin with a fish-shaped gold and gemmed clasp.

'What do you think of it?' He heard the suppressed excitement in her voice.

'The portrait is from Egypt, or perhaps Syria,' he said. 'Brought back by a crusader, probably. This must have been a holy woman, perhaps an early martyr.'

'Saint Luke, they say, was artist as well as physician,' Mother Rohese said eagerly. 'He painted from life the divine features of God's Mother.'

'Yes,' said Straccan thoughtfully. 'If this was mine, I should like to believe that. But there is nothing to say so. Unless you know whose it is, you can only make guesses.' He turned the cylinder, angling it to the light to see the inscription, but the strange glyphs were like nothing he had ever seen. 'This case isn't Egyptian,' he said, 'nor Byzantine, nor from anywhere I know of. It's much older than the picture and they don't belong together. Someone just found the case convenient to keep the picture in.' He rolled it up and slipped it back in the cylinder. 'What do you want me to do?'

'I hoped that you might know the picture,' said the Prioress. 'These precious things are your ...' She paused and actually looked embarrassed.

'My line of business,' Straccan smiled.

'Exactly. I hoped that this might be known to you, that you could tell me whose it is.'

'I'm sorry.'

'The dead man also carried this letter.' It was written in an angular cramped non-secretarial hand and bore neither salutation nor signature. It simply said: 'Do as I ask, for my soul's sake.'

'What should I do?' she asked. 'With someone's soul at stake, how do I find out where the man was going?'

'Easier to find where he came from,' said Straccan, who was wondering that himself. 'That will lead to the answer. Do you have an intelligent man among your servants: someone you could send back along the road to make enquiries?'

'Our bailiff's son is a man of some sense,' she said.

'See what he can discover. Meanwhile, if you wish, I will make some enquiries. See what I can find out.'

'That is what I meant to ask of you. Thank you.'

'At your charges,' said Straccan.

'Of course,' said the prioress with a wintry smile. 'You will give us your accounting.'

Chapter 4

Straccan's house was built on four sides of a square, in the style and on the site of an old Roman villa. Roman-worked stone still formed part of the walls, and red roof-tiles, hypocaust tiles and multicoloured mosaic tiles turned up everywhere the ground was dug. The roofs were now of furze and thatch and much of the building was new wood. Straccan's office was at the back, and there he sat at a table, checking items on a long list while his clerk opened and sorted oddly-shaped packages taken from a small hide-covered chest. This mild late-March morning the shutters were off, letting in light and noise unhindered. In the yard a supply cart was unloading, men and women going back and forth with sacks and bundles, shouting, laughing, whistling.

'Item,' said Straccan. 'Six threads from the chemise of Our Blessed Lady.'

'Here,' said the clerk.

'Item, rib of Saint Cecilia.'

'Here.'

'Item, dust from the tomb of Saint Thomas Becket.'

'Yes, about half a pound of it in a leather bag. I'll put a new label on, this one's too hard to read.'

'Item, bone fragment from the arm of Saint Mary Magdalene.'

'No. Cross that off. The Prior of Winchelsea bought that while you were away. And you remember he wanted that foot of Saint Martin?'

'He couldn't afford it.'

'Right. But he's come up with a bright idea. He suggests

22

borrowing it, just for two or three years. Reckons it'll rake in enough offerings in that time for him to be able to buy it.'

'Fat chance,' said Straccan, drawing a line through the Magdalene's fragment. 'Some of Becket's dust has got in my throat. Let's have a drink, Peter.'

The clerk poured beer from a jug into two pewter cups. Straccan walked to the window, leaned through and shouted, 'Has anyone seen Bane?'

'Gone to the village, Sir,' someone called back.

'I want to see him as soon as he gets back.' He picked up the list again. 'Ready? Item, jawbone of Lazarus.'

'Here. Looks more like a woman's jawbone. Oh well, never mind.'

'Item, ear of Saint Marcellinus.'

'Can't find it. An ear? Haven't had an ear before, have we?' Peter turned over several small boxes, pouches, bundles. 'No. Oh is this it?' He held up what looked like a withered blackened folded scrap of leather. 'I suppose it *might* be an ear.' Both men stared doubtfully at it. 'Who was Marcellinus, anyway?'

Straccan consulted his list. 'It says here, an early blessed martyr. Let's have a look.' He turned the darkened scrap over in his fingers, sniffed it, shrugged and handed it back. 'Keep it dry. It'll start to smell if the damp gets at it.'

'What else is supposed to be in this lot?' Peter poked about in the sheep's wool packing.

The sound of hooves cut through the cheerful racket outside. Straccan glanced over the rest of the list. 'We should have the Virgin's binder, a swaddling band of the infant Christ and two of his milk teeth, a thorn from the crown, a kneecap of Saint Peter, three hairs of Saint Edmund, a splinter of the true cross, sundry bloody clouts from sundry martyrdoms, an arrow that pierced Saint Sebastian, oh, and three teeth of Saint Apollonia.'

An ugly gap-toothed face frowned round the open door. 'Sir, a man to see you.'

'Who is it, Cammo?'

'Him,' said Cammo, with obvious disapproval. 'From that Master Wotsit.'

'Master Gregory?'

'Aye.'

'Well put him in the solar. Have his horse seen to. Tell Adeliza to wait on him and I'll see him as soon as I've put this lot away.'

Master Gregory's messenger sat at his ease on the cushioned window seat, dipping his hands in and out of the bowl of warm water Adeliza held for him. He had been doing this for some time, apparently absorbed in letting the water run and drip from his fingers. Adeliza looked unhappy, and her arms had begun to tremble with the strain of holding the bowl. After a few more moments it shook sufficiently to spill a little water into the man's lap. He smiled at her.

'Clumsy slut,' he said very softly and pinched the back of her hand sharply. His nails were very long. 'Pretty, but a clumsy slut. Calls you his housekeeper, does he? Keep his bed warm, do you?'

Tears gathered in her eyes and she stepped back.

'I haven't finished,' he said.

'Yes you have,' said Cammo from the doorway. He leaned against the door frame, huge hands hooked into his belt, staring at the man. 'Take the bowl away, Liza. I'll wait on him.' As she hurried out of the room he snatched the towel from over her arm and threw it at the seated man.

'Your master is ill served,' the man said, still smiling. 'Clumsy cattle and insolent serfs.'

'Do you want something to drink?' Cammo asked, lumbering forward and looming over him.

'No. Wait . . . Yes.'

Outside the window, a little girl had run into the yard and was talking to one of the carters, who laughed and swung her high on to the driving seat of the cart, behind the four great oxen whose heads were well tucked into nosebags, tails swishing at flies and glossy hides twitching occasionally.

The messenger watched the child and licked his lips. 'Whose brat is that?' he asked. Cammo ignored the question and plonked a beaker of beer on the seat beside the man, resuming his stance by the door. Outside, Gilla chattered happily and gee'd up the oxen until she was lifted down and taken to meet each beast in turn, her clear voice repeating their names – Dumpling, Blackbird, Belly-wise and Bracken – until Adeliza appeared from the kitchen and scooped her back into the house.

Peter came in. 'Master says sorry to keep you waiting, will you come with me now?' The messenger pushed past Cammo without a glance.

'Good day to you, Sir Richard,' he said. 'My master has another commission for you.'

'What does he want?'

'He requires a relic of Saint Thomas.'

'Then he should apply to Canterbury.'

'No, not Becket. Thomas the disciple. Thomas Didymus.'

'Doubting Thomas?' Straccan looked thoughtful. 'His remains are said to be in India.'

'As you say. But the King of France has the skull, or part of it, in his Halidom.'

Straccan took a large thick book from the table beside him and began riffling through its pages. 'Ah yes,' he said. 'Saint Thomas. The Pope has a finger. But he won't sell anything for less than a kingdom, and trying to deal with his agents can take years. King Philip, well, just possibly *he* might, if the price was right.'

'My master trusts that you will negotiate on his behalf, as you have done before. Funds can be drawn in Paris from the Jew, Rohan, or in Rome from the banker, Tolomei.'

'I'll make enquiries,' said Straccan. 'My fee is one hundred gold pieces, half before I go, and mine whether I succeed or not. The other half on delivery.'

'One hundred? Your charges have gone up, Sir Richard!'

'The cost of living's gone up. It's the Interdict, you know. Everything's dearer: travel, inns, food. Besides, it's always costly dealing with royalty. Palms to grease, friends to buy, favours to spread around.'

The man unbuckled his belt and upended it over the table. Gold coins fell out, one after another. Straccan counted twenty.

'Present yourself at the house of the Jew Eleazar in Nottingham, and give him this.' He took a roll of parchment from his pocket. 'It is my master's authority to pay the rest.'

The messenger's escort, two men-at-arms, was ready and waiting when his horse was led from the stable. A boy held its head while he mounted. He sat in the saddle for a moment, gazing round the yard at the various doors and windows. From an open door came the sound of a child singing. The man smiled. 'Who is the little wench?' he asked. 'I saw her earlier, sitting in the cart.'

'That's our Gilla,' said the boy, beaming. 'The master's little girl. Don't she sing pretty?'

'Like an angel,' said the messenger, and listened a moment more before touching spurs lightly to his horse and trotting under the arch out of the yard.

I've got a job for you,' said Straccan when Bane returned. He recounted the story of the dead man at Holystone while Bane listened, whistling softly. 'The nuns sent their bailiff's son to try and backtrack this fellow and find out anything about him. When Gilla came home, the prioress sent word with her their man came back with no success. I want you to have a go. Find out where he came from and who sent him, where he was going, and what that picture is.'

'Right. When?'

'Tomorrow will do.'

'I met that Gregory's man and his escort as I came back. What did he want?'

'He wants a relic of Doubting Thomas,' said Straccan. 'Have you ever seen one of these?' He offered Bane a gold coin. It was small and very thick. On one side was some unknown script and on the other the image of an ugly little tentacled creature.

'Some sort of octopus,' said Bane. 'No, I've never seen one. Where's it from?'

'I've no idea. I thought I'd seen all monies, especially eastern. D'you think this is eastern?'

'Probably. But it's strange to me. Where'd you get it?'

'Gregory sent it. Up-front money for his relic.'

'Just so long as it's true gold,' said Bane.

'Oh, it's gold right enough.' Straccan held up one of the coins which bore his testing teeth-marks.

Chapter 5

Straccan knew very little of Bane's previous life. He had a story but how much of it was true was anybody's guess. Various more-or-less colourful adventures were let slip from time to time. Apprenticed to a physician, he had run away and joined the army – been wounded in a skirmish in France – survived and gone pilgrim to Saint James at Compostella, come home penniless and turned beggar, tried thievery and joined a band of wandering players.

Straccan first saw him in the pillory in the market square at Evesham where a small crowd had gathered, not to pelt, but to laugh at the prisoner's jokes, songs, and facial contortions. Towards curfew folk drifted away to their homes and a couple of large young oafs started throwing rubbish. Straccan, watching from the alehouse door, saw the prisoner's head jerk and his body suddenly slump, hanging from the neck and wrists like a sack, and realised that a stone had been flung. Just then the sherrif's underdog came to open the pillory, letting the man fall like a dead thing into the mud. The two youths had fled, the sun was sinking, the curfew began to ring and three or four people hurried past, ignoring the huddled body.

'What was he in for?' Straccan asked the alehouse keeper.

'His mates buggered off without paying their score.'

'Why did he stay?'

'Pissed.'

Straccan hauled him up, so light a weight that he staggered back, braced as he was for something more substantial. He carried the body to the alehouse, laid it on a bench, fetched water and a rag, and wiped the blood and muck from the face. A darkening lump was swelling from the edge of an eyebrow up into the hair. The man groaned, tried to sit up and was violently sick. It was a couple of days before he could stand again, and meanwhile he lay on straw in the stable-loft at Straccan's charges.

When Bane emerged from the nightmarish vertigo that had kept him, kitten-weak, on his back, Straccan packed him on his led mule and rode to Peterborough. At the abbey gate he said, 'This is as far as I go.'

'I'm in your debt,' Bane said.

'Forget it.'

'I'd like a chance to work it off.'

'I don't need any help,' Straccan said curtly.

'Roads aren't safe. Two's less like to be set upon than one.'

'I can take care of myself.'

'Expect you can, Master. So can I, when I'm sober.'

'Anyway, I wouldn't want a piss-artist around.'

'I'm not,' said Bane, stung. 'It was rotten bad beer!'

'That's what they all say,' said Straccan. He took the mule's leading-rein, rode in under the arch of the abbey gates and didn't look back.

His business there took longer than expected, for His Reverence the Abbot, abed with gout, would see no one until he felt better. Three days later when Straccan rode out again, an insubstantial figure detached itself from the mud-splashed wall and limped barefoot after him. Near the town gate the rider stopped and let the man catch up. The swelling over his eye had gone down but that side of his face was all bruise, the same yellowing purple as the threatening morning sky which promised storm.

'What are you called?' Straccan asked.

'Hawkan Bane.'

'Well, Hawkan Bane, you don't owe me anything.'

'No? Reckon you owe me, then.'

'What?' Straccan laughed. 'How's that?'

'You saved my life. I'd've probably died. They'd've let me lie in the mud and drown, if I didn't freeze first. So it's up to you to look after me now! On Tuesday I ate my coat and yesterday I ate my shoes. Now all I've got left's this shirt, and if I sell that for food too, I'll go bare-arsed. So I'm your responsibility!'

'I never heard such crap in my life,' said Straccan, 'but I admire the cheek of it, I suppose. What use could you be to me?'

'I can do things. You'd be surprised.'

'Surprise me.'

'I can cook. I can mend, tend livestock. I'm skilled with wounds, fevers and such. I can read and write a little, and reckon. I can kill your enemies and entertain your friends.'

Straccan snorted. 'Sounds like a reference for a wife! Can you really read and write?'

Bane bent and wrote in the mud with his finger: God, Kynge, Engelond. Straccan peered at the words as the mud absorbed them into itself again. 'Fair enough,' he said. He nudged his horse gently with his knee and it walked on slowly, with Bane holding the stirrup and limping beside. 'So what did you do before you were brought to such straits?'

'I've travelled,' said Bane. 'I was a soldier.'

'Where?'

'France. I was with King Richard at Gisors. I was left for dead there. The night-frost stopped me bleeding to death and a woman helped me – one of the scavengers that loot the dead after any battle. But she took a fancy to me. She was all right.'

'I was there,' said Straccan. 'My horse was badly hurt: I thought he'd die, but he didn't. I took a pike-thrust through the thigh. It's still stiff in foul weather.'

'A horseman?' Bane was startled. 'What were you, a sergeant?'

'No. I am a knight. And must be on my way, so go you yours, and let go my stirrup.'

'Let me along of you for a week! If you still don't want me, then I'll go my way!'

Four years later he was still with Straccan.

Bane's travelling kit contained the essentials: spoon in its case, provender, cup and water bottle, fish-hooks and line, a change of clothes, spare shoes, bandages and salves, and an inventive collection of concealed weapons as well as the short sword worn at his back, the dagger in his belt and the axe strapped to his saddle. There were also some less usual items including a flute and small bagpipes. His rangy bony cheap-looking horse would attract no attention, and Bane himself, a small skinny figure cloaked and hooded in drab greys and browns, would pass as nigh invisible. His peculiarly elastic countenance could assume at will the appearance of a man much older, with sucked-in cheeks and puckered toothless-looking mouth. So that the old man seen in one village was obviously not the much younger fellow met with further along the road.

He made first for Holystone, to learn all he could of the dead man, his appearance and the circumstances of his end. The stableman, Martin, fetched a sack and tipped it out.

'This is what he was wearing. Bailiff's son Tom, he looked at it all, before he went.'

Bane fingered the small pile of clothes: leggings, boots – the boots looked new, the soles dirty but with scarcely any wear – a torn and bloodied tunic and jerkin, a knitted bonnet, a rough frieze cape with thistle-burrs caught along its hem. 'This is all he had?'

'There's his pack,' Martin said, taking a satchel from a hook on the wall. 'Just a spare pair of shoes and a tunic. There was some bread, and some bacon and cheese.'

'What happened to that?'

'We ate it. Me, that is, and Oswyn the scullion. There's a bottle, too. This one.' He unhooked a thonged pewter flask. 'It had ale in it.'

'I take it that's empty now too.'

Martin gave him a scornful look.

'Was it good ale?'

'Aye, it was.'

'And was the bread fresh or stale?'

'No more'n a day old.'

'Good cheese?'

'Oh aye.'

'Local cheese?'

'No. From east of here, I reckon. Like they make in Trundle. They sell it there on fair days.' And, with pride, 'I've been there!'

'A travelled man.' Bane picked over the coins in his purse and put a pie-wedge silver piece in Martin's ready hand. 'Did you tell bailiff's Tom about the food and the ale?'

'No. He never asked.'

While Bane rode east then north, as his enquiries led him, Straccan sent to his agents in France and Italy concerning the relics of Saint Thomas, and awaited replies. It was his habit to ride around his farm every morning, and now she was at home he would set Gilla on the saddle before him. On this mild wet morning they halted to watch men clearing the rubble of collapsed walls where the new stables and mews were planned. In their straw rain-capes the men looked like little mobile haystacks with arms and feet. Straccan rested his chin a moment on top of his daughter's head and smelt the sweet herby scent of her soft hair.

'You've had your hair washed,' he said, fingering a fine fluffy strand which curled and clung to his fingers.

'Adeliza washed it last night. She washed hers first and then mine. Her hair is so long she can sit on it. Will mine grow like that?'

'If you don't cut it.'

'The nuns cut their hair, they cut it all off, short as yours.'

'They have to. They're not supposed to be vain.'

'But they are married to Our Saviour! Wouldn't you think he'd like them to be pretty?' Straccan opened his mouth but she hurried on. 'And that's another thing! How can he have so many brides? There are seventeen nuns at Holystone, and hundreds more all over the world.'

'You'll have to ask Mother Rohese to explain, when you go back,' said her father, feeling the firm ground of precise earthly matters turning to treacherous theological quick-clay beneath him.

'Mother Rohese is too important, she's always very busy. Dame

Januaria says good Christians don't ask questions, that questions are the tools of the devil.'

Straccan felt even more at sea. 'I suppose it depends on the questions,' he said.

'Yes, but if no one tells you what you want to know, how can you find out, if you don't ask?'

Chapter 6

For Sir Richard Straccan, Knight, at Stirrup, near Dieulacresse, into his own hand, read the superscription, and Straccan cracked open the seal with his thumbnail, holding the letter to the window's light. From his Paris agent, encoded, it began without preamble and tackled all essentials.

> The item in question is an especial treasure of the king in his Chapel Royal. There is no possibility of it being sold. The chapel is never unattended. The relics are locked in, under, and behind the altar. Masses are continually sung, at least two attendants always present. The doors are guarded.

The letter continued with a list of relics dispatched earlier that week in the vessel *Sainte Foy*, together with several orders from clients and a short list from the pope's agent of minor relics for sale.

It was three more weeks before the reply came from Rome. He read it and sent for his clerk. 'His Holiness no longer has the finger of Saint Thomas. He gave it to His Grace of Canterbury.'

Peter whistled. 'Langton's got it! Is he still in Rome?'

'No. He's in Becket's old hideaway, Pontigny. I'll have to go. We might come to an agreement. If ever a man needed money, our exiled archbishop must!'

'I thought the Holy Father was his friend.'

'Since boyhood, I believe. The pope will sprinkle archbishoprics and relics among his cronies, but he hates to part with true coin!'

'You be careful,' Peter said. 'The king'll take a dim view of anyone known to visit Langton.'

'This isn't politics,' said Straccan. 'It's only a petty piece of business.'

Looking across the muddy tidal river down to the town and the grey sea beyond, Bane let his horse crop and sat with his back to a boulder out of the wind. A huddle of heather-thatched roofs, liberally blotched with seagulls' droppings gleaming white, spread out from the castle which crouched threateningly over the River Tweed. The tide was in, the river busy with boats, and two large merchant galleys lay at anchor below the castle, with several smaller vessels by warehouses along the waterside. The town embraced the castle closely. While Bane watched, carts and riders and people afoot moved in and out of the town. The offshore wind spread the chimney smoke thinly out over the sea.

Berwick looked busy, peaceful and squalid. Scars of its old sufferings showed. Gangs of repairmen clustered here and there along the castle walls, new stone patching looked raw and pale. Seagulls swarmed in the air like bees, circling and screaming, a continual raucous din as they swooped on rubbish and rose triumphant, small birds pursued by larger. Everything and almost everyone below was splashed with their droppings.

He had watched the town since early light, seen the fishing boats go out, the tiny distant guard on the castle walls change, the morning rush of farmers into town with milk and produce. Travellers departed in their various directions. Some had passed him, going south. With Nottingham, York, Durham, Newcastle and Alnwick now behind him, Bane had covered more than two hundred miles since leaving Holystone.

At Nottingham, he'd found a woman who remembered the dead man for his outlandish speech. 'A foreigner,' she said. 'Welsh, or Irish, or something. Yes, he drank here, and I filled his bottle for him – he tried to drive the price down! I told him, there's an Interdict on, you know!' No, he had no horse. He had asked for a shoemaker.

The shoemaker, primed with a quarter penny, delivered his information. He had taken the man's boots in part exchange for a new pair. The old were worn out, and no, he didn't have them any more, he'd reused the salvageable leather, which was just common stuff. He didn't recognise the workmanship; they weren't local boots. The man said his mule had broken its leg at Newark, and he'd had to walk thereafter.

At Newark, Bane found the farrier who'd bought the mule and still had its harness. 'Not English work,' the farrier said, running a grimy thumb along the stitches. 'Foreign, that is.'

'Any idea where he came from?'

'No. But I picked up the mule on the Doncaster road.'

At Doncaster his luck seemed to run out until by sheer good chance he sat at dice with the off-duty gate guards, one of whom remembered winning two shillings from a traveller whose description was very like the murdered man, and who had been a sore loser.

'Quite a tasty little fight we ad,' the guard said cheerfully, 'till one of me mates dropped a sack over im, and we bundled im into the lock-up for the night. Went off next morning swearing murder.'

'Murder's what he got,' said Bane. 'Where'd he come from, do you know?'

'York.'

York was a big place, and Bane, asking about a tall man, probably foreign, riding a grey mule, learned nothing for two days but then found a blacksmith who had shod the mule. It had cast a shoe a mile or so outside the city. The blacksmith was talkative and had a good memory. The man had paid him with a Scottish coin and asked about the road ahead. He was going to Doncaster.

'I know where he went. I need to know where he came from,' Bane said.

'Dunno where from, but he'd come through Durham,' said the blacksmith. 'Prayed at Saint Cuthbert's shrine, he told me so, for a safe journey.'

'Saint Cuthbert wasn't listening,' said Bane.

At Durham he tracked him to a brothel, where a disgruntled whore remembered him for his roughness and the false coin he gave her.

'A foreigner,' Bane said. 'Welsh, Irish, or something.'

'Scottish,' said the girl.

'Are you sure?'

'My mum was Scottish. Course I'm sure.'

'Did he say where he'd come from?'

'He said I wasn't a patch on the whores in Newcastle, and they charged less for the pleasure of him,' she said, and spat. Bane gave her a penny. 'It better be real.' She scowled.

'It is, never fear. I'd give two more if you'd had his name.'

'Oh, that. Grimmer, or Grimmon, or something like,' she said. 'Gimme my tuppence.'

Newcastle was cold, dark, foggy and reeked of fish. Its whorehouses were nothing to write home about and its whores had seen better days, but at the eighth establishment Bane struck lucky. His tall Scot with the grey mule was remembered unlovingly. The man's name was Crimmon, and he was from Berwick.

Wondering if he was going to have to traipse right to the very top of Scotland, Bane had set out for Berwick and now sat watching the town as it yawned and got up in the morning. Scratching the bug bites from last night's bed, he hoped to find a stable to sleep in tonight. Years of experience had taught him that prized horseflesh lay cleaner and sweeter than Christians. When the morning rush in and out of the gates was over, he rode down and entered the town, asking for the sheriff.

'Crimmon, you say? That's all, just a name?'

'Just a name. He rode a grey mule.'

'Why are you looking for him, English? What's he done?'

'Got himself murdered. The Prioress of Holystone thought his kin should know.'

'That was mighty kind of her, to send someone all this way.'

'It was her Christian duty,' said Bane.

'Well, I'll find out where he lived and tell his folks,' said the sheriff. 'You can go back home now, English; your Christian duty's done, and I wouldn't hang about here if I was you. You're on the wrong side of the border!'

Chapter 7

Straccan had waited six days at Pontigny. The group of people hoping to see the archbishop changed daily, some arriving, others leaving; a few had even seen him. Nobles and peasants, monks and nuns, priests and merchants, came and went. There were occasional messengers from Rome, bringing papal encouragement for the exiled archbishop, and from King Philip of France, stirring mud for all it was worth. It suited him well to have England and the Church at each other's throats. The archbishop's absence from his appointed place did not mean he was out of touch. Far from it. A constant stream of representatives from various English foundations poured in with complaints and problems, asking his advice. On arrival, they gave their names and some stated their business to the guest master of the great monastery at Pontigny, where Stephen Langton, the latest in a long line of disaffected English churchmen, passed the time while waiting to enter into the see the pope had bestowed upon him, and King John so indignantly refused to hand over. Then they waited to be summoned to the archbishop's presence.

Straccan found himself in a small stuffy dormitory with three other would-be visitors: a plump Paris merchant who whistled constantly and tunelessly through his teeth; a silent grey-haired nobleman in rich but soiled clothing who eyed the rest suspiciously and spoke to no one, biting his nails all the time; and a shabby little Irish monk, Brother Dermot, who carried a scroll from his prior and the gift, for the archbishop, of a precious thumb-bone of Saint Brigid. This he showed Straccan who eyed it with professional interest and made an offer; whereupon Brother

Dermot hastily wrapped it up again and stowed it back in his bosom, abashed.

Straccan sat and waited, stood and waited, walked about and waited, ate and slept and rose again, and waited. The Paris merchant was summoned in the middle of the night and departed, still whistling, to be seen no more by the rest of them. Familiar faces in the courtyard disappeared as the days passed, and new ones took their places. On the evening of the sixth day, as the sky began to turn all shades of gold and the shadows to grow long, a cloaked and hooded man red with the dust of travel, rode in just as the gates were about to close for the night. Dismounting, he handed his reins to a lay brother who appeared at a trot from the porter's lodging. The guest master himself, a venerable broad-bellied monk, appeared to lead this new arrival in at once.

'God's bones,' cried the grey-haired nobleman, the nail-biter. 'Who is *he* to be whisked in at once while we wait day after day? You, Sir!' to the dusty traveller, 'When you see His Grace, tell him Lord Beltrane waits on him still!' And he rushed forward, seized the man by the shoulder and shook him furiously. Brother Dermot stuck out a dirty sandalled foot and the nail-biter tripped, falling heavily. Starting to rise, he grabbed at Dermot and pulled his dagger, but Straccan's boot connected with his elbow and the knife went flying.

'Lord Beltrane, whoever he is, needs a quiet place to recover himself,' he said to the guest master. It was quite dark now and monks came running with torches and lanterns. Light and shadow danced and flickered on faces. Two monks led Lord Beltrane away. At Straccan's words the dusty visitor swung around and reached towards him.

'Sir Richard? Sir Richard Straccan?'

'Yes?'

'Richard! It *is* you! I know your voice! Don't you know me? See . . .' He dragged his hood back. 'I am Sulpice de Malbuisson.'

'My God,' said Straccan, staring at the thin bearded face with its one-eyed eager stare. 'Jesus, Sulpice, is it really you? I thought you were dead!'

*

'I usually eat in the refectory with the rest of the community,' said Stephen Langton. 'But when I have guests we can be private here.'

Straccan sat after supper with the archbishop and Sulpice de Malbuisson. The young monk who waited on them cleared away the dishes and crumbs and trimmed the candles. Langton leaned back in his chair and gazed at Straccan.

'My nephew has talked of you before, Sir Richard,' he said. 'He owes his life to you, and I owe you much thanks. Sulpice and my brother are all the kin left me. His mother – my sister – died when he was very young, and his father died before he was born.'

'I thought you were dead too, Richard,' Sulpice said. 'After you got me back to the camp, they told me you had disappeared. Then we were all bundled into wagons and taken to the ships. When I came to my senses I asked for you but you were not aboard. I asked and searched at Cyprus when we landed but you weren't on the other ship. Many of the wounded had died on the voyage and been thrown overboard. Not all their names were known. I have prayed for your soul ever since!'

'I'm sure I'm the better for it.' Straccan smiled. 'I never made it to the ships. I was still in the camp when the infidel raided it and I was captured. I had a year in a galley until it was taken by a Spanish vessel, a pilgrim ship that took me back to Acre.'

'What then?'

'I had no money to reward my rescuers, so they ... leased me you might say, to a Jew in the town, a spice merchant. As a servant.'

'How shameful,' said the archbishop, his face dark with anger, 'for a Christian to sell another Christian to a Jew!'

'Oh, it is often done, Your Grace. To a Jew, to a Saracen, to another Christian, even. But I was lucky. Simeon was a good man. Compassionate. He fed and clothed me, and when he found I could read and write he used me as a clerk to write to his associates in France and England. I had the good fortune to apprehend a thief in his storeroom and Simeon rewarded me by paying my debt to the Spanish captain.'

He remembered vividly the brief murderous struggle in

Simeon's storeroom – he bore a welted scar across his ribs to remind him – the heat, the overpowering scent of spices, the panting, grasping, sweaty grappling with a body unseen in the darkness, the knife scorching across his chest, then wrenched away, dropped and kicked among the sacks. All the power of his galley-toughened muscles was behind the fist he drove into the robber's belly. Lights and shrieks as Simeon's men, hearing the fight, arrived with lamps. Himself slipping down into the puddle of his own blood. The smell of blood and cinnamon . . .

'So you lost the eye,' he said to Sulpice.

'The arrow pinned eyelid to eyeball.' Sulpice frowned. 'They got the arrowhead out but it went bad on the ship. It was all very nasty, cautery and that, you know, but here I am and the other eye still serves me. I don't remember how you got me away when we were ambushed.'

'The arrow hit you and you fell from your horse. I took a slash across the collarbone but it wasn't too bad – it knocked me out of the saddle, though, and I fell on you. We rolled down a sandbank. You were dead to the world with the arrow sticking out of your eye socket. I just dragged you. There were some rocks and a hollow behind and beneath them. We tumbled into it; I remember praying there would be no snakes. Nobody noticed. It was a nasty hot little fight up above us. Our lot was wiped out. The Saracens cut their heads off and dragged the bodies away behind their horses. When it grew dark and you had come round, we started walking.'

Sulpice turned to his uncle, smiling. 'He dragged and supported me twenty miles,' he said. 'At the end, I kept passing out and he carried me like a child, on his back.'

'We propped each other along much of the way,' Straccan said. 'It was only the last mile or two that you couldn't stagger.'

The archbishop leaned forward, his elbows on the board and his chin in his hands. 'Tell me, Sir Richard, what is your errand here?'

'I want to buy one of your relics, Your Grace.'

'Which one?'

'The finger of Saint Thomas.'

*

Bane reached Stirrup again a few days after Straccan's return.

'You're thinner,' said Straccan as Bane hobbled into the central courtyard, leading his limping horse.

'I've got a blister the size of a duck egg,' grumbled Bane.

'Adeliza! Bring food and ale! Come into the office. You can stick your feet in a pan of water, and tell me your story!'

Chapter 8

'Robert de Beauris of Skelrig is your man,' said Bane. 'It's his picture. He sent his servant Crimmon with it to his sister at Arlen Castle.'

'Arlen Castle?' Straccan rubbed his unshaven chin with a rasping noise. 'What does the lady there?'

'She's the baron's wife.'

Startled, Straccan said, 'What was the man doing, carrying such a precious thing to a noble lady with no escort? Why a man alone, skulking through the country like a felon?'

'It's all a bit queer,' said Bane. 'After they shuffled me off at Berwick I asked around, quietly, and found people who knew this Crimmon. He came from Mailros, they said. So I rode south out of town, as if I was going back home, and then turned back west. There are three big hills; make for them and you're there. There's a fine abbey and a bit of a town, not much, but growing. I presented myself at the abbey, told them Prioress Rohese had sent me and showed her token. Here it is.' He pulled a cord over his head and dropped the prioress's token on the table. 'They were hospitable and the lay brothers were gossipy. They fed me and gave me a bed, and told me all they knew about the lord of Skelrig. He's some sort of nephew to Gerard de Ridefort.'

'Exalted circles we move in,' said Straccan. 'Barons and their ladies, and now de Ridefort! He was Grand Master of the Templars at Jerusalem, twenty years or so gone – which makes the business of the paltry messenger stranger still.'

'This Robert has been away from his barony for some time, they said, on knight-service. He returned just after Christmas. Seems he asked to enter the abbey at Mailros as a novice, but the abbot wouldn't have him. Robert got very worked up and begged to be let stay, even as a lay brother, but the abbot said no and threw him out. He went back to Skelrig, and hasn't been seen since.' Bane yawned and stretched, wincing as stiff muscles pulled. 'So I went there, and as soon as I asked to see Lord Robert I was grabbed and shoved into a nasty little hole next the stable, and locked in. They seemed scared stiff of me. They shouted through the door, who was I, what did I want. I said I had business with Lord Robert and they'd better let me see him or they'd be sorry, all the usual stuff. Everything went quiet after a while and I reckoned it must be night-time so I had a go at the lock, but there was a bolt outside as well.

'When they opened the door it was mid-morning, and there was this little priest standing there shaking and as grey as my shirt, and half a dozen fellows with bows and swords huddled behind him like children behind their mother. He started shouting Latin and suddenly chucked a cup of water over me – holy water as it turned out – cos when I didn't vanish in a puff of sulphur he turned pink again right away, and the others shoved him aside and took over. Before they could really get started on me I shouted, 'Crimmon, Crimmon's dead,' and they listened to the rest. Someone went off to tell Lord Robert and I was taken into the tower. It's just a very small tower with a few outbuildings, though they say he's a very rich man. Anyway, three floors up, there he was, behind a closed door and shouting through it just like we'd been doing below!'

'Mad?'

'Barking. And terrified.'

'What of?'

'Demons.' Bane poured and drank more ale. 'He's shut himself up in this room. He let me in after I'd yelled all about Crimmon and the picture and the Prioress of Holystone. Well, *he* didn't let me in, he had a lad in there with him, a dumb boy, to do things like that – fetch and carry, open doors, empty pots – because *he*, de Beauris I mean, is sitting up there inside a great circle, all made of candles and incense-burners and bowls of holy water and

45

crucifixes and relics and bunches of herbs. No one else goes into it, and he won't budge. He's got a bed in the circle, and a table and chair, and a chest full of money. He's wearing a monk's robe over a hair shirt, he's festooned with relics and crucifixes and he stinks to high heaven.

'I told him the whole story: how his man died, how the prioress got his letter and the picture and wanted to know what to do with them. And after going over it again and again for hours, he finally told me he'd sent it to his sister Julitta, the lord of Arlen's wife. She knew what to do with it, he said. Then he opened the chest – that's how I know it was full of money – and took out a handful of coins and threw them into one of the bowls of holy water, and told me to take it, and thank you very much, and why didn't I start back right away?

'I headed straight for Alnwick. The roads up there are unbelievable. Thank God it was dry; if it had been wet I'd never have got there. I might never have got back home either; it's all bog when it isn't flood. On the road a galloper passed me, going my way head down, but I'd seen him before back there at Skelrig. And there he was again, in Alnwick when I stopped for the night, lurking about and watching me. So when I'd had enough of it I gave him the slip and followed *him* for a change. He panicked about a bit when he realised he'd lost me, and then went into a house and presently came out again with another man. And this is where it gets queerer still. Guess who the other fellow was.'

'Who?'

'That Gregory's man, the one who came here after the finger of Saint Thomas.'

'His name's Pluvis,' said Straccan thoughtfully. 'You're sure it was him?'

'No mistaking him, ugly sod.'

'Did he see you?'

'He didn't know me. I watched them while they talked, and then the Skelrig man got on his horse and set off back the way we'd come. And wotsisname, Pluvis, shouted to a servant and went back inside, and presently five horses were brought to the door, and out he came with two other men and two archers. Now one of the men I've seen before; he was Eustace de Vesci. The other I didn't know. White face, black hair and moustache. He and de Vesci wore mail. The archers looked foreign, I think they were Saracens. I whined for charity and one of them threw a handful of horse shit at me. De Vesci went off by himself and the others rode north. I hung around a bit to ask who the pale man was.'

'Well?'

'Nobody wanted to talk about him. I couldn't find out a thing beyond his name: Rainard, Lord Soulis.'

Chapter 9

The small thick gold coins felt unpleasantly greasy, and Straccan rubbed his hands on his tunic after counting them, glad to be rid of them. Pluvis had taken the relic, paid the balance due and gone. The strange figure on the ugly coins wasn't an octopus, it was no creature Straccan had ever seen – something like a toad with tentacles round its mouth. Whatever it was, he disliked it *and* the gold it decorated, and took it all to Eleazar the Jew to change for other coinage, keeping just a few for curiosity's sake. That done, clean silver in his purse and more at home in his safe place, he rode again to Holystone to tell Prioress Rohese what Bane had discovered.

'I am amazed that your man was able to learn so much,' she said. 'Our bailiff's son had no luck at all, and was a week away.' (Straccan had given her an edited version of Bane's account and a list of his expenses.) 'He ate and drank enough for two,' she observed sourly, casting a critical eye down the listed items.

'Bailiff Ambrose's son?' said Straccan.

'No, your man Bane!'

'I told you he was intelligent. I never said he was abstemious,' Straccan protested with a smile. 'It was a long hard journey, and he was ill used by Skelrig's ruffians as well.'

'I am sorry for that, indeed. I suppose this precious thing must now go to the Lady Julitta. Do you think she might be persuaded to sell it?'

'Who knows? I'll ask her, if you wish.'

'I know nothing of her brother,' the prioress said. 'I wonder where he got the picture.'

'His uncle, or whatever he was, the Grand Master, would have been able to lay hands on almost any holy thing,' said Straccan.

'Julitta de Beauris was no great heiress,' the prioress observed. 'Her mother was Alice de Ridefort, the last of twelve daughters if I remember right, and her father some petty lordling, a Scot, I suppose. However, Julitta inherited nothing. What there was went to the heir, her brother, who was niggardly with her dowry. But she's a great beauty. I have seen her, and all they say is true – a *great* beauty. Arlen *would* have her, dowry or none. It made quite a stir.'

'Do you want me to take the picture to her?'

'Yes. I will write and tell her how we came by it, and if you will be my messenger I'll be in your debt.'

'Not forgetting my charges,' said Straccan. They smiled at each other with perfect understanding. 'I'd like to see my daughter, while I'm here.'

The lady was not at Arlen Castle but at her summer hall, which had no drawbridge. Its modest gate was guarded by men-at-arms and the largest hounds Straccan had ever seen: two enormous bandogs the size of small ponies, chained one at each side of the gate, straining at their collars and growling savagely, all white teeth and scarlet tongues. A thin dirty boy much marked by ringworm, sat by an iron winch from which chains ran to the dogs' collars. As Straccan approached, the boy turned the wheel and the dogs were reluctantly hauled aside. As he passed into the inner court, one threw back its head and bayed after him, a chilling deep-toned sound that echoed back and forth from the surrounding walls. A steward called a boy to escort him to the lady's solar above. There, a waiting woman looked up, harried, from piles of scattered garments and open clothes-chests trailing silks, velvets, cambrics and ribbons. She led him up a winding stair to a window, and pointed out across another inner yard.

He found her at last in the stable, sitting in the straw in a tumble of soiled silks with a colt lying across her lap, its sides heaving as it drew in one painful breath after another, eyes bulging and suffused with blood, foam from its mouth everywhere. Her hands soothed the suffering creature and she bent to whisper in its ears, blowing her own breath into its red nostrils, regardless of the froth and muck on her gown and veil. The narrow long-fingered hands held the colt's shaking head and, as Straccan watched, it grew quieter. The stertorous gasping eased, the congested eyes closed and opened, closed and opened, bulging less and less.

The woman wiped its nose and mouth with a wet cloth, taken from a bucket behind her, that reeked of wine, squeezing the cloth so that a trickle of liquid ran into the animal's mouth, keeping up a constant flow of whispered words, soft and soothing, just beyond Straccan's hearing. Suddenly the colt, which had appeared dead a moment before, sucked in two or three deep breaths and raised its head to look round. It lurched to its feet, staggered, half fell, regained its footing, stood trembling on its thin long legs and uttered a lamb-like bleat which was answered instantly by a shrill anxious whinny from another stall.

'That's his mother,' she said. 'He'll be all right now. Milon!' A groom's head appeared over the partition. 'Take him to his mother.'

Straccan stood aside to make room as the groom led the colt away. 'What was the matter?' he asked, extending a hand to pull the lady to her feet.

'He began to cough, and couldn't stop,' she said, wiping her hands on the soiled silk of her skirts. 'Then he had one fit after another.'

'I thought he was dying. What did you do?'

'Oh,' she gave him a sideways smile, 'I talked him out of it. Who are you?'

'My name is Straccan. I come from your brother, lady. Indirectly.'

'Give me the icon.' she said. She had washed, and changed her clothes. Her skin glowed, flawless, in the candlelight and her pale silver-blonde hair escaped in slippery gleaming waves from a red gauze veil. She sat with Straccan alone over the remains of their meal at a small table in her solar while her women came and went, chattering like birds, giggling and filling the room with scents and colours.

'The what?'

'The picture.'

He unbuckled the pouch at his belt, laid it on the table and took out the cylinder, handing it to her. She held it but did not open it. 'There is also this,' he said, taking out the brief message the unfortunate Crimmon had carried, 'and this, from the Prioress of Holystone.' He proffered Mother Rohese's letter. To his surprise, she cracked the seal and read the letter like any clerk.

'I must reward you, Sir Richard, for all your aid and trouble.'

'Prioress Rohese deserves your thanks, Lady. As for me, I ask only one thing.'

'What?'

'Tell me about the icon.'

It was said to be a portrait of Christ's mother, she told him. It had been found in an ancient monastery in Egypt by an infidel king, the Emir Bahadur al-Munir, who gave it – in gratitude for the sparing of his life – to the Lionheart, King Richard. Richard, who valued nothing unless he could turn it to money to finance his crusade, sold it to the Grand Master of the Sovereign Order of Knights Templar. How it passed from his hands into those of his great-nephew was not dwelt on, but the lord of Skelrig wanted his sister to sell it for him; and she had a ready eager buyer.

'I might outbid your buyer myself,' said Straccan, eating dates, 'if you would name your price.'

'Are you so rash, Sir, as to outbid the king?'

'Which king?'

'The Lord John, of course.'

'In that case, probably not. It would be a reckless man who tried to outdo His Grace in any matter.'

She smiled and said nothing.

'The Prioress of Holystone however is a formidable lady, and his kinswoman. She might reck to outbid His Grace,' said Straccan. 'Would you name a price for her?'

'I would not. *I* am not his kinswoman, nor willing to incur his displeasure,' she said. She leaned to pour him more wine and the scent of her was heady indeed.

'I doubt if even a king could be displeased with you, Lady,' Straccan heard himself say, dazzled.

Riding away again, with a letter from the lady in his saddlebag for the prioress, he could not forget Julitta's face. It shone in his memory all day, and when he stopped for the night he realised that the whole day's long riding had passed unnoticed like a mere hour. He had left his pouch on the table in her solar and she had come after him with it herself, catching up with him at the gate; she took both his hands in hers, surely she didn't farewell every messenger like that? Her hands were cool and light, and at their touch he felt a little static shock and a sudden rush of uncomfortably sharp desire.

In the morning, after an explicit sensual dream which he found hard to clear from his mind, he touched spurs lightly to his big bay's sides, eventually shaking off the dream's sticky memory in the leaping delight of hard riding. At Holystone before noon, he gave Julitta's letter to Mother Rohese.

'A proper gratitude,' she said. 'Properly expressed. She has made over the revenues of her vineyard at Edgeley to the priory for a year.'

'I hope that will comfort you for the loss of the portrait,' Straccan said. 'I did my best for you but it's to go to the king.'

'Oh, him,' said she, dismissing her brother with a shrug. 'I might have guessed. It's said the lady is his *very* good friend.'

For a moment Straccan didn't take her meaning, and then he did and was conscious of a decided pang.

Chapter 10

The first thing Gilla could remember was her mother holding her, walking up and down and singing softly. She'd been plucked up from her cot, screaming from a bad dream. Even now, years and years later, she could still remember bits of the dream: running along narrow stone passages, closing door after door behind her but knowing some awful Thing was on her heels until in a tiny room behind the last door of all she could go no further. Long bony brown fingers poked impossibly through the keyhole, picking the wood of the door away like bread, until a dreadful bark-skinned face leered through at her while the gnarled and twiggy fingers crumbled more and more door away to make a hole big enough for the witch to clamber through ...

Her mother smelled of flowers and held her so safely nothing could hurt her, nothing could ever get her as long as Mama was there. But then Mama wasn't there any more, and Gilla's next memory was of a plump soft kindly woman in black and white robes, who took her hand and led her to a small covered cart full of cushions and drawn by two white mules. The swaying sleepy motion of the cart seemed to go on for days while the black and white woman and another in exactly the same clothes sat with her on the cushions in the tented space. Occasionally they got out to walk and stretch their legs a while and to pee behind the bushes, but at last they reached this house, the Priory of Saint Catherine at Holystone, the only place Gilla could remember living in at all, for of her first home with her mother she had no memory, being only three years old when her mother died.

Time passed, and the child laid down more memories as life

took on shape and pattern, ordered by bells and peopled entirely by women in black and white, save for Sir Bernard, the nuns' priest, and Ambrose the bailiff, who was frequently glimpsed stumping along the passage to report to Prioress Hermengarde.

Prioress Hermengarde was Gilla's great-aunt, sister to her mother's mother, and to her surprise Gilla learned that somewhere far away, over the sea – 'Outremer' they called it – she had a father! No, pet, not like Sir Bernard, and no, certainly not like Bailiff Ambrose. Your father's a knight, a brave warrior fighting the Infidel. The Infidel are wicked heathens who captured God's Holy City, Jerusalem, and make slaves and prisoners of poor Christian pilgrims.

Knights and heathens took their place in Gilla's mind-world, along with saints and angels, dragons and wizards, nuns, priests, peasants, horses and dogs. She longed for her father's return, but by now her mother's face was fading from her memory, overlaid by Aunt Prioress, dear Dame Domitia who told such splendid stories, and Dame Perdita who tucked Gilla into bed and fussed over her when she had the cough, or the spotted fever, or the earache.

She was seven when her father came back. Sent for to the guest parlour, she saw the man waiting – a face almost blackened by sun but with blazingly blue eyes and a smile that broke over the little girl like a glorious sunrise as he swept her up into his embrace and held her close. His chin was scratchy, and when she pulled her face back she was horrified to see tears in his eyes and spilling down his cheeks.

'Oh there, there,' comforted the child. 'Don't, don't cry! Everything will be all right!' And loved him with all her being.

The little girls played in the priory orchard on fine afternoons, watched by a lay sister or one of the nuns. Dame Matilda would sometimes teach them a new game; Hoodman Blind had been such a success that their immoderate mirth brought sharp rebuke. Dame Margaret would sit under a tree and doze while they played. Dame Hawise had produced from her capacious pocket knuckle-bones from the priory's own mutton, which occupied them for days and could be played with in the cloister when it was too wet to go into the garden.

Today it was Dame Margaret, nodding under a pear tree, more than half asleep, only just aware of their light voices and laughter on the edge of consciousness ... until there was silence, which the nun realised had lasted some time. She sat up and stared about, seeing the children standing by the orchard wall. Why so quiet? No one hurt, no one crying, but something not as it should be ... What? Yes!

Only three little girls. Not four.

'Where is Devorgilla?' she called.

Three little faces turned to her, pale and worried, and three voices answered all together, mixed and muddled.

'We were playing hide-and-seek ...'

'Gilla climbed the tree.'

'This one, here, by the wall.'

'Someone sat on top of the wall and called her.'

'He called Gilla's name, and she climbed higher ...'

'And he pulled her up ...'

'There were horses, we could hear them.'

'And she's *gone*, Dame.'

'I shall go myself,' said the prioress. 'Dame Januaria will go with me, and Sir Bernard, and Ambrose. A message will not do. I must go.'

She sat in Chapter with her nuns, the officers of the community, the morning after Gilla's disappearance. They were all shocked and very distressed, but even more upset by the notion of Mother leaving to ride twenty-five miles to some petty farm at the edge of beyond, quite out in the wilds, and in this appalling weather. It had begun to rain in the night and blow hard, and looked as if it intended to rain and blow for ever.

'The child was in our care,' said the prioress. 'I must tell her father myself and lose no more time about it.'

Voices were raised in protest but the prioress stood and raised her hand, silencing them. 'I am going. There's no more to be said. Sub-Prioress Domitilla will take my place while I'm away. It will only be overnight; I shall be back tomorrow. Dame Januaria, get Sister Hawise to pack our bags, tell Sir Bernard to ready himself – you'll find him in the mews with his mangy sparrowhawk – and tell Ambrose to put pillion-saddles on Sorrell and Roland.'

Dame Januaria, who had no cushion of flesh on her bones and detested riding, whispered 'Yes, Mother,' and fled unhappily out of the room. The others crowded round the prioress, still protesting, several even weeping, but she shook them off as a mother cat shakes off her kittens, blessed them in total and marched to her room. There she took silver from a small coffer and put it in a worn leather purse buckled to her belt. She kicked off her sandals and rummaged in a chest for a pair of sturdy boots. A great hooded cloak over all, and she was ready.

Presently the two horses clattered out of the priory gates, Sir Bernard with the Prioress behind him and the bailiff with Dame Januaria on a thick-legged mare. Rohese dreaded the meeting ahead and as they rode prayed non-stop for Gilla's safety.

Business having taken Straccan to Nottingham, he called at Eleazar's narrow unobtrusive house to collect a sum due from a client, and found his money-man unhappy and worried.

'Haven't you heard? No, I see you haven't. News just came. That Pluvis, Master Gregory's man, he met with a dreadful accident. He's dead, Sir Richard.'

'How? What happened?'

'They found him, well, just bits really, not all of him, by the crossroads at a place called Shawl. Torn to pieces by wild beasts, so they say.'

'What of his escort? He had two men-at-arms.'

'Asleep in their beds, as *he* should have been too. They saw him to his room, and slept by the fire downstairs. How he came to be wandering about alone in the forest in the middle of the night, no one knows.'

'Anyway,' said Straccan, '*what* wild beasts? Wolves are no trouble at this time of year. Did he fall foul of a boar?'

'Wolves, boars, whatever it was it tore him to pieces. And in truth, they may say wolves, but they don't believe it. They think some evil spirit got him, they really do, they *believe* it! You Christians have some very odd notions.'

'We do indeed,' said Straccan, tucking his money into the breast of his coat and fastening it. It had been a long day. He'd be glad to get home to Stirrup.

By the time he reached home he was tired and hungry, and none too pleased to be dragged from his supper by the watchbell's clank, announcing the approach of strangers.

'Who's coming?'

'Looks like nuns,' said the watchman, frowning against the sun.

'Nuns?' Straccan ran up the steps to look out. The three riders were close enough now to recognise. 'Open the gate,' he said, feeling sudden dread clamp round his heart as he went down to greet Prioress Rohese.

Straccan shut his eyes, his mind crying, No, no! He clenched his fist and struck the wall, and again, bursting the skin and leaving blood on the stone. No, no! He leaned, shaking, on the table edge until the shocked stiffness of throat and tongue abated and he could speak, at first with his back to her, but then able to turn and look at her.

'A monastery is not a prison, after all,' he said harshly. 'Nuns are not jailers. Why should little girls in a garden need warders?'

'That is generous,' the prioress said. She too was shaking, partly from weariness after the long fast ride and partly with relief, because he had, in the instant of knowledge, looked as if he might kill her.

'Why Gilla?' he asked, as if to himself. 'Why was there a man on the wall? To steal fruit? But took a child instead, the nearest within hand's reach? There are children everywhere, far easier to steal than from behind a monastery wall. I'll ride to Holystone with you. I want to see for myself just where it happened, and how. Bane! Bane!'

When Bane did not come, Straccan flung back the door and went to find him. 'In the yard, Master,' said Cammo. And there, in the yard, was a stranger, his string of laden dejected ponies straggling in through the gate and around the inner courtyard. A pack-driver, talking to Bane; Bane turning to Straccan, holding out a roll of parchment.

Straccan unrolled it. A few lines of writing and a soft curl of hair, so fine it fluffed up instantly and the wind took it, scattering bright hairs in the mud.

She is unhurt. You will find Saint Thomas his finger. Send it to the Jew Eleazar, at Nottingham. When I know he has it, she will be returned to you.

He seized the pack-man's baggy jerkin and heaved him forward. 'Who gave you this?'

'A m-m-man at L-L-Lincoln.'

'What manner of man?'

'Oh, a f-f-fine lor-lor-lord, on a f-fine b-b-black ha-ha-horse.'

Outside the convent wall where the great old apple tree overhung the road, Straccan searched the ground not knowing what he hoped to find. It had rained since Gilla's abduction, but he found hoof marks in the soft earth beside the road. Someone had dismounted, tied the horse to a bush and waited. The marks of a man's feet were plain enough beneath the wall. *There* he had stepped back to catch the child, and *there* the footprints were deep, deep with the added weight as he caught her.

A clump of ancient holly grew about fifty yards along the road. Behind that he found the hoof marks of two more horses, the dung of one and something strange. A small circle of fieldstones had been made on the ground; in it were some wet feathers, palely stained with rain-washed blood, the blackened and half-burned skull of a bird and the remains of charred twigs and leaves. He crumbled one of the leaves – some herb, by its smell – valerian maybe, he thought. It seemed too much of a coincidence to think that the stone ring was not associated with Gilla's abductors. But what was it? They hadn't just been cooking a meal there. Poking about in the holly, he came upon some rat-gnawed remains which seemed to be the headless body of a small white hen. He had no idea what to make of it.

They'd been seen at Salterhill, ten miles from Holystone. A very beautiful young man, said the giggling girl who remembered him vividly. 'Fair as a prince in hauberk and leather bonnet.'

While she eyed the questioners hopefully, her young brother butted in. 'He had a helmet laced to his saddle bow and a little girl asleep in his arms. There was an older man, wrapped in his cloak and two black men with him, archers— Ow!' Earning a cuff from his sister and a silver penny from Straccan.

After that they could find no trace.

'I'll waste no more time like this,' said Straccan. 'Fair man or none, this is to do with that Pluvis and his master, Gregory. Gregory sent word that he'd not got his relic. I sent back that his man had paid for it, taken it and gone, and it was no more business of mine. Now my Gilla is stolen away and there's that message to find the relic and send it to Nottingham. But we know that Pluvis is dead, at this place called – what is it? Shawl. He was there, and the relic was with him. We'll go there!'

Chapter 11

The crossroads at the forest's edge near Shawl was a peaceful spot, birds singing in the trees, bees droning in the clover, the view into the gentle valley below bright and fair. In the centre of the crossroads was an ancient weathered lichen-crusted grey stone. There Straccan leaned, holding his bay's reins, and Bane sat forward in the saddle of his scrawny grey. It looked to be some two miles or so to the village and manor of Shawl below. A few threads of smoke stood straight up above the thatched roofs. Distant small dots moved in the field-strips, and to their right where the forest's edge curved down the hill and most nearly approached the village about half a mile from the outlying huts, two children followed a small herd of pigs trotting purposefully to their foraging.

A man had been torn apart here by wolves or perhaps demons. If they hadn't known that, they'd have eaten their bread and cheese there, but decided instead to ride into Shawl to break their fast. The church or the manor, Straccan wondered, where to ask first? The church was nearer; he'd tackle the priest.

But Father Osric lay abed, solidly unconscious, snoring wetly, and by the pot-house reek of his foetid hovel which leaned against the church wall, he'd be less than conversational when he *did* wake. A few very small children played in the spaces between the huts, but as soon as horses were heard an old man, kipper-coloured, swathed in ragged wadmal and limping cruelly on a bandaged foot, shot out from a doorway and hauled and herded every infant inside. He planted himself stick in hand, in his open door, glaring at them.

'Good morning,' said Straccan. 'Is your lord in his house?'

'Sir's away.'

'Where will I find the reeve?'

'Reeve's at Sir's.' He jerked a thumb along the road to where the manor roof could be seen over its surrounding trees.

Straccan rode on but Bane dismounted and picked up his horse's right forefoot, examining the shoe. 'Where's your smith?' he asked.

'Forge. Down by river.' The thumb indicated the opposite direction. Bane turned and led his grey that way, kicking aside a bunch of thin yapping limping curs that sought to follow.

'The body, Sir? It was horrible. I've never seen anything like it. I don't want to talk about it; it brings it all back!'

'Torn apart, I was told,' said Straccan implacably. 'But was it eaten?'

'Eaten? I suppose so,' said the reeve. 'That's what wolves do, isn't it? A foot was missing and, er, innards.'

'Were there teeth marks? Were there bites, man?'

'For God's sake, Sir, I didn't peer that closely at him! He was torn apart; wild beasts do that, what else could do that?'

'For my part I'd settle for wolves,' said Straccan, 'but there's talk of demons.'

'Demons?' The reeve crossed himself several times rapidly. He looked pale and sick, and sweat sprang out on his forehead and chin. 'Let's have no talk of demons and such, Sir, please! I'll have no hope at all of getting any work out of anyone if they think the forest is full of demons!'

Straccan stared at the wall hanging – shabby, stained, and rat-nibbled along its bottom. It depicted lovers in a woodland glade. The woman had golden hair in disarray under a red veil and reminded him quite painfully of the vivid dreams that had continued to plague his nights since he met the Lady Julitta; dreams that clogged his memory and worried him by day. He rubbed his tired eyes.

'Tell me what happened,' he said.

'No one knows what happened,' whined the reeve. 'He went to bed and next morning he was found up there!'

'Who found him?'

'Forester.'

'What did he do?'

'Came and got me out of bed. I had a look, then I went to tell Sir Guy.'

'Got *him* out of bed, did you?'

'Well, no. Sir Guy sleeps heavy. No need to upset *him*. The man was dead.'

'So when did you tell him?'

'After he'd broke his fast.'

'Then the body was lying up there for what, several hours, after you saw it?'

'For a while, yes.'

'And anyone might have searched its pockets.'

'No one was about.'

'The forester. What happened to him?'

'He went back into the forest. King's man. I can't tell him to go, stay, whatever.'

'And when your lord had seen the body?'

'He sent for Father Osric.'

'What did he do?'

'Nothing. Said it was too late to do anything. Puked in the bushes.'

Straccan sighed. This didn't seem to be getting anywhere. But Pluvis and the relic *must* lead to Gregory, and Gregory had Gilla. Thin as the thread was, he must follow it. It was all he had. 'What then?'

'Sir Guy went back home, sent men with a litter. They took the body into the stable, put it in an empty stall. Sir Guy, Father Osric and me, and Sir Roger—'

'Who's he?'

'The lord's son. He was to travel to the wedding with his father.'

'What wedding?'

'It was *his* wedding day, Sir Roger's! They wanted to be off

62

before noon to fetch the bride. They're all away now, visiting her manors. So this nasty business was doubly unwelcome, coming then, with all to do. Sir Guy was as angry as ever I've seen him! Sir Roger wasn't best pleased either. They sent me to the inn to see the dead man's servants. One of them was still asleep, the other was just up and out back pissing in the cabbages. I asked him where his master was and he said upstairs. I went up and looked in the room. There was his pack beside his bolster and his cloak over the foot of the bed, and the bed had been slept in, and he wasn't there. And he wouldn't've been, would he, seeing he was dead.'

Sir Guy had questioned the two men-at-arms, the innkeeper, his wife, the scullion and the grubby serving woman, and no one had seen or heard a thing. The man had gone upstairs to bed, and then somehow out to his death.

'So in the end, to save trouble and fuss, the lord and Father Osric decided on wolves,' said the reeve. 'And he was buried over by the hazel wood, away from the ditch where we're stowing everyone else. You know, until they can have proper burial, when there's no more Interdict.'

And that should have been that, except that two days later the grave was found open, empty, and the remains were once again at the crossroads.

'What?' said Straccan, startled. He shivered slightly; it was damp and very cold in the hall.

'They dug him up,' said the reeve patiently. 'They dug him up, they carted him back up there, and they dumped him by the stone, right where he'd been in the first place.'

'Who did?'

'Oh, the villagers, the buggers. I don't know who, I don't know which actual ones, but I know and they know and Sir Guy knows, and Father Osric, we all know! They think it was demons killed him, so they won't let him lie in earth anywhere at all.'

'What did you do then?'

'Father Osric tried to make them see reason. He preached to them out in the churchyard and they listened like sheep, and then sexton took and buried him again. And the very next morning, there he was, gone.'

'Back at the crossroads?'

'Yes. And none the sweeter.'

'Then what?'

'Sir Guy ordered a party to take what was left into the forest and bury it somewhere. Father Osric said that wasn't right, but Sir Guy said he'd had enough, and he didn't want to hear any more about it, *ever*.'

The smith was more than willing to give his waiting customer the creeps while he dealt with the grey horse's shoe. With a dreadful relish, he described the corpse, the mutilations in detail, and speculated righteously on the probable sinful causes of the stranger's ghastly end.

'I elped carry im down to the stable,' he said. 'All the bits. It was orrible. I seen dead men a-plenty, but never such a mess as that.'

'I suppose you have trouble with wolves every year, so near to the forest,' said Bane.

'Wolves? Well, now and then, if winter's ard. Then the lord sends is unters out. Goes imself sometimes, if e feels like it. Five shillin fer a wolf, you know, that's what the king pays! Five ole shillin! But that wasn't wolves. I seen what they do. I seen what they leave of sheep, and once when I was a boy they got an old woman. What they do ain't the same. There's demons in the forest!' He looked hard at Bane to see if he was convinced. Bane looked suitably concerned. He paid the smith and went and sat on a bench outside the alehouse to wait for Straccan.

Chapter 12

'Any one of them could have taken the relic,' Straccan said, trying to ignore the buzzing in his ears and the tiptoeing approaches of a headache. 'The forester, the reeve, Father Osric, Sir Guy – but not his son – Sir Roger apparently didn't even see the corpse. The reeve seems unlikely, too squeamish by half, and the only thing that bothered Sir Guy was that they would be late for the wedding. Father Osric seems too much a drunken sot for any sort of enterprise. Which leaves—'

'The forester,' said Bane with his mouth full of dinner.

'Aye, the forester. So where do we find him?'

They found him at home, at his ease and with his feet up, peacefully sewing rabbit-skins together to make a winter vest. His neat sturdy well-thatched hut was tucked away in a clearing just off one of the main forest paths. The door stood open and some hens scratched and crooned just outside where a scattering of crumbs and scraps had been thrown for them. The man looked up at their approach but did not move as Straccan dismounted giving his reins to Bane. As he did so he felt a spasm of nausea and the headache began to tread more heavily. Not now, God, please, he muttered, and aloud said, 'Good day,' through the open door.

'Sir.' The man laid his needlework down, one hand coming to rest negligently on the hilt of the businesslike knife at his belt. His face was as brown and seamed as bark, with a great dark ugly scar on the right cheek. His rolled-up sleeves showed arms welted with scars. An old soldier.

'I am Sir Richard Straccan,' said the knight, at which the man stood up – he knew his manners – but kept a hand on his hilt, for he knew his way around as well.

'What can I do for you, Sir?'

Straccan's headache was getting hard to ignore, and the sunlight was too bright for comfort. 'I need information,' he said. 'I'll pay for it.'

'Folks usually do, Sir,' said the man easily. 'A time-honoured custom. Won't you come inside?' He hooked a stool forward with one foot, and waited until Straccan sat before himself sitting down.

'There was a man killed here a while ago. You found his body. At the crossroads.'

'Oh, that. Friend of yours?'

'No. Tell me how you came to find him.'

'I was patrolling that way. I do random night patrols, so they never know where I might pop up. When I got to the crossroads, there he was.'

'Did you hear or see anything else? Wolves? Men?'

'No.'

'How did the body lie? All in a heap or scattered?'

'In a heap.'

'Did you touch it? Move it at all?'

'I kicked over the bit his head was attached to. To see who it was.'

'Did you know him?'

'No.'

'What about the clothes?'

'What about them?'

'He was dressed, not naked?'

'Yes.'

'What had he on?'

'One boot – there was only one foot, we never found the other – his leggings, tunic. All torn. Nothing worth the saving.'

'Nothing else at all? Not even a saint's medal round his neck?' Straccan had to force his mind to think, his tongue to utter. He was feeling very ill now; there was no doubt his crusader's legacy, the ague – Saladin's Revenge, they called it – had chosen today to lay him low.

'No.'

'No jerkin? No belt?'

'No.' The man half-turned to swing his stewpot off the fire and set it in the hearth. Turning back, he looked hard at Straccan. 'You look sick, Sir. Shall I call your servant?'

'Did you find *anything* on him, man? I'm not here to inform on you. I've nothing to do with the king, or his justices, or the law.'

'What might it be you're looking for, Sir?'

'He stole something from me. It might have been round his neck. A little metal case about this big.' He showed a gap of two inches or so between finger and thumb and saw the uneasy shift of the forester's eyes.

'He had nothing round his neck. God smite me else,' said the man.

Straccan sighed and put both hands to his pounding head. He felt very cold and clenched his teeth to keep them from chattering. 'You might find it,' he said. 'Perhaps it was dropped, and lost in the forest. If you should find it, I will be generous.'

'I'm sure you would, Sir, if I found it. How generous, might I ask? I'm perfectly willing to look for it as I make my patrols, you know, if it's worth my while.'

'A gold piece,' said Straccan, pulling one of Master Gregory's nasty little coins from his purse and slapping it on the table. The forester stared at it and paled under his tan. 'You've seen that stuff before, haven't you?' said Straccan. 'You've seen these queer coins; he had them in his belt, didn't he? I *know* he did, and you took 'em. Bane!'

Bane was off his horse and through the doorway as if by magic, with his sword's point at the forester's throat. 'Take that knife off your belt. Drop it. Kick it out the door!' The man hesitated, Bane jabbed slightly, and the knife skidded over the door sill scattering the hens outside.

Straccan was holding on to the sides of his stool with both

hands. 'He knows where it is,' he said hoarsely. 'He had Pluvis's belt.'

As Bane stepped forward the forester stepped back, and back until he was against his hearth, and still Bane pressed forward. With a yelp the man fell backwards and for a moment sat in his own fire. He rolled screeching away from it, making a desperate grab at the hot stewpot – to throw – but Bane's foot sent it flying, stew everywhere, and the forester lay in the corner, swearing dreadfully.

As Bane raised his sword, the man cried, 'Yes! I took his belt! There were two gold pieces in it, just like that one!'

Straccan scooped his coin off the table and flung it into the corner. 'Now you've got three. You've been well paid so what about *my* thing?'

'I never saw it!'

'He's lying,' said Bane with an evil grin. 'Let's have a look at his lights. There's truth in entrails, they say.'

'No, don't!' The forester scrambled back against the wall and sat up in his corner. 'Yes, all right, I had it! It was some sort of relic – a bone, a bit of finger, nothing else – and a common little latten case, not even silver. Just a fake. I threw it away.'

Straccan said earnestly and with effort, 'I swear by God and his most Blessed Mother, we mean you no harm. Just tell me where it is . . .' and pitched forward off his stool into a whirling fog of pain and cruel cold.

Chapter 13

First the shivering. Blue to the lips, blue to the fingernails, toenails; rigor after rigor. Hot stones, well wrapped, packed all around him, light soft warm coverings, these made no difference, the cold phase took its relentless course. There was a woman. She tended him with extreme gentleness; he was aware of her, a shapeless figure in grey homespun, a dark shadow moving between him and the light. There was the clean fragrance of herbs, the sharp smell of a bitter drink forced between his chattering teeth.

Then the hot phase. She wiped his face with cold damp cloths that smelled of rosemary; his skin was uncomfortably hot to her touch, dry, burning as the fever soared.

He was burning. He could see and feel the desert sun, the pitiless sun of Palestine, a vast white-hot glowing disc that filled the sky and boiled the blood in his veins. They had got him, the infidel dogs, staked him out for the sun to fry his brains, while somewhere behind him, out of sight, they watched and laughed. Or was he already dead, scorching in hell? His clothes were on fire, he could see them shrivelling and browning, then blackening, with wisps of smoke . . . He struggled to break free, but there were chains, red-hot chains holding him down. His world shrank to a tiny inferno. He called for Bane, for Marion his wife, and for his daughter. Something had happened to Gilla; she was lost; he must find her, he must escape from hell and find her . . .

The sweating stage broke suddenly and violently. It seemed impossible that so much water could come from a human body, and keep coming, pouring from him, drenching the straw mattress beneath him, sour and acrid. He heard voices – he tried to open his eyes, but the leaden lids would not lift – Bane's voice and another man's. Strong hands lifted him, laid him on a fresh straw pallet while the saturated one was taken away. The smell of herbs again, and savoury cooking smells. Devils had ceased using his head as an anvil. Cool hands raised his head, holding a cup against his lips, a hard cold pressure, the same bitter taste.

'Marion?' he said.

'Hush now.'

'Gilla! I must find her—'

'Don't talk. Just sip. You'll be better soon.'

He was as weak as a new lamb, no, weaker, for they struggle to their feet, and he was barely able to raise his head or move his hands. Conscious at last, fully awake, he was aware that a curtain hung between his bed and the rest of the room, and that firelight showed through a small rent. Now and again a woman moved between the light and the curtain, casting her shadow on it.

Hands raised to her head, she shook loose the plaits which tumbled down over her shoulders; unwinding them, combing with quick strokes before re-braiding and tying their ends. She unfastened her girdle and reached up to hang it on the wall. Then, still in her gown, she moved out of his sight. He heard the rustle of her mattress and the creak of a box bed.

He opened his mouth to speak, to ask who she was, where he was, how came he there; but while he was thinking about it he fell asleep, and once again he rode the nightmare: another evil violent dream. They had troubled his nights for weeks now, leaving him weary and sickened on waking; their ugly memories swimming up in his mind during the days, so that he had begun to dread sleep.

When he woke in the morning the curtain was drawn back and tied against the wall. The door was open, letting sunlight stream in. No one was there, but on the table a cream-coloured kitten sat washing itself. Straccan began to sit up but a wave of diziness made him pause, resting back on his elbows until his head cleared. He heard Bane's voice outside, and a moment later his servant came in, carrying a leather bucket full of water. Seeing Straccan, he smiled. 'She said you'd be better today.'

'Who did? What's this place?'

'It's Mistress Janiva's house.'

'Janiva? Is that the woman who's been looking after me?'

'Aye. That Tostig, the forester – you remember? Him and me brought you here when you passed out. He said she'd put you right. I told him if she didn't I'd cut his throat and throw his liver to his hens.'

'That must have made him very helpful.'

'Yes, well, he was all right once he knew we really weren't friends of Pluvis, or spies for the Justices. That Pluvis was even nastier than we thought, and it wasn't wolves killed him.'

'Nor demons,' said Tostig, coming in with a huge bundle of dead branches and sticks, which he dumped noisily by the fireside and clumped out again.

'Nor demons,' Bane agreed. 'It was the men of the village. Cunning bunch of buggers! Never does to underestimate us common folk. Seems Pluvis made away with one of their little uns, a girl, five or six years old.'

The nails of Straccan's clenched fists cut into his palms as a cold horror struck through him. Bane went on, 'Cecily, her name was. The other children said he'd been talking to her, gave her a ribbon. He walked away and left them, but presently she was gone. So they reckoned it was him.'

Straccan found he was shaking and lay back again to let the weakness pass. Cecily, he thought. Five or six years old. Please, God, Lord of Pity, no! Not Gilla!

'They got in at his window,' Bane said, 'when he was asleep, and half-throttled him. Gagged him, tied him up, dragged him out, and packed him on the priest's mule. Osric was dead to the world, that was one thing they could count on, he wouldn't hear anything. Somewhere in the forest they'd taken their oxen, four oxen. When they got him there, they threatened to castrate him unless he confessed. So he sang. Like a linnet. Told them he'd flung her in the river. They found her a few days later, eight miles downriver at

Cubberswick. He told them a mark she had, a little red mark on her belly. That was true. Offered them gold! So they put away the knife and he perked up, reckoned they were going to spare him, started to grin and say now they were seeing sense. He hadn't realised what the oxen were for.'

Bane's voice went on, soft, almost a monotone. They had tied him, arms and legs, each limb to an ox. When he began to scream, someone shoved a wad of sheep's wool down his throat. He struggled, jerking and plunging madly, his face blackening, and the noises he made behind the gag were dreadful. They drove the oxen forward. The beasts took a few steps and the ropes pulled taut; they hesitated but their drivers coaxed them on. There was a sound, not very loud, like wet sticks breaking. The great placid beasts lurched, steadied and stopped.

'How did Tostig come into it?' Straccan asked.

'He was patrolling. He came on them as they were dumping the bits at the crossroads. They told him the story. He agreed to keep his trap shut, for a consideration.'

'The money belt.'

'Right. And the relic was in it as well.'

Straccan was silent. The only sounds were the crackling of the fire and outside the soft patterings of a sudden squall. He drew a deep breath, pushing away with great effort the ugly remains of last night's dreaming.

'They've got away with it, too,' he said, groping for the solidity of here and now. 'No one will ever talk and no single man is a murderer: *they* didn't kill him, the animals did. God's Mother! If anyone *guessed*! All the men of the village would hang, the manor would be fined out of existence, the beasts forfeit that brought about a man's death. Sir Guy would have a sticky time of it too, when the Justices got hold of him. The whole thing is his responsibility, ignorant or not. So no one will ever let *this* cat out of the bag!'

Bane agreed. 'Tostig won't, because he pinched the money belt. And the lord doesn't want to know: all he wanted was to sweep the whole affair under the mat and get on with the wedding. The village will hold together as solid as rock. And as far as the manor records show, one village infant was drowned in the river and one stranger, passing through, was killed by wolves.'

'What about Pluvis's men?'

'Sir Guy let em go. They asked the quickest way to Altarwell.'

'Where's the relic?'

'Tostig *did* think it was a fake. Well, it doesn't look like much, does it, in that cheap little case? He gave it to Mistress Janiva, thought she might have some use for it.'

'Who *is* she?'

'I think she's some sort of wisewoman,' Bane said. The fact obviously disconcerted him; he looked and sounded astonished.

'She lives here alone?' Straccan was no less surprised.

'She's looked after,' Bane said. 'Someone from the village comes morning and evening to see what she needs. They think a lot of her. She looks after them when they're sick. And Tostig, he comes by every day, brings her rabbits and wood, and stuff. He thinks the world of her. No –' seeing Straccan's questioning eyebrow – 'nothing like that! He's got a woman of his own in the next village. But a year or so back, he got in the way of a boar – you saw the hole in his face? He says he was near dead when his woman fetched Mistress Janiva. She healed him.'

'God healed him,' said the woman coming in just then. 'I nursed him.'

Bane jumped up and bowed. Straccan said, 'As you have nursed me. I thank you, Mistress. How can I repay you?'

'I need no payment, Sir. You'll be abed today, and still weak on the morrow. But perhaps while you remain here you may do me some service, if you will.'

'Gladly.'

He was staring. He had expected her to be old. She was less than twenty. Her face was oval, lightly tanned, slightly freckled, the skin very clear and smooth as an egg. Reddish-brown hair in two plaits wound with green wool. Brown deer-lashed eyes, neat eyebrows. Tall, and under the baggy grey wadmal gown, slim and long-legged. Her tanned hands, marked with many little scratches, were clean and cool on his forehead. Her presence somehow was as refreshing as spring water. 'No more fever,' she said. 'Did you sleep well?'

'I was sore beset with evil dreams.'

'Fever brings bad dreams,' she said, 'but that has passed. Are you hungry?'

Straccan discovered he was famished and made short work of bread and rabbit stew. When he had finished, Janiva pulled a stool to his bedside and sat down. 'Your man has told me about the relic you seek,' she said. 'Tostig gave it to me but if it is yours, I must restore it to you. Yet any man could say it belonged to him. Can you prove your claim?'

Straccan smiled. 'As it happens, I can. In my saddlebag, you'll find a parchment. A bill of sale from the Archbishop of Canterbury.'

While she looked for it, he said to Bane, 'No use you hanging about here too. I'll be on my feet tomorrow, on my horse the day after. You go ahead to Altarwell and nose around until I come. See if you can spot that bastard and his black horse, or get some news of him and my Gilla. I hope to God she was with him, and not—' He swallowed the ugly thought. 'See if you can learn anything of Gregory. I'll find you. What's today?'

'Tuesday.'

'You'll get there some time Thursday. I'll be there Saturday.'

Chapter 14

Janiva stirred the water with her fingertips. She signed the cross over it, breathed on its surface and looked. An observant watcher would have seen her sudden pallor when the pictures came.

They always came fast upon each other, a new one rising through the old – scattering it – taking its place; clear, small, intensely bright. Often she saw strangers and strange places, but when she had a purpose, seeking a certain face or place, she always saw what she sought. She had seen the pictures since she was a child. Her mother made her swear never to tell anyone, and said *her* mother, too, had known this power – curse or blessing.

The moon had waxed and waned and waxed again since she first had seen the traveller, this man, the sick knight, in her bowl. She had seen him several times, so that when Tostig and the man Bane brought him to her door she recognised him at once, although most of the pictures had shown him younger. She had seen him riding a great war stallion, in gashed and bloody chain mail, swinging a mace. She had seen him kneeling among a great press of other kneeling men, on the floor of a church or crypt lit by a thousand candles and lamps; one lamp, hanging from the vaulted ceiling on long chains, was close to the traveller, who raised his head from prayer and stared at it with tears in his eyes. She had seen him thin and ragged, scrambling along the deck of a small boat, all blurred and gone in an instant.

Now he was here in her house, and when she dipped water from the stream and looked into the bowl she saw him sleeping there, safe, with her own familiar things all about him. But as she watched, some dark foul shadow rose and covered him, sank and lay alongside him, over him. He struggled but his eyes were closed. There was no strength in him. The evil shadow lay thickly upon him, its edges expanded to fill her room and she felt a cold gripping nausea as a vile reek rose from the bowl of water. The stench was in her nostrils, in her throat, choking her. She felt it in her mind, clogging her thoughts with half-seen visions that started fair but ended foul in blood and torment.

Jerking her head back from the bowl she crossed herself and flung the water on to the ground. An evil taste lingered in her mouth. She blew her nose hard and spat, drank clean water from the stream and splashed it on her face. The sweat on her body stuck the gown to her skin, and turned chill.

This strangling slime had a name. This clarty reek had a name. It was ... it was ...

She had never met this evil before, but something within her, older than Janiva herself, knew it, knew it for the enemy, knew it as a thing to be vanquished and destroyed.

It had a name. It was a succubus.

From the sick episode by the stream, Janiva plunged into the village's May Day celebrations with a fierce hunger for normality and fun. The greensward beside the church was packed with Shawl's own villagers, and people from neighbouring settlements. A maypole was set up, topped with a green bush and twined with flowers and leaves already wilting in the heat of the fine day. Stalls hemmed the green selling food and drink, secondhand clothes and shoes, pots and pans, knives and spoons, tawdry trinkets and patchily-dyed coarse ribbons. Sir Guy had sent three sheep to be roasted, and these, turning on their spits, scented the air with mutton grease, promising well for growling bellies later on. Sir Guy and Lady Alienor were in the church talking with Father Osric, who was hoping for a money gift to pay for new shutters. The winter blasts through the window-holes were crippling; the old boards were rotten and would never stand another winter. Sir Guy's little group of family, friends and servants stood in the churchyard waiting for him, talking and laughing, an occasional high-spirited shriek of mirth from one of the women shrilling over all.

A relic-pedlar-cum-quack-doctor had set up shop against the churchyard wall beside the gate, offering unguents to heal the bone-ache, powders to sprinkle into husbands' ale to increase potency and potions to cure everything else. He also offered salt from the pillar that was Lot's quondam wife, fingernail clippings from Saint Peter and some of the clay from which God had made Adam. A small crowd stood staring, unimpressed and ready to jeer. 'Put er in yer stewpot,' shouted one, of Lot's wife. The pedlar glared, but just then the lord and lady came out of the church; he redoubled his enthusiasm but the fine folk jostled by laughing and chattering, and took no notice.

The locals, who took great interest in such matters, noticed that Sir Guy wore his old red hat but had a new blue cloak with fur trimmings. Lady Alienor was wearing her second-best blue gown but with a new girdle. There were little bells on the girdle's ends, which chimed and tinkled as she walked. Shawl folk grinned, nudging one another, and pointed to make sure no one missed this novelty. Pog's wife, who was selling ale, poured a brimming beaker for Sir Guy who downed it in three heroic gulps then rocked back on his heels looking surprised – Pog's wife's brew was particularly potent this year. Sir Guy braced himself and beamed in all directions before plunging on. Miller gave him a sausage, Blacksmith's wife gave him a pickled onion. Tanner's little girl, scowling ferociously, thrust a bunch of drooping flowers into the lady's hands. Lady Alienor patted the child's cheek kindly, looked with resignation at her bouquet, and yawned, longing to go home and get her shoes off. Her husband had bought them for her in York; they were too narrow but she didn't want to disappoint him by admitting it. Her face brightened when she caught sight of Janiva, and she sent a servant to fetch her.

'God save you, My Lady,' said Janiva. 'I thought you were still away, following the bridal pair.'

'We got back last night,' said Alienor. 'My lord *would* have us back for May Day! Thinks nothing can happen without him. Let's sit down in the shade for a little while. My feet are killing me!'

'How is Sir Roger?' Janiva asked. 'And how do you like your daughter-in-law?'

'The boy does well,' his mother said, 'and the girl will do, though he'd sooner have had you, as well you know.'

'Ah, but I am dowerless.' Janiva laughed. 'A poor match for a knight! Besides, I think of Roger as my brother. There is no blood bond, I know, but nothing can make me think of him in any other way. And truly, Lady, I don't want to marry! Not just Roger, I don't want to marry at all! You know how I feel.'

'It's against nature.' Lady Alienor sniffed. 'I don't hold with female education! It overheats the brain.' She looked round quickly to see if her husband was near. He wasn't, his red hat showed at a safe distance over the heads of the mud-coloured crowd, like an exotic poppy. She slipped her shoes off and tenderly massaged her toes. 'Look, there's a blister already! And I haven't had them on any time at all. You always were an ungovernable creature, Janiva, and my lord indulges you sinfully, letting you be taught to read and write. But he'd find a good match for you, if you'd let him.'

'Sir Guy has always been like a father to me; and you, My Lady, kindness itself. But I'm a free woman. I have my bovate of land, my house and the allowance my lord settled on me when Mother died. There's no one to bid me or forbid me. Not many women can say as much.'

Alienor looked hard at her, then patted her hand. 'Wilful,' she said. 'Not that there isn't some sense in what you say, and your mother was no fool; I liked her. But for her milk and her care, my son would have died a baby. Now, God willing, he'll be fathering his own sons. That plump little fig he's married should have no trouble feeding them – breasts like bolsters!' She wrestled her shoes on again, grimacing, and held out her hands for a servant to pull her up. 'I must catch up with my lord,' she said, 'before he eats anything else. He'll be groaning and farting all night! God be with you, Janiva.'

'And you, My Lady.'

The sunny cheerfulness and general goodwill cleaned the stink from Janiva's mind. She shared the ale, enjoyed the mutton, bought a pretty latten belt buckle and watched a group of gaudy players perform a short bawdy play about Saint George and the dragon. This ended amid waves of hilarity as the dragon's component parts – two men, the front and back ends – collapsed in terror at the sight of the saint's enormous wooden phallus and fell off the stage altogether, having imbibed too much of Pog's wife's ale.

When she felt clean again, *right* again, she went back to her house. The sounds of revelry, singing, bagpipes, whistles, recorders and surges of mirth could be clearly heard, and Straccan had tried to get up and have a look. His legs were still shamefully wobbly, but he'd pulled her stool to the open doorway, and was sitting in the sun with a blanket round him and her kitten in his lap. He looked very tired.

She set a pot of water on the fire and put greens, carrots, turnips and dried peas in it. 'I've brought mutton from the feast. I expect you're hungry, but first take your medicine.' She poured a mugful of the bitter brown liquid he'd been swallowing obediently for the past couple of days, and he downed it, making a face.

'What *is* that stuff?'

'I make it from willow bark,' she said. 'It is sovereign for fevers and the ague. Sir Richard, I must talk to you.' She brought her other stool out and sat opposite him. 'What did you mean, when you said you had evil dreams?'

He looked away from her towards the green and shifted uneasily on his seat. 'Well, you know, nightmares.'

'Not just from the fever. You had them before you were ill.'

'Yes. How do you know? For some weeks. It seems forever.'

'Falling? Drowning? Monsters chasing you? Rooted to the spot, with danger at your throat?'

'Nothing so commonplace.' He coloured and looked embarrassed. 'I can't describe them. About women, you know? God help me, children, even. I'm not like that! Lust and torment, night after night, till I'm afraid to close my eyes! Nastiness.' His eyes, very blue in the open air and under the bright sky, had a desperate haunted look.

'Yes,' she said softly. 'Nastiness. That's it.' She felt a cold anger that this man, her traveller, an ordinary decent man, should have been poisoned by this thing. 'Sir Richard, I believe you're bespelled.'

They turned out his saddlebags, his purse; examined his clothes, his boots, even the harness and saddle, all the straps, buckles and rings. 'There will be something. A charm for ill,' she said. 'I'll know it when I see it.' From his clothes and belongings she only sensed a confusion of everyday matters and a strong anxiety shot through with a vivid anger, nothing else. She handed him his belt satchel. 'What's in there?' she asked.

'Only the relic, the finger. Bane put it there before he left. You've seen that, anyway.'

'No, not that,' she said. 'Is there anything else in this bag?'

'No.' He tipped the latten reliquary into his hand and upended the satchel, tapping its bottom to show its innocent emptiness. They both stared at the small bright thing which fell out.

'What's that?' He reached down, but she put her foot on it swiftly, to stop him touching it. He looked up in sudden shock at her fierce face. 'Is that it? What *is* it? How did you know?'

'It's like a cloak around you, a smell. I can smell it inside, in my mind. Sorcery has a stink to it.'

'Sorcery?' He said it violently, making her jump. 'Sorcery! It's Pluvis – or was!' He told her about the ring of stones and the decapitated white hen. 'That was it, wasn't it? Some sort of filthy witchery he used to call my Gilla to him!'

'I think so. Who is this Pluvis? Why is he your enemy?'

'He's the man who was killed here at Shawl. And a week ago I would have said I had no enemies! I'm a quiet man. I live peacefully. I go about my business honestly. I don't mess with the supernatural.'

'You trade in it.'

'What?'

'Of course you do. Relics. What are they, if not supernatural?'

'They're not sorcery!'

'They're power,' she said flatly. 'Power can be used for good or ill.'

'Relics are good,' he said angrily. 'They heal.'

'They can harm, too. I've heard of relics that struck down thieves, paralysed evildoers and smote blasphemers dumb, liars blind, oath-breakers dead. Power works both ways. You trade in the uncanny, Sir Richard, and you deal with powerful folk. Among them is one at least who seeks your harm. *Think!*'

She fetched the tongs from the hearth and picked up the charm. It was a bright tangle – a few strands of hair, a bit of red thread – twisted and stuck together with some sort of gummy stuff in a ring-shape, its sole intent to do him hurt. Looking at it with loathing, he felt the fear coiling coldly in his belly swiftly replaced by a burning fury.

He followed her into the house, wishing the enemy was there to strike through and through, slash, hack and destroy. The lack of a foe to strike was almost more than he could bear. He watched as Janiva snatched her pot from the fire and threw the charm into the flames. The kitten swore and streaked out of a window, tail a-bristle like a small comet. The thing burned quickly, a flare that died to a ring of ash which she scattered with the poker; but the stink of it grew and became enormous, a gorge-heaving reek of corruption.

'Oh Christ,' he gasped, swallowing hard as the willow-bark medicine strove to rise again. He fought it back. Janiva's face was white and sick. He saw the convulsive movement of her throat, snatched her hand and ran lurching through the doorway into daylight, where he gulped the clean air until his mind felt scoured. In place of the sick obsessions, bright clean anger burned, at whoever sought to mire him in such filth.

When they went back inside the choking stench had gone but something still smelled rotten. Janiva looked about, sniffing, and came to the covered clay pot which she had carried back from the fair. She lifted the lid, cried out, clapped it down again and hurled the pot outside as far as her arm could send it.

'What is it? What's the matter?'

'It was the meat,' she said miserably. 'Cut fresh from the roasting. Oh Richard, it was full of maggots!' She sobbed suddenly and leaned against the doorpost. He tipped her face up with a hand under her chin and kissed her. She clung to him. There were tears on her lips.

Chapter 15

Bane had spent a comfortable night, warm and dry, in a barn away from the high road. He was about five miles from Altarwell where he was to wait for Straccan. There was a famous shrine to Saint Felicity there, and yesterday the road had been busy with pilgrims coming and going. It was a fair fresh morning. Bane ate his breakfast and made his way to the river, which he could hear in the trees not far off, to have a wash and water his horse. Then he heard the noise.

He listened. There it was again. Pigs, he thought. As it was much too early, only just dawn, for domestic pigs to be out and about, these must be wild pigs. Perhaps there was a piglet among them to which he could help himself without anyone being the wiser. He tied the grey to a tree, took his small bow and a couple of arrows, and cautiously slipped through the trees and under-growth in the direction of the sound.

He found himself on the edge of an open space: not a clearing, an ancient place ringed with low grey irregular stones, a broken ring with several stones missing. Within the circle on the trampled grass, lay a clutter of ragged folk and a no less ragged little monk, all of them equally thin and dirty, huddled asleep. They lay, snoring and wuffling, in various abandoned positions, as if God had shaken them out of a great bag in the sky and left them as they dropped.

Puzzled, Bane saw that several of the sleepers had ropes tied round their middles leading to latches on a stout leather belt round the monk's waist. Three of the sleepers were thus attached, and six others lay a bit apart with no bonds. Under the monk's outflung right arm lay his hooked pilgrim staff, and fastened to it a worn obviously empty provender bag. Some of the sleepers, Bane now saw, were women. Although their shapelessly-bundled bodies gave no clue, the rest were all to some degree bearded.

The little monk suddenly woke himself with a prodigiously raucous snore and sat up staring about, patting the ropes on his belt and swivelling round on his bottom to count his companions.

'... five, six, seven, eight, nine, thank God and his Blessed Mother ...' All in a hasty soft babble. Then he scrambled to his knees, clasped his hands together and had a quick pray, before rummaging in the breast of his gown for a small bundle which he undid to reveal a brass bell. This he rang very gently. The musical jingle at once woke the others, and one of the women, sitting up, looked straight into the surrounding trees, saw Bane, and screamed like a trapped rabbit.

'What? Where?' The monk leaped to his feet, seizing his staff and staring fiercely into the trees in the wrong direction. The others set up a dreadful din of howls and screeches. One began tearing at his hair, actual strands coming out in his fingers, while another rolled himself into a ball of arms and legs, rocking on the ground like a huge baby, and yet another turned and bent over, raising his rags to expose his bare backside.

Bane stepped out of the trees. 'I didn't mean to scare you,' he said. 'When I saw you lying there, I thought you'd been hurt.'

The monk glowered at him and shook his staff threateningly. 'Don't you come nigh, you go your way! Don't bother my loonies, and they won't bother you.' Noticing the bare bum, 'William! Stop it! Don't be rude!' And to the rest, 'Quiet, now! Quiet! The stranger's going. Shut up!' At which, bit by bit and rather reluctantly, the odd group stopped its caterwauling and capering, and William stood straight, grinning gummily. 'Clear off,' said the monk to Bane, 'before they gets troublesome.'

There was a sudden burst of noise on the far side of the ring, bushes shaking, voices raised in jeers and whoops. A shower of stones flew into the small company, striking heads and bodies, making them scream and hurl themselves to the ground in terror.

Louts throwing stones! Bane's instinctive reaction was to loose his two arrows, which struck tree trunks just above the bullies' heads, and to leap across the ring at them, drawing his backsword as he ran. Flushing them out, three big hulking boys, he whacked at their heads and shoulders with the flat of the blade, driving them squealing down the bank into the river where they slipped and stumbled on the slimy stones and fell, cursing and crying.

'Why'd you do that?' shouted the monk.

'I don't like sods who throw stones,' snarled Bane, rubbing the knotty scar beside his eye.

One of the roped men gave a braying laugh and wiped his nose with his fingers, saying fervently, 'Thass right, thass right!' One of the females had pulled her ragged skirt right over her head, revealing all else but hiding her fear from her tormentors. The little monk gently tugged the fabric from her white-knuckled grasp and patted the garment down over her body.

'There, Alice, they've gone. Don't cry, now. This gemman drove em all away, see?' He pointed across the river where the dripping stone-throwers sloshed up the farther bank. 'Ere,' he said suddenly to Bane, 'they mighta drowned.'

'No loss,' said Bane.

'Souls' loss,' said the monk. 'You meant it kind, but they could ave drowned and gone to ell.'

'Well, they didn't, did they,' said Bane, exasperated. 'Who *are* you? Who are these people?'

'My loonies? Poor buggers, they're just my loonies. I looks after em.'

Bane shared the remainder of his food with them. He had some very dry bread and cheese, some cold bacon and a handful of raisins. It only made a mouthful apiece, but they sat companionably chewing while Brother Celestius talked.

His own priory, far away in Dorset, was very old, very small, very poor and down to half a dozen elderly monks and just one weakly twelve-year-old novice. No relics, other than a disputed toe of Saint Jerome. No shrine. Nothing to attract moneyed visitors. Nonetheless the monks were obliged and happy to give hospitality to guests, and refuge and help to the sick. Brother Mark, infirmarian, himself feeble, could potter about dosing the ordinary sick with potions but was quite unable to care for the lunatics, dumped at the priory by their families when they'd had enough of them. There was no secure ward for them, and no hope of cure. 'So we all put our eads together and prior decided, and I got the job of lookin after em, being I'm the youngest. It's all right and proper, we got our dispensation to leave ome. Ave to ave permission, see?'

Ever since the prior's decision five years ago, they had traipsed from shrine to shrine around the country in hope of miracles. 'This year, we been to Saint Thomas and Saint Winifred and Saint John and Saint Edmund.'

'Any luck?'

'Taint luck! Tis Grace of God, shown through Is blessed saints. But well, no, we ain't ad any luck this year.'

Now and then one of them actually did improve. In the five years of their wanderings, two had got better. And sometimes they died, or sickened with other ailments. 'Fevers, coughs, agues, you know.'

'Are they troublesome?'

'What d'you think? Course they are. Not always, but they needs watchin. William, now, you seen im brandishin is bum, and e shouts rude things, and people laugh, and e waves is cock at em. And there's Alice, always pullin er frock up. Sigbert ere can't be trusted with a knife, e cuts imself up, silly sod. Cuthbert there, e as fits. Walter thinks e's John the Baptist and dunks folk in water, only e olds em down too long. E drowned is wife and kiddies. That Maudlin steals babies if she gets arf a chance. It's all go with this lot, but the poor buggers can't elp it. They're not too bad, as long as folk don't tease em, but folk *will*, and once they're upset it's a long job gettin em settled. Nor we can't beg proper, not if one of em's displayin is bum, or oikin er clouts up, or chuckin turds at folk, or pinchin their babies, or pissin in their washtubs.'

'So you beg.'

'Between shrines, a course. We gets fed at all the proper oly

86

places, we're proper pilgrims. I got my prior's token, and most of em as word of us by now. And sometimes we earns a bit. They be'aves emselves quite nicely when they wants to. Walter, if e gets a chance, can play the bagpipe jaunty as ever you eard. Tom's a wonder with beasts, ain't you, Tom? Cattle, orses, sheep, pigs, dogs, they do anything e wants. E can whistle just like a bird and birds'll come and sit on im. E does it sometimes to cheer us up, if everything's quiet.'

Walter had a small sack hanging at his belt from which he produced a folded wad; this, opened, became a large-brimmed shapeless hat studded with badges, which he identified for Bane, with pride. 'This is Saint Thomas of Canterbury, we been there, thass where Brother got is bell. This one's Saint Winifred, we been there. This is Saint John, we been there, too. This is Saint Dunstan, we was there last summer. And Saint Cuthbert.' He frowned unhappily at Cuthbert's badge. 'We went there, but we couldn't go in, cos e don't let women in, and we can't leave our women outside. Thass where Pernella died. We cried. Brother cried too. You cried, dint you, Brother? This one's from somewhere foreign; I swopped it for another Canterbury one.' He spat on his finger and rubbed the dull lead badges tenderly, humming; then abruptly stuffed the hat back in its bag, glaring suspiciously at the others. 'It's *my* at,' he said, low and urgently. '*My* at!'

'No it ain't, Walter,' chided the monk. 'That at belongs to all of us, *you* knows that. But it's you what takes care of it, ain't it, cos we all knows you'll look after it proper.'

They made their way back to the road, collecting Bane's horse on the way, and headed for Altarwell at an easy pace, passing between them a bottle of ale from Bane's saddlebag.

'They does dreadful things to loonies,' Celestius said, 'cos they say God's punishin em for great sins. But I thinks they're just sick, like anyone else. Like fevers, or lung rot. Sort of mind rot, maybe, poor sods. Just sick. And sick folk should be elped, not urt. Look at Millie.'

Millie shuffled along behind the rest, both hands to her face, holding her cheeks. A greasy stained cloth cap was pulled well down over her forehead and ears, and her eyes looked up nervously beneath its floppy overhang.

'Millie,' said the monk, 'show Master Bane your poor ead.' She shook her poor head violently and began to cry.

'E won't urt you, Millie, will you, Master Bane?'

'Of course not,' said Bane, gently.

Millie slowly untied the capstrings at the back of her neck and pulled the thing off. Her head had been shaved recently and was a mass of bristles, jagged shallow cuts and great scabs, some still angry, with clots of unguent here and there. She wiped her eyes on the cap, fumbled it back on and pulled its strings tight again.

'That's supposed to cure madness,' said Celestius angrily. 'They ties em down and shaves their eads and burns em with ot irons. I'd like to put the irons to *their* eads. God forgive me, I'd like to stick the irons up ... Oh dear, mustn't think uncharitable thoughts. They means well, but it's ard to remember that when they dumps these poor buggers after the doctors and priests ave been at em. Dumps em, they does, at the nearest monastery if they're lucky, or just any old where, so long as they gets rid of em. So ere we are, tryin to find a saint as will be merciful to us.'

'Aren't you afraid of them?'

'Lord no! They won't urt me, won't urt each other neither, not now. We been on the roads a long time together – me and William and Maudlin and Tom the longest – we been together five years. Some dies, and every now and then we gets a new one tagged on. We got Millie last month. We looks after each other. I keeps em out of trouble, and we keeps moving. There's always ope over the next ill.'

Chapter 16

The door of Prioress Rohese's chamber burst open without ceremony admitting a flushed dishevelled young nun who, before the irate prioress could utter her rebuke, gasped, 'Madam! The lord king is here!'

'Here, now?'

'He's at the gate, Madam.'

'With what company?'

'Well, none yet. He's alone, he's left them behind.'

'Just like Father,' muttered the prioress. 'Tell cellaress to prepare for twenty attendants, that's his usual lot. The rest of his household will have to quarter in the vill. Have fires lit in the refectory. Send to the vill for kitchen help; and make sure the silver candlesticks he gave us last year are somewhere he'll notice them. Prepare the guest rooms, put two braziers in his, and hang the Penitent Thief tapestries in there. Oh, and make sure there's a tub ready, and plenty of water heating, in case he wants a bath.'

As she snapped her orders, the prioress swept the clutter of parchments, rolls and books off her table into the document chest, locked it and pocketed the key. The flustered nun sped off on her errands, and the prioress just had time to set two cups and a flagon on the table when once again the door was flung open and the king bounced in, beaming. His face was nearly as red as his hair and glossy with perspiration. He was clad all in reds and purples, and brought with him a strong smell of horse, leather, perfume and sweat – not unpleasant but shockingly male and startlingly vivid in the pale quiet room. His colour and scent filled the place and seemed to use up all the air. The prioress felt breathless just looking at him and had a headache coming on even before he swooped to one knee before her, grabbed her hand to kiss her ring, then bounced up again and embraced her fiercely.

'Dear sister,' he said, letting go and smiling broadly as she smoothed her rumpled veil and adjusted her wimple.

'I wish you wouldn't do that,' she said.

'Ah, rubbish, you know you're glad to see me! Breath of fresh air in this arid sanctuary. All the news, all the gossip, a damn good dinner; I've got a present for you.'

'I don't want your present,' she said ungraciously. 'What are you doing about this damned Interdict?'

'Ah! That. Well. Exploring all avenues of mediation, of course....'

'That means you're doing nothing at all and waiting to see what'll happen next,' she snapped. 'Have you any idea what a nuisance it all is?

'Of course, of course, but it's not *my* fault, Rosy. Even you must admit I've done my best. Anyway, I didn't pop in to discuss politics.'

'What did you "pop in" for, then? And don't call me Rosy!'

'To cheer you up. Break the monotony. Give all your hens something to talk about. I'm on my way to Arlen, and Holystone is only a step out of the way.' (The 'step' was a detour of some forty miles all told. 'I've got some fellows coming along behind with stuff for the Priory: fish and flour, and wine, and oranges, and some cloth – I think – and some splendid venison. Rosy, I had good hunting yesterday ... I hope you'll find it useful.'

For a moment he looked oddly anxious, and the prioress, who had never needed to complain of his lack of generosity, said sincerely, 'Thank you, My Lord, you have always been a loving patron to our house.'

'And I brought this for you,' said John, flinging himself down on the window seat and rummaging in pockets and layers of garments, eventually fishing out a small jewelled bauble on a heavy gold chain.

'What am I supposed to do with that?' The prioress sounded cross. 'I can't wear jewellery.'

'It's all right. It isn't jewellery, it's a relic. Look.' He held it up, a square gold locket set with a large emerald that caught light from the window and gleamed green flame. 'See, it opens.' He pressed a catch, the locket sprang open and something small fell out and rolled across the floor.

'Oh bugger,' said the king. 'It's come loose again!' And down he went on hands and knees, crawling across the floor patting the boards. 'Where did it go? Did you see? Under the table?'

'I didn't see anything. What is it?'

'Get round the other side.' He had his head under the table now and, furiously, she stalked round the other side and got on her hands and knees, peering back at him underneath the table. 'There it is!' He pointed. 'Look, under your chair.' She saw a small grey object like a little stone and picked it up. 'Give it here,' said the king, and she handed it to him between the table legs. He scrambled backwards awkwardly and got to his feet panting.

'John,' she said, exasperated, 'whenever you come here, it's just like being back in the nursery! What *is* that thing?'

'A tooth of Saint Ursula.' He beamed at her. 'I *knew* you'd love it. It cost a fortune!' He fumbled with the locket and the blue-grey much-decayed tooth. 'See, here? It fits in this setting. One of the claws has pulled away a bit. I thought I'd fixed it.' He pressed the claw setting hard with the royal thumb, squashing it well down on the saintly tooth. 'There! It can't come out again now.'

He took her hand, turned it palm up and dropped the locket and chain into it. She looked at it and at his flushed face, and down at her dusty creased skirt, and began to laugh.

After dinner, the lord king sent for his sister to attend him in his chamber. He had bathed. All had been cleared away but the room was still steamy, and heady with scents. The sturdy plumpish royal body was comfortably enveloped in an elegant dressing gown. The king's short curly hair was still damp, and he sat in his chair with his feet on a stool while his bath woman cut his toenails.

'Come in, come in, no ceremony,' he cried cheerfully as the

prioress hesitated in the doorway. 'Sit down, make yourself at home. You've heard all my gossip at dinner, now it's your turn. What have you been up to lately? Give Madam Prioress a cup of malvoisie and some macaroons. Dinner was splendid, Rosy! Squabs in honey and almonds, delicious. You must give my cook your recipe. Here, have a cushion.' He pulled one from the pile behind him and tossed it to her. She caught it and held it on her lap.

'My Lord,' she said, 'I must thank you for your generous gift of provisions. The waggon arrived while we were at dinner. The oranges especially, a great treat for our sick and infirm. It was very thoughtful of you.'

'Well, there you are; I'm a very thoughtful man,' said the king, and, to his bath woman, 'Have you done? Right, sling me my slippers and you can clear off.' He pulled his jewelled velvet slippers on and admired his feet. 'You must tell me if there's ever anything you need, Rosy. You're not wearing your reliquary.'

'It's in my prie-dieu,' she said. 'I can't walk about jangling with gold and emeralds. It is a rich gift.' She eyed him cautiously. 'Where did you get it, My Lord?'

'The Archbishop of York had it from a relic-pedlar, who got it in Naples from the Count of Ischi,' said John. 'I bought it from York. I intended it for my Halidom, but then I thought of you. I know you have a passion for relics.'

'Passion? Hardly. The priory has a decent collection, of course. We add to it from time to time.'

'Got any new ones lately?' The king was peeling an orange, on his face a look of innocent unconcern which didn't deceive his sister for a moment. Something was up.

'No, I haven't. What are you on about?'

'Oh? I heard – just heard, you know, can't recall who mentioned it – that you'd hired some relic-merchant to find you something choice.'

'Well, you heard wrong,' she said, annoyed that his spies had been, well, *spying*, but aware that all his friends, lovers, relatives and of course enemies, as well as anyone who caught his interest, were under constant surveillance. 'I haven't hired anyone. Sir Richard Straccan very courteously did an errand for the priory, that's all.'

'Straccan! That's the fellow! One of the best in the business, I'm told. Turned dealer when he came back from the Holy Land. Funny thing for a knight to do, but then, live and let live, that's what I always say. It was *him* went to Naples to get that tooth, what a coincidence! A busy man. A man whose time costs money. How very kind of him to be your errand boy.' He was still smiling but the gooseberry-coloured eyes were hard.

The prioress kept her hands relaxed on the cushion. She wanted to say, testily, What's worrying you, John? But dared not. She said nothing and stared at him.

He let the silence go on, stopped smiling and began to clean his fingernails with a small jewelled pick. She noticed he was getting long-sighted, holding his hand away to inspect it. After a while he said, 'We have reason to distrust this Straccan of yours.'

'We' was a bad sign. She arched her brows enquiringly at him and waited.

'Damn it, Madam! He consorts with the usurper Langton! Don't deny it!'

'How can I deny it? I don't know anything about it. It's no business of mine.'

'Right,' said the king, 'but it's very much *my* business. I'm keeping an eye on Straccan: where he goes, who he meets.' His expression softened. 'Rosy, can't you see how it looks? The man visits Stephen Langton, is *privately* entertained. Visits you. Visits the Countess of Arlen, who then makes over some of her revenues to you!'

So that's what's got him going, she thought. Julitta. Him and his spies! Spying on his half-sister; spying, of course, on his mistress. Spies everywhere. 'My Lord King,' she said, 'I know nothing about Langton. I know Straccan because his young daughter has been lodged with us since her mother died. His errand to the Lady Julitta was a priory matter. We did her a service, she thanked us appropriately. It's nothing to worry about. I promise.'

'You always kept your promises,' he muttered, nibbling at a hangnail. Then, jumping up, again the jovial beaming brother, 'Well, well, let's forget all that, shall we? Have an orange. I'll peel one for you.'

She stood up and laid a hand on the silky velvet of his sleeve. 'My Lord,' she said, 'let me tell you about Straccan's errand. It's a strange story. I think you'll be interested.'

Chapter 17

Saint Felicity's holy spring at Altarwell had brought prosperity to the monks, their abbey and the neighbouring town. Pilgrims came in a never-ending stream, gifts and legacies with them, and twice a week the well chamber in the crypt was opened to give the faithful, sick and supplicant, access to the blessed water. Evidence of its healing power was there for all to see. The walls of the crypt were festooned with discarded crutches, hand-trestles, soiled dressings and bandages, and hung with wax models – some lifesize – of legs, feet, hands, arms, hearts, ears and eyes, all representing the once-diseased but now cured, bodily parts of the grateful and fortunate. Rank upon rank of candles burned in the low arched chamber, giving a queer flickering realism to the wall paintings – scenes from the life of the blessed martyr, Saint Felicity, whose holy power had caused the spring to burst forth from a rock five hundred years ago.

The main door stood wide open to admit the crowds, but not much daylight reached the far end of the crypt where a low stone basin caught the steady flow channelled through three lead pipes. The basin was on a stepped stone dais, and on the Watering Days, relays of sturdy monks in pairs dealt with the sick and infirm, helping them up the steps, sitting them on the parapet or leaning them over the edge in a proper and respectful manner – no spitting or splashing or acting the fool – and baling the water over them with wooden dippers.

Bane waited for Straccan as he'd been told, while watching for the unknown fair man. He wandered the streets, visited the alehouses, patronised the bear-baiting and the dog fights, and stared hard at every fair head and every black horse, with no luck at all. Nor could he learn anything of the man Gregory. Today, Saturday, Watering Day, along with half a hundred other idlers he had come to the well chamber to watch the show, and now stood below the steps of the well in a sweaty smelly press of hymn-singing hopefuls. He was not at all surprised to see Brother Celestius and his charges in the crowd a little way off. There was no need to worry about William or Alice, Bane thought. The crush of bodies was too tight for them to do anything but shuffle slowly forward waiting their turn.

Hung about with filthy rags, a shivering beggar crouched on the lowest step beneath the well, as offensive an object as could be. The skin showing through his rags was covered with sores, great pustules, raw wet lesions, maggoty ulcers and broken scabs. The stench was so powerful that people pressed away from him and he sat in a small space all his own, a mute huddle of misery. Bane noticed he was quietly secreting coins among his tatters, ragged quarters and halves of silver pennies, and even the occasional whole coin, dropped beside him in charity.

Brother Celestius and his people had reached the bottom step, where they fell to their knees, faces rapt; all but Walter's, who was staring at the basin and watching the steady flow from the pipes.

The hymn rose to a crescendo, a huge volume of sound which echoed back and forth from the curves of walls and roof. It was followed by a moment of intense silence, before the cries and pleas of the imploring sick rose in a great clamour and the packed bodies surged forward. The two strong young attendant monks rolled up their sleeves and began bawling. 'Wait!' and 'Stoppit!' and 'Shut up there! Two at a time,' shoving back against the pilgrims with considerable force.

In pairs the pilgrims ascended the steps, sat on the parapet, or leaned over the basin shouting their prayers, battering at the ears of the Blessed Saint with their grievances, illnesses and troubles, while the monks dipped and poured, dipped and poured. Two by two by two, men and women, children, babies in arms, all dipped in the water as if in a second baptism. There was a brief disturbance when one of the babies was found to be already dead. Its mother would not let it go, and was dragged away screaming.

In a sudden flurry of movement Walter eeled through the crowd, rising suddenly on the bottom step. He reached for the neck of the smelly beggar, hauling him from his seat and plunging his head and upper body into the well. Water surged up and overflowed, deluging the legs and feet of those nearest. The unfortunate victim struggled and plunged, breaking the surface with a yell of 'Leggo!' but was thrust under again in Walter's iron grip. 'I baptise thee, I baptise thee,' Walter cried, 'all clean from sin!' Both monks had hold of him, trying to pull him back without success. Bane pushed forward and snatched Brother Celestius' staff, thrusting it between Walter's ankles and jerking him off balance so that he toppled down the steps, dragging monks and half-drowned beggar all in one splashing yelling heap. As they separated and began to scramble up again, there was a sudden silence, then gasps, murmurs and rising cries.

'Look!' 'Praise God!' 'Praise Saint Felicity!' and 'What?' 'What's appened?' 'Soddit, get your great ed out o me way and lemme see!'

The beggar's body was clean of sores! Some scabs, drowned maggots and other repellent debris floated in the basin. The beggar coughed and spat up water, then, realising everyone was staring at him, looked down at his breast and arms, and ran a wet hand over his face and scalp. 'Shit,' he said, and launched himself at Walter, ramming his head into the madman's belly. Walter, still held between the two monks, doubled up and began to cry.

'E tried to drown me,' the beggar said, furious.

'E can't elp it, don't urt im, e's a loony,' cried Brother Celestius.

'I'll give im loony,' shouted the beggar, and swung his fist at Walter's eye.

Bane caught his hand before connection. 'Reckon he did you a service,' he said with a wink. 'Came here to be cured, didn't you?'

'Cured? Oh! Yes, of course! Cured! That's right! It's a miracle,' said the beggar fervently.

97

The magic word echoed and re-echoed and leapt from tongue to tongue. – Miracle ... Miracle ... The beggar smirked at the monks. The monks looked at each other, a spark of intelligence jumped from eye to eye; one raised an eyebrow, pursing his lips interrogatively, the other nodded and they made the best of the opportunity.

'A miracle,' shouted one brother in a great bass bellow. 'Praise be to God and Saint Felicity.' While the crowd sank to its collective knees the other monk hustled the beggar away behind screens and out through a back door into the abbey garden, where he administered a swift kick and several slaps. Sounds of protest drifted back before the door was firmly heeled shut.

In the crypt, the prayers and howls and praises were deafening, a solid battering of animal noise, its purpose to grab and hold the saint's attention. Women swooned. Men wept, tearing at their hair and clothes. On their knees the sick, the penitent, the lame and blind and wronged, lurched and shuffled forward, dabbling hands and faces and torn bits of cloth in the water puddled on the floor.

'How'd he get loose?' Bane asked Brother Celestius, seeing him reattaching Walter on a shortened rope.

'Cunning old git, ain't e?' The monk sighed. 'E asked the man standing next to im to lend is knife. Cut the rope. Gave the knife back. In all that squash, I never noticed.'

Bane made his way to the door, shoving through the kneeling pilgrims, and as he went out he met Straccan coming in. Together they walked out into the courtyard.

'What's going on in there?' Straccan asked.

'Signs and wonders,' said Bane. 'You all right now?'

'Yes. Any sign of that fair bastard, or news of Gregory?'

'No. What happens now?'

'I want you to stay here a bit longer in case the fair man turns up. I'm going to the Temple commanderie at Durham, to find out about that man you saw in Alnwick, Soulis. Wait for me at Burnhope if you get there first.'

'You reckon he's got something to do with this?'

'I think he's the man we know as Gregory. Those children said the fair man was riding with Saracens, and you saw Soulis with them too. He may have been a crusader, and if he was, or if he was a pilgrim to the Holy Land, the Templars will know.'

Chapter 18

When Straccan had gone, Bane bought some bread and bacon and leaned back against the abbey wall, munching and waiting. Presently the miraculously cured beggar was flung out, bruised, dusty and cursing. Picking himself up, he shook a fist at the brawny gate-porter and limped off along the street, not noticing that Bane followed. A Saturday market was in full swing outside the Westgate, and the beggar pushed through the crowd, past the stalls and in through the gate, making for the brothel district, and nipping swiftly in at the front door of one whose signboard proclaimed it to be the Bishop's Mitre.

Bane tucked himself inconspicuously in a doorway at some distance, and waited again. An hour or so passed before the man emerged, washed, decently dressed and carrying a bundle. In ordinary trews and tunic he was not readily recognisable as the disgusting vagabond from the crypt. Bane followed him back to the abbey, where streams of pilgrims were passing through the gate and in and out of the wellchamber, from which a sustained roar of praise and pleading continued. The beggar pulled up his hood and pushed his way into the chamber. Bane waited and after a while the man came out again, gazing around anxiously now, peering at people and faces, looking for someone. Bane followed him back to the market, where he waylaid the beggar by the simple means of ducking around a stall and colliding forcefully with the startled man. Allowing his bread and bacon to be knocked from his hand, he grabbed the fellow to steady himself and said cheerfully, 'Oh, it's you!'

'Eh?' said the beggar.

'You. From the well chamber. The miracle man! I was there, remember?'

'Er ... yes.'

'Here, pick up that loaf, will you? I've only just started on it. Where did the bacon get to? Oh, there ...' He snatched it up, brushed the dust off and blew on it. 'Hungry?' he asked. 'There's enough for two.'

They sat on the ground outside the Westgate, leaning against the town's defensive wall, watching the ebb and flow of the market and sharing the food.

'The maggots were a nice touch,' said Bane. 'Original.'

'I thought so,' said the beggar. 'A good idea, though I say it myself. I keep some here.' Delving into a pocket he produced a small round wood-shaving box, eased off the lid and displayed the seething contents.

Bane eyed them critically. 'What do they eat?'

'That's a bit of mutton pie they've got there.'

'Oh.' Bane's gaze wandered along the stalls and over the people, selling, buying, arguing, laughing, haggling. He saw a cutpurse slip his trophy to a woman partner who shoved it down the bosom of her gown, caught Bane's eye, grinned cheekily and stuck out her tongue before melting into the crowd. 'Funny bumping into you like that,' he said. 'You look a bit more prosperous than you did this morning.'

'That's my working clothes,' said the beggar, picking his teeth.

'Did they take your earnings?'

'Every penny, the sods! Every half, every fourthing! Said I was lucky not to be flogged.'

'You were.'

'I know. But that monk, the fat one, he gave me such a kick up the arse I won't sit easy for a week.'

They sat quietly for a while, chewing. A group of well-dressed pilgrims on mules clattered and jangled their way out through the gate, heading west. Two knights, one a Hospitaller dusty with travel, rode in.

'How'd you make that stench?' Bane asked.

'Professional secret,' said the beggar. 'But seeing as you've shared your breakfast with me, I'll let you in on it. Rotten fish and dead moles. Nothing stinks as bad as a mole, ever notice that?'

'Can't say I have. Where will you head for now?'

'Not sure. Newcastle, maybe. What about you?'

'I'm waiting for someone.'

'Perhaps we'll bump into each other again somewhere,' said the beggar matily.

'I shouldn't be surprised,' said Bane. 'Seeing as you've been following me ever since I got here. You going to tell me why?'

The beggar looked taken aback. 'I don't know what you mean!'

'Yes you do.'

'No, honest!'

'Honest my arse,' said Bane. 'You were a leper at the gate when I got here on Thursday. I chucked you a penny. I've a bloody good mind to have it back now! And I've seen you several times since, dressed as a pilgrim, keeping an eye on me.'

'Don't be daft,' said the beggar uneasily. Bane's arm moved quickly. His dagger appeared in his hand in no more than a blink, its point at the side of the beggar's neck just under his ear.

'Open your bundle!' And, as the man hesitated, '*Open* it,' pressing slightly until the point broke skin.

'All right! All right!' Opened, the neatly strapped bundle revealed among other things a leper's cloak, clapper and alms bowl. The cloak, reversed, became a pilgrim's cloak, and there was a badge-studded hat very like the one poor Walter cherished. 'How'd you know?' the beggar asked resentfully.

'I've had some experience in the same line. And there was that smell. It's a bloody powerful smell. I noticed it when you were the leper, and by God, there it was again in the well chamber. So I took a good look at the face that went with the stink and realised I'd seen it in lots of other places lately.'

'It's a small town,' the beggar suggested hopefully. 'Bound to keep running into the same people.'

'Bollocks,' said Bane. 'Why are you following me?'

'I was told to,' said the man sulkily.

'Who told you?'

'I don't know! I do it for a living. Follow people. When I'm told.'

'So who told you?'

The beggar looked uncomfortable. 'I don't know,' he muttered, 'I *don't*!' The point nicked a little deeper and a trickle of bright blood ran down to his collarbone. 'I get messages!'

'I can push this in a bit further each time. You'd really better tell me about it.'

'Like I said, I get messages! Someone tells me. Might be anyone – beggar, child, whore – someone who's been given a penny or two to pass it on. Saying who I'm to follow.'

'I don't believe any of this.'

'Look,' said the man, 'I was a player. You know? Mummery and mysteries, buffoonery? Keep em laughing, make em cry? One day, well, night it was, back in Bristol, I had a spot of trouble. The company I was with got into a fight and a fellow got killed. They buggered off and I was the only one taken. I was locked up. I expected to hang. Then someone offered me this job.'

'When was all this?'

'Last Michaelmass. Not this one just gone, the one before. Steady wages, he said, and a good bonus, just to follow folk. I've been doing it ever since. Bristol, Peterborough, Lincoln, York, all over. Tell where they go, who they meet. That's all. In disguise. I'm good at disguise.'

'Very painstaking,' said Bane.

'Well, so I get carried away a bit now and then. It's an art! And no one's ever twigged before.'

'There's always a first time. Go on.'

'It seemed a good idea at the time. Better than being hanged. And I didn't really have any choice, did I? What d'you think would've happened if I'd said no? Pat on the head and sorry we troubled you?'

'The man who hired you, what did he look like?'

'Oh, Christ. I never got a look at him. It was dark. The candles were behind him. He was just a shape.'

'Make some guesses.'

'Thin. Oldish. Croaky voice. Spoke English like a Frenchman.'
Bane thought about it. 'So you got a message to follow me?'

'No, not you. Your master what's-his-name, Straccan. Only you
turned up alone so I hung about watching you. Reckoned he'd be
along.'

'Well, you missed him,' said Bane with satisfaction. 'He's been
and gone again, while you were having your sneaking arse kicked
out of the abbey.'

The beggar flashed him a look of pure dislike and sat dumb.

Chapter 19

It took Straccan three days to reach Durham. Heavy rain turned the roads to sucking swamps, showing no sign of relenting when he at last reached the Templars' commanderie by the Cow Gate. It was an outpost, a unit of knights and sergeants seeing to the administration of the Order's properties in the area and offering banking services. The black and white pennon, Beauseant, hung sodden from its pole. Straccan sat on the bench inside the gatehouse, looking out at the steady drumming grey rain.

As he sat, he thought of Gilla and of his dead wife, Marion, and of Janiva. He had thought a lot about *her* since leaving the house at Shawl. After the destruction of the charm, she had told him about her gift of scrying and had tried to see in the water where Gilla might be. She could not. He remembered her anger and frustration at the failure. A barrier, she said. Some sorcery that baffled her seeing.

Sorcery! What could a man do against invisible unknown enemies? How could he fight intangible evil? He needed something to attack with sword and lance, and all he had to fight were shadows against which he was helpless. Surely only Holy Church could stand against sorcery? Yet Janiva had found that ill charm and destroyed it, and he was no longer weakened by evil dreams.

'What?' he said, startled, looking up at the squire who had come to attend him.

'Sorry, Sir. I didn't mean to make you jump. I only asked your name and errand here.'

'I'm Sir Richard Straccan of Stirrup. I want to talk to the master.'

The squire led him through passages, up stairs, across galleries, and down more stairs to a small comfortless damp-smelling room, no more than a cell, where the spare and shrivelled master, Sir William Hoby, sat at a desk sealing letters. A smell of hot wax filled the room.

'William,' said Straccan, relieved. 'I hoped someone I knew would be master here. How are you?'

'Older,' said Hoby morosely. 'Riddled with rheumatism. You look fit enough. What do you want?'

'You needn't bristle. I'm not after your money and I'm sorry your old bones ache, but you probably deserve it. I need information, William.'

'Sit down,' said Hoby. 'Shove the cat off that stool and have a drink. Stay and eat with us. Spend the night. What's the matter?' He rocked his chair on to its back legs.

'I have to find out about a man. He was probably in Palestine, but I don't know when. All I've got is his name. Lord Soulis.'

Hoby's chair banged down on all four legs again. 'Soulis? Where'd you come across him?'

'Our paths haven't exactly crossed yet, but they're going to. Do you know him?'

'Saw him a couple of times,' said Hoby. 'He was pointed out to me at Acre. Saw him again a few years later on the road from Joppa to Jerusalem. A troop of us camped at the waters at Lydda, and this bunch of tame Saracens appeared, looking like it was more than they could bear not to slit our throats. You know that look they have for Christians. Not Saladin's men – they belonged to Soulis. He was in the middle of them – Saracen armour, robes, the lot – on the most beautiful horse I've ever seen. We asked him about the road ahead. His infidels jabbered at him; not a dialect I knew at all, couldn't make out any of it. He said something to the master, I never heard what, then he and his creatures went their way. After a little while we went ours, smack into a nasty little ambush in that gorge, you know it, at Khatrak. The master was killed. They impaled Isumbras of Drayton, remember him? And poor old Martin of Andover. Can't be sure, but I've always thought Soulis let us ride into it.' Hoby stared ahead, not seeing Straccan at all, only the remembered treachery.

'What became of him?'

'Ah, now. I heard he became a *very* rich man indeed. Found a lost city somewhere in the desert. Brought out a lot of gold. *My* opinion, nasty piece of work altogether. All sorts of rumours.'

'What rumours?'

'Folk said he studied the black arts. Found his treasure with the aid of demons. There was a queer old fellow he brought out of the desert, supposed to be some kind of Arab sorcerer. Probably all rot. But *still*, *I* don't like him. He gave me the creeps!'

'Any idea where he is now?'

'Scotland, I suppose. That's his country. Want me to find out?'

'Yes, William, I *do*! As quick as you can. I'll tell you why.'

A damned queer story, Hoby thought after Straccan had left, and it worried him. Worried him so much that he couldn't sleep and in the middle of the night got up, lit a candle and wrote a letter in his own hand, no secretary.

To Sir Blaise d'Etranger, at the Priory of Coldinghame, in Scotland, greetings . . .

Chapter 20

There was a lot of unusual activity in the enclosed yard at the foot of Skelrig tower. A huddle of derelict wattle outbuildings had been pulled down and burned, the remains of the huge bonfire glowing in gusts of warm wind. Flames leapt up each time more rubbish was dumped on, as serving men emerged from the tower's arched door with loads of rags, bones and festering slimy rushes. Just inside the outer gate were four loaded waggons, now horseless; the horses stood heads down in the walled hay-meadow which ran down to a pretty lake where ducks, coots and moorhens ignored the rumpus, bobbing about at the far end with their backs turned. It all looked very domestic, a tremendous long-overdue spring-cleaning.

'. . . and clear out that filthy stable. I want it swept and washed, clean and fit to put the horses in tonight,' said the Lady Julitta, appearing in the doorway and continuing the stream of orders she had been issuing ever since her arrival that morning. 'Faugh, what a sty! You! Yes, you,' to a servings lad trying to escape her eye. 'Tell my steward to have the beds and hangings unloaded and put up on the second floor.' The boy scooted off on his errand. Julitta took a deep breath and surveyed the bonfire, the yard, the meadow, the lake and the track along which her retinue had travelled. Apart from a couple of huts in the middle distance, the landscape was empty of humanity; just rocks, gorse, sheep-cropped grass, heather and reeds.

Her steward trotted towards her. 'My Lady, the floor is still wet upstairs.'

'Have it flogged dry, then,' she snapped. 'I want all the stuff inside before it rains.'

The steward cast a wary eye at the pure blue sky, not a cloud in sight, and kept his thoughts to himself. Men began shouldering bundles of bedding and the dismantled parts of beds.

'Has the kitchen been scoured?'

'Yes, My Lady.'

'And the cook?'

'Doused in the horse trough, My Lady, and scrubbed.'

'Then let him get his fires going and get to work. What about my brother?'

'Not a cheep, My Lady. Door still barred. Lord Robert doesn't answer.'

'He will when he gets hungry.' She looked up at the tower where two men-at-arms, keeping watch, leaned on the rampart overlooking the approaches. 'Get the ale and wine unloaded. And don't forget to take some ale up to those two.'

She went back inside and climbed the uneven spiral steps to the bedchamber. There the beds had been set up, some with slatted bases and some with lacings, and mattresses and covers were being shaken and laid on. Two women with long mops were beating the floor to dry it. Light and a little breeze came in at the windows on the western side. On the recessed stone seat by one of the windows a child sat looking out over the empty hills. A little girl.

Julitta went and stood beside her. She laid one hand gently on the child's shoulder but the girl took no notice. On the horizon, a line of clouds had appeared. Julitta put two fingers against the child's face and turned it towards herself. The dark blue eyes met hers without expression, but a shiver shook the small body.

'Are you cold?' Julitta asked. The child shook her head. 'Hungry?' Another shake. 'Well, you will eat something soon, and then go to bed. You are very tired, aren't you? The blue eyes closed and opened, and the girl nodded. 'Yes,' said the lady, satisfied. 'Very tired.'

Gilla yawned.

The clouds were nearer now, and darkening.

Chapter 21

Sir Miles Hoby lowered his head and muttered, 'Thanks *so* much,' as a deluge of rainwater escaped from a market-stall canopy and descended upon him. It hardly mattered. He was soaked to the skin already, and the blue dye of his cheap padded jerkin had run, staining his wrists and hands and even his fingernails pale blue.

It had been one of those days, one of those weeks, really. In fact, looking back from this sodden standpoint it had been one of those years, culminating in the series of accidents, incidents and misadventures of the past seven days. Nothing had gone as planned since he left Durham. First his servant had come to grief, drunk; toppled off his mule on to a pile of bricks, broke his collarbone and had to be left behind. Then the packhorse had gone lame and Miles had exchanged it for a mule, all he could get, and *that* proved a wilful, peevish, ill-conditioned, lazy, cunning brute, given to biting, jibbing, kicking and bolting. Miles's hand was bandaged, there was a piece out of the flesh of his shoulder, his shins and one hip were blackly bruised and he hadn't run so far so often since he was a small boy. Still, he was young, healthy and delighted to have a job at last. Full of righteous goodwill he had stopped to render thanks and praise to his favourite saint at Nettleham and discovered his purse missing when he got out of the crowded church, the cut ends of its strings flapping forlornly. He could and would, of course, indent for expenses at the next commanderie or preceptory, but it cast a certain blight over the whole business.

Then, only this morning, this exceptionally warm sunny

morning, riding through the small town of Dale, he had encountered an abjurer being led through the town by soldiers and a priest. Pelted with filth and stones and buffeted in the face and body by any man's fists that could reach him, the poor devil's few remaining tatters of clothing had been torn from his body, and even the town's stray dogs were baying and snapping at his bleeding heels. Limping along behind him, almost as ragged, thin and runny-nosed was a young woman, massively pregnant. His wife, the priest told Miles, who would not stay behind in their home town, who insisted on following her man into exile and almost certainly to death; and there was nothing they could do about it.

Miles unbuckled his cloak from the saddle behind him, leaned down and draped it over the woman's shoulders. She flinched as if from a blow, then stood still clutching the cloak to her, staring open-mouthed with astonishment at the young knight. Before he could snatch his hand away she seized and kissed it, plastering it with snot.

Such a fine morning! And now look at it! He was cloakless, drenched and dripping, and if he wasn't sneezing and snuffling by morning *that* would be a miracle of some sort! But at least he wouldn't have to tether the beasts and sleep saturated under a hedge. Here at Fenrick was a pilgrim hall, built by the bounty of a local nobleman now dead, where travellers could dry out, be fed and bedded, and enjoy some company and conversation. He might, though he doubted it, be able to pick up another servant, perhaps even find a man who could manage the brute; now that *really* would be a miracle. Miles's hopes, damp and deflated, began to fluff up and dry.

When he opened the door of the hall an overpowering smell of wet people, mingled with that of fried onions and burnt sausages, rolled out to greet him. Miles still had most of his strong young teeth, and there was little he loved more than a crusty blackened sausage. His spirits revived so much that he began to hum a cheery tune.

There was no reason at all why a knight should not use the

pilgrim hall, but very few did, preferring to keep among their own kind, camping off the road, or seeking hospitality at a house of religion, or a manor, or the castle of a relative, friend, or friend of a friend. Miles stood out in the crowd like a grape among currants, his tall figure drawing all eyes; nudges, whispers and admiring looks among the females, and resentful glances from the men.

He sat at the long board set on trestles in the centre of the hall. Many pilgrims had brought their own food and shared it with those nearest them; but the hospitality of the hall tonight ran to sausages and onions. Along came a warty little man in a grubby apron who slapped a bread trencher down in front of each guest and was followed by another as like himself as to be a brother, doling out the food with a generous hand. Smoke and cooking fumes hung in visible blue veils and the atmosphere was eye-watering, but Miles was glad to be warm; and his jerkin, which he'd hung on the rack by the fire, was steaming heavily.

There were several piles of straw pallets at one end of the hall, ready to be laid down for the night. They looked third- or fourth-hand, Miles thought, but never mind, what were a few fleas set against the relentless deluge outside? A great flash of lightning cast a blue and sinister light on the upturned startled faces at table, and thunder bowled around the edges of the sky. Folk crossed themselves and muttered the names of saints. Miles picked his teeth, sat back, surveyed the company and thought about the job.

'You can make yourself useful at last,' his uncle William had said. 'And if you don't cock this up, my boy, well, perhaps we can think about you joining the Order. If you still want to, that is.'

'Of course he still wanted to! Had wanted to be a Templar since he was seven years old. Wanted *nothing* so much, especially as a certain young woman, Hilda daughter of Sir Brian Jourdaine, remained stubbornly unimpressed by his efforts to attach her interest. But once he wore the coveted Templars' white mantle with its crimson cross, she'd look at him with different eyes. Too late then, of course! Warrior monks were celibate, and she'd have lost her chance, but the fantasy was tempting, and he half-dozed over it for a while in the increasing fug.

Outside, the wind changed, and rain began to blow in through the windows. Someone fetched the hide shutters and hooked them up. Talk and laughter began – jokes, travellers' tales. Someone sang an old love song which was very well received, and a little wiry chap leapt on to the board itself and walked along it, back and forth, on his hands, somersaulting neatly down again and pretending to stumble into a plump and jolly woman's lap; cheers and helpful suggestions were not wanting.

Miles listened and laughed, got up and turned his jerkin over to steam the other side, and with a fine bow accepted a honey cake offered by a blushing young matron. Thanking her, he admired the swaddled baby she carried – a pallid pungent larva-like bundle. 'Fine little lad,' he said cheerfully.

'It's a girl,' said the mother irritably.

He'd taken off his wet boots and hung them round his neck, and now he sat with his feet in their damp darned hose near the fire. He'd sleep dry if itchy tonight. Tomorrow he'd make an early start, and if he could coax the brute into anything like a decent pace, he hoped to catch up with Sir Richard Straccan in two or three more days.

'A good man,' his uncle had said. 'Dependable, honest. Having a rather worrying spot of bother. Catch up with him and lend a hand. I've a feeling he'll need it.'

'How shall I know him?'

'Some thirty years old or so, about my height. Rides a big bay with one white fore. Wears a blue cloak, carries his hauberk rolled behind him strapped to the saddle. Old saddle, patched, with worn red leather trimmings. Axe at the saddlebow and an old-fashioned sword worn at his back. One manservant, I've not seen him. Making for the border turning west for Liddesdale. Soulis's hold Crawgard is there. My information had Soulis there at Christmas, though he may be elsewhere by now.'

'What is Soulis like?' Miles had asked.

'I haven't seen him for twenty years. He was a black-haired, white-faced, lipless creature, proud as Lucifer. About thirty years old then, fifty or more now. Miles . . .'

'Sir?'

'There may be something else behind it all. Soulis is an evil man. Wear this.' He produced a small flat silk packet stitched all round, with a cross embroidered on it and suspended from a silken cord. 'It is the Blessed Host,' said Sir William. 'I got it from Father Alphege. It will protect you from all evil. Keep it close.' Miles hung it round his neck and tucked the little packet under his shirt. His uncle took a chain and locket from his own neck and put it on his nephew's, saying, 'Wear this also. It is a relic of Saint Cuthbert. Don't lose it, I want it back!'

Miles knelt to receive his uncle's blessing, quite touched at the old man's concern and absolutely thrilled to have a job, an errand – by stretching the imagination only a very little he might even be able to call it a quest. He'd kicked his heels at York and then Durham, hoping to be taken on in some capacity by the Order, ever since his father's death last summer had left him penniless and landless with only his youth, strength and skill at arms to recommend him.

The little chap who had danced on his hands was an entertaining fellow. During the evening he told a long and robust tale concerning a monk, a goodwife, her spouse and an ale barrel, which made all but a few sour folk laugh long and loud; and he made astonishing shadow-pictures with his hands – animals, birds, an old woman nagging – which drew cries of delight. Not a few fourthings and ha'pence were tossed his way. He didn't look like a pilgrim – no staff or hat or badges – just a mountebank, making his living from the others. But a merry fellow.

Or so Miles thought until he was leaving the backyard privy on his way back to fug, fleas and bed, and found the merry fellow's knife at his neck.

'I never took you for a robber,' he said indignantly, 'and anyway, you're out of luck, I had my purse cut two days gone.'

'I'm no robber,' the merry man hissed, 'but I heard you, when you arrived, asking the porter at the door about a friend of mine. What do you want with him?'

'Do you mean Straccan?'

'That's the name.'

'Funny way to enquire about a friend,' said Miles. 'Why not come over to me in hall and say, Here, I think we have a mutual acquaintance?'

'Never mind that. Why are you after him?'

'Oh, I've had enough of this,' said Miles, smashing his elbow into the mountebank's windpipe, catching the dagger as it dropped and raising one knee to propel the collapsing body back inside the privy. Before the man could recover his breath, Miles had him suspended by the ankles, head down inside the noisome hole, wheezing, squeaking and trying to pray.

'My turn to ask questions,' said Miles. 'What's your business with Sir Richard Straccan?'

'Let me up, oh, God, let me up! Christ . . .' Miles shifted his grip and leaned comfortably against the wall. 'Let me up!'

'When you've sung,' said Miles. 'Meanwhile, let's hope no one else comes out here, because he'll just have to piss all over you. Or whatever else he needs to do.'

Sir Miles kept a firm grip on the mountebank's arm when they re-entered the hall, steering him to the corner where he'd prepared his pallet, and hooking his feet from under him when they got to it so that he fell on to the bed. Miles sat beside him.

'It's an odd story,' he said. 'I'm not saying I believe it, but it *could* be true, I suppose. It doesn't seem the sort of tale a chap would invent, even if tales and suchlike were his business. How do you report back?'

'What?'

'You're paid to follow and spy. So who do you tell and how, if you don't know who's paying you?'

'Someone turns up,' said the merry man sullenly. 'It's never the same person. There's a password. When someone comes up to me and says the password, I go where I'm told and tell all I know to whoever's waiting for me.'

'Clever,' said Miles. It was dark in the hall now, and the light from the fire had died down. All around them straw mattresses rustled as folk shifted and settled to sleep. There was some murmuring and a stifled giggle or two, and a volley of coughing. Miles rolled his captive over and used the man's belt to tie his hands behind him. 'You're not the bedmate I'd choose,' he said, 'but we'll share this place tonight. I'll decide about you in the morning. Don't think of scuttling off. I'm a light sleeper.'

He was, too, for the mountebank had two goes at taking his leave and each time was jerked back painfully, the second time nearly dislocating his shoulder. After that he lay quiet, fuming, until morning.

'There seem to me three ways to handle this,' said Miles, after their dole-breakfast of porridge, bread and ale. 'But before we go into that, you can help me get my beasts ready. Get my saddle and gear.' He noticed with approval that the man was quick and neat in his movements and handled the animals with confidence. The mule eyed him balefully and he scowled back at it.

'You got a right one here,' he said.

'Get it loaded,' said Miles, and watched as his prisoner cinched the brute's bellyband, waiting a moment before punching it hard in the gut and cinching it tighter while the mule was gasping. When it nuzzled his shoulder and bared its great yellow teeth he jabbed two fingers up its nostrils, and when it lashed out with the left hind foot he chopped it so hard on the nose with the edge of his hand that its eyes watered. Miles grinned.

'The first way,' Miles said, 'is I can kill you. I don't really know what to make of you, and that way I'd be rid of the nuisance. But you've done me no harm apart from annoying me in the privy. I doubt you are in a state of grace, and I am unwilling to send a man's soul to hell for no great matter.'

'The second?' asked the man hopefully.

'The second is, I can let you go, you can take to your heels and I'll go my way. But this doesn't do anyone any good, as you will still have your job to do, as I have mine. We must both find Straccan. So the third way may be more profitable for us both.'

'Go on.'

'You come with me. I need a man; mine was injured and left behind, and you can be useful. I will even pay a wage, which is not to be sneezed at. If you cheat me or try to hinder me in any way, I can always kill you after all. What do you say?'

The merry man looked along the road, and back at the horse and mule tied to the rail by the hall door. The brute showed the whites of its eyes in a promising manner. 'All right,' he said.

'Good,' said Miles. 'What's your name?'

'Larktwist. Starling Larktwist.'

Miles grinned. 'We all have some cross to bear,' he said.

Miles privately thanked his favourite saint – without reproaching him over the loss of his purse – for the turn of fortune which had brought him Starling Larktwist. And Larktwist, having twice in one week been compelled to tell his story in circumstances he preferred to forget, thanked his talisman (a grubby cloth bag round his neck, containing, so the witch who'd sold it to him said, a charm to ensure that come what may he would come up smelling of roses) for the lucky chance that had brought him Sir Miles, a young man not only in need of a manservant but heading in absolutely the right direction.

Heavensent, thought Larktwist, as they made their way to Alnwick, where Miles obtained more funds and a cheap but sturdy border nag for his new companion.

Heavensent, thought Sir Miles, as the unusually docile brute trotted quietly behind them. 'You've got its measure,' he said encouragingly.

'Up to a point. But it's watching for any chance to get back at me. It'll learn though ... Whoa!' The brute surged suddenly forward and tried to scrape its packs against Miles's knee. Larktwist took off his muffler and bound it over the animal's eyes. It reared and squealed, but presently trotted along in a docile fashion. 'It'll learn,' said Larktwist.

Chapter 22

Julitta placed a shallow black pottery dish, glossy with glaze, on the table. For a moment she contemplated her own fair face in the mirror-like water, then dropped a few fresh rose petals on to the surface and stirred the liquid with her finger, setting them circling.

'Look, sweeting,' she said huskily. 'Look at the water. Watch the petals go round.'

'No.' Gilla tipped her head back as far as she could, staring at the ceiling, the beams and the crumbling painted plaster.

'Look, honey,' said the soft persuasive voice. 'Look!'

Gilla's head rolled on the slender neck. She stared at the window, the walls, the hangings, anywhere but at the woman or the water which dragged at her will.

'Look at the water, Gilla.'

The child resisted. And resisted. Until eventually her dulled gaze slid past Julitta and settled on the black bowl. The petals circled slowly, and then were still.

'What do you see?'

'Nothing.'

'Look again. See my brother. Where is he?'

The child's lips moved stiffly. 'Sleeping. Above us. The candles are nearly burned away.'

'Good, that's very good, sweetheart. Look again. See our master. Where is he?'

'I see nothing. Only—'

'Say!'

'Sky, clouds, the tops of trees. Hills.'

'Look again. See him!'

Gilla's face convulsed and tears ran from her eyes. 'I don't want to!'

'Look!'

'Please . . .' But the woman's will was too strong and soon the child leaned over the bowl, staring.

'He is coming,' she whispered. 'He is on the road.'

'When will he be here?'

The child sobbed. 'Soon.'

'Who rides with him?'

The child bit her lower lip so sharply that blood came. 'Two men. They are wearing white veils,' she whispered. 'Archers. I see their bows.'

'There,' said Julitta. 'That is well done, little one. It will be easier in time; you'll get used to it. What else do you see?'

Gilla bent over the dish, her breath ruffling the surface. Tears fell into the water. The picture she saw, the unnaturally bright small moving picture, faded, and another took its place: a cream-coloured kitten, sitting on a stool delicately washing itself. At Gilla's sudden smile Julitta frowned. In the water a woman's hands picked the kitten up, lifting it high until her face came into view. Oval, smooth, tanned, full-lipped, with hair in two plaits twined with green wool; reddish hair gilded by sunlight at her back. Brown eyes looked straight into hers.

'Gilla? Gilla!' The words were in her head; all she could see now were the woman's eyes. 'Gilla, don't do this! Oh Lord, protect her! Sign the cross, Gilla! Move your hand, I'll help you.' As if someone else had taken hold of it, Gilla's hand jerked from her lap and moved up, down, left, right, over the water.

And now there was just a black dish with dull scummy-looking water and floating dead brown petals.

'What did you see?' Julitta, furious, grabbed the small offending hand, twisting it cruelly. 'Why did you do that?'

'She told me to, the lady told me to,' said Gilla, in a clear angry voice. 'You're hurting me! Let go! I hate you!'

Julitta sat back and stared at her. 'Who did you see? Who told you to do that?'

'I don't know! I *don't*! Leave me alone! I want my father!'

'Oh, him,' said Julitta with a thin smile. 'He is most likely dead by now.'

When the quietly weeping child had been taken back to her small bare chamber and bolted in, Julitta stood by the window biting her lip. She could not understand what had happened. The child had been docile, that was to be expected with drugs in her food and drink, and the results were most promising.

When that foul creature Pluvis and his startlingly beautiful but equally unpleasant companion Hugh de Brasy had turned up at Arlen Castle with the little girl, Julitta thought her just another serf brat, of no importance except to keep Pluvis quiet. He had a taste for small children. Best not to dwell on what he did with them in his hot little turret-top room. Once, passing the door, she heard a child singing, before its voice broke into tears and pleading, shouted down by his laughter. The servants were told to stay away from the tower. Pluvis's own man carried food and emptied slops, kept the fire going and took away the ashes.

Carried up the tower stair wrapped in a cloak, the child had seemed asleep, as they usually were, but suddenly a fold of the cloak fell away and the bright soft hair fell loosely over Pluvis's arm. Julitta saw before he could cover it again. Clean hair.

'What have you got there?' she demanded.

He stared at her, an insulting mind-your-own-business stare that infuriated her. He was always an insolent creature, and his loathing of women showed in the contemptuous way he looked at them. She knew what he was, but he was the master's creature and she had never interfered. He did as he pleased, and they were only beggar brats.

Not this one. This one was clean.

He was furious when she made him give the girl up. But there she stood, Lady of Arlen, in her own castle with her men-at-arms within call. He dared not defy her.

'Not this one,' she told him. 'Find another if you must, but remember the master's waiting for that relic.'

Robbed of his toy, sulking, Pluvis rode away from Arlen, heading north, with the finger of Saint Thomas.

She put the child, deeply drugged, in her own bed. The drug made its victims docile even after they woke – dreamy-eyed, slow of movement, above all obedient. If not renewed, the effects wore off in a few days. She questioned the girl and learned who she was: of all people, Straccan's daughter! That stupid relic-peddling fellow who had brought the icon and who'd sat staring at her like a landed fish, goggling with idiot admiration. It had amused her to bespell him; she'd disliked him on sight, and anyway, it was as well to be rid of anyone who knew about her brother and the icon. The spell was slow but sure. It would destroy him in time.

She had a feeling about this child. The power in Julitta sensed it in others. She gave Gilla a quartz crystal, smoky yellow at one end but otherwise clear. 'Look, sweetheart,' she said. 'Look in the stone.'

'What for?'

'It's a game. Some people see pictures in there. Can you?'

Gilla could.

Julitta sent de Brasy to Scotland, to tell the Master of her prize.

At the gate of the monastery at Shipwood, Straccan asked for the travellers' dole for himself and Bane. At each town and vill, abbey, priory, hospice and inn, he asked the same question.

'Have you seen a man, fair-haired and very fair of face, who rides a fine black horse? Has such a one stopped here? Stayed here? He might have had a small girl with him.'

'No, my son, I haven't seen him.' said the gatekeeper, passing bread and cheese and ale through the wicket into their hands. 'But if you wait, I will enquire of guest master if such a man has been here. What is his name?'

'I wish to God I knew,' said Straccan.

Chapter 23

Hugh de Brasy was his name, and one of his women once said of him that he was fair as an angel of God. That had amused him at the time, and even now, some years and many women later, he would smile when the thought recurred. All things considered, it was an excellent jest, though it must be said of de Brasy that he served Satan with no more ardour or enthusiasm that many a man served Christ.

Fair he was, with features like the Archangel Michael in a church window: straight nose, full lips, firm chin, large blue eyes and silver-gilt hair. His hands were well kept, clean and mani-cured. He bathed often and smelled of perfumes. He could play both lute and dulcimer, and sing in a pure tenor; and with sword and dagger he was more talented than most.

He rode a splendid blue-black Andalusian stallion, his saddle and gear ornamented with silver, and anyone could be pardoned who mistook him for a prince, or at the least, one of great worth and noble blood.

In truth, he was the son of an unnamed drab and an unknown sire, ditch-born and ditch-abandoned, found near death by a kindly miller on his way to market and deposited at the abbey he passed on his road for the monks to save or lose. They saved him.

And he grew to an abiding hatred of them, because of their coldness, the merciless Rule, poor food and many beatings; because of the rape of his body when he was eight years old by the fat kitchener, who thereafter shared him with his cronies. His savage hatred encompassed all of them, the God they prayed to and the Church they served.

When he was twelve he stabbed the kitchener to the heart with the knife used for scraping wax from the candlesticks, and fled, lucky beyond belief to tag on as servant to a cavalcade of crusaders setting out for Palestine. There he passed the years until his eighteenth birthday, though he knew not the day itself, only that he had been found, birthwet and bloody, early in May.

He learned many ways to please and serve the knights in those six instructive years. And he learned several of the languages of the East, for he had a quick ear and was gifted that way. He learned to steal cunningly, to kill noiselessly and the art of poisons. Purged by his experiences of either hope or faith in God, he was perfectly willing to give Satan a try, only to find the king of hell equally unresponsive. By the time he was eighteen, he believed only in himself and his luck.

His luck held, and he came to the notice of Rainard, Lord Soulis.

This Soulis rewarded loyalty with a liberal hand, and in his service a man could rise very high, no matter his birth, providing he was obedient, not squeamish, and truly wished to please his master.

He had served Soulis unquestioningly for more than fifteen years, ever since the master came out of the desert with his sacks of gold coins and the madman, Al-Hazred. All that time he had been Soulis's man, body and soul, but recently Hugh de Brasy had begun to form other plans.

For at thirty-three a man is nearer the end of his life than at eighteen, and whereas in the prime of young vigour, old age and death, heaven and hell, are too remote to matter, once past thirty those inevitabilities seem nearer.

On this fair day it was good to be away from Crawgard, from the tower where the Arab laired among his spells and stinking drugs. Good to be under blue sky in green hills, riding a fine horse and listening to the pure song of a thrush high above him; very good, even if one's purpose was murder.

Murder had *never* bothered de Brasy.

Nor did his master's devotion to sorcery, for he had no belief in it. He thought the Arab a cunning trickster, a parasite feeding off the master's gullibility. Like the beast he was, de Brasy had a highly-developed sense of danger. One way or another, he was certain Lord Rainard was heading for disaster, and when he fell, like a great tree he would drag lesser trees, his servants, with him.

It was not an easy decision. He had worried over it for months, considering and rejecting one plan after another. Responding to that warning nudge of danger's knuckle, he knew the time was ripe for a career move. He had money hidden, not enough to content him but he knew where there were gold coins a plenty, so much that a few handsful would not be missed. And by the time *he* was, he would be far away.

In the branches above, the thrush was still pouring out its torrent of joy. A little bone whistle hung from de Brasy's belt. He put it to his lips and blew a shrill piercing call that stunned the thrush into resentful silence. He listened. Nothing. Dismounting, he looped the reins over a deadfall and sat down with his back against a big ash tree to wait awhile. Presently he blew once more, just as the thrush was getting into its stride again. This time an identical note came back from among the trees to his left, and soon a figure appeared between the brambles, silent as a shadow.

It walked upright on two legs and had a whistle like de Brasy's hanging round its neck, but that was all there was to show it was human. Clad in wolfskins, all features hidden by a massive filthy beard and matted thatch of hair, it stood and stared sullenly at de Brasy. The breeze, blowing towards the seated man, carried the odour of old blood and decay.

'Well, Sawney? I see you're still this side of Hell,' said de Brasy. 'How long for, I wonder.'

The creature growled like a dog, deep in its chest.

'Does it never worry you? Hell? Eternal torment? No, I don't suppose it does.' De Brasy stood up and leaned gracefully against the tree. 'I've got another job for you. Or would you rather I gave it to someone else?'

The creature grinned showing big brown teeth, and shambled forward shaking its head. 'Na, na, master.' It seemed quite shocking to hear words emerge, recognisably human. As shocking as if a bear or a dog had spoken like a Christian. 'Sawney'll do it, good old Sawney. What'll you give us?'

'Meat,' said de Brasy. 'Venison. Mutton. Man. I know which you prefer.'

The brute chuckled. 'Aye,' it said with dreadful relish. 'Meat! Man! Aye. What's to do, master?'

'Same as you always do. Travellers are coming, Sawney. Two men. One on a big bay horse, the other on a grey. Take em, kill em, eat em if you want, horses and all.' He slipped the reins back over his horse's head and swung up into the saddle. 'Enough to feed your disgusting tribe for a week. Two sheep and a fat doe, as well; they'll be here for you afterwards. But I want the men's heads. Understand? Recognisable. Not gnawed! So I know you got the right ones. And anything they may be carrying – except money, you can have that. Anything else – jewellery, lucky charms, letters, swords, knives – I want those. *Anything*, understand? Put the heads and everything else in a sack and hang it in this tree. I'll come and get it.'

'When they coming, master?'

'A week, maybe less. Wait and watch, Sawney. Have fun.'

The creature laughed and turned back to the bushes. 'Fun,' it gloated. 'Us'll do that, master.'

De Brasy looked up at the sun and down at his shadow. Time enough to reach the town and have a bit of fun himself.

Chapter 24

The Cistercian monks of Saint Mary the Virgin at Altraham, shockingly hard up after floods drowned their flock of sheep and a storm threw down their barns, had decided to prod the conscience of the laity by putting the relics of their house in a wicker handcart and trundling them round the country to rouse sympathy and raise funds. A peep at Saint Joseph for a penny, or a halfpenny, or a fourthing, or – as they got hungrier – even a couple of eggs.

It chanced that by the bridge at Hexford they met a similar turnout, the Austin canons from Saints Peter and Paul at Fimberly, a small priory in like straits and blessed with the same bright idea. They had the corpse of their Saint Osric, not a patch on Joseph, even if Fimberly had all, or almost all, of their saint while Altraham had only the skull and one hand of theirs, and a dubious leathery hairy object hotly defended as Saint Joseph's scalp.

The two parties approached the bridge from opposite ends, each leader waving his great cross and bawling to clear the road. Neither would retreat or give way. It was obvious, said the Cistercians, that Saint Joseph had precedence, a great saint whom all the world revered. A mere Saxon saintling, a petty local hermit of whom no one had ever heard, must take second place.

Fair enough, retorted the Austin canons, if Joseph was genuine, but all the world knew Altraham's saint – the dying bequest of a lecherous local lordling, who hoped thereby to get a leg-up into paradise – was a fake, just the skull and paw of an old monkey and a bit of dog skin. Remarks were also passed about the Cistercians going bare-arsed, all the world knowing, jeered the canons, that they wore no drawers under their habits!

Matters proceeded *a verbis ad verbera*, and during the mêlée an enterprising bystander made off with Saint Joseph, what was left of him, and so poor Altraham lost its only treasure, and must now go home in disgrace.

They sat at the roadside, bruised, torn, muddy and sullen, and didn't even look up as two horsemen approached.

'Brothers,' said Straccan, 'have you seen a fair-haired man riding a black horse pass this way? Perhaps with a little girl?'

They had not, nor would they have noticed so despondent were they. But Brother Udemar still clutched his collecting box and, without hope, just out of habit, he rattled it under Straccan's stallion's nose. Zingiber shied violently and nearly unseated his rider.

'What a bloody silly thing to do,' said Bane. 'I've a mind to stick that box up your arse!'

Brother Udemar gave him a belligerent look but thought better of a retort. Zingiber curvetted and pranced a bit more but let himself be soothed, although showing the whites of his eyes to the monks.

Straccan surveyed the row of tattered churchmen. 'What happened to you?'

They told him.

'Well,' said Straccan, 'you've still got the cart.'

What good was that? They had no bones to show!

'Bones are bones,' Straccan observed. He looked absently at the church and churchyard a short way from the bridge. 'I doubt anyone could tell one old skull from another,' he said.

They followed his gaze. Possibility dawned. They looked shiftily at one another. Brother Stephen, the youngest, just out of the novitiate, stared blankly with one eye; the other was closed and blackening fast. The penny dropped. Scandalised, he shouted, 'You mean, dig someone up?' His brethren fell to hushing and shushing him, and one even clapped a hand over the boy's mouth.

'Is there a decent place to spend the night on this road?' Bane asked. There was a Templars' hostel, they told him eagerly, four leagues along, easily reached before dark.

'We must be on our way,' said Straccan. 'Here . . .' He leaned over and dropped a penny into Brother Udemar's box. 'God be with you, Brothers. I hope you find your lost bones.'

Out of sight of the battered troop they began to laugh.

Sir Miles and Larktwist reached Hexford bridge at dusk and decided to spend the night in the church porch. There was no alternative, Hexford being nothing but a huddle of mud hovels, a church and the priest's house – a slightly larger hovel than the rest. There was a half full moon swimming between scudding clouds and frequent showers of stinging rain.

Knocking at the priest's door brought his frightened hearth-mate from her bed, wrapped in a ragged blanket. 'Father Leonard's away,' she said. 'You ain't goin to lock me up again, are you?'

'What?'

'Cos Father's paid the ransom, all but a bit, and he'll pay that, honest!'

'What ransom?' Miles asked, puzzled.

'What Father Len had to pay to get me back, when the king's men took me away.'

'Oh,' said Miles. 'That!' He hid a smile. Annoyed by an upsurge of opposition from the clergy, all of them inconvenienced and many impoverished by the Interdict, King John had locked up their barns and storehouses, demanding payment before he would restore them. Far worse, he had ordered all their unofficial wives, mistresses, hearth-mates, bidie-ins, whatever, to be locked up until their partners bailed them out. Country-wide, from panic-stricken parish priests left to mind their own babies, wash their own drawers and tend their own cook-pots, and from arrogant bishops deprived of their nocturnal consolations, a great stream of silver poured into the welcoming royal coffers. After a brief separation from their masters, the ladies were returned home unhurt, many of them having quite enjoyed the enforced holiday from their bed-and-board obligations. The whole country was still giggling.

'No,' Miles reassured her. 'It's nothing to do with that. We just want to pass the night in the church porch.'

'That's all right. You can put your horses in the byre if you want; it's out back.'

They settled the horses and the brute in the priest's byre, company for his scrawny cow, and made themselves as comfortable as they could among their packs in the porch. It was cold and the flagstones were damp and slimy with moss, but it was out of the wind. Larktwist mumbled as he rummaged in their packs for food.

'Think yourself lucky, spy,' said Miles. 'You are sitting here a free man, out of the rain about to eat your dinner, instead of being head down in the turds back at Fenrick. Have a bit of pie.' He cut and passed a slice.

'Lucky, is it?' Larktwist scowled, chewing and spitting. 'Well, I'd as lief not be dead, but it's no great good fortune to be sitting here eating bat-shit pie!'

'Eh?' Miles took a bite and spat it out. 'The swindling old besom! It's green with mould inside!'

'Not the only thing that's green,' muttered Larktwist, hurling the rest of his portion out among the graves. 'Here, I've got a pasty somewhere ...' He burrowed in his layers of clothing and produced a flattened object wrapped in dock leaves. He broke it in half and gave one piece to Miles. 'This was baked this morning. I bought it hot from the oven. Remember? I suggested you might do the same but would you listen? It's not enough for two, really, but better than nothing.'

After eating their meagre supper they slept the sleep of the just.

Miles was woken by a sharp poke in the ribs and Larktwist's hand over his mouth to stop him crying out. He removed the hand, none too gently. 'What's the matter?'

'Something funny's going on. Out there. Look!'

In the graveyard among the hummocks and rampant weeds, knee-deep in mist, were figures moving about, bending, standing up again, making strange gestures. There was an occasional soft thud but otherwise silence. Owls hooted. Miles felt the short hairs at the back of his neck prickle as they rose.

'What is it?' he whispered.

'Dunno. Ghosts?'

Miles crossed himself. 'Lord, protect us!' They pressed back into the deep blackness of their shelter, watching. There were five figures, weird shapes in the moonlit mist, and their eerie silence was unnerving. 'It might be witchcraft,' Miles hissed. 'Some evil rite. They must be stopped! The priest—'

'The priest's away,' Larktwist reminded him.

'Well, we must do *something*!'

'Keep our heads down?' Larktwist suggested hopefully.

Miles swallowed. An enemy, a siege, a battle, a mêlée, these he could cope with. The powers of evil were outside his experience. Then he had an idea. Very quietly, praying it wouldn't screech, he eased the church door open and slipped inside. He found the holy water stoup, made a cup of his leather bonnet and scooped some water into it. Turning, he almost fell over Larktwist who had crept in behind him.

'Get out of the bloody way,' he snapped.

'I was just making sure nothing happened to you. Besides, it's safer in here. They wouldn't dare come inside the church. Where you going? There's no need to be brave, is there? Oh, Christ, I hate heroes.'

Miles moved stealthily out into the porch again where he lit their hand-lantern, closing its sides to hide the flame and, half-crouching, he began to creep across the mounds and hollows towards the uncanny group.

He was within a few feet of them when there was a loud crack and one hooded ghostly shape said, 'Shit!'

'What's up?'

'The sodding shovel's broken!'

'Use your hands.'

'You come here and use *yours*,' said the first phantom furiously. 'Why should I do all the bloody work?'

Crossly, because his legs were still shaking, Miles stood up, spilling his capful of water. 'Oi,' he said. 'What are you lot up to?'

The first ghost squealed and fell prostrate at his feet. The others grabbed hold of one another and stood, shaking and stammering. 'W-what is it? Is it an angel? B-blessed Saint Joseph, is it you?'

'No it's not,' snorted Miles. 'What's going on?' He stepped forward, and just then the moonlight slanted into the shallow hole they'd been infilling, and on a knobbly sack lying among their feet. 'Let's have a look at you.' He uncovered the lantern and held it up.

Monks! White monks, probably. Their robes, drawn up and tucked into their belts as if they were reaping, were so stained and torn it was difficult to be sure. They had obviously had a hard time of it recently. He had never seen a bunch of monks so tattered and battered, to say nothing of shifty. They might as well carry a banner with UP TO NO GOOD blazoned on it. But it was not for him to interfere with what must be Church business, however peculiar it seemed. Still, curiosity prodded him.

'What's in the sack?'

'What sack?' Brother Paul looked round wildly for inspiration.

'There. By your foot.'

'Oh. That sack. They are the . . . the bones . . . the bones of holy Saint Joseph,' babbled Brother Paul desperately. A small gasp came from the others who had stopped clutching one another and looked poised to run at any moment. 'They were stolen from us,' Brother Paul continued. 'We have recovered them.'

'A likely story!'

'I swear, Sir, we were set upon, here, on the very bridge itself, just yesterday. And abused! They called us a bunch of bare-arsed sheep-shaggers, may they rot in hell! And we were beaten. And robbed.'

'Who robbed you?'

They all spoke at once. 'Misbegotten black canons! Those Austin buggers! Them with their beards!' That at least had the genuine ring of indignant truth.

'What?' Larktwist had silently appeared at Miles's side. 'You were robbed by other monks?'

'It isn't funny,' said Brother Paul angrily. 'God and Saint Joseph will punish the ungodly!'

'Is it true?' Miles asked. 'You swear it before God?'

Another collective gasp, but Brother Paul – who would end his days, greatly revered, as Abbot Paul – was equal to it. 'It's perfectly true. They beat us; and we were robbed. I swear it before God!'

'Oh well, if that's your story and you're sticking to it,' said Miles resignedly, 'you'd better be on your way before someone else decides to have a go at you.'

'Yes, Sir, thank you, Sir.' Three bags full, Sir, thought Brother Paul resentfully. He picked up the sack and slung it over his shoulder. It rattled. One of the others picked up a collecting box. Another slyly kicked the broken shovel out of sight under a bush.

'Here.' Miles rummaged in his pocket and dropped a halfpenny in the box. 'Now, Brothers. Have you seen a man and his servant on this road? He rides a tall bay, the servant rides a grey.'

'Yesterday. They passed us here just after the fight,' said Brother Udemar helpfully.

'*He* gave us a penny,' said Brother Paul.

'Well, a halfpenny's all you'll get from me and lucky at that, seeing you woke us up! Were they heading north?'

'He asked if we knew a place to sleep. We told him there's a Templars' hostel, a pilgrim station, twelve miles on.'

'Thank you, Brothers.' And to Larktwist, 'Get the horses.' They spurred across the bridge and were soon out of sight.

'Let's get out of here quick,' said Brother Paul.

It was early afternoon when they sighted two riders on the road ahead. A bay horse and a grey. Miles gave a happy cheer and the riders halted, looking back as he spurred towards them.

'Sir Richard Straccan?'

'Yes. Who are you?'

'I am Miles Hoby. My uncle bade me follow and find you. He said you might find me useful.'

Straccan beamed. 'Did he? Good old William! Thank you and welcome, Sir Miles.'

Larktwist grinned sheepishly at Bane. 'Hallo.'

'What are you doing here? This chap's some sort of spy,' Bane said. 'I came across him at Altarwell. Someone has paid him to follow us. What's he doing with you, Sir?'

'It's all right,' said Miles. 'I can explain but it's a bit of a story. Have you had your dinner yet? I've come a long way on an empty stomach, and if you're willing, we can stop a bit, have something to eat and I'll tell you all about our friend here.'

Chapter 25

A small boy sat on Janiva's table, dirty, tear-streaked and scared. His mother, a tanned earth-coloured woman drab in muddy wadmal and clutching a basket of eggs, stood watching impassively.

Janiva coaxed the boy to calm. When her cool fingers touched his brow his blue eyes flickered and closed.

'Now, Peter,' she said. 'Open wide!

He gaped obediently.

'Put your tongue out as far as you can.'

The pink tongue, startlingly clean as it emerged from the filthy little face, moved a little but not very much.

'Lift it up for me, Peter. Stretch it as high as you can.'

The boy was tongue-tied, and now she could see why: a taut membrane held the tongue captive. She unclasped her scissors from the chain at her belt and snipped quickly. There was a small spurt of blood which stopped at once, and the boy blinked and grinned.

'There you are, Peter.'

Janiva lifted him off the table and gave him a mug of water. 'Go outside, rinse your mouth and spit.'

'Well,' said the boy's mother, 'if I'd knowed that's all it was, I coulda done that.'

'Of course you could, Madge. It's just a matter of knowing what to do.'

'Well, thanks. Thanks, Mistress. Them other little sods won't tease im all the time now. Ere . . .' She placed the basket of eggs on the table.

'Thank you,' said Janiva.

After they left, she wiped away the muddy marks left on the table by her small patient and stroked her little cream cat, which dabbed at the ends of her braids with its tiny pink-padded paws. She set the kitten down near the fire, where it patted at the moving shadows of leaves outside the window, before settling down to serious washing in the middle of which it fell asleep. Janiva swept the hearth and mended the fire before turning to a row of small pots on the table, their contents now cool enough for her to push in the rolled leather stoppers and tie a thin skin disc over each top. This done, she put them away in a cupboard and returned to the fire to stir the soup in its hanging kettle. A testing sniff prompted her to add some dried herbs and raise the kettle higher above the heat. Then she dipped water from the tub behind the door and poured it into her scrying bowl. She closed the door, setting its bar in place before seating herself at the table with the bowl between her hands.

Since she had seen Gilla in the scrying bowl the barrier was broken; now she could call the child's image to the bowl every day, praying for her safety and thanking God and his Blessed Mother that she still lived.

But she had no idea *where*.

She was familiar now with the isolated tower and its surrounding bare rocky hills. But it could be anywhere: England, Normandy, Brittany ... And she knew the woman now, the witch. Knew her for the one who had glamoured Straccan; knew her by her taint, the first time her image appeared in the bowl.

Closing her eyes, she breathed deeply and evenly for a few moments until her thoughts sank down into the quiet place where they could stand aside and let the pictures come.

She saw the tower for a few seconds only, clouds above and the little lake beyond, and then, fast, fast, the images rose to the surface, one pushing through another. Gilla, asleep on a truckle bed in an otherwise empty small room, its cold curved stone walls red in the light that came through a high slit window. A group of ragged grimy children in a subdued huddle outside a closed iron gate. A gaunt young man, his clothes soiled and crumpled, kneeling in a chalked circle, his lips moving in prayer. Sun-bright blue sky. A hawk stooping to its prey, a flurry of feathers and the splash of the lark's blood on the outstretched gloved hand of the rider below, the beautiful woman whom Janiva knew was holding Gilla captive.

'It's you again, is it,' she said with contempt. 'Mother of maggots!'

The pictures tumbled up, one through another to the surface, and broke there. For a moment she saw Straccan, riding along a narrow stony riverside path. Then the woman again, this time indoors, standing over the sleeping child with a candle. On the little bed Gilla turned over uneasy in restless sleep. Now the woman was standing outside a closed door on the spiral stair of the tower, her pale hands pressed to the planks of the door, her face alight with triumph, eyes full of hate. Janiva tried to hold on to the picture but it was gone. There was just the still surface of the water.

A lark was singing, soaring high and joyously over Skelrig tower, its pure fluting outdoing all other birdsong. On the slope of the hill, a woman flew her falcon and the lark's song stopped. Presently, with blood staining her glove, the woman rode back to the tower.

Attracted by the novelty of new arrivals, a few children from the smoky cluster of thatched hovels half a mile away had come to gawp and beg.

'Shall I see them off?' her sergeant asked.

'No. Give them some bread, then send them away. They may come again tomorrow, if they choose.'

When the master came he might have use for a brat or two. Their mothers were always pleased to see them taken into service. For the children it meant an end of bare backs and empty bellies, and if they were never seen again, well, that was only to be expected, living now among the fine folk, going with them when they moved on, the shivering poverty of home never missed, gladly forgotten.

Later in the morning she climbed to the top floor, to her brother's door.

He couldn't stop her. He didn't even try.

'Be still,' she said. Just that, and he had frozen where he was, helplessly staring as she dismantled his defences.

'Juli,' he said, 'he will destroy us all!'

'You are mad,' she said, and madness gave a lunatic caper, a gargoyle grin, as it sprang to life somewhere in his mind.

'They're coming, the Master and the Arab,' she said. 'They will deal with you!' And terror made him shake. 'What's this?' She laid her hand on the coin chest.

'Money,' he said. 'Julitta—'

'Be silent!' His mouth worked desperately but no sound came from it. 'You fool,' she said. 'You selfish grasping worm. You'd give me nothing in my need but for your own sake, to save your paltry soul, you'd give Skelrig to the Church!' She laughed, and he wondered how it was that she could still appear so beautiful.

'The Church shan't have it, Brother. Our master wants it, because of the Nine Stane Rig.'

It was an ancient stone circle, cresting a low hill about a mile north of the tower; a faery ring, shunned for fear of elvenfolk. And surely it was an uncanny place. Within the circle, it seemed always colder than outside. At certain times of the year folk claimed to see strange lights moving within the ring. They gave it a wide berth. Wild creatures, too, avoided it.

'It is a special place.' Her voice was gloating. 'Sacred, and so old, Brother. Much blood was shed there in olden times, to please gods that are forgotten now. The Arab says that power lingers in such places, power the master can use to become stronger. And don't think that pocky little priest of yours can help you now, for I've sent him off.' At the door she turned. 'The master has the icon. I sent it to him. He knows you tried to betray him.'

The door slammed behind her. Released as abruptly as if he'd been pushed, he fell on both knees and a howl of despair burst from him. He knelt on the floor looking at the damage she had done.

The chalk circle, so carefully and accurately drawn, was broken, wiped away by her feet. Two bowls lay on the floor, one inverted the other still rolling back and forth on its side, the holy water they'd contained soaking away into the broad dry planks. Protective charms and precious relics which had ringed him in security had been scooped up and flung on the brazier where they flared, stank and smoked. Frills of ash lay on the charcoals.

She had betrayed him. There would be no help. All these weeks he'd waited, praying, living and sleeping in his pitiful circle, sure that help would come. But now there was no hope.

Chapter 26

Robert shared his lord and patron's interest in the black arts for as long as it only involved the sacrifice of beasts. But children, baptised souls, were another thing entirely, and horror had overwhelmed him. He had panicked and fled to the isolated safety of Skelrig. From there he wrote to his sister, bidding her have no more to do with the murderer, de Soulis. He, Robert, was surely damned, he wrote, for his part in such evil, unless God could be persuaded to forgive him.

Priests could persuade God, and money could persuade priests. He must confess and be absolved of his sins, but before he even dared to confess he must be sure of eventual forgiveness. For that, naturally, he was prepared to pay. God had his price like anyone else. Robert would make a gift of his Hoplaw estate to the abbey at Mailros. That should smooth the way, and then, when they agreed to accept him as a novice, he would give them Skelrig as well. After all, he'd have no use for it any more once he was safely in the cloister.

Then he'd remembered Martin. Martin Brus.

They'd been boys together: friends, quarrelling and making up, brawling and being punished, enduring together the years of brutal training, gashes, bruises, broken limbs and physical exhaustion. They'd shared boyhood illnesses, boyish crimes and the aspirations of idealistic youth. For nine years they had been as close as brothers; first pages, then squires, until the culmination of all those years of discipline, violence and endurance – knighthood.

Robert had been exalted. They would be perfect knights without sin or stain, chivalrous, brave, undefeated. Minstrels would make songs about them, ladies beg to give their favours, princesses would pine, infidels and heretics fall like bulrushes to their swords.

And, just a few days after their dubbing, Martin packed his few possessions in his saddlebags and rode away.

'I have to go,' he said. 'There's something else I have to do. It is more important.'

'What? In God's name, what's more important than being a knight?' Robert shouted.

Martin clenched his fists, and tears ran down his cheeks, but he just kept saying he had to go; there was something he must do. Over and over.

'You're throwing away all you've worked for. Your uncle will never forgive you!' Martin was his uncle's ward, his parents being dead.

'It's all right. Uncle Blaise knows all about it.'

Robert had an idea. 'It's not the Church, is it? God's Blood, Martin, tell me you haven't decided to be a bloody monk!'

To his astonishment, Martin began to laugh. 'No, no! You're wrong, Rob. That's not it at all.'

'Then what? Are you ill? Is that it? Something's wrong with you!'

Martin sighed. 'I can't explain. Forgive me, but I gave my word. Believe me, Rob, there is another task for me. I am going to serve my uncle, and he will teach me.'

'Teach you what?'

'I can't say. But it's very important, more than being a monk or a priest, and much more than joining the troop of some lord, no matter how great he may be.'

'If you say so.' Robert scowled. 'I can't stop you. God's Bones, Martin, I thought we would stay together, take service together, be friends for ever!'

'I hope you will always be my friend, Rob. I will surely be yours. But this I have to do.'

He rode off alone just after dawn with only Robert to see him off. He was going, he said, to Sauchiehill, to his uncle's holding.

Soon after Robert took service with Lord de Soulis, he asked leave to go home and see to his affairs and decided to ride to Sauchiehill. Martin might be having second thoughts. Besides, Robert wanted to show off the fine gear and garments his patron provided.

He found his friend in the tiltyard, sparring, both of them shirtless, with his uncle, a tall old man still very strong and quick. They were at it hammer and tongs, the old man wielding a gaveloc, Martin an axe. Robert, unnoticed, sat on a bench and watched. The sweating grunting combat ended abruptly with Martin's axe flying through the air and Sir Blaise thrusting the gaveloc between his nephew's ankles to bring him down. Robert clapped enthusiastically.

Before the antagonists put on their shirts, Robert noticed that Sir Blaise wore a curious amulet round his neck of some greenish-grey stone. It was quite large and looked something like a star. He only saw it for a moment, and then it was hidden under the shirt and he forgot all about it.

They made him very welcome; his friend was delighted to see him again but there was no hope of Martin changing his mind. Whatever it was he had to do, he was committed to it.

When Martin saw him off next morning, Robert said, 'I'll come again, when I can.'

'Not for a while,' Martin said. 'We're for England next week.'

'England? Will you be long away?'

'Quite some time I think. An old friend of my uncle has died at Salisbury and left him some property in bequest, so we are going there. But I'll send word when we're back. It was good of you to come, Rob.'

'God be with you, Martin.'

'And you. And Rob—' His plain kindly face was suddenly creased with concern.

'What?'

'If you're ever in trouble, need a hand, you know? Send to me.'

'Why should I have trouble?' He laughed. Fame and fortune beckoned, and the world was his.

'No reason,' said his friend. 'But remember, if you need my help, if the day comes, I'm your man.'

Again Robert had written to Julitta, telling her he was sending, by a sure hand, the old icon that had belonged to their grandfather. She was to find Sir Martin Brus, companion and nephew of Sir Blaise d'Etranger, perhaps at Salisbury. When the icon arrived, she must give it to Martin saying to him, 'The day has come.' Just that. It was not the icon that mattered, of course, precious though it was; it was the case but to send just the empty cylinder would seem most strange.

He knew Martin would come. He would see the star symbol on the case which Robert had stolen from the Arab's reeking room – the same device as on the talisman Sir Blaise wore round his neck. Robert knew now what it was Martin had to do, and what his uncle was. Blaise d'Etranger was one of the few who could stand against such as Al-Hazred and his master.

He could trust Julitta. Of course he could. She was his sister, after all, and would do as he told her.

When Abbot Renwal of Mailros refused to admit him as a novice, Robert was first incredulous and then, when he realised the old man meant it, mad with terror. How, outside the holy abbey, could he hope for protection? Worse still, when the abbot heard his confession he denied him absolution and ordered him on pilgrimage to Jerusalem!

'Did you think that the slaughter of God's innocents and dabbling with devil-worship could be wiped out with ten Paters and an Ave? Pray, fast and wear a hair shirt day and night until you return,' he said, nevertheless pocketing Hoplaw without so much as a thank-you. 'When you get back, you will walk here from Skelrig, barefoot, in just a shirt with a rope round your neck, to show penitence. Then we'll see whether there's any possibility of absolution. And understand that's not a promise! Now get out of here! You defile this holy ground.'

Of course, he didn't need to go to Jerusalem himself; wealthy penitents seldom hazarded themselves on such a journey. He asked around for a reliable substitute and paid him handsomely to undertake the pilgrimage, promising to care generously for the man's family meanwhile. Crimmon he despatched south to Julitta, with the icon in its tell-tale case.

Then he waited until the man Bane turned up and Robert learned how all had nearly been lost. But God was merciful, it could still be put right. Thanks to Hawkan Bane's master, Straccan – Robert blessed him fervently – Julitta would get the icon, find Martin and give it to him.

All he had to do was wait: praying, fasting, itching unbearably in his hair shirt, drinking only water and eating just enough to stay alive. Above all, he must keep his nerve. In the circle the Arab's spells could not reach him. The dumb boy, Hob, was a good lad and cared for him well enough. Martin would come soon.

But, before the end of May, Julitta came.

She was older than he by four years, the first-born. He remembered trotting after her when he was small, clutching at her dress when they walked down the stairs, holding her hand when they crossed the yard to see the hawks or the horses, calling to her when their father set him on his first pony, 'Look, Shuli, look! Shuli, look at *me*!'

When he was sent away at seven, raw material to be turned first into page, then squire, then knight, she ran after the horses waving, but he knew he must not look back nor wave, because he was a man and she was only a girl; so he sat very straight and stared ahead. It was ten years before he saw her again. He didn't recognise the beautiful woman at all, just stared, feeling clumsy and tongue-tied as most men did when they first saw Julitta.

Their father was ill. Grey-faced and gaunt with a sick-room smell of liniment and drugs, he shuffled about the place sour with illness, fierce eyes glaring under overgrown eyebrows. He was certain no one could manage as he had and that all would be wasted and ruined when he died.

'There's just enough for equipage,' the old man said without preamble, cornering Robert in the mews. 'The land's mortgaged;

I owe the Jews forty marks. There's nothing for your sister's *dot* if you're to be fitted up properly, so don't expect money to fling about when I'm gone! There's a man at court says he'll take you on. He has to provide four knights in the king's service, and one of em died at Yuletide. He'll pay my debt, you'll have your keep, and whatever you can win at tourneys will be yours.'

'Who is he?'

'Rainard de Soulis.'

'I've heard of him.' So he had. Very rich. Favoured by the king. An old crusader.

'See that you please him, and you'll do well enough. He's generous to those who serve him well.'

Julitta found him in the chapel. 'Robbie,' she said, straight to the point like their father, 'he'll not give me a dowry. Will you?'

'I've no money,' he said, embarrassed because he couldn't help noticing the swell of her breasts and the fragrance of her, so close to him.

'I know. But when he dies, Robbie?'

'He's told me there's nothing but debts.'

'Is it true?'

'Why should he lie? He can't take anything with him.'

'Robbie, will you help me?'

'When he's dead,' he said, 'we'll see what there is.'

And there was nothing, just as the old lord had said.

Robert entered the service of Lord Rainard de Soulis. A great man. In the king's favour and himself of royal blood of the old Celtic line. Proud, distant, splendidly dressed. Anyone seeing him with the ageing shabby king would mistake man for monarch, monarch for servant. Although in his youth King William had been a brave fighter, in sick and disappointed old age, debt-ridden and in thrall to the King of the English, he spent his days recalling past victories, dreaming and scheming to regain the lands south of the Tweed, once Scottish but now firmly, intolerably, in the grasp of England.

Soulis was always with the king: leaning on his chair, passing his cup, whispering in his ear, offering an arm to help the feeble old man rise and walk, closeted with him alone for hours on end. He seemed to have no interest in reward and God knows he was rich enough, if rumour and appearance marched with truth.

His household and knights kept to themselves. The knights were renowned for their uncommon success in tourneys, and whenever serious fighting was required they were a byword for ferocity. Robert found them polite but, like their master, aloof. In the first few months of his service he was more than once surprised by their viciousness, far removed from the casual brutality he was used to.

But after a while and little by little, they accepted him. A clap on the back from one, a comradely grin from another, then the invitations began — to come hunting, come hawking, come drinking, come wenching — little by little, drop by drop. Like the potion in his drink of which he was unaware, and the drugged smoke of the candle in his small chamber which brought strange dreams — often delicious, but sometimes terrifying — steadily his easy comfortable morals and flimsy principles were eroded ... week by week, little by little, drop by drop.

They were at Lord Rainard's domain of Soulistoun when, one morning, returning from the mews, he saw a woman on the steps ahead of him. The early sun was in his eyes as he looked up to greet her.

'Good day to you, Lady.'

She turned and looked down at him. To his astonishment, it was his sister.

'Juli! What are you doing here?'

'The same as you. Brother. Seeking my fortune.'

He took her hand and led her back down the steps, across the yard and through the little gate that led to the pleasance. But the benches were wet with dew, so they must walk.

'I didn't know you knew My Lord de Soulis,' he said.

'Did you not? He has been good lord to us both, Robbie, since our father died. You he took into his service and I hear you have had good fortune in the tourneys.'

At Easter he'd unhorsed two knights; one whose stallion, armour and weapons he had sold back to him for a helmet full of silver. The other, a poor knight, could not afford to redeem his horse and armour nor replace them, but in desperation offered instead to wager property he owned near Stirling – Hoplaw, a small fortified house, farm and woodland – against his ransom price. It was unethical, against the rules which would have the loser forfeit cheerfully or pay up and look pleasant, but after a moment's surprise, Robert agreed. He won.

'Robbie,' his sister said, and he knew what was coming, of course he did. 'You've been lucky. You have two demesnes now, Skelrig and this Hoplaw. It is only a small place, I'm told. Will you not let me have it? You are in the way of making your fortune. If I had Hoplaw, I could be wed.'

But he had plans for Hoplaw. He had discovered in himself a managing mind and an eye for potential. It was a small place, as she said, and run down, with neglected woodland and a mismanaged farm. The bailiff was too old, half-blind and cheated left right and centre by the estate's people. But it was more valuable than it appeared and could be greatly improved. He had some money now, would certainly get more and could afford to put the place in order. He intended to do something for Julitta, of course, one day. It wasn't all that important. There was plenty of time. She was young, beautiful. Time enough to think about her dowry when he could arrange a marriage for her which would bring *him* some advantage.

'I won't part with Hoplaw,' he said. 'I'm having it put to rights, a lot of work's being done—'

'Then borrow on it, Rob!'

'I'll not go into debt for—'

'Me?'

'For anything, I was going to say. It's foolish and ruinous, and something I'll not consider. Be patient, Julitta. And tell me, why are you here?'

'I came to say goodbye, Rob. I'm for England. Lord Rainard

spoke of me to people he knows there, and one of them found me a place in the service of Queen Isabelle.'

A glorified chambermaid and body servant, but nevertheless a place of some honour with plenty of other ladies pushing to get in if there should be a vacancy. 'Though you might wonder,' she said discontentedly, 'why any noblewoman would jostle for the privilege of emptying the royal stool-pot, or combing lice from the royal hair, or kneeling to latch the royal shoes.'

'Why do it, then?' he asked. 'You can always go home.'

To Skelrig? The back of beyond? She'd had enough of it. What chance of finding a husband there? She'd be better placed at the English court, even if she had no dowry. She smiled at her brother, a smile as false as the cheap pearl trimming on her mantle. From that moment she hated him entirely.

Linking her arm through his she said gaily, 'It doesn't matter, Brother. Don't worry about me. I may surprise you.'

And surprise him she did, and a good many others, when a few months later the Earl of Arlen, one of King John's close circle of trusted lords, demanded to marry her.

'She has no dowry, you know,' said Robert, when Arlen made his formal approaches.

'Oh, that,' said the Earl. 'I know. It doesn't matter.'

He could hear her two great bandogs howling outside in the bailey as if they sensed the approach of something detestable.

The birdsong faltered and died, and the birds flew off in sudden startled flight. Ducks and coots on the lake panicked across the water and out of the reeds, labouring into the air. A vixen and her cubs ran, heedless of cover. The dogs had stopped howling and after a few minutes of soft whining were quiet.

The master had come.

Chapter 27

He had bolted the door from the inside, and Julitta called for help: two of her own men and Robert's dirty dumb serving boy. But when they broke the door down it was too late. He had looped his girdle over the shutter and kicked away the stool beneath him. His body hung against the wall, the bare blue feet scarcely clear of the floor.

Julitta entered the foul-smelling room, holding her skirts up away from the clotted rushes. 'Get him down.'

They laid him on his soiled pallet in the broken circle.

'Carry that chest to my chamber.' She pointed to the money box. One of the men picked it up and stumped off down the steps. 'Take those things off him,' she said, pointing at the string of crosses and relics round his neck. The other man looked uneasy and shuffled his feet but did not move, and the boy, Hob, began to cry.

'Get out of here!' She bent over the body and tugged at the string. It broke and the amulets fell with a clatter to the floor. She heard a gasp and, looking up, saw the dumb boy cross himself, his shocked gaze fixed on the dead man's engorged face. Blood trickled from the corpse's nose and mouth. Blood crying for justice, the infallible sign of murder.

The girl was proving difficult. Her food was drugged but now she refused to eat, refused to talk, refused to obey in any way. Faced with the mutinous child, Julitta's anger surged.

'You sullen brat,' she said, and gave the little face a stinging slap. The dumb boy, bringing in peats, jumped at the sound and dropped them. 'Clear that up,' the lady snarled. 'Get out and take the peats with you. The child needs no fire.'

Gilla's hands and bare feet were cold; she had only her shift and an old blanket. The lady had taken her shoes and clothes when she shut her in this cold bare little chamber.

'You'll do as you're bid, or I'll let Red Cap get you!' Julitta said. 'You don't know about Red Cap. He lives beneath the tower, down there in the rocks, in tunnels. He comes up at night, for he can't abide the daylight. He is old, so old! A filthy creature, teeth like a boar and long twisted claws on his hands and feet. The claws have grown right through his shoes! He wears rags stolen from the dead in their graves. You will do as you're told, or I'll let him in to you this night.'

The mark of her fingers was scarlet on Gilla's pale cheek. The boy swept up the broken peats, packed them back in the basket and scuttled out of the room trembling, not daring to look back at the little girl.

As the late evening light shone through the slit window of the garderobe chamber, Gilla watched the shadow on the wall cast by an iron boss in the middle of the window bars. She had looked at it for a long time and now, she thought, it began to seem like a tunnel. After a while she got up out of her body and went into the tunnel. It felt warm and familiar as if she had done this many times before. It was dark in there, but the walls and floor shone faintly and she could see quite well. She walked steadily down the tunnel, knowing it would lead to daylight.

It opened on to a small garden, green and fragrant with meadowsweet and roses. Birds sang there. A stone bench was set on a little rise amid beds of herbs. The bench had carved arms: one a dragon the other a unicorn. A lady was sitting there. She held out her arms and Gilla went into them. The lady smelled of flowers.

'There now, sweeting,' she said. 'It's all right now. This is your safe place.' She took the child on her lap and Gilla rested her head against the lady's breast. 'Sleep, little one,' the lady said.

In the morning, Lord Rainard stood on the donjon roof beside the iron beacon-basket which was always kept full and ready to fire. He looked north, south, east and west, and for as far as he could see there was no habitation, though faint smoke from the village half a mile away hung over the hill. Below, at the gate, half a dozen ragged barefoot children waited hopefully for bread. Lord Rainard sniffed at his gold pomander. His pale lipless face was severe and would not have looked out of place under a cowl or mitre. His clothes were of the costliest fabrics, but dark and plain.

The watchman kept as far away as he could. Never at ease near great folk, he was more than usually uncomfortable in the proximity of this lot. The self-murder of poor Lord Robert had set any number of nasty rumours afloat, and the watchman, conscious of the contemptuous stares of the two infidel archers, was seriously thinking of taking to his heels as soon as he got the chance.

The Lady Julitta was talking about the child.

'She must have some sort of protection,' she said, her perfect brow creased by an angry frown. 'Something happened when she was scrying. I could do no more with her. I keep her quiet with valerian, but to be useful her mind must be free. Even drugged, she resists me. She resists me! A child! Beating has no effect, nor hunger. Where does she get such strength?'

'Fetch her,' said Soulis.

When Julitta returned with the child, he picked her up and set her on the waist-high wall with the sheer drop below. She sat with her hands in her lap, her expression calm and dreamy.

'What is this?' Julitta demanded. 'She doesn't seem to see or hear.' She waved a hand in front of the child's eyes. Gilla did not blink.

Lord Rainard put a finger under the small chin, tilting her face up and turning it towards the morning sun. The pupils did not contract. The faraway look never wavered. She simply did not see him.

'I've seen this before,' he said. 'You overplayed your hand, my Julitta. You terrified her so badly that, somehow, she found a place to hide. Remarkable! I could bring her out but there is no time; we have much to do. It's a pity. She is rarely gifted. But there it is, if we can't use her one way, we can in another.'

He stared at the rapt face. Bending close, he whispered, 'If you do hear me, maid, listen well and think on this. Whether you will or no, you *shall* serve me. I will write my spells on your body with sharp pens and bloody ink. It would be better to obey me and live.' And, to Julitta,

'Lock her up again. We've work to do.'

Chapter 28

Now they were a company of four; and with four to talk, joke and share the chores of the journey, to argue and to laugh, the journey seemed less slow. But they could not ride fast enough for Straccan who fretted with impatience over every mile of the road, such as it was. It got rougher and rockier, with mud holes that could swallow a donkey, until eventually it was no more than a track which they followed from hint to hint – a dislodged stone, the scrape of a cartwheel, the blackened remains of someone's cookfire – all there was to show that other travellers had come this way.

They passed through clumps of birch and alder, bright hazel woods and denser tracts of oak and ash. They crossed deep quarrelsome streams in sinister gorges. The travellers' way led up, day after day, into hills where storms and mists closed in, soaking and chilling them, only to speed away to the south and east to let the hot sun dry and warm them all too briefly. They camped by small streams full of trout, and slept uneasily with the crashing roar of waterfalls never far.

Great bulwarks of hills rose around them, the way grew steep and wild and they led their beasts beside tremendous precipices, over raging river gullies and through pools aboil with foam. They grew used to the screaming eagles circling overhead, and to long silences among themselves.

When at last they came down out of the hills, they hit upon the remains of an ancient stone road, running from the west to the north-east coast. Broken in places, it was still a miracle of easy going after the way they had come, and they were able to follow it for several miles before their way took them north of it, and into forest.

They passed the ruins of deserted farms and villages swallowed by the forest, crumbling walls and roofless ivied chapels. This was Northumberland, torn to pieces over centuries by raids and warfare, stuck together with the blood of martyrs and slaughtered innocents.

They met no one but a tinker with his donkey, whistling his way south; they passed none nor did any catch up with them. For a day the forest track was wide and dry, but then it steepened and worsened, rough and rocky for a mile or two, then boggy and foul. They forded streams, circled deadfalls, and led their beasts round swampy places. Once, far away, they heard a hunting horn, but it came no nearer and they heard it no more. That night it rained, and though they made a shelter of branches, they slept little and lay cold. Next day, the forest started to thin. Then there was a sudden smell of woodsmoke, their rough track crossed another wider, clearer, and they met their first souls since the tinker: a family of charcoal burners, with their low snug huts and wagon.

Straccan asked about the road ahead but they gaped at him, the women giggling and whispering to each other, the men unable to understand him or he them. Bane fared no better, their dialect was as foreign a tongue as Greek to him.

They rode on, their footing muddy and slippery after the night's rain, leading the horses for long stretches and plagued by mosquitoes and vicious tiny midges.

There were great hills again, climbing to the east, west and ahead of them. Once, from a hilltop, they saw the distant sea to the east, blue as the sky, and on it a ship with striped sail bellied, scudding south.

At last a vill, a poor place but they could buy black bread and ewes' milk, and pay for a night's lodging on fairly clean straw in a farmer's brew house reeking of old ale, but dry. Soon after dawn they were on their way again, given knowledge of the road ahead by their host. 'Two vills, Lords, Muchanger and Haccledun, and then a hard way through the forest for three leagues or so, but after that the road's level and easy and meets other roads, and you will cross into the Scots' country soon after you pass through Crantoun.'

They made good time, stopping in Crantoun at noon for ale and pottage at a hovel reckoned an inn. The house was poor and so was the pottage, but the ale was potent and yes, they were on the road for Crawgard, the innkeeper said sullenly. Go another mile to the ford, then turn west and follow the river road.

They could hear the man cursing long before the path brought them upon him and the reason for his profanity became plain. A loaded cart had overturned spilling sacks of oatmeal, peas and salt, sides of bacon and other goods into the reeds. One of the shafts had snapped, and a knock-kneed horse, freed of its burden, stood in the cool of the river, head down smugly sucking up water. The driver's curses died on his lips as the riders came in view, and he looked no whit reassured by Straccan's amiable greeting.

'Who're you?' he demanded.

'Travellers,' said Straccan. 'Is this the road for Crawgard?'

'Crawgard? Aye.'

Straccan slid from his horse. The carter snatched up a piece of the broken shaft and clutched it competently, like a quarterstaff. 'Keep off,' he snarled.

'We mean no harm,' said Straccan. 'Truly, we are just travellers. Have you an axe?'

'Axe? No. Why?'

'To cut another shaft.' He unstrapped his own axe from the saddle bow. 'Well, do you want a hand or not?'

The new shaft was cut and fitted, the cart righted and reloaded and the melancholy horse harnessed. The driver was friendly now and full of thanks. 'Crawgard's about two miles,' he said. 'I'm going there myself; this lot's for them. It's a rough path – crosses the water three times before it gets there.' He took a leather bottle from under his seat and passed it round.

Miles drank and coughed. 'Sweet Jesus,' he croaked, 'what's that?' He handed it delicately to Straccan. 'Be careful. I think it's poison.'

'It's whisky,' said the carter indignantly, 'and wasted on Southrons! Give it back if you don't want any.'

The bottle had gone from Straccan, who was wiping his eyes, to Bane, whose startled expression didn't worry Larktwist at all. He tilted the bottle and took three swallows before the carter wrenched it away, shoved the stopper in and poked it back under his seat. 'My brother makes it,' he said. 'Mild as milk. Bairns are raised on it.'

'God help us all if we meet any of your bairns,' said Straccan hoarsely. 'I'm afraid we've drunk most of your bottle.'

'That's all right. I've got another.'

'What's your name?'

'Magnus.'

'Magnus, how would you like to earn some money?'

'How much?'

'Funny,' said Bane. 'I'd've thought "what for?" would come to mind first.'

'Sixpence,' said Straccan, holding the thin silver coins out on his palm. 'And sixpence more when the job's over.'

'What for?'

'My friend here,' said Straccan, clapping Bane's shoulder, 'has a fancy to ride in your cart.'

'Have I?' Bane said, surprised. 'Oh. Yes. Lucky me!'

Coming up from the leaf-shadowed water into the sunlight, they saw the donjon of Crawgard, the loneliest fastness of the border, stark against the sky. Crowning a low hill, it was an ancient tower, small by English standards, the lower storey built of stone, the two upper floors of wood thickly plastered. A few small thatched buildings leaned against the outer walls. Sunlight gleamed on the helm and pike of the guard on the roof. The great gate stood half open, and two sloppy-looking men-at-arms watched the wagon as it crawled up the road. A couple of hobbled cows and a few newly shorn stunted sheep grazed. There was a powerful sheepy smell and constant bleating as they neared the gate. The guards pushed the gate wider open to let the familiar cart roll through.

Inside the yard, penned shaggy sheep were packed tightly and two bent ragged figures were busy with shears. A steady trickle of shorn beasts dashed out through the gate to join the rest on the slopes below. Within the rough circle of the outer wall, the donjon rose tall and grim. An outside stair of stone led up to the first floor where the door to the great hall stood open and a thin haze of smoke leaked out. The ground floor storeroom at the base of the donjon was entered by a broad doorway at the foot of the stair. Smaller timber buildings clustered round the base, rather like the hovels outside: brewery, wash-house, dovecote, stable and byre. Only the kitchen was stone-built. The cart stopped at the kitchen door which also stood open.

Bane followed Magnus inside. In the impenetrable darkness of the farther corners, rats squeaked and scampered over piles of stinking kitchen refuse. A huge sullen fire cast a lurid hellish glow. The cook, a fat dirty man with a pustulant nose, lay on a heap of smelly fleeces behind the door, hiccuping and clutching a leather bottle very like the carter's. A scullion with a black eye and split lip applied himself drearily to the turning of two spits. Mutton smoked on one and a row of plump little ducks blistered on the other. Under the great table, a small boy, soot-streaked and snotty, dabbled wooden platters in a bucket of unspeakable water.

'You're late,' said the cook, waving his bottle at Magnus.

'Had an accident. Broke a shaft. This fellow gave me a hand.'

'Well, bring it all in,' said the cook. 'I'd give you a hand, but you know what my back's like.'

Magnus nudged Bane and winked.

It took an hour or so to unload the waggon, stowing the sacks and tubs in the dark storeroom, which smelled of cheese and onions and had its own population of rats. When they'd finished, the cook offered his leather bottle. Bane declined with a shudder but Magnus took several swallows before handing the bottle back. 'Where's Marget?' he asked.

'In the wash-house,' said the cook. 'There's roast duck for dinner, if you're not too tired to eat it.'

Magnus waved a scornful hand. 'See you later,' he said to Bane.

'I'm leaving at first light. You can get a mattress in the hall and have your dinner there.' He made off across the yard to one of the buildings.

'Who's Marget?' Bane asked the scullion.

'His sweetheart,' the man said. '*His* sister.' Jerking his head towards the cook.

'What time's dinner?'

'Dusk. Will you help me carry it up?'

'I might. How many feeders?'

'Twenty.'

'That's not the full garrison, is it?'

'Ach, no. The lord's away, he's no been here since Yule, and the young lord's gone off and took twenty with him. So there's just us,' gesturing round the kitchen, 'and Marget, and the young lord's friend in the gatehouse, the lady of course, them upstairs, and the infidel.' He spat and crossed himself.

'No children?'

'No.'

'You sure?'

'Told you, I feed them. Twenty mouths.'

'Who's the lady?'

'The old lord's wife. Puir thing, she's away with the fairies.' He made a gesture universally understood, twirling a finger beside his ear.

'What's this infidel, then?'

The scullion looked uneasy. 'Ach, he's an auld body, belongs to the lord. Ah've nivver seen him. He keeps his room.'

Bane found a barrel of wizened but still-sweet apples, pocketed half a dozen and helped himself to a chunk of cheese. He made his way across the yard and up the outside stair to the door of the hall. Standing in the doorway, he looked into the cavernous smoky room. Rows of straw pallets lay alongside the walls, several of them occupied by sleepers. A roaring fire burned at one end of the hall and beside it lay two huge boar hounds, one asleep, the other scratching with mindless persistence. A few stools and a bench were grouped at a comfortable distance from the fire around a board resting on trestles and half a dozen unshaven unbuttoned men were playing without enthusiasm a game involving dice and small stones.

The stair continued in a spiral inside, its uneven steps curling out of sight.

Bane walked over to the table watched by six pairs of unfriendly eyes.

As Straccan – a stranger and therefore dangerous – rode up from the river, the watchman atop the donjon had a crossbow bolt aimed at him and the two guards at the gate held their pikes ready to rip his guts out if required. He reined in at a suitable distance.

'Sir Richard Straccan, to see Lord de Soulis.'

The guards stared at him and glanced at one another. One shook his head. 'The lord's away,' he said.

'Where?'

Before the man could reply, a voice from above drawled, 'Well, God-a-mercy! Someone from civilisation has found this godforsaken place!'

Straccan looked up at the small window above the gate. A pale but cheerful face peered down at him. 'A knight, are ye? And seeking Lord Rainard?'

'I have something to deliver to him,' Straccan said. 'Who are you?'

'Turlo FitzCarne of Dun Carne. Oh, let him in. Let him come up,' he cried to the guards who still stood at the ready, looking uncertain. 'He's alone; are you afraid of one man? They probably are, you know,' he added to Straccan. 'Couldn't fight their way out of a haystack!'

The pikemen let him pass. His heart hammered hard and fast beneath his ribs. Somewhere in this place he might find Gilla. If she was here, he'd find her, and God help anyone who tried to stop him.

'Up here!' The voice from above again. A wooden stair led up to the door of the room over the gate and, in the doorway, leaning on rough crutches, was Sir Turlo FitzCarne.

'FitzCarne,' said Straccan, as he mounted the stair. 'Haven't I heard of you?'

'Lord, I should hope so,' said Sir Turlo, crutching rapidly over to a fleece-heaped chair by the window.

'Tourneys,' said Straccan. 'That's what you do. The circuit! You were champion at Chester and Windsor. What on earth are you doing here?'

'You may well ask,' said the champion morosely, pouring wine into two horn cups. 'Sit down and have a drink. *I'm* here because of this blasted broken leg. What brings *you* to the back of beyond?'

Not that he listened. He was an addict deprived of his drug – talk – and once started, it seemed nothing could stop his flow. He had broken his leg in a fall three months before at an unimportant little tourney in Carlisle. Not his sort of thing at all – a piddling little local affair, not even licensed – but seeing he was there and it was going on, well, he entered, just to keep his hand in. His girth broke and down he went just after unhorsing and vanquishing Bertran de Soulis, son of Lord Rainard. Sir Bertran had chivalrously insisted Sir Turlo be his guest until he was fit again, when he could collect his ransom and rejoin the tourney circuit at his pleasure.

'It's taken much longer than I expected,' said the champion. 'But I think it's really on the mend now. Another two or three weeks, and with the blessing, I'll be on my way at last.' He had missed the great tourney at Edinburgh, alas, which was just a few days ago. That was where Sir Bertran had gone, leaving him bored and kicking his heels. 'Well, not actually kicking them, do you see, in the circumstances, but I can't sit a horse yet, and there's *nothing* to do here, and no one to talk to.'

In a corner, Sir Bertran's hawk, loaned to his guest, glowered on its perch and loosed a dropping which splattered on the floor. 'I hobble about a bit outside and fly her at ducks and pigeons, but it's clumsy like this, and she resents me, the creature!' He had moved to the gatehouse when his friend departed. 'It's quieter. The men make more row day and night than pigs at trough! And there's that creepy little fellow upstairs. I'd rather be as far as I can get from him.'

'Who's that?'

'Some old madman Lord Rainard looks after. An Arab, for God's sake! A scholar, they tell me. Bertran wouldn't go anywhere near him, and I've never even clapped eyes on him. He lives in the top chamber in the tower. I couldn't get up all those steps even if I wanted to, which I don't, and anyway, he's an infidel, so he is.'

'They told me below that Soulis is not here.'

'Lord Rainard's with the king.'

'In Edinburgh?'

'Wherever the king is – Edinburgh, Dunfermline, Roxburgh, Stirling – and he has his demesne, Soulistoun, but I've no idea where he is right now.'

'Then I must go on,' said Straccan, putting his cup down. 'Unless you can put me up for the night?'

'Ah, sure, you'll not be leaving now, not with night coming and the fairies about! Stay the night and go on in the morning,' cried the hospitable invalid. 'There's been no human being to talk to since Bertran left.' He crutched to the door where an iron triangle hung and rattled at it with a short iron bar. The clanging resulted in the emergence from the main hall on to the outside stair opposite, of the garrison captain, a burly sloven holding aloft a torch.

'What d'ye lack?' he bellowed.

'Sir Richard will stay the night,' FitzCarne bawled back across the yard. 'Bring another mattress over, and blankets. And supper for two.'

'Thank you,' said Straccan. Now he would have time to search. 'Is there no one here but yourself then, and the garrison, and the old heathen?'

'Well, there's the lady; she never leaves her room either. There's a fat slut that serves her, serves the garrison too, all comers. But they're all scared spitless of the old man! It's my belief he's a sorcerer, I sign myself to the Trinity every time he comes to my mind.' Suiting action to word, he crossed himself and devoutly kissed the crucifix he wore on a silver chain. 'God and Mary and Patrick protect us from all evil,' he said.

'Amen,' said Straccan. It was almost dark now and he wondered where Miles and Larktwist were waiting. At least Bane was here, ready if needed.

Bane was settled comfortably in the hall, throwing dice. He had brought his own – or, rather, a pair borrowed from Larktwist – guaranteed to give him an edge. He'd lost a sum sufficient to endear him to his companions and was now teaching them 'the latest game from France', at which he intended to lose yet more, before eventually winning a respectable amount; not so much as to arouse undue suspicion, but enough to show a profit. The others crowded round the flat stone slab on which Bane had chalked the game's ground, a square divided into smaller squares decorated with serpents, dragons and siege-ladders. A little pile of ragged half- and quarter-pennies went back and forth among them.

The carter was in the stable with his doxy, and Bane had supped on scorched mutton wondering who got the ducks. (The cook, his sister and Magnus.)

'What this game needs,' said Bane, casually, 'is a drink to wash the dust off my luck.'

'Mine too. Will, run down and tell Sandy we need another jug of ale!'

'Ale?' said Bane, with a slight sneer. 'I was thinking of this.' He produced the carter's reserve bottle, stolen and hidden in his capacious pocket. 'Whisky.'

Good fellowship and a hefty swig from Bane's bottle compelled the captain to produce a similar bottle of his own, and the new game proceeded, noisily enough for Straccan to hear it in the gatehouse where FitzCarne was at last snoring on his pallet. From the window, which looked out for miles over the dale, not a light could be seen. Crawgard felt like the only human habitation left in all the world.

Out there, according to his sleeping host, the Queen of Faerie and her Court would be riding even now, passing like a mist of stars threaded with music, unseen by Christians, bent on their cold, malicious sport. Elf-archers would shoot the farm dogs that gave warning of their coming. Nimble elf-maids would steal sleeping babies, as yet unbaptised, leaving in their place in the cradles bundles of rags, roots and dead leaves, casting their callous glamour on the substitutes so that for days after, poor bereaved mothers would nurse and rock and sing to the things, while husbands, families and neighbours feared them mad.

Elves it was who called up the marshlights to lead night travellers to swampy death, and blighted the barley as it grew, and charmed axe-blades to turn on woodcutters. They soured and clotted the milk in cows' udders in the byre, and laid tanglefoot spells on the paths and trackways, so that horses stumbled, and people afoot fell in the mud. Their hatred of humankind was very great, and only the cross of Christ could baffle their tricks. Fitz-Carne, a mine of faerie lore and an unstoppable story-teller, had kept going until, in desperation, Straccan feigned sleep, fearing he would otherwise talk all night.

As silently as possible, boots in hand, Straccan tiptoed to the door and down the steps, praying they wouldn't creak. At the foot of the stair he sat and put his boots on. He crossed the yard, pausing by the open stable door when he heard a woman laugh inside. A man's voice mumbled something in reply, and Straccan could hear hay rustling. Moonlight through the door silvered limbs in a flurry of amorous activity. He glided past and climbed the donjon stair.

Just before he reached the main door, there came a sound from above. He couldn't make out any words, but after a deep-voiced cry there was a pause and then a strange droning chant accompanied by piping – an extraordinarily disquieting sound that stopped him in his tracks. It came from a narrow window on the top floor.

There was nothing to see. Nothing moved in the moonlit night. There seemed no reason for the hairs to prickle and lift at the back of his neck and the sweat to run cold down his sides. For a moment, impossibly, he thought he smelled snow coming, and sensed air shifting, not behind or before him, but above. It was cold, so cold that the breath crackled in his nostrils as if it was mid-winter.

Then, as suddenly as it began, it was gone. The chanting and piping stopped. The June night was warm but Straccan was shivering. He crossed himself. Damn that garrulous idiot, Fitz-Carne, with his spooks, he thought angrily. What in the name of hell just happened? His heart was thudding, and it was some minutes before he could move on up the steps and peer in through the half-open door of the hall.

There was a small group of men, Bane among them, clustered round the table over some sort of game. The stair continued, spiralling inside the wall now, to the chambers above. If Gilla was here, that's where he would find her. Ghost-like, he faded in through the door on to the inner stair, swiftly up, round the curve, out of sight of the hall.

At the first door he paused. No sound. He eased it open and was greeted by the smells of stale sweat, urine and sickness. He was in a large bedchamber, stone-chill and fireless, its windows shuttered but with enough moonlight filtering through cracks and round edges of the shutters to show the towering mass of the curtained bed.

A woman's voice from the bed said, 'Marget?'

'No, Madame.'

The voice, now shrill with terror, began babbling prayers in a mixture of bad Latin and Norman French. Straccan shut the door and moved to the bedside, his eyes searching the darkness for the shape within the curtains.

'Madame, I mean no harm! I'll not hurt you.'

The babbling stopped on a catch of breath, and a thin strong hand clamped on his arm, making him jump.

'You're real,' she said. 'I can touch you! You're a man!'

'Of course I'm real,' he said, puzzled. 'Did you think I was a ghost?'

'No. I know all the ghosts here,' she said. 'They do no harm. Poor lost things. When I die, shall I join them, do you think?'

'I don't know,' he said, disconcerted. 'Are you the Lady de Soulis, wife of Lord Rainard?'

'Oh, hush,' she said sharply. 'Don't speak his name! He'll find us, if you speak his name. Naming calls, has no one told you that?'

'No, Lady. I don't know what you mean.'

'That's why I lie here in the dark. I could have lights, you know. I could have hundreds of candles if I wished; he is rich enough. But even he can't see in the dark, he can't see me here.'

FitzCarne was right, he thought, the poor woman was wood-mad. Gently he patted the hand that quite painfully gripped his wrist. 'Madame, I am looking for my daughter, Gilla. Is there a child here at Crawgard?'

'Your daughter? No, no child here. Why should she be here?'

'I think Lord Rai— your husband, I think he has her.'

'Not here. Perhaps at Soulistoun. Is she young? That creature of his, Pluvis, he's the one who steals children. Ugh! He used to bring them here, but I forbade it. That was long ago. Is it spring?'

'It's June, Madame.'

'Summer already? I've not seen a summer day for seven years.'

'Are you too ill to leave this room?'

'I'm afraid, afraid to be out there, under the sky. It isn't heaven, you know.'

'What isn't?'

'The sky! It's hell. Holy Church teaches that the devil and his realm are under the earth, but that's wrong. Hell is in the sky, among the stars.' Her free hand began patting about on the smelly quilts. 'Where is it? Have you taken my charm?' She began to cry, a thin weak sobbing.

'What charm, Madame? Let me strike a light, then you may find it.'

'No! No light! I told you! Here, here it is!' She clutched something and touched his hand with it – it felt like a warm stone. 'Yes, you're just a man. I thought you were, but I have to be sure.'

'Madame, are you certain there is no child here?'

'No child, no. My son was here a while ago, but he's no child, and he's gone away again. He came to say goodbye to me. He begged me to have candles, you know. But he has never seen the devils. *I've* seen them. They come down from hell, when that infidel wizard summons them. I heard him a little while ago. I felt their bitter breath.'

'Madame, I must leave now,' Straccan said, gently trying to prise her grip loose. She resisted.

'I can't let you have my charm,' she said distractedly. 'It's the only one I've got.'

'I don't want it, Madame.'

'Don't you? Are you another of his creatures, then?' She snatched her hand away. 'Flesh and blood, no demon, but you're one of *his* people! I should have known! He sent you here!'

Straccan stood up and backed away from the bed. 'No, Madame, I'm not one of his people. I am sorry to have disturbed you. God be with you.' He shut the door behind him, glad of its thickness, for even if the mad woman cried out, no one would hear, not with the racket downstairs. So that was Soulis's wife, poor lady. And she was sure Gilla was not here. But she might not know. How could she know, shut in that room in the dark? A hundred children might be brought and slaughtered here without her knowing.

Up the stair again. Another door opening into another bed-chamber. No one there. Two small rooms in the thickness of the walls full of chests and boxes, some roped, others standing open, books and clothes inside, the dry smells of fleabane and lavender.

He reached the top floor. The door opened silently on to a muffled darkness. Straccan tugged the heavy curtain aside. A reek of spices overlay a smell of rottenness. The room was high, narrow and hot – two glowing braziers accounted for that. At one end of the room was a low bed, a tumble of soiled cushions and grubby blankets. At the other end, a table was littered with parchments and books, and a small shrivelled man sat in a big painted chair. He held a pen in one hand; the other rested on the open pages of a massive volume. He wore the robe and corded headdress of a desert Arab, and with revulsion Straccan saw that although the hand wrote steadily, the man's eyeballs were rolled back and only the blind whites showed.

There was no one else in that foetid place, and certainly Gilla was not here.

Straccan's boots made no sound on the rugs, nor did the old man look up to see who had come in; he went on writing. When Straccan drew his dagger and laid its point to the writer's scrawny neck, the scribbling hand did not cease and the blind eyes did not flicker.

'Who are you?' Straccan spoke in the tongue of the desert people. The wizened little mummy went on writing. Straccan looked at the pages, not recognising the script; it was similar to the Arabic he was familiar with but not the same. He took hold of the wrist of the writing hand and lifted it. The flesh was cold and dry, and he felt a nauseating dislike of the skin he touched, dark yellow, wrinkled and papery like a shed snakeskin. The fingers continued to wag, the pen to write invisible signs in the air. Straccan dropped it. The man must be drugged. An empty beaker lay on its side among the parchments. He sniffed it. A pungent smoky odour, but no drug that he knew.

He walked round the table, looking at the scattered parchments. Many of them were very aged. There were bundles of that curious Egyptian stuff, papyrus, and wax tablets, as well as some ancient-looking dirty clay slabs covered with impressions like the tracks of birds. Among the clutter, he spotted a familiar bronze cylinder, green with age, engraved with a spiral of strange symbols. He reached for it and fingered the star on the lid. How in God's name did that get here? It must be the same one, there surely couldn't be two! He twisted the lid off, and yes, there was the icon.

A yellow hand shot out and grabbed the cylinder. Straccan, shaken, saw the white eyes move and turn black, shark-like, lightless. The old man gabbled something he did not understand and scrambled to his feet, making not for the door but for the nearest brazier on to which he flung a handful of black glittering powder. Thick smoke rose. Straccan felt his sanity waver as shapes from nightmares and beyond nightmares began forming in the smoke. The chamber, so hot a few moments ago, suddenly seemed winter-cold. The old horror was giggling, drool on his chin. Straccan, chilled to the bone, snatched the cylinder back from the feeble hand, tore the door curtain aside, saw a key hanging beside the door, snatched that and got out of the room.

He'd moved faster, he thought, than he'd ever moved in his life. He locked the door behind him and leaned against the arrow slit in the stair wall, sucking in clean air. He'd not breathed in much of the hallucinogen, and his head cleared quickly.

He crept down the steps, past the open door into the hall where the gambling had reached the rancorous stage and was promising to get physical, and ducked out of sight through the outer door. As he crossed the yard he heard the sharp scrape of a pike against stone atop the tower, and the watchman began to cough, ending with a curse. A few minutes later he was back in his bed, listening to the champion's peaceful snoring.

Chapter 29

Straccan left at dawn, with just the yawning champion to see him away, naturally unaware of the Arab's whirlwind departure an hour later, escorted by two of Crawgard's bowmen who'd almost rather have been skinned and salted than ride with Lord Rainard's pet sorcerer. They were even more unhappy when they realised which road he was taking. He didn't utter a word, and no one could have understood him if he had.

When the kitchen boy, bringing breakfast, unlocked his door, the old man had pushed past him and scuttled down the steps straight out to the stable, where a frightened groom found him saddling Sir Bertran's prized Arab mare.

As he spurred furiously through the gate, two of the garrison, less lucky than the others, grabbed bows and helmets and followed cursing. If any harm came to him, Lord Rainard would have them killed.

Straccan made his way along the river path to where Miles and Larktwist had camped overnight. All was peaceful, Miles shaving while Larktwist fished; there were already four trout lying on a leaf-lined bark platter, and as Straccan arrived Larktwist pulled out a fifth.

'What news?' Miles called, waving his razor.

'Gilla's not there.'

'I'm sorry,' said Miles. 'There's no doubt?'

'No.' He recounted what had happened at Crawgard, but did not mention the strange episode the previous night when the summer evening had turned to mid-winter for a few fleeting moments. He was almost sure he'd imagined that, but now and then, on the very edge of his disquieted vision, the nightmare shapes of the old man's lair lurked. When he tried to look straight at them, like faint stars they were gone.

Before long they heard the rumble of Magnus's wheels and the wagon lumbered into view.

'Have you had breakfast?' Straccan asked Bane, when Magnus, pocketing his second sixpence, had rattled away with an occasional pig-like squeal of ungreased axles.

'If you can call it that,' said Bane grumpily. 'That oatmeal just makes a man hungry.'

'How about some fine fresh fish?' Larktwist said, bearing the platter, now with eight trout, up to their fire.

'Jesu,' said Bane admiringly. 'That's what I call a catch!'

'The river's full of them,' Larktwist said. 'You could pull them out all day. You want to help me clean them?'

'Not especially,' said Bane, 'but if it means they'll be cooking quicker . . .' He and Larktwist went into a private huddle: Bane returned the borrowed dice and counted out a share of his winnings.

'So what do we do now?' Miles asked, as they packed up their camp after breakfast.

'We'll make for Soulistoun,' said Straccan. 'I asked FitzCarne about it. It's Soulis's chief demesne, east of here towards Edinburgh. I don't know what else to do. Gilla may be there, please God.'

They rode east, and in the late afternoon, to Straccan's frustration, Miles's horse cast a shoe, which slowed them down. Luckily the road was soft, and after a couple of miles they saw smoke over the trees. A farm perhaps, or a village. A village it was, and a blacksmith in it, cheerful at the unexpected business coming his way.

'Bane and I'll ride on,' said Straccan. 'We'll keep to the road and find a place to camp tonight. You follow when you're done here.'

The smith gave them an uneasy glance. 'It's a bad road, noble Sirs,' he said.

'Gets rough, does it?'

'Rough, aye, but that's not what I meant. It's a bad road for travellers. You gentlemen should go back towards Crawgard, and north from there to Hawick, and then turn east.'

'But it's much shorter this way,' said Miles.

'It's dangerous, Lords,' the smith said.

'Bandits?'

'Some say so, but none's ever been caught. People just vanish. It could be wolves, of course, but . . .' He crossed himself and kissed the little brass crucifix that hung round his thick neck on a plaited cord. 'We call it the devil's road,' he said.

'You think the devil snatches travellers?' Straccan asked.

The man lowered his voice. 'There's an ogre,' he said.

There was a thoughtful silence. Then Bane said. 'Seen it, have you? This ogre?'

'No, Sir, and please God I never do. But it's there, and it eats people. Well, I've said my piece. Do as you please, but don't say I didn't warn you!'

The family numbered thirty creatures; eight males, twelve females and ten juveniles from infants to about ten years of age. At fifty, Sawney was an old man, but unlike other folk he had never gone hungry. There was always meat of a sort to fill his belly, so instead of being half-starved and feeble like most outlaws, he was a powerful brute, heavy and surprisingly, dangerously fast. His was the blind savagery of the boar, bowling down prey with a grunting irresistible charge. All flesh was his family's prey, but their choicest delicacy was human.

For years they had waylaid, slain and devoured travellers. They fell on solitary walkers, or pairs if they looked unlikely to put up much of a fight, with the ferocity of a wolf pack, and even ambushed and dragged down riders. Although all folk carried weapons of some sort – dagger, sword, axe, club – none of the family was ever badly hurt. So swift, so shocking were their attacks that victims often stood staring in disbelief, too amazed even to run until too late. But if they ran, oh when they ran, that was sport indeed! The reeking baying pack was inescapable, attacking as they did on their own ground, the steep rough paths and desolate boggy places they knew so well.

They would hurl rocks and trip-sticks to bring their quarry down, batter the skulls in with stones, drag the bodies a little way off into the dense gorse and bracken and often tear the warm quivering flesh from the bones there and then.

Their lair had never been found. The brave few who sought it were never seen again. In that wild empty land the family had flourished for twenty years, since Sawney and his woman Kate, running from justice in Carlisle with the hue and cry after them, had stumbled on their refuge and denned there ever since. She bore a child each year, of which some lived and grew; brothers and sisters incestuously mated, and so they multiplied.

De Brasy had come upon an injured female in a boar trap a few years ago, and for amusement kept it alive, fed it and perversely made some sort of pet of the thing. He had tamed it to muzzle and collar and kept it chained and obedient for fear of the whip.

Eventually, he could almost trust it – never quite – but in its halting barely recognisable speech it told him about the family and led him to the lair. With gifts of food, especially sugar for which they had a desperate greed, he persuaded them to his will. He found them useful. More than one of his enemies – he had many – ended up in the family's larder, and several of his creditors, of whom there were even more, went the same way.

They had watched several days with feral patience, and these were the men; these were the horses they must look for, the white-foot bay and the grey.

The path ran beside the river for miles, and then climbed above a rocky gorge, narrowing at a bend with a nasty drop on the right and a wall of rock on the left. Out of a cleft above the riders sprang three of the males, hanging on Zingiber's neck, stabbing and hacking to bring the stallion down. Straccan tore the axe from his saddle bow and struck at the filthy hands that grabbed him. A severed hand fell like a loathsome great spider, the male screaming and waving his spouting arm as he toppled into the gorge. The other two drew back as Zingiber fell bleeding to his knees. Straccan leapt clear as the horse rolled in agony, and with sword in his right hand and axe in his left, flung himself after the two retreating males.

Behind him on the path, Bane had time to draw his sword and spur forward, leaping Zingiber's body and thrashing legs. He caught up with Straccan where the path widened, curving away from the gorge between thickets of rowan in dense gorse and bracken broken by rocky outcrops. From this shelter, in a pincer movement, flinging stones with deadly accuracy, came a dozen more of Sawney's tribe.

Straccan was forced back against the rock, facing half a dozen of the creatures. His axe and sword kept them off but several stones struck him, one opening a gash above his left eye from which the blood blinded him while a blow over the ear made him dizzy and sick.

Bane kept his horse turning, turning, its hooves jabbing at the attackers, while he slashed left and right with his sword, but a fresh shower of missiles brought him toppling from the saddle, and with howls of triumph the creatures rushed at him. The grey neighed and galloped back the way they had come, leaping Zingiber's lifeless body, hooves clattering on the rocky path, round the curve, out of sight.

Three of Straccan's attackers turned to join the pack swarming over Bane, and the other three hesitated, glancing at their kindred. Straccan dropped his axe, tugged the horn from his belt and blew long and hard.

Almost at once came the ringing of hooves on rock again, and here was Sir Miles coming full tilt up the path, straight at the pack worrying Bane. Mace whirling, he scattered them, and Larktwist, coming up behind leading the mule and Bane's runaway horse, jumped down and dragged Bane out of the road on to the grass at the side.

Straccan brought down two with his sword, sickened when he saw that one was female. One more fell to Miles's mace, and the rest dashed into the cover of the rowans and tall bracken, and were gone as if they'd never been, leaving their stench, and their dead.

'This one's alive,' said Larktwist, rolling a body over with his foot. Miles dismounted, took straps from his saddlebag and bound the creature's hands and feet.

From some distance ahead and still out of sight, came the sound of another horn, tan-tan-ta-ra-tan, and soon a rider came in sight, wearing an old-fashioned plate hauberk and steel cap, on a big dusty black gelding.

'Who's that?' Straccan gasped, bending to retrieve his axe and almost falling as sick dizziness surged over him.

'Haven't the faintest,' Miles panted.

Larktwist rummaged in the packs for the first-aid kit and bound a rough dressing round Straccan's head. Bane, however, was unconscious and breathing stertorously, almost snoring.

'I don't like the look of this,' Larktwist said. 'He's in a bad way.'

As the newcomer – an old man, and a knight by his bearing and gear – drew nearer, Straccan knelt by Bane, whose eyes were closed and whose face looked shrunken and collapsed. 'Hawkan,' he said. 'Hawkan, can you hear me?'

'He can't,' said Larktwist.

The rider slowed to a trot as he came close, then to a walk, and halted.

'Is he badly hurt?' the old man asked.

'Yes,' Straccan said. 'We were set upon by – I don't know what they were – savages! There were women too. I killed one.' Struggling against vertigo, he bent over Bane touching his face gently. 'Hawkan, they've gone.'

The old man dismounted. 'I am Blaise d'Etranger,' he said. 'They won't come back now; we are too many, and armed. Let us carry your companion. A little way ahead there is a place where we can tend him, and you can rest.'

Sir Miles cut two rowan saplings and crossed them at one end, using a blanket to make a travois. They wrapped Bane like a baby, fastened him into the travois so he could not be dislodged, and fixed the contrivance to his horse, which Straccan now must ride. The captive they hauled upright and gagged, loosing its feet so it could walk but fastening its strapped hands to Miles's saddle, so it must trot alongside the horse.

As they rode slowly, led by the newcomer, Straccan pushed forward to ride beside the old man. He was tall and very thin, with fierce hawkish features in which the marks of old suffering were plain. From under his steel cap long white locks fell on to his shoulders. His white beard was neatly braided and great moustaches hid his mouth. A heavy two-handed sword hung under his mantle, and strapped to his saddle was an odd sort of staff, forked and iron-clad at one end, pointed and iron-tipped at the other. A nasty weapon, the Scottish gaveloc, and one that Straccan had never seen.

'You are Sir Richard Straccan,' the old man said.

'You know me, Sir? Yet I don't remember you, and I am sure I would.'

'Sir William Hoby sent me a letter. He said you were seeking Rainard de Soulis, the Lord of Crawgard.'

'He has stolen my daughter,' said Straccan. 'I've been to Crawgard. All I found were a disabled tourney champion, a madwoman and some foul old Arab. Soulis isn't there. We are going to his demesne, Soulistoun, to seek him.'

'He's at Dunfermline with the king,' said Sir Blaise. 'Or was when I left Coldinghame. But he'll leave there soon, for Skelrig.'

'Skelrig?'

'Aye. There's a man there, a knight in his service, who is sick, so I heard.'

'Robert de Beauris?'

'Yes. You know him?'

'I've had some dealings with him. But until now, I didn't know he was Soulis's man. Sir Blaise, it was good of my friend William to write to you, and gracious of you to come seeking me; but why?'

'William is an old friend of mine, too. He told me your errand. He thought I might be of help.'

174

They had come about a mile from the ambush; the road went downhill again and levelled, meeting the river and running alongside. There was an ancient beehive stone hut, an abandoned hermitage, on a small spit of rock that stuck out into the river. A heron, disturbed by their coming, laboured heavily away dropping its fish. An otter splashed in after it, disappearing in a swirl of silver bubbles to emerge at the opposite bank, where it vanished into the reeds with its booty.

They carried Bane into the hut, which was cold but blessedly dry, and while Miles cut bracken to make a bed, Larktwist got a fire going and heated water to bathe the blood off Bane and Straccan. Blaise wordlessly produced needle and sinew and competently stitched the flap of skin that had been torn loose over Straccan's eye. It was quite numb, and Straccan felt nothing. 'Thank you,' he said. He lifted Bane's unresponsive hand. It was cold.

'Will he die?' Miles asked.

'It's in God's hands,' said Blaise.

'Can we do nothing for him?'

'Only pray, and keep him warm.'

Later, as they sat round the fire eating supper, the old knight produced Sir William Hoby's letter and showed it to Straccan.

'Why is he so concerned?' Straccan asked. 'He has sent me his nephew, Miles, God bless him, and now you.'

'When Soulis's name came up, he was concerned; and so am I.'

'You know him?'

'I've met him, in Outremer. He lived there some years, first as crusader, later as a pilgrim. Tell me, Sir Richard, have you heard of a black pilgrimage?'

'No. What is it?'

'It is for an evil end. Soulis made his pilgrimage far into the southern waste. He was gone two years and reckoned dead. But no, out he came after all, and with great treasure. It was whispered that he had found the lost City of Pillars.'

Miles said, 'Sir, what is the City of Pillars?'

The old knight was silent so long that Miles thought his

question had not been heard, but he did not like to ask again. Then Sir Blaise said, 'The City of Pillars, fabled Irem, was lost in the waste for a thousand years. But Soulis went in search of it, and found it. That's where your old Arab came from.'

'You know him, then?' Straccan said, surprised.

'I've heard of him.' The man spoke softly, as if to himself. 'Abdul Al-Hazred, of the Tribe of Ad. All those ancient tribes of desert dwellers are long dead, like the Romans who once dwelt in these parts. Irem was lost and buried in the sands for a thousand years. Yet it seems Soulis found it, and came away not only with much gold, but brought Al-Hazred out.'

Miles looked puzzled. 'How had the old man lived in such a place?'

'God knows! There is neither meat there, nor anything that grows. There must be forgotten wells, but water alone cannot keep a man alive for long. Perhaps the wandering desert folk supplied him, although most of them would shun the place. They say it is magic, ensorcelled, and only demons dwell there now.'

The rhythm of Bane's breathing changed. It hitched, and caught, and after that was barely perceptible. Straccan wiped the grey face tenderly. Sir Blaise, watching him, said, 'If we could get him to Jedburgh . . .'

'Is there a chirurgeon there?'

'A monk-physician, at the abbey. But it is a long way to carry your servant.'

'My friend,' said Straccan. Despite the fire and the warm evening, he was shivering. He grieved for Bane, who was surely dying, and guiltily suppressed the fear that the days it might take would be days lost in his search for Gilla. Once, after a siege, he had seen a man stumble away from his wife's violated corpse, and beat his own head against the wall until he fell senseless and bleeding. Now, in his agony for Gilla and despair for Bane, he understood why. He mourned too for Zingiber; Zingiber who was only a beast and soulless, but his companion for eleven years. He sat staring into the fire, and then, blinded by it, into the gathering night outside the hut, where horses and mule were tethered. Now that the numbness had worn off, the wound above his eye felt as if it had been sewn with red-hot wire. Yet despite his fears, his nausea and the pain, he eventually slept.

Miles stood watch until an hour or so before the dawn, when he shook Larktwist awake to relieve him.

'How's Bane?'

'Still breathing.'

'God save him.'

'Amen!'

Straccan woke a little after dawn and found Sir Blaise sitting beside Bane. Bane's face was skull-like, damp and grey, the sunken eyes ringed in bruised circles. 'He is cold,' the old knight said, chafing the dead-feeling hands, trying to warm them. 'I have put another blanket over him, and made up the fire.'

'Who *are* you?' Straccan asked. 'How can you help me?'

'Yes,' said Miles, who had woken when the fire was mended, 'and how do you know about what's-his-name, the Arab, and the lost city, and all that?'

Sir Blaise sighed, 'I am the Lord of Sauchiehill. My domain lies north of here. I am an old man, as you see, so I have put my holding in good hands, and live in retirement near the priory at Coldinghame. Prior Aernald and I were squires together, years ago. He lets me live in one of the priory's houses, for friendship's sake. Once, long ago, I was a knight of the Order of the Temple of Solomon, in Jerusalem.'

'A Templar!' Miles breathed reverently.

'In Outremer,' Blaise continued, 'I learned the legends of the desert. I spoke with the wise men of Arabia and learned much of their lore. I also learned some of their ancient languages, only to be found in old books. In short, I made a study of Saracenic magic. This was forbidden by the Church, and I was punished and disciplined for it. I "lost the Order"; do you know what that means? I was cast out, no longer a knight of the Temple, and I spent six years in a Church prison until they judged me repentant and broken to their will.'

There was a shocked silence. After a while, Miles said hesitantly, 'Wasn't that heresy?'

'So they called it,' Sir Blaise said. 'I call it knowledge. But I have told you the truth, and it's for you to decide. If you prefer to manage without any help from me, I understand. Heresy's a fearful word. I am bound to tell you this; it is a duty laid on me by Prior Aernald that I may offer my help, but must tell my history.'

Straccan had taken the bronze cylinder out of his pocket and was turning it in his hands. This was the thing he had given to the Countess of Arlen, and which she had said would go to the king. It had no business being at Crawgard, but she was the sister of the Lord of Skelrig, where Soulis was going ... They were all connected.

'May I see that?' the old man asked. He looked closely at it. 'Lord protect us,' he said. 'Where did you get this?'

Straccan told him. It all seemed very long ago now: the murdered messenger, Bane's journey north, his own visit to the lady Julitta. 'The picture inside, she called it an icon,' he said.

The old man uncapped the cylinder and slid the rolled portrait into his palm, untied it and studied the sorrowful face. 'Egyptian work,' he said. 'But the icon is nothing to do with this business. *This*,' he tapped the cylinder, 'is what matters. The case.'

'Look,' said Straccan. 'Can we please make sense of all this? What do you mean about the case?'

'I believe this came from Irem,' Blaise said. 'Although,' he smiled slightly, 'the scholars of Arabia will tell you it is not of this world at all, but came from a star.'

'That's rubbish,' said Miles. 'The stars are holes in the floor of heaven made by God's finger for the light to shine through, so we will know where heaven is!'

Blaise put the icon in its case and gave it back to Straccan. 'I have heard it said too, that all that great spray of stars in the night sky is milk from the breast of the Holy Virgin. Another view is that stars are the souls of the righteous who died before Christ was born to save mankind. Although spared the pains of hell, they may not enter paradise, where only true Christian souls may go. They are set in the sky instead, which we can only hope is some comfort to them! A priest at Canterbury told me stars were the tears of angels, weeping for the folly and wickedness of men. But I have also been told that angels are in a state of perpetual exaltation, and if that is the case they'd hardly spend time weeping. There are lots of stories about stars, young Sir, so why shouldn't the Saracens have stories, too?'

Miles looked unhappy and didn't answer.

Blaise continued. 'They believe that demons dwell among the stars and that a sorcerer who knows their names can call them down, force them to do his will. But he must be powerful indeed, for always they seek to break free and turn upon humankind. Soulis,' he added, 'must have studied these matters deeply, or he would never have found the City of Pillars.'

'What can a man want,' Straccan wondered, 'enough that hell's fires hold no terrors for him?'

Blaise shrugged. 'With Soulis, we may rule out love. He is a man that has no need of women. Although he has gold, he may crave more; some have a great lust for riches. Then, too, he is growing old. If he believes eternal life can be his for the asking, that might be worth any risk. Also, he is proud: he may desire to make men his puppets, command them, raise or put down kings, throw down kingdoms. In the ancient lore books of Arabia, Al-Hazred is said to speak the tongue of demons and to know their names. Without its name, no man can summon a demon or compel it to obedience. If Soulis cherishes the old madman, it may be because he believes him the key to power beyond most men's dreams.'

'Can devils give him such things?' Miles asked.

'The Church itself does not deny the power of Satan. Didn't he say to the Lord Christ, "All the kingdoms of the earth will I give thee, if thou wilt fall down and worship me"? The summer solstice is near, a time when the old magic of this world is said to be strong. In pagan times, it was a great festival. Whatever Soulis has in mind to do, that will be the time.'

Straccan and Miles crossed themselves. There was no scepticism. The reality of their time contained God and Satan, saints and demons, miracles and magic, angels and ghosts, priests and sorcerers, nuns and witches, castles and faery halls, heaven and earth, horses and cattle along with unicorns and dragons, basilisks as well as everyday poultry, all as much part of existence as themselves.

'I met Robert de Beauris once,' Blaise said. 'He was a friend of my sister's son Martin, my pupil who died last year, God rest his soul.' He sighed. 'I am old, past the days of my strength, and now I have no young successor to learn from me.'

'Learn what?' asked Miles.

'As much wisdom as I could push into him. I'm not a Templar any more, but I honour the vows I took: to watch and guard pilgrims in their search for Christ. Men strive to reach Him here, just as much as in Palestine, and are beset by evil here too. There are others like me throughout Christendom. While we live, we watch and guard, lest evil prevail.'

Just then Bane drew a few fluttering breaths and seemed to stop breathing altogether for a few moments, before beginning again even more faintly than before.

'He must have the last rites,' Miles said urgently, looking at Blaise. 'In extremity, anyone may do it.'

Chapter 30

Outside, full morning had come. A hind and fawn drank at the opposite bank, and faded back into the dappled shadows beneath the trees. Birds sang. The sun shone. It promised to be a fair day.

Far along the road there was a little cloud of dust. Travellers approaching. Pilgrims, for as they came nearer they could be heard singing a hymn. They came slowly, all on foot, and gradually the dust cloud resolved itself into a group of odd-looking men and women in the charge of a small skinny monk. Several of the trudging singers appeared to be tied to the monk by lengths of rope attached to his belt.

Brother Celestius, said Straccan to himself wonderingly. Striding forward to meet them he cried the name aloud, whereat the dusty gang shuffled to a halt staring at him uncertainly. The monk stepped in front of them, spreading his arms as if to hold them back.

'Let us pass in peace,' he shouted. 'We're pilgrims!'

'Brother Celestius,' said Straccan again. Who else could it be?

'We don't know you,' said the monk. 'Ain't seen you before.'

'You know Hawkan Bane,' Straccan said. 'He met you at Altarwell. He told me about you.'

Celestius' worried expression switched to one of pleasure. 'Oh yes! We remember Master Bane. Stop that, William! *You* remember Master Bane. Alice? Walter? Course you do. E was kind to us.'

'Raisins,' said William hopefully. 'He gave us raisins.'

'So e did,' said the monk. 'You must be is master, Sir. E talked about you. What you doin ere?'

'We were ambushed by outlaws, savages,' Straccan said. 'Don't go on along this road, Brother; it is deadly dangerous. Bane, they have killed Bane.'

Celestius stared at him. One of the ragged women began to cry and in moments all the tattered company was in tears.

'Master Bane's dead?'

'Dying. He's in there.' Straccan nodded at the stone hut. 'Brother, God will surely reward you if you will give him the last rites.'

Celestius cast off his umbilical cords, gathering them together and putting them in Straccan's hands. Ducking under the low lintel, he entered the beehive hut. They could hear his voice, low, mumbling, then sing-song in prayer. Silence followed. Then they heard an odd sound, a sort of hiccup, a weak cough. Bane! A few moments later the ragged monk crawled out on his hands and knees and scrambled upright.

'Better get im a drink of water,' he said. 'E ain't dyin. E's feelin much better. But e's very thirsty.'

'He *was* dying,' Straccan said obstinately, after the monk and his people, fortified with a little whisky, had departed by a different way. Celestius had refused the coins they pressed on him but accepted some of Bane's private store of raisins. The sound of their cheerful singing died away in the distance. 'I've seen enough men die to know!'

'Yes, he was,' said Sir Blaise. 'And if that's so, we have been privileged to witness a miracle.'

'That little chap ...' Miles crossed himself. He was pale and shaking.

'Yes,' said Blaise thoughtfully. 'That little chap!'

Chapter 31

They stayed where they were for two days while Bane recovered his strength. Straccan restrained his burning impatience to be on the road again. Indeed, the miracle of Bane's healing gave him hope. God was good, surely He would safeguard Gilla. A litany of desperate prayer ran through his mind day and night: *Lord, keep her safe, bring me to her, save her!*

The captive savage they kept on short commons: water twice a day, dried meat only in the evenings, like a dog. Much like a dog it ate, worrying at the food with black and loosened teeth, mostly gulping it entire. It whined a lot, dog like, when not gagged, and shivered at night, tied to a tree at some distance from their fire where its stink wasn't right under their noses. Its only garment was a filthy old shirt, inside which infested rabbit-skins were crudely sewn, fur against flesh, for warmth. The shirt, heavy with grease and old blood, contributed a large part of the creature's stench.

It made no human sounds, just animal grunts when fed and squeals when frightened, and their efforts to get it to talk were useless.

'*Can* it talk?' Miles wondered. 'It's more beast than man.'

'They were men before they were beasts,' said Blaise. 'I'm sure it can talk, though we might not understand it.'

'You seem to know all about everything,' said Miles ungraciously. 'Have you heard of these things?'

'Rumours,' Blaise said. 'But I can guess what happened. Once they were men, but times were hard, they were hungry and they found a simple solution to the problem. They needed meat and, after all, it was everywhere around them, but on two legs. Probably to begin with, years ago, they raided a farm here and there, a vill by night, stole children as well as sheep. Then they began to waylay travellers, and grew fat. They bred and flourished. Now and then some local lord would send a troop to hunt for outlaws or wolves; they might find an outlaw or two, a wolf or two, but not these creatures. They don't find them because they're cunning; they lair in some hidden place where men can only scramble afoot, and no horsemen can go.

'In the villages they are a tale to frighten bairns, and so it's gone on for years because no one believed it.'

'If you want it to talk,' Larktwist said diffidently, 'I think I know a way.'

There had been two hares in his traps that morning, a welcome change from fish and dried meat. When he bled them, he noticed the riveted attention of the prisoner, its slobbering lust for the blood. He held the basin under its nose, and it writhed and plunged and whined, begging.

'Clever,' said Blaise admiringly. 'The blood craving! I'd not have thought of it.'

Bane was on his feet again and able to ride, when the savage led them to its tribe's hiding place. It was wild country, with desolate hills and deep gorges where the sunlight never reached bottom, and streams gurgled in darkness.

'Watch out for the Elven-Queen,' said Blaise, teasing Miles.

'What do you mean, Sir?'

'This is faery country, boy. Didn't you know?'

Miles crossed himself. 'No!'

'Here in these hills, the elves dwell, so it's said.' Blaise smiled. 'On these very paths, the fair folk ride at night, gleaming and deadly, to meet with their kin, wage their wars, seduce Christian men and women from their homes and change their own soulless birthlings for human babies, when and wherever they can. In olden times this was the very heart of their realm. These hills are supposed to be full of their gold.'

'Why do they want human children?'

'Because *they* can go about by daylight, among Christian folk, to work ill, and because they can handle iron; elves can't abide it.'

Now they were in a scrub-choked rocky valley. They had followed a deep-cut stream for some time through gorse and quickthorn, and when Blaise, hearing the rustle of a small animal, prodded at the bushes with his gaveloc, the prisoner yelped and jumped up and down waving his hands, jabbering and making strange buzzing noises.

They realised why when a cloud of wasps rose and hummed angrily about them. Before they could win clear Straccan had been stung twice on the hand, and Larktwist on the neck. Now, too late, they saw the oval whitish nests, like huge corrugated eggs, in the thorns.

'Bloody nests,' said Larktwist. 'Let's get out of here! My neck don't half hurt!'

Their guide led them, at last, in a difficult scramble up the side of the valley. No wonder the lair had never been found: it was no more than a horrid hole in the ground among tumbled boulders which screened it from anyone passing below. And even when they had clambered up they would not have noticed it, for it lay under an overhang of rock, in perpetual shadow.

Having found it, they descended as quietly as they could back to where they'd left the horses tethered. It was late evening now, and they made a cold meal of bread and cheese while discussing what to do next.

'We could only get down there one at a time, so that's no good, and we can't smoke them out,' said Straccan. He itched to be on the way to Skelrig, to confront Soulis, but at least this was action, which his body craved. 'If we dropped fire down there they could easily beat it out.' He sucked the swollen wasps stings and then paused, looking at his hand. He laughed.

'What is it?' Miles asked. 'Have you had an idea?'

'Yes! I know what'll do the trick!'

'What?'

'Wasps!'

'You clever devil, you,' said Miles, grinning.

'How do we handle them?'

'There were ... what? Half a dozen nests back there? So we need as many lidded baskets, that's all. Clip the nests off gently tonight and let them drop into the baskets ...'

'And chuck them down the hole,' finished Miles. 'It's splendid!'

'Wait and see if it works,' said Straccan. 'If it does, you can sing my praises then, and I'll bask in the glory.'

'I bet he will,' whispered Larktwist to Bane. 'Want to wager on who'll be the poor sod that gets to collect the nests?'

'I hate to throw cold water on your bright idea,' said Bane sourly, 'but we don't have any baskets.'

'Then we'll get some,' Straccan said, 'at the nearest vill.'

God alone knew what it was like down there when the enraged wasps came boiling out of their shattered nests. The screams began almost at once, and when the savages tried to get out they were driven back by blades.

It seemed a long wait as the morning sun rose and beat down hot on their backs, but eventually the screaming subsided. When nothing had tried to escape for some time, they judged it safe to go down. What they saw would haunt them for ever.

Cavern led into cavern, and the damp and foetid murk was ill-lit by a few rag wicks in bowls of stinking fat. There were pieces of meat hanging, like any housewife's store of bacons and hams, but these were the quartered flesh of men and women. The place was full of the droning of huge blue flies which clustered on the rock walls and on the ripe meat, and lit on the searchers' faces and hands.

A few wasps still buzzed angrily, but most had found their way out again through various crevices in the rock, through which came narrow shafts of light. Five of the beast-folk, three of them children, were dead, stung on lips and tongues and eyes, swollen, blue and asphyxiated. The rest were alive, but of those, four were so badly stung that they could not walk. Straccan and his companions fetched up the dead and the living, the dead dragged by their feet, the stumbling sting-blinded living fast bound.

Coin the creatures had kept – it was found scattered all through the caverns – for their brats had played with it, as they had with human bones and skulls. Savages they were, but they had the cunning to realise that jewellery might be recognised if they tried to sell or barter with it; so that too, they had kept. It was trumpery stuff, for they were clever enough not to attack the better-off travellers, anyone for whom search might be made. Their tawdry treasure was piled here and there in pathetic heaps – a little silver but mostly brass or latten, with glass gems – buckles and brooches, rings and pendants, amulets and pilgrim badges.

'So much for faery gold,' said Miles bitterly, stirring one of the piles with the tip of his sword.

'Eh? Oh, aye,' said Blaise. 'The people under the hill, the fair folk!'

They gathered it all to take to Jedburgh, where perhaps someone would recognise this buckle or that ring, and learn at last what had become of their missing kin.

Their captive guide, whimpering and cringing, led them to the far end of a low tunnel, where a charnel reek came from a dreadful natural oubliette. With gestures and jabbering – Straccan thought that whatever their language was, it sounded like nothing but a fit of coughing – it made them understand that the victims' remains, and their clothes and possessions, had been flung down there. Miles dropped a stone to test the depth, and they listened long before they heard it strike bottom.

They felt they would never be free of the stink; their hair and clothes were befouled, it penetrated their flesh and filled their lungs. Later they burned their clothes and sat in the stream, scrubbing their hair and skin until numbed and sore. Even then, the smell still seemed to be with them, and it was some days before they no longer complained of it.

'We will take them to the abbey at Holywood,' said Blaise. 'It lies less than a league away. The abbot is my cousin.'

'What then?' asked Straccan. 'I must get to Skelrig. God only knows what's happening there. These beasts have cost us time enough already.'

'You and Bane must ride on. There's no need for you to tarry for this. The lad and his servant can help me take the savages to Holywood. My cousin has the right of High and Low Justice,' said Blaise with grim satisfaction. 'Pit and gallows, life and death in his domain. We will leave them in his hands to be justified, and catch you up on the morrow.'

The creatures were put to death a week later, after a dreadful interval of torture and confession that exhausted even the hardest of the servants of justice, innured to anguish and depravity though they were. Under torture, several of the condemned told of the fair man who rode a black horse and paid them with meat and sugar to kill travellers of his own choosing.

Because of the nature of their crimes, they were regarded as beasts, not as human beings with immortal souls. No priests attended them, no prayers were said for them, and the day of their execution was a local holiday, the event itself a piece of theatre, a Roman circus, amusement and entertainment on a grand scale, a huge release of public hatred. Had they not been guarded as they were dragged to their deaths, they would have been torn apart by the baying multitude. But men with pikes kept the crowd back, and on the scaffold, built unusually high so all could see, the survivors of Sawney's family were butchered, gralloched and dismembered, as they had used their victims.

Sawney was kept until last, and baited like a bear before the executioner got his turn. With its bowels heaped between its feet, and first one arm, then the other, and one leg, then the other, struck off, the huge heaving carcass clung to life longer than any of the others, howling and blaspheming while its guts were burned before its eyes, until the final shuddering agony at last silenced its tongue.

The remains were pitchforked into a blazing fire and consumed, the ashes and calcined fragments raked up, pounded to powder and thrown into the river, where children threw stones at the greasy clots until all were swept away.

Chapter 32

The dumb boy, Hob, was sitting on an arrow chest in the window alcove just outside the garderobe room where Gilla was imprisoned. When he heard footsteps ascending, he swung round and slipped down behind the chest, where he crouched and made himself as small as he could, holding his breath, sure that the loud beating of his heart must be heard and he would be dragged out. But nothing happened. The lord, and Lady Julitta went on up to the top floor, talking quietly together.

Something was going on in the upper chamber. They had put that horrible old man in there who had turned up yesterday. One look at the Arab had frightened Hob half to death. Nothing as old and desiccated as that should be walking around alive.

What was going on? De Brasy had ridden out this morning leading a pack pony laden with brazier, charcoals and torches; he had returned without the burden. The kitchen was in a state of chaos, for a feast had been ordered for Lord Robert's men and the servants who had come with the Lady Julitta and the shuddersome new lord.

Above, the door closed behind them. Hob let his breath out and felt the sweat chilling on his skin. Tears leaked from his eyes; he wiped them and his nose with a dirty hand. Lord Robert was dead. Hob had seen his poor body and the blood, mute witness of murder.

Hob, dumb from birth but neither deaf nor stupid, was accustomed to the casual unkindness and deliberate cruelty with which dumb creatures are used. He had loved his master, Lord Robert, who always treated him kindly, but, above all, *talked* to him. Hob was proud of that. He did not realise that the terrified man had only been talking to *himself*, never dreaming the boy listened and learned. He had learned a great deal. He could understand the everyday Scots tongue used in the vill and the tower, and also some of the Norman French which the great folk sometimes spoke.

He knew the lady was wicked. She had forbidden Hob to look after Lord Robert and was guilty of his death. True, he had hanged himself, God shrive him, but it was *her* doing. The dead man's blood was proof. She and the new lord meant to bring the devil here. Hob knew all about the devil, whom Lord Robert feared, hiding in his magic circle. He knew all about the green metal case with a picture inside, too, which Crimmon had taken to England, wherever that was. Lord Robert had sent it to the lady his sister, to give to a great warlock who would come and destroy the devil, so that Lord Robert could leave his magic circle, ride his horses again, fly his hawks, and laugh and sing as he used to before he made the devil angry with him. But the lady had betrayed her brother, and his blood had cried out against her.

And there was the little girl. Hob had seen her slapped and shaken, heard her crying shut in that cold little room. The lady had even taken away her dress and shoes and the silver medallion she wore, and left just her shift and a blanket. Hob carried her food and knew she did not eat it. What would happen to her? She was so pretty, and small.

Hugging himself, trying to ease the misery of loss and fright, Hob huddled in the alcove wondering what to do. He wanted to go home; his grandfather would be glad to see him, and he'd be safe there; hungry and cold, but safe. The devil wasn't after *him*. But what about the girl? Suppose he let her out of her prison? What could she do, where could she hide? Suppose . . . suppose Hob took her with him?

There was a new bright bolt, fitted by the lady's orders to the garderobe door, but Hob could reach it. He touched the child's hand. She was asleep, poor wee cold thing, and didn't move. He squeezed the small hand and touched her gently on the cheek. Still no reaction. He saw the bruises and welts on her thin arms and on her soft throat, and made a little shocked pitying sound. He watched the rise and fall of her breathing, wondering how to wake her.

Wake up, he called desperately inside his head. Wake up! Wake up!

Gilla opened her eyes on Hob's anxious tear-smeared face. A boy. The boy who brought her food and peats for the fire. She didn't know his name.

'Who are you?'

He touched his lips, shook his head and made his sound, a soft grunt.

'Are you dumb?'

He nodded vigorously and smiled.

'Have you come to take me home?'

He nodded again, thinking he'd sort 'home' out later. Getting her out of here was enough to be going on with.

'Be off with ye. Go on, get oot!' The harassed cook, furious at this invasion of his steamy domain, laid about him with a heavy ladle, clouting heads, shoulders and elbows indiscriminately. Damn the beggar-brats; they were supposed to wait at the gate until the cook sent a scullion with yesterday's trenchers and any other leftovers. For some reason, today they had taken it into their stupid heads to run in through the gate and across the bailey to the kitchen door, half-terrified at their own daring.

'Ye wee skemps, I'll skelp ye! I'll set the hounds on ye! Oot! Oot! Oot!'

Yelping, they ran like a pack of grey and brown rats in their dirty sacking hoods and ragged shirts towards the gate, dodging the laughing guards who pretended to chase them. But one man, sharper of eyes and wits than the rest, noticed that while eight had run in, ten were running out.

'Shut the bloody gate!'

Hob's hideout, his secret refuge from the fears and torments of his silent childhood, was about three miles from Skelrig amid the small clustering braes, where rocky outcrops and deep narrow burns broke the bare hills. He had spent much time there in his short life.

Hob was seven years old when his father died, and his uncle, a tavern keeper in Dalkeith, claimed him for an unpaid slave. Hob's grandfather, his mother's father, objected strongly, but Uncle Willie bore him down, wore him down – the old man was frightened of the bellowing giant – and one morning Hob was put up behind his uncle on a tall bony horse, silently weeping.

His uncle was a bully who, by noon, had earned the boy's hatred. He slapped him till his head rang and shouted at him as if, being dumb, the boy must be deaf as well. Mid-morning, the fat man dismounted, pissed noisily against a rock and ate an excellent packed meal by himself, giving the child nothing. Mid-afternoon, when he stopped again and disappeared behind a tree, Hob took to his heels.

His hidden place was a small cave in the rock wall above a deep-cut burn, only gained by a desperate scramble upwards after following the stream bed for some way. It could not be seen from above at all and was well off any beaten track. He stayed there a full week while his furious uncle raged and searched, and finally gave up, riding back to his tavern alone.

Hob had meant to bring Gilla here. They'd have been safe, at least for a while.

He believed in the elven-folk, but he also believed firmly in the power of iron which they dreaded. In the past couple of days he had brought as much small scrap iron, stolen from the smithy, as he could carry, his chief pride and defence being a rusty length of chain which, like Lord Robert, he laid out in a protective circle. Several horseshoes and little heaps of nails reinforced his defences, and he had built a small stone hearth, now crowned with an old iron pot lacking its handle, likewise pilfered from Skelrig. He had also fetched a great heap of bracken and grass for some warmth and comfort.

Now he burrrowed into it alone, a small animal crying quietly as he made his nest. He'd failed her. He'd done his best and he'd failed. The gates had slammed shut before they could get through, and the man who had shouted had picked Gilla up by her hair and carried her, screaming, back into the tower. Hob and the rest had been knocked about a bit but there were no orders to hold on to them.

This place was safer than his grandfather's hut in the vill. If the bad people realised what he'd done, they would look for him there. Food was the first necessity, but Hob had been catching fish by hand in the burns since he was three years old and he was a dead shot with sling and stones, able to knock a squirrel out of a tree and even bring down a bird on the wing. Flint and steel he had. He would not starve.

Hob slept briefly, twitching and whimpering in his sleep like a puppy, but when he woke he knew what he was going to do. His stomach twisted with fear when he thought of returning to the tower but the bad people were up to something and, whatever it was, it would be done soon; no one would leave a brazier and coals lying about outside for long. It would be very soon, perhaps even tonight.

The lass was wee but brave. He could be no less brave. He must go back. If he got the chance, he would slip inside. If not, he would wait and watch until he could.

'How far now to Skelrig?' Straccan asked.

'Eight leagues or so,' said Blaise.

'Then what?' Miles asked. 'We five can neither siege the place, nor storm it.'

'I hope it will be a simple matter of exchange,' said Straccan. 'I have his relic. It *is* his, bought and paid for. He has my daughter. One for the other.'

The old knight's expression was bleak. 'When you have her, what then?'

'I will kill him.'

Chapter 33

Unlike Lord Robert, whose sleeping conscience had been inconveniently jolted awake by murder, de Brasy didn't care who suffered, as long as it wasn't him. While still with Soulis he must obey, and if that meant more killing, what the hell. It would make no difference, anyway. He didn't expect Al-Hazred's filthy ritual to have any more effect now than before; for all the old devil swore he could draw upon the power in the Nine Stane Rig to ensure success this time.

That was the trouble with the Arab. He had promised success *this* time both times, and had explanations for each failure. The stars were against them, other influences opposed them, the place was wrong, the time was not right, even the bloody *wind* had changed!

How the master could still believe in the old fraud was beyond de Brasy's understanding. They had tried his great ritual at Soulistoun – that's where the stars were against them – and at Crawgard – that was the wrong place – but never mind, third time lucky. They would try again, this time in the Nine Stane Rig.

Soulis had read in some old book that power was often concentrated in ancient stone circles. He bought old books, manuscripts, letters and documents from all over the world. Agents in Bristol, Paris and Marseilles, Rome and Nuremberg, Valencia, Athens, Egypt and Jerusalem, sent him antique parchments, papyri, clay tablets and linen scrolls. He and the Arab pored over them. Most were rejected as rubbish, but now and then some scrap of ancient lore was discovered that promised to be useful.

Al-Hazred found the summoning ritual in a crate of crumbling clay tablets from Outremer, and at Soulistoun they tried, and failed of course, to tempt a demon with new-spilled blood – the blood of hens and lambs – for the ritual demanded blood without saying what kind. But the blood of birds and beasts did not coax a demon into the lead and silver cage prepared for it. And then, for the first time, the master turned upon Al-Hazred and struck him in his rage and disappointment. De Brasy saw the Arab's face slack with astonishment and sudden fear, and the quickly-veiled glare of hatred in his lightless black eyes. If looks could kill . . .

De Brasy would never have drunk anything offered by anyone who looked at *him* like that, but once again the master allowed himself to be placated, and swallowed the Arab's prescribed potion 'to restore My Lord's spirits, to comfort My Lord in his disappointment'.

To polish My Lord off more like, thought de Brasy, awaiting developments with interest. But he was wrong, this time. Restored and comforted, Soulis listened, nodding dreamily as Al-Hazred poured the soothing oil of his plausible explanations. What they had offered, he said, was not precious enough. The demon scorned the blood of soulless creatures.

So next time, at the winter solstice at Crawgard, they offered blood *and* souls.

There were a few nasty moments when, in the disorienting haze of incense and smoke from the powders and herbs the Arab burned, de Brasy actually thought there *was* something there, shadowy hints of a dreadful ever-changing shape, trying to form. Urged on by Al-Hazred, they tried to capture it with an orgy of slaughter, but to no avail. It faded away, leaving them with nothing but the stink and what was left of the bodies.

But this Nine Stane Rig was a place of power, of ancient sacrifice, where blood had been offered to the old dark gods; and the master was all the more determined to go ahead tonight, since the special child who was to be their offering had almost got away.

'Such purity. An innocent soul, a fledgeling seer. The perfect offering,' Soulis gloated.

'Even so, it would be as well to have more than one,' Julitta said. 'There are plenty of *neyf* brats in the vill. Take one of them.'

'Common stuff.'

'Their souls are probably every bit as innocent as hers,' said Julitta tartly. 'Send de Brasy.'

De Brasy shivered. Tonight in the Nine Stane Rig they would try again, and he had a nasty feeling that, in spite of all his careful planning, his stolen gold, the ship waiting at Leith, something was about to go wrong. In his bloody eventful life, he had learned to trust the uncomfortable sensation of cold feet.

'We still lack one relic,' Julitta said.

Lord Rainard gnawed his lip and touched the necklace he wore, a heavy silver chain from which hung a number of small reliquaries. 'True. But I have all the others, except Thomas's finger. I don't believe that just one missing will matter in the end. If the Arab cannot control the demon, we still have the protection of ten great saints. Even Peter,' he sneered, 'against whom the gates of hell cannot prevail!'

He passed the little reliquaries through his fingers like rosary beads, lingering over the one which held a knuckle-bone of Saint Peter. It, and the relics of the other disciples of Christ had been collected over several years at enormous cost. Next to a relic of Christ Himself, those of His disciples were the most powerful, sure and certain protection against the being from outer darkness which the Arab swore he could summon.

There *should* be eleven relics: one of each true disciple. Even so, ten great saints would surely suffice to keep him safe, and compel the demon's obedience. Providing it was first fed and satiated.

'There may be something in what you say, My Lady.' He turned to de Brasy. 'Get a child from the vill. Let no one see you. After tonight,' he added triumphantly, 'nothing will prevail against me!'

Not for the first time de Brasy wondered what was so desirable that Lord Rainard would be willing to traffic with hell for it. It had something to do with letters he wrote to, and received from, France and England. The bitch Julitta's husband, the Earl of Arlen, was in it, and others of King John's lords – de Cressi, de Vesci, FitzWalter and Mowbray among them – even the king of France, Philip Augustus, whose seal de Brasy had seen on some of the letters. If he could read, he would have known all.

Overnight, a cold grey North Sea haar had rolled inland, settling as far west as Selkirk and pouring over the Eildon Hills in a dense gloomy torrent. Here to stay.

About ten miles from Skelrig, Straccan and his companions saw it ahead and gave a collective groan.

'That's all we need,' said Bane.

At Skelrig, the sleepy watchman on the tower roof could not see the ground below at all. Mist clung to his clothes, beaded the iron plates of his hauberk and gathered to drip from his helmet straight down the back of his neck. The uncanny silence that had prevailed since the new lord and his sinister bodyguards had arrived continued, with the place blind now, as well as deaf and dumb.

Fog didn't hinder Hob who knew every inch of the ground for several miles around Skelrig. He crouched inside the low-walled stone stell just outside the bailey gates. No one had gone in or out, and the gates had remained shut since he got there. Even the elves, Hob thought, would surely have the good sense to stay at home on such a night! He had secretly pocketed the broken necklace of charms and amulets which the lady had torn from Lord Robert's dead throat, and wore it, mended with a bit of string, round his neck. This, and the short length of rusty iron bar thrust through his belt, would make any elf think again before giving him trouble.

There was a sudden shouting and calling inside the gates: horses, people's voices, the sound of the great bars being lifted. The gates squeaked and jerked and opened. There was the smoky glow of torches. Now!

But as Hob tensed to begin his dash he saw the first rider come through the gate. It was Soulis, and the little limp body held before him on the saddle bow, fair hair hanging loose, was Gilla. Dead, Hob thought with sudden anguish but, as he looked, one small hand clenched and unclenched. The cruel lady followed, then the wicked Arab, then that man de Brasy carrying another child. Hob gave a small grunt of dismay. Last came the bad lord's Saracen archers, and the gates squealed and juddered shut behind them.

De Brasy had thought to be safely away by now. He had intended to leave the tower before the others, ostensibly to light the brazier and torches and make the circle ready, but instead riding hell-for-leather to Leith, to catch the tide and the ship bound for Cyprus. A man of means could live well there. The gold he'd stolen from Soulis would set him up in comfort, even in some style. But before he could slip away, Soulis had bidden him ride with them to carry the second sacrifice, the drugged boy he had plucked from the vill placating its mother with coins and promises of the brat's good fortune. As the party rode out of the gate the Arab looked over his shoulder at de Brasy and showed his fangs in an unpleasant grin. He was certain the old devil could read his mind. Earlier he'd come upon Al-Hazred muttering with the Saracen archers who had bowed and kissed his hands. When they saw de Brasy, they scowled, one even set hand to the hilt of his curved sword, but the old sorcerer held the man's wrist, shaking his head, his dead-looking eyes fixed on de Brasy.

For the present there was nothing for it but to obey and ride with the master to Nine Stane Rig. However, the haar was so dense they must go slowly, letting the horses feel their way. A blessing, de Brasy thought. He would seize his chance.

Hob kept up with them easily.

He watched as the bad people left their horses with the bowmen and climbed the mound, carrying the children. They passed out of his sight into the ring of stones. Shivering, Hob crept round to the far side of the mound, and began to crawl silently up.

Midnight was near. At Skelrig, the men of the garrison and the servants slept after their drugged meal. Some sprawled at the table, others had slid to the floor and lay in the rushes. To be sure none would wake, the Arab had also doctored the candles, and soporific smoke hung heavy and sickly in the hall.

In the Nine Stane Rig the ritual began.

A few miles away to the south-west, where Sir Blaise kept watch by the night fire, he raised his head and stared into the foggy darkness. The hairs on his arms and the back of his neck were prickling, but he heard and saw nothing. Nevertheless, he stood and drew his sword.

Straccan, wrapped in his cloak, sat up. 'What's the matter?'

'Something's happening,' the old man said. 'Can't you feel it? Sense it?'

Straccan threw his cloak aside and got up. 'I don't know,' he said after a minute. 'It's like being on watch and knowing the enemy is out there somewhere, only you can't see him or hear him. But he's there, and at any minute he'll be at your throat.'

'Rouse the others,' said Blaise. 'We must go on.'

'We'll lose the way,' Straccan said, nevertheless prodding the others with his toe.

'I don't think so,' Blaise murmured. 'I feel the pull of it. Like a lodestone.'

They rode slowly, unable to see more than a few feet ahead. The haar was denser now, and cold wet droplets clung to their hair and clothes, and slicked the horses' sides.

As he crawled up the hill, Hob heard a shrill far-off piping, which seemed to come from the darkness above; a thin dismal wail that had nothing of music in it. Hob loved music, and this dirge set his teeth on edge; it seemed to get inside his skull. Shaking his head, he crept to the man-high base of the fallen King Stane and peered round the edge. He could hear chanting, words he couldn't understand. His thin body shook with the hard hammering of his heart.

There was no fog in the Nine Stane Rig. Lit by the reddish light of a brazier and by candles and torches stuck in the ground, the

Arab stood with his back to the unsuspected watcher, his skinny arms raised to the night sky; it was his sing-song voice Hob had heard. At his feet was a heap of small bodies – decapitated doves, lambs with their throats slit – and before him a stone trough which steamed. There was a coppery-sweet smell of blood. The bad lord and the cruel lady were bending over something on the ground which squirmed and cried like a hurt animal.

Hob couldn't see Gilla or de Brasy. Where were they?

The bad lord lifted the thing on the ground and passed it to the Arab. Hob nearly bit his tongue through as he saw the limp legs and lolling head, the small naked body slick with dark blood from cuts that laced the skin from brow to toes. Not Gilla. A boy.

The Arab laid the boy in the trough. Hob began to cry, swiping at his tears with both fists. He desperately wanted to run away, to run and never stop, but the wee girl must be in there and he couldn't leave her.

The Arab raised his arms again, and so did the lady and the bad lord. Within the circle, frost glittered on the grass and the stones. From nowhere, a small cold wind rose, lifting the lady's hair as she stood, swaying. Hob smelled ice.

Outside the circle, the fog wreathed and swirled. Inside, the air seemed to quiver and a black pit opened in the sky. Those in the ring felt a sensation of intense downward pressure, which hurt their ears. A thin snow began to fall, tinged red by the torchlight.

Something was there.

It shifted shape constantly, at first impossibly huge, cloud-vast, then contracting to cow-size, to man-size, a black shadow in darkness, its shape only suggested by the stars it blotted out. Now and then there was a faint glint like the edge of steel, and a dry rustling sound like snakes.

The brazier's glow dimmed, the torches dwindled to small red eyes, the candle flames went blue, and shrank, and went out, and a cold luminescence began to pulse from the stones.

The Arab's wailing rose to a howl, his hands wove shapes in the air. *There* was de Brasy; he moved now from the other side of the great stone into Hob's line of sight, carrying the little girl in his arms. The bad lord, his pale face triumphant, clutched at the necklace he wore and turned, looking, Hob thought, straight at him.

'Sssh,' said Straccan. 'Listen.'

They stopped and listened. Nothing. Then ... yes, the distant chink of shod hoof on stone. Gently they eased swords from scabbards, making no sound. There! A rattle of pebbles, and, quite clearly, the harsh blowing of a horse ridden hard. Now they could all hear the regular fall of hoofs on turf and the jingle of harness.

The rider was some way above them, coming downhill. Straccan and Miles moved up the slope, waiting. The fog muffled then magnified sounds, so they could not tell how close the rider was until suddenly he was upon them, his mount rearing with a squeal as Miles snatched its reins. Straccan seized the rider's leg and dragged him in a heavy tumble to the ground.

It was a very fine black stallion.

The rider was very fair.

Miles was upon him instantly, rolling him over, pinning him down. The fair man snatched the young knight's own dagger from its sheath and slashed, a stroke that would have disembowelled Miles but for a swift kick from Straccan which sent the knife spinning off into the fog. The rider fought like a wolverine, with fists and feet and teeth, until Straccan kicked him so hard in one knee that they all heard the bone crack. De Brasy screamed, then gasped as Straccan dropped with both knees on to his unguarded belly, winding him and setting a dagger at his throat.

'Where's my daughter?' he snarled.

'Who ... are ... you?' de Brasy gasped, trying to pull away from the business end of the blade.

'You know me, you hellspawn scum. I'm Straccan.' With a jerk of the point he sent blood flowing over de Brasy's leather hauberk. 'Is she at Skelrig?'

'No!'

'Liar!' Straccan switched the knife to his right hand and thrust it right through de Brasy's left forearm, pinning him to the ground.

The man howled like a dog. 'Murderer,' said Straccan. 'Where is she?'

'Dead!'

Straccan gave a great sob of grief and despair.

De Brasy had handed out a good deal of pain in his time, but hadn't been on the receiving end for years. He was shuddering with shock. Leaning over him, Blaise saw the pupils of his staring eyes were mere dots. He gripped the man's chin, turning his head until the vacant gaze held his own.

'Who is at Skelrig tower?'

'Just servants and men-at-arms.' De Brasy hiccuped. 'The others are at the stones.'

'What stones?'

'The circle, the Nine Stane Rig. Let me go! I'll pay. I've gold— Aah!'

Straccan tugged his knife out of de Brasy's arm. 'Get up.'

De Brasy tried to stand but could put no weight on his damaged leg. He groaned and fell back.

'Let me tickle him a bit with my dagger.' Bane drew the knife from its sheath and fingered it hopefully as de Brasy moaned, clutching at his knee.

'Hurts, does it? Good,' said Straccan. 'We'll tie you on your horse. You will take us to this stone circle.'

'No! I beg you! Let me go!'

'Help us, and we might,' said Blaise.

De Brasy was babbling, shrill with panic. 'It's not my fault! It *was* real after all, it was terrible! I didn't want to be there! I took his money. I had to get away!'

'What was real?' Blaise asked.

'The Arab's devil! I never believed in it, but there *was* something there. I couldn't really see, I didn't *want* to ... but *something* ... Oh Christ, just for an instant ...'

'Go on.'

'I had hold of the girl till they were ready for her.' Straccan tensed as de Brasy went on. 'The master called me to bring her to him. I tried ... but, oh God, I couldn't, with that *thing* at his back.

I dropped the brat and threw my knife at the Arab. Got him, too. He screeched and fell. The bowmen came running.' His voice broke on a sob. 'The master rushed at me . . . *He* was all right, God rot him! He had those relics to protect him. I tried to snatch them but they broke and I ran. Julitta started screaming. Perhaps the demon got her, I hope it did! Let me go! You promised!'

'I made no promise.' Blaise grasped de Brasy's bloody collar and hauled him upright. His legs folded and he hung for a moment, like something dead, in the tall old knight's grip. Then, faster than seemed possible, he pulled Blaise's dagger just as he had Miles's, and struck at him. Blaise jerked back as the blade slit his coat, but as de Brasy lurched awkwardly towards his horse the hilt of a knife sprouted from his back between the shoulder blades, petals of blood like a great flower blooming around it as he fell among the horses' shifting feet.

Bending over him, Straccan wrenched his dagger free, wiped it on the dead man's coat and stuck it back in the sheath at his belt.

Bane and Larktwist bent to lift the body. 'Hamstring that,' said Blaise curtly, 'and cut its head off.'

Miles opened his mouth to protest, but Blaise said, 'Rainard de Soulis is skilled in devilry. He could put a lich to use.'

'Oh Christ,' said Miles, looking sick.

They packed the body over the black stallion's saddle. Bane, efficiently checking the saddlebags, found two small heavy linen sacks which chinked richly as he tossed them to Straccan.

Chapter 34

At the foot of the hill they found two horses and the ground much trampled. Dismounting they left Larktwist to hold the animals. The stones bulked tall and pale out of the fog as they climbed the hill. Reaching the ring they saw that there had been torches lit, on spikes stuck in the ground, but only one still burned. Straccan seized it and held it up.

From an overturned brazier a fan of spilled charcoals spread across the turf, still sending up coils of smoke which hung in layers in the circle. Right in the centre of the ring was a stone trough, half-full of jelling blood. Huddled against one of the great stones was Lord Rainard, an arrow in his shoulder. The woman lay near the fallen King Stane, looking dead. There was no sign of the Arab or the archers. There was a thick reek of blood, and a stupefying sick-sweet perfume which Blaise recognised as hashish.

'Lord Christ! Gilla!' With a great cry, Straccan knelt by a small broken body flung down like rubbish upon a heap of bloody feathers and carcasses. His shaking hands turned the body over. It was a boy, five or six years old.

'She's not here,' said Blaise.

Straccan knelt by the body. 'Lord Jesus, into your care, receive this soul . . .' His voice broke.

The woman moaned and moved slightly. Blaise stooped over her, drawing aside the long hair, wet with blood, that covered her face.

Straccan came to look, stumbling as he trod on something in the grass: it looked like a cage, trampled, crushed, silvery-grey. He stared at the woman's face. 'Julitta,' he said, his face twisted with revulsion.

Blaise's fingers had found a great lump above Julitta's ear. 'She'll live,' he said. 'It looks as if someone struck her down.' He held up an iron bar. 'With this.'

'De Brasy?' said Miles.

'I don't think so. She was screaming, he said, when he fled.'

The all-pervading smell reminded Straccan of the Arab's room at Crawgard, and as he breathed it the wreathing smoke seemed to take form, just as it had there, shifting, changing ... Cold sweat ran down his back and when he spoke his tongue felt thick and clumsy. He pointed. 'Look! There!'

'There's nothing,' Bane said, staring.

'I thought I saw ... It's gone now.'

Miles crossed himself. 'Lord, protect us!'

'This air is deadly,' said Blaise. 'We must get out of here, or we'll all see horrors and run mad!'

They dragged them out of the ring and down the hill; the woman limp and unresisting, Soulis struggling feebly and crying out in a foreign tongue as they secured him. Whatever the language, Blaise recognised it. He ripped a piece from Soulis's cloak and gagged him with it.

'What was he on about?' Bane panted, as between them they heaved Soulis over Larktwist's saddle.

Blaise shrugged. 'Those were the names of demons; he was calling them to help him.' His teeth gleamed in a quick smile as Bane crossed himself. 'Don't worry, my friend. As you see, they have not come. Still, no point in taking chances.' He tightened the gag and wrapped the reins round his wrist.

Away from the stones, their heads began to clear. A damp wind, rising, tore at the fog, and a bleached moon slid out between retreating clouds. By its light they could now see the distant top of Skelrig tower, gaunt against a paler sky.

In the hall they found the sleepers, who they slapped, pummelled and threw water over. Dully at first, but soon growing angry, the garrison listened as Sir Blaise told them what had been found at the Nine Stane Rig.

'Lord Rainard is my prisoner, and Lord Robert's sister has no authority here,' the old man finished. 'Until King William decides what to do with Skelrig, take your orders from us.'

'Let's burn the witch,' said the captain of the tower guard who had served Lord Robert. A growl of approval rose from the others.

'Burn she will, no doubt,' Blaise said, 'but after a trial, and in Edinburgh for all to see. You will not touch her, do you hear me?'

They shuffled their feet and looked resentful, but nodded, and some said, 'Aye.'

They laid Julitta on a narrow pallet in the small room where, although Straccan did not know it, his daughter had been confined. The snick of the new bolt that imprisoned her penetrated Julitta's stunned consciousness. Her eyelids flickered opened and she stared around the little chamber. When she tried to sit up there was a savage jolt of pain in her head. Probing carefully through her hair she found the lump and winced. Carefully she lay back and closed her eyes. Memory returned in disjointed images.

Snow . . . cold wind in her face, lifting her hair . . . The ever-changing shape descending from the black pit of the sky . . . De Brasy dropping the girl . . . the Arab screaming . . . arrows in flight . . . Soulis falling, crying, 'Now! Kill her now!' Two strides to the fallen child. She raised her knife and heard Soulis call, 'Look out!'

And knew no more until now.

Whoever had brought her here would be back soon. She must find a way to escape.

The savaged body of the boy they took to the chapel, where Bane and Larktwist laid it on a bench before the stripped altar and rummaged around in the priest's deserted room until they found a linen cloth to cover it.

Lord Rainard, still trying to mumble through his gag and staring past them at nothing with eyes like de Brasy's, pupils contracted to pinpoints, they fettered in the vault. The arrow had pierced muscle but nothing vital. There was very little blood. Blaise snapped the shaft, leaving the arrowhead in the wound. They searched him and emptied his belt purse which contained a few coins, a nail-paring knife and a small key.

They searched the place. In Soulis's baggage they found a barrel of gold and silver coins, tight-packed in linen sacks. The lid was askew and the bags didn't fill the barrel, accounting for de Brasy's getaway fund. The silver was of all kingdoms, but the gold was that which they had seen before, small greasy coins with something like an octopus stamped on them. Sir Blaise picked one up. 'Irem,' he said, and threw it back wiping his fingers in disgust.

'How does this open?' Miles had flung a pile of garments aside and found an iron casket. It was a marvel of the locksmith's art with no less than seven intricate locks, each looking as if it required a different key.

'Let's see.' Larktwist took it from him and turned it round in his hands, peering intently at the locks. There was thick dust in all of them. 'Dummies,' he said. 'German work. They think it's clever; as if anyone could be bothered to use seven keys.' He upended it and scrutinised the elaborate wrought design on the bottom. 'There, look.' A small keyhole, hidden in the arabesques of foliage. Soulis's little key opened it.

Letters. Spilling them on to the bed, Blaise recognised the seal of the King of France. There too was the seal of the Lord of Alnwick, Eustace de Vesci, and the wolf's head of Arlen. Blaise began to read. 'God's eyes, he would be King of Scots,' he said, amazed. 'Here's treason. You go on, I'll read.'

Sitting on Soulis's unmade bed, he went through all the letters while the others continued to search. At last, in what had been the lady's bedchamber, Straccan found a little grey dress and a pair of small scuffed shoes.

He pressed the dress to his lips and his tears ran, blotting the fabric. Clutching Gilla's crumpled dress and little cloth shoes, his last hope died.

Chapter 35

De Brasy's corpse had been shovelled underground with unceremonious haste, no one bothering to waste a prayer, for it was certain that his torments now entertained the fiends, and serve him right. And a good thing too that someone'd had the sense to hamstring the body before burying it, lest it walk again. Better safe than sorry. But in Skelrig's earth-floored chapel, tacked on to the side of the tower and roofed with leaky old gorse thatch, many candles had been lit. The floor had been swept, the dust wiped away where the slaughtered child lay.

Sir Blaise knelt and prayed before turning the linen cloth back. As he examined the slashed and inscribed flesh, a shadow fell over the body and he looked round to see Miles standing behind him.

'Who did this? Soulis?' The young man's eyes were full of shock and pity.

'He, or the Arab,' said Blaise grimly.

'Where d'you suppose *he*'s got to? There was no sign of him at that Rig place, although de Brasy thought he'd killed him.'

'That one would not be so easy to kill. He fled, and his countrymen with him. This poor child may have come from the vill. Someone must go and ask. Has the woman come round yet?'

'Yes.' Miles gently covered the body again. 'I sent food and water in to her.'

'It's time we talked to her.'

Julitta denied everything. She had come to Skelrig only to see her poor sick brother, and then, when he died so shockingly, his terrible overlord arrived and forced her by threats, to be an unwilling partner in black sorcery.

'Thank God, good Sirs, that you came when you did,' she said, speaking to Sir Blaise but turning her green gaze pleadingly upon Miles, who blushed. Straccan, standing in the shadows by the door, she did not appear to have seen. 'Will you not untie my hands? You can see I couldn't manage to eat much with them bound, and I spilled the cup. It is against courtesy to keep me bound like this. And it hurts,' she added, her voice small and pained.

Miles took a step towards her but Blaise blocked his way. 'Leave her,' he said. 'We know well, Lady, that you are accomplice and creature of the Baron de Soulis.'

'It isn't true,' Julitta said pathetically. 'How can I convince you?'

'We have his letters,' Blaise said. 'Letters from your husband among them. You may as well speak the truth, Lady, before you die a traitor's death. I doubt if King John will be any more tender of your fair body than of any other traitor's. You know better than I what mercy you may hope for from him.'

She lowered her eyes, but not before they saw the malevolent gleam in them.

'As for your brother, God have pity on his soul, he asked for your help,' Blaise continued. From his belt pouch he took the icon in its case. They heard her indrawn breath. 'He asked you to find his friend, Martin Brus, whom he knew would understand what it was and whence it came. But you betrayed your brother, Lady. You sent this thing back to your master. The letter you wrote is in his casket with the rest.'

She glared her hatred at him.

'Martin was my nephew,' said Blaise. 'He would have recognised this perilous thing and brought it to me, and *I* would not have failed your brother. His death is your blame, Lady, as surely as if you put your own white hands to it; and the death of that poor child, butchered in the ring of stones. Who was he?'

'I don't know. De Brasy brought him.'

'What of Sir Richard Straccan's daughter?'

Straccan's hands clenched and he took a step forward.

Julitta spat at him. 'You damned bone-pedlar! I knew you'd bring trouble! How you fancied yourself, you interfering fool, sending your servant to my brother, meddling in my affairs! And you wanted me, didn't you? In your arms, in your bed, skin to skin ... You *burned* for me.'

Straccan bowed his head, shame and revulsion scorching him.

'If you wanted to avoid his attention, you shouldn't have stolen his daughter,' said Blaise.

'I didn't! It was Pluvis, the damned perverted fool! He and de Brasy reft her from that nunnery and carried her to Arlen castle. I took her from him and brought her here. What else could I do? Hand her back to her father and hope he'd do no more than thank me?'

'Where is her body?' Straccan asked.

Julitta looked at him and saw the glimmer of a chance. 'I can show you the place,' she said slowly. 'You'll not find it else.'

They had brought her palfrey, ready saddled, to the mounting-block, and led her into the bailey. A rumble of anger and a few shouts of 'Witch!' came from the men-at-arms and servants watching. She did not seem to hear.

'That horse is lame,' she said.

Bane trotted it forward and round, and back to the block. It limped on the right fore.

'There was no sign of that before, Sir, I swear,' said the puzzled stableman. 'It must be a sprain.'

Straccan was impatient. 'Get another horse.'

'There's only that black stallion,' said the stableman, 'or one of the ponies.'

'I can ride the black,' she said.

They rode east, Julitta between Straccan and Miles, the stallion on a rope tethered to Straccan's saddle bow. It was a dull cold morning with a venomous north-east wind, and the masses of dark cloud piling up in the north promised heavy rain before long.

She rode well, handling the stallion with no effort, her head bowed, the bright blood-spattered hair hidden under an old hunting cap. Miles, glancing sideways at her, saw her lips moving constantly as if in prayer.

Halfway down a rock-littered slope the path narrowed and they rode single file, Straccan leading, Julitta in the middle. Suddenly she cried out, pointing. Straccan caught only the word boar. He looked, and saw the side of the hill above them begin to move.

A great tusky boar was barrelling down upon them, as unstoppable as an avalanche. How in God's name came such a beast here, so far from its natural forest lair? Stones rattled around them, raising a fog of red dust. The feet of Miles's horse were swept from under him, horse and rider tumbling down the hill.

Julitta leaned low in the saddle and heeled the stallion hard. The great animal leapt forward, jerking the tether violently and dragging Straccan's horse, which lost its footing on the shifting ground and fell, rolling sideways. The strain on the rope was too much; it snapped, and she was away.

In the tumbling debris Straccan rolled aside to avoid being crushed by his horse. His girth broke and the saddle pitched downhill. The animal tried to get up, shaking and snorting, but fell back. A fore-leg was snapped. Bitter at heart, Straccan drew his knife and gave the mercy stroke.

Through the cloud of dust he saw the lady, her great horse moving so fast and smoothly it seemed to fly over the ground. In a few more moments she was out of sight among the little hills.

There was no boar, only a great rolling rock: loosened by the recent rain, it had slid from its place and brought down the rockslide. Bruised, bleeding and swearing furiously, Miles ran to Straccan, who was kneeling in his horse's blood.

'Are you all right?'

'Help me up.' He held out a hand and was tugged to his feet. 'She's got away,' he said. 'What a God! No pity.'

'I'm sorry,' Miles said. He'd been saying it for ages. Sir Blaise sat in Lord Robert's great chair in the hall and Straccan, bruised and scraped and limping, paced back and forth by the window. They had been over and over the sequence of events, and Miles was sick at heart and sick of apologising. 'She had too good a start; and anyway, I couldn't follow her and leave Richard,' he said helplessly.

'You should have, boy!'

'I'm sorry!'

'Leave him be,' Straccan said. 'It wasn't his fault.'

The old man glared at him, then covered his eyes with his hand. After a moment he looked up at Miles and said, 'No. Forgive me. You did what seemed right. But that woman is deadly as a viper in a glove! She knows us and has cause to hate us. We shall rue her loss.'

'I'm sor—' Miles began.

Blaise interrupted. 'No. *I'm* sorry, boy, for rating you. It's not your fault.'

'Now we shall never know what happened to the little girl,' said Miles unhappily. Sweat streaked his face and he was only just becoming aware that his body seemed to be all one great bruise.

'Tend to yourself,' said Blaise. 'Get that man of yours to bring you water and towels. There'll be salve somewhere in this place; if anyone can find it, he can.'

Miles went in search of Larktwist, and Blaise turned to Straccan. 'You should see to your hurts as well,' he said.

Straccan stared out of the window, gripping the bar. 'Do you think she truly knew where Gilla lies?'

'No, I don't. She led you out only so that she might escape.'

'Then what has become of her? If that devil Al-Hazred took her, she must be dead like that poor innocent in the chapel.' His knuckles whitened.

Blaise was thinking hard. 'The Arab went off with his countrymen,' he said. 'Their horses were gone. He had no reason to take Gilla. It was Soulis who needed her dead. Al-Hazred was making his getaway; your lass would only hinder him.' He tapped his fingers on the arm of the chair, frowning. 'All we know is that she was in the Nine Stane Rig and we have not found her body. Perhaps because there is no body to find.'

'De Brasy said she was dead.'

'She was alive when he ran.'

'Julitta said it too.'

Blaise stared at him. 'No. No, she didn't. Think back. She said nothing about Gilla being dead. You asked where her body was. She simply said she'd show us.'

'But her dress, her shoes . . .'

'Don't dwell on that. Richard, I do not believe God is so pitiless. I believe there is hope of her. Take a party and search. If she got away, she can't have gone far.'

'Look,' said Gilla. 'There's my lady.'

Hob crouched on a rocky ledge beside the burn, his skinny bare arm in the water stroking the smooth side of a fat trout. Ssh, he said mentally, and with a jerk of his arm flung the fish into the reeds where it flapped and twisted. He sprang up, beaming, but the girl wasn't looking at him or the fish. Her gaze was fixed further along the stream and her smile was beautiful. Suddenly it felt warmer – as if the sun had come out – but the sky was dark with cloud and the cold wind rose to howling pitch over their heads outside the gully.

The lady stepped delicately through the water, but the water was not stirred nor did she get wet. She walked away along the bed of the burn, stopped to look back at the children and beckoned, smiling.

'Come on,' Gilla said, tugging at Hob's ragged tunic.

Hob couldn't see anybody, but there was something – a shimmer, glints of brightness – over the water where Gilla stood. She put her hand up as if to take the hand of someone Hob couldn't see.

She turned her radiant face to Hob. 'We can go back now. The lady says it's all right. My father has come.'

No! No! Not back there, she couldn't mean that! Not to the bad people! The bad lord had fallen to an arrow but he'd still been moving, calling; he was alive. As for the cruel lady, the witch, she *might* be dead. He had given her a grand crack with his iron bar. He regretted its loss; a worthy weapon, as good as any magic sword in a story. She'd gone down like a stone but he wouldn't believe her safely dead unless he saw her corpse.

Hob shook his head violently and seized Gilla's arm, grunting and crying in distress.

'It's all right, truly! I know! She told me.'

Who did she mean? Hob clutched his string of charms and prayed urgently. He had his own concept of God, nothing Father Kenneth would have recognised. Skelrig's old priest would have been very disturbed if he'd realised the unorthodoxy of Hob's beliefs.

There were paintings on the chapel wall at Skelrig's – old, peeling, damp-stained – but enough remained to show that God-and-Mary wore golden hats like platters and walked about on clouds. The clouds looked soft and woolly, and Hob thought they kept the holy people's feet nice and warm. They were one being in Hob's mind, God male and female, though sometimes God was a baby, and sometimes he was a man nailed to a cross. That had troubled Hob when he was younger, but he had decided that it couldn't have hurt because God's face was so calm, not screwed up in pain. Hob no longer worried about it.

He prayed now to God-and-Mary and saw them standing on their little fleecy cloud between him and Gilla, nodding and smiling at him. Make her stay, he pleaded, but they shook their heads and moved along the burn on their cloud. After a few steps they turned and gestured to him to follow. Gilla was slipping and splashing among the stones. Hob gave a great humphing grunt, which meant wait for me, and floundered after her.

Straccan and his party had ridden for hours, first searching the village, then fanning out around it. They examined bields, bushes and reed-beds, dovecotes, shepherds' bothies and clumps of trees, finding nothing. As time passed, Straccan felt hope leaching out of him and rode hunched in his saddle, as if to ease a wound. Aching, wretched, he stopped to let his horse drink where a small burn fell from a rocky lip into a deep brown pool. The sound of the waterfall was clear and musical. It almost sounded like laughter.

It *was* laughter! He looked up. A boy was peering down from the rocks above, a ginger-haired local lad, scrawny and in rags like dozens Straccan had seen in the Border villages. Before he could call out, the boy drew back to let another child take his place. Straccan held his breath and, for a moment, was perfectly still. Then he gave a great cracked shout.

'Gilla! My Gilla!'

His echoing cry brought the others spurring back. He hurled himself from his saddle into the pool, reaching desperately for holds among the slimy stones behind the falling water, unaware of his throbbing ankle or the rocks tearing at his flesh. He called her name over and over as he strained upwards to reach her, and she dropped safely into his arms at last.

Chapter 36

While Gilla and Hob slept safely on mattresses by the wall where Straccan could see his daughter whenever he raised his eyes, Sir Blaise laid out Soulis's letters on the table in some sort of order and rested a finger on two which bore King Philip's seal.

'These are all the proof we need of his treason,' he said. 'King Philip promises men to back a rebellion, once King William and his son have been killed. William himself believes the French will support *him* in an armed sweep to retake the lands south of the Border that were once part of Scotland. But Soulis has some claim to royal blood, descended as he is from the quondam Kings of Scots, and he covets the crown. His plan was to kill the king in the first skirmish and make it seem that the English did it. Then he and de Brasy would murder young Lord Alexander with poison.'

'Where is the prince?' Miles asked. 'Is he in safe hands?'

'Safe enough at Dryburgh, with the queen his mother. With King William out of the way, Soulis planned to take Lord Alexander to Stirling Castle and appoint de Brasy as his body-guard. He would use a subtle poison that would take weeks to kill him, and all the while the new young king would be comforted and advised by his father's good friend and counsellor, Rainard de Soulis. When the boy died he would step over his corpse to the throne.'

He picked up a roll with the seal of Eustace de Vesci. 'Here is treason against the King of the English too. The Lord of Alnwick gives the names of other barons who may be bribed or persuaded to turn traitor, Mowbray and de Cressi among them.'

'De Vesci,' Straccan thought aloud. 'Bane saw him with Soulis at Alnwick.' He touched a letter with the seal of Arlen. He'd carried one just like it from Julitta to the Prioress Rohese. It seemed years ago, instead of just a few months. 'What is Arlen's part in it?'

'Murder,' said Sir Blaise. 'Like Judas, he has sold his lord. King John's price is higher than Our Saviour's: Arlen demands three thousand marks.'

'How were they going to do it?'

'He loves the chase above all things, your king. Arlen plans to invite him to a great hunt, using false news of a magnificent stag. It wouldn't be the first time one of your kings died in a forest, by chance or misfortune.'

'But Arlen is one of the king's favourites, high in the royal household.' Straccan paused, considering. 'Julitta is the king's mistress. Is that why Arlen wants him dead?'

'They're in it together. They'll have Soulis's blood money, and favour and reward from the French king too. Arlen's plan is simple. Once the chase is under way, Julitta will entice the king into some romantic greenwood glade, out of sight of the others. And then Arlen will kill him, saying he heard his wife crying for help and thought she was being raped; he didn't know it was the king until too late. He'd be believed. With John dead, the French king's son Louis will have England.'

'Never!' Miles banged one fist into the other palm. 'He has no right to the crown of England.'

'Neither did the Conqueror,' said Blaise. 'But Louis has the pope on his side, just as the Bastard of Normandy did. The French have papal blessing for their enterprise against your king, because, so these letters say, he murdered his brother's son, Arthur of Brittany, and has never confessed nor done penance. It is King Philip's sacred duty to depose an excommunicated ruler and lift the Interdict from his sorely tried people.'

Straccan gave a derisive snort. 'No one knows what happened to Arthur; and he was a traitor too. God's grace, he was taken in armed rebellion, besieging King John's own mother at Mirabeau.'

'Well, Prince Louis is married to John's niece, Blanche of

Castile,' Blaise said, tapping one of the letters with his finger. 'It is intended he shall rule England in right of his wife.'

'It's a mongrel claim,' Straccan said hotly. 'And there's the little Lord Henry who is rightwise king when his father dies. What do they plan to do with John's children? Are they to be slaughtered, like the young Scottish heir? King John must be told of this!'

'King William also,' said Blaise, returning the letters to the casket. 'He believes Soulis his friend.'

'We should divide the letters,' Straccan suggested. 'You take those that concern your king, and I'll take those that concern mine. It will save time. I don't want to be kept dangling about the Scottish court. I just want to take Gilla home.'

Larktwist came in. 'The guard says Soulis is asking for you, Sir Blaise,' he said.

'Come to his senses, has he? Well, I suppose I must hear what he has to say.' Blaise got up stiffly, swaying.

'Are you all right?' Miles asked. 'You've gone a funny colour.'

'I'm all right, just weary. What about you, boy? You took a bad fall.'

'Just bruises. May I come with you?'

'Curious to see the great warlock? Come on, then.'

Straccan yawned hugely, 'I can hardly keep my eyes open,' he said.

'Lie beside your little lass,' said Blaise gently. 'You can surely rest awhile, now all is well with her. The boy and I will see what our captive warlock wants.'

The vault under Skelrig was like any other, dark, damp and smelly. 'Get lights,' said Blaise. The guard brought two crusies and hung them on hooks in the wall. They cast a wan and spluttery light over the soiled bloodstained prisoner, who sat cross-legged on the wet stone floor and scowled at them.

Miles looked curiously at him. There were dark blotches in his cheeks and his face looked oddly lopsided, one eyelid drooping, one corner of his mouth pulled downward. There was plentiful grey, even some white, in his rumpled hair. He looked, Miles thought, thoroughly nasty but not dangerous.

'You have no right to hold me,' Soulis said. He spoke with slight hesitation as if he had trouble managing his tongue, but his words were clear enough. 'What authority have you here? I have done you no wrong and I am not your enemy.'

'As to that,' Blaise said, looking hard at him, 'a traitor is every true subject's enemy, and a warlock is the enemy of God and all mankind.'

'Traitor, warlock? What nonsense is this? You're mad! I am a friend of King William and, believe me, you will pay for this outrage, whoever you are!'

'I am Blaise d'Etranger.'

'Ha,' sneered Soulis with vast contempt. 'That old heretic! I thought you were dead long since.'

'Not yet, Lord Rainard. Do you want food or drink?'

'No.'

'There is no leech here to tend you, but I will take the arrowhead out if you wish.'

'Don't touch me!' Spittle ran from the sagging corner of his mouth, but he seemed unaware of it. What do you mean to do with me?'

'We will take you to your friend, King William, with the proofs of your treason and sorcery.'

'There are no such proofs.'

'We have your letters,' said Blaise calmly. 'And the statements of the Lady of Arlen, and your man de Brasy.'

'Forgeries! Lies! I give you one last chance. Release me, or, I swear, you will wish you had never meddled with me.'

'We'll waste no more time down here,' said Blaise to Miles. 'It's a bit chilly and does my rheumatism no good. He has nothing to say worth hearing.'

They unhooked the lamps and opened the vault door.

'Wait,' de Soulis cried. 'Is it day or night?'

'It's all the same down here,' said Blaise. 'But you'll see the sun again, My Lord, I promise you, from the scaffold.'

'I shall be laughing when *you* cry mercy,' said Soulis viciously. 'This coming night my demon will rock your reason from its pedestal!'

'What did he mean, about his demon? And what's happened to his face?' Miles asked, when they had bolted the vault door and were climbing the steps.

'I think he's had a stroke. It smites upon one side only; folk call it the half-dead disease. It has damaged him and he is weaker than he knows. If he has some evil in mind or hope of escape, he'll be helpless alone. Lucky for us his bowmen turned against him. As for his demon ... I wonder ...' Frowning, Blaise leaned against the stone sill of an arrow loop and looked out at the clouds and bare hills. 'I think I'll just ride out to the stones again now, and have a look round.'

'You can't,' Miles protested. 'You've not had the clothes off your back, nor any rest since we got here.'

'It's not far, boy, and I can ride well enough. I'll not be long.'

'I'll go with you.'

'You won't. There's nothing you can usefully do. I just want a good look at the place in daylight, to see what's lying around. You'd get in the way.'

'I won't. I'll stay wherever you tell me while you get on with whatever you want to do. But, I mean no offence Sir Blaise, you are tired and, well, not as young as you were. I'm going with you. That's it, and all about it!'

'Damn your impudence!' The stubborn old man glowered at the stubborn young one. Miles shrugged and looked belligerent. After a moment, Blaise laughed. 'Very well! But you will do *exactly* as I tell you. If I say silence, you won't utter. If I say stay, you won't budge. But if I say go, then, boy, *promise* me, you will obey me.'

'I promise.'

'Well, if you're coming anyway, go and find the biggest hammer in this place.'

'Hammer?'

'Just bring it along.'

*

'Where is Sir Richard?' Miles asked, as Larktwist helped him on with his boots.

'Sleeping like a baby. Got the little girl in his arms, both of them in dreamland, and that dumb lad has curled up in the straw alongside.'

'He's a good boy,' said Miles. 'Give me my leather hood, and here, can you get that buckle round the back? Thanks.' He stamped his feet comfortably into his boots and settled his sword belt.

'Where you off to?'

'Sir Blaise wants another look at the stones.'

'Rather you than me.'

'Bring the hammer,' said Blaise.

They left the horses hobbled at the foot of the low hill and climbed, batting at flies and thrips, to the Nine Stane Rig. Just before they reached it wan sunlight escaped through a split in the clouds, and Miles's spirits, depressed by the dismal place and memories of last night, lifted a bit. In sunlight, the stones lost much of their brooding menace. They had seemed vastly tall in the mist and darkness but were now seen as grey-blue granite flecked with quartz, nothing like the reddish local stone and not much taller than a man and a half high. Eight were roughly similar in height, depth and breadth. The ninth, the King Stane, taller and tapering, had fallen long ago into the circle and lay pointing to the west.

The grass inside was trampled and in one place dark with blood. The brazier, toppled by the bowmen in their flight, lay on its side, coals spread across the charred turf. Fragments of glass phials lay in an oily stain. Bending to sniff cautiously at it, Blaise saw something else lying in the grass: a broken neck-chain from which hung several small reliquaries. Each bore the incised name of a different saint. Twisting the lid off one, he emptied a scrap of bone into his palm. Was this Soulis's armour against whatever demons he hoped to summon? Stowing the necklace in his belt pouch, Blaise stooped to the crushed cage and ran his hands over it.

The headless carcasses lay in a sodden heap, just as they had last night.

'That's odd,' said Miles, squatting by the remains.

'What?' Blaise was walking from stone to stone, pressing the palm of his hand to each one.

'No foxes. You'd think they'd've been at this lot by now. No flies, even. Come to think of it, there's none here in the ring at all, though there's plenty outside.'

'Hmmm?' Blaise wasn't listening. He crouched by one of the stones, his hand splayed on the rough glinting surface, his expression absorbed.

'I *said*, nothing's been eating these. No foxes.'

Blaise looked at him and got up quickly. 'What did you say?' He came over to the heap of carrion and looked at it. 'No flies.'

'That's what I said.' Miles looked worriedly at the old man. 'No foxes, no flies, nothing. It's queer.'

'Will you fetch my horse?' Blaise asked. 'Just lead him up here gently. See how far he'll come.'

The horses were in the usual cloud of flies, flicking their tails and stamping. Sir Blaise's black gelding, an elderly dignified animal, walked willingly enough up the hill as far as the reach of the stones' shadows, where it stopped abruptly. Miles chirruped encouragingly, but the gelding laid its ears back and showed the whites of its eyes.

'Take him round the other side,' said Blaise, squinting up at the pale sun.

On the west side, the shadows lay inside the circle and the animal walked to within a yard of the stones before balking. Blaise came out and tried to lead it forward, but it pressed back hard on its hind legs and would not move. Blindfolding had no effect; it still refused. Blaise mounted and urged it on. The animal's skin began to quiver, its legs trembled, it squealed and reared, and almost threw its rider.

'There, there, Saladin!' Blaise soothed it, turning the horse away from the stones. 'Before you take him back down, smash that thing to pieces, will you?' He kicked the stone trough. Miles grinned, spat on his hands and raised the hammer.

'What now?'

'Take my horse down and wait there for me.' As Miles began to object, Blaise went on, 'Fear lingers here, and he smells the blood. Horses are wise enough to shun it. Go on with you. I shan't be long now.'

'Why are there no scavengers?'

'The place is polluted. It must be cleansed. Go on, take the horses. I'm coming.'

Miles led Saladin down to where its stablemate whickered anxiously in greeting. But the big gelding was quite recovered and began cropping the grass as if nothing had ever alarmed it.

Presently the old man came down the hill, and they headed back to Skelrig.

It was about two hours before sunset, and the rain that had threatened all day now began in earnest. Miles had been wetter this year than ever before in his life.

'I shall have to come back alone,' said Blaise as the tower came in sight.

'We can come again in the morning,' Miles offered, ignoring the old man's last word.

'Tonight,' said Blaise. 'And, bless you boy, but this time I *must* be alone.'

'Why? What did you find back there?'

Blaise looked very old and tired. His face was ashy and drawn, his lips mauve. 'That is what Soulis meant. They didn't finish what they started. They opened a gate, God help us, to summon something.'

'What?'

'A creature, a being, you might call it a lord of hell.'

'Jesu protect us!' Miles crossed himself three or four times and devoutly kissed the Blessed Host which his uncle had given him and which he wore round his neck. 'But it's gone, surely, back to hell!'

'What is hell?' The old man murmured, as they approached the tower. 'Another place than this, a world where God's Writ doesn't run, inhabited by beings we cannot comprehend. And sometimes perilously close to our own. At such times—'

'The solstice,' said Miles.

'Aye, boy. At such times, my old teacher said, it is possible to pass from one world to another, through a gateway such as Al-Hazred opened.'

'Back there.'

'Aye. But it all went wrong and the gate was never closed. Their demon went back where it came from but the gate is still open. It can come back any time.'

Chapter 37

Sir Blaise sat in the window seat of the upper chamber, turning the pages of a great book he'd found among the Arab's magical paraphernalia. It was the same book Straccan had seen at Crawgard, written in one of the ancient languages of Arabia. So antique was the writing that Blaise could only read it with difficulty. Some of it he did not understand, but he could comprehend enough to know that this monstrous volume was both a demonary and an instruction manual of the evil rituals of Irem. It must be burned, but first he must learn all he could from it.

During his dangerous forbidden studies years ago, his teachers in the Holy Land had spoken of Abdul Al-Hazred and of this very volume. Most had doubted the existence of both the Arab and his fabled book, but one gentle old mystic maintained that the book at least might still exist, and if ever found must be utterly destroyed.

He should not read it; it should be thrust straight into the flames. But his curiosity, that thirst for answers which had got him into trouble years ago, could not resist. Here were instructions on the use of colours in magical defence, something he had never heard of; and this must surely be the ritual the sorcerer had attempted in the Nine Stane Rig. Here were listed the names of all lesser demons, and greater, the very lords of hell. Beside each name the Arab had written the conjuration to raise that particular demon with the spell to bind it to his bidding and, God be praised, the incantation to banish the creature again. He read and reread it, puzzled and worried. It was almost the same as that which he had learned long ago from his teachers in Egypt and Syria, but there were differences: a word here, the order of words there. Which was right, his version or this? Blaise rubbed his aching eyes and wished he was twenty years younger.

Straccan woke soon after sunset, not that the sun had been visible, and the rain looked like setting in for a second Noah's Flood. Gilla was still deeply asleep, and the boy, in the straw under a blanket, never stirred as Straccan carefully stepped over him. In the hall, half a dozen men were finishing their supper and Bane was mending a rip in his shirtsleeve by the light of the fire.

'Where's everybody?' Straccan asked.

'Sir Blaise rode out an hour or so ago and Sir Miles went after him a bit later, and I think some of these buggers –' he jerked his chin towards the men-at-arms, a sullen group at the far end of the hall '– are up to something.'

'What?' Straccan had piled cold meat and pickles on a bread trencher and had his mouth full. He swallowed. 'Is there any milk?'

'Whatever for?'

'For Gilla, when she wakes.'

'Oh, of course. Sorry! Well, there's two cows in the byre and half a dozen nanny goats wandering round the yard, so there must be some milk somewhere. I get the feeling it's not much in demand, though. I'll get some for her.'

'What did you mean when you said they're up to something?'

'They were *seriously* pissed off when the witch got away,' Bane said. 'They don't want Wotsisname to leg it as well. Soulis, I mean.'

'He's in chains. The only place he'll go is to King William's gallows.'

'He may be in chains but he's not gagged, and he's been carrying on something horrible down there, so the guard says.' Seeing Straccan's questioning eyebrows – his mouth was full again – Bane added, 'Curses, threats, and sometimes he laughs; they *really* don't like that! He's got them very nervous.'

'I'll go and have a look at him. What's in that barrel?'

'Ale. Want some?' He held out a horn cup.

Straccan downed it in three swallows. 'Has Soulis been victualled?'

'Buggered if I know. Probably not. No one's exactly keen to open the door down there.'

'And who are *you*?' the prisoner demanded.

Straccan held up his torch. Whether or not he'd been fed, at some time someone more tender-hearted than the rest had pitchforked a few trusses of straw into the vault which Soulis had raked together to make a couch. Chains were fastened to an iron belt round his waist and one to a fetter on his ankle, long enough for him to walk three or four steps, no more. Now he sat on the straw with his arms round his knees. In the impenetrable blackness of the vault beyond the flaring torchlight, rats scampered and squeaked.

'I'm Straccan.'

'Oh, *are* you? Julitta said you'd be a nuisance. She thought she'd taken care of you. She must have been quite shocked when you turned up.'

'Why did she put that spell on me? I never did her any harm, or wished her ill.'

'To keep you from interfering further, or ever putting two and two together. Didn't work. Pity. Primitive enchantments like that are notoriously unreliable. Women's rubbish! How did you break it, by the way?'

'I had help.'

'*Did* you? How interesting. From whom, I wonder? Someone with a little knowledge, was it? Among your comrades, perhaps? You seem to have wandered the country collecting misfits as you go. That old heretic d'Etranger, how did you come by him? And that penniless youngster, so full of futile good intentions.'

'Have they given you something to eat?'

'No, and don't trouble yourself, Straccan. I'll not eat while I'm a prisoner.'

'Then you'll get hungry.'

'Hungry? My demon is hungry. You drove it away before it was full-fed, but it has starved for centuries, it will be back.' He laughed shrilly. 'We are done for, all of us. Nothing can stop it now!' He laughed more wildly, rocking to and fro, saliva flying from his lips as his head jerked back and forth.

'You're mad,' said Straccan, shivering. 'Mad, a murderer and traitor both. The king you meant to betray will have his justice of you.'

'That old fool?' Soulis sneered, and spat in the straw. 'The Lion, they call him, that toothless senile luckless nithing. A laughing stock throughout Christendom. It'll be a cold day in hell before he can harm me! Is it night yet?'

'It's getting dark.'

'It will get darker. You've seen the light of day for the last time, you and your party of fools. You think you've saved your precious daughter? I told you, *nothing* can save her now!' His braying mirth sounded like something bawling in the torments of hell. No wonder it made the guards nervous; it turned Straccan's own nerves to water. He turned his back on the prisoner and slammed the door of the vault so hard the draught blew his torch out.

'Sod it,' he said with feeling and stumbled up the slimy steps. He was still shivering and felt the unwelcome nudge of a headache.

'What's going on?' Larktwist, clattering down the tower's irregular steps, almost collided with Bane coming out of the hall. Outside, below in the bailey, could be heard shouts and a woman crying.

'Trouble! The mother of that kid turned up. Saw the body before anyone had the sense to stop her. Went crazy. You can hear her. She'd brought folk with her – neighbours, friends – they're howling for blood.'

'I don't blame them.'

'Nor me. Thing is, the men here wouldn't mind seeing a bit of blood; they've seen the kid's body. They know how Lord Robert died, too. They feel cheated of the witch so they want to be sure of the warlock.'

'Where's Sir Blaise got to? He means to take Soulis to the king,' said Larktwist.

'They went back to the stones, him and the youngster.'

'What the devil are they doing there?'

'Unfinished business, the old man said.'

'What did he mean?'

'Don't ask me! They were up there earlier, and after they came back the old man had his nose in that Arab's book for hours. He ought to have been resting, he looked like death warmed up. Then he got on his horse and was just leaving when Sir Miles came down and caught him; said he ought to be in bed, not buggering about in that bloody circle. They had a proper row, hammer and tongs, just like married folk. The young un wanted to go along, and the old man wouldn't let him. *Ordered* him to stay behind, he did. So Sir Miles just watched him out of sight and then saddled up and followed.'

'It's getting on for midnight. They should be back by now.'

The angry noise below grew louder and more insistent. 'They mean to have him,' said Bane uneasily.

'Let em,' said Larktwist. 'Good riddance!'

They had planned to leave on the morrow: Blaise to the King of Scots with Soulis under guard, Miles to his Templar uncle, Straccan and Bane, with Gilla, home to Stirrup and Larktwist wherever his peculiar occupation called him. But as Straccan struggled to get his scarred boots on, the symptoms were unmistakable. Not now! I must get Gilla out of here. What did he mean, that devil, that nothing could save her now? God, Christ, I *can't* be ill now! That lot below are thinking of lynching Soulis, or I'm no judge. Not that I give a damn. Where the hell has Blaise got to? I need to talk to him.

The familiar iron band screwed itself tightly round his skull, pain shot down the back of his neck, he was cold and his legs felt watery. By the time he found Bane his teeth were chattering.

'Pox on it,' said Bane. 'Not now!'

'Never mind that. Where's Blaise?'

'You should be in bed.'

'Not yet. Where is he?'

'Him and Sir Miles went back to the stones.'

There was a rushing noise in his ears, swelling, fading and returning, and the disorienting visual effect of seeing everything apparently at the far end of a long tunnel.

'Get me a horse,' he said, clinging to the door frame as the floor rose and fell and the walls advanced and retreated.

'You're not going anywhere,' Bane protested.

'Yes I am. They're in trouble, I know it. Something's wrong there. You stay here. See no harm comes to Gilla.' He gripped Bane's arms and almost shook him. 'You hear me? Look after her!'

At the foot of the hill he dismounted, but before he could wrap the reins round a branch his horse reared, screaming, and bolted. He could see nothing that might have spooked it and stared after the thudding hooves, astonished.

The pain in his head was worse now, and vertigo made him feel sick and weak. Had the hill been this steep last night? Christ, help me, he prayed. Christ, who guarded my girl, guard me now! He went down on all fours, scrambling towards the stones. It felt as if he was pushing his way through water. It was darker up there, too. Or else it had taken him a damned long time to climb, for he'd been able to see quite well in the lingering northern twilight when his horse ran off. There were no stars. Thunder rumbled in the distance.

The gaps between the stones were doorways into deeper blackness. Lord, help me! Suddenly he thought of Janiva: her strength and courage the day she found Julitta's ill charm; and the children, Gilla and Hob, armoured in innocence and brave beyond reason in the face of evil. Taking strength from their courage, he forced himself to keep moving. The thunder was nearer now.

Sweat poured from him as he stepped between the stones. He was immediately aware of a painful pressure which hurt his ears and made it difficult to breathe. It was pitch dark but then lightning split the sky and he saw Blaise, fallen in the centre, and

Miles crouching by one of the stones, hacking desperately at the turf with his dagger.

Crossing the circle through the resisting air took for ever, as if in a nightmare. His legs were as heavy as lead. Even his words came slowly. And Miles's replies.

'What's . . . going . . . on?'

'Bury . . . these.' Miles clutched the broken reliquary chain. 'One . . . by . . . each . . . stone.' There were two left. 'This . . . in . . . centre.' Gasping for breath, he shoved the last one at Straccan. 'Take!' He fell forward on hands and knees, his head hanging.

Straccan closed his hand on the reliquary and turned to Blaise, seeking the pulse at the side of his neck. It beat faintly, erratically, but the old man was alive.

'Blaise. What happened?'

Blaise opened his eyes. 'It's coming,' he whispered. Straccan bent his head to catch the slurred words. 'I made circles of power to contain it. Won't hold for long. Close gateway. Quickly.' His icy hand grasped Straccan's. 'Must be eleven relics. Only ten here. You have . . . last one . . . finger of Saint Thomas. Quick! No time! Bury them here.'

Straccan heard Miles cry out. He turned.

What was that? Pouring down from the black starless vault above, a blacker shadow in darkness, glinting wetly as it moved.

'Too late,' whispered Blaise.

Straccan drew his knife and stabbed the turf. One. Two. Into each slot he pushed a reliquary, the second the little latten case he had carried for so long. He thumped the palm of his hand down hard to flatten the earth over them.

Whatever *that* was, didn't like it. The demon screeched and writhed, and as it strove to break through the circles of power Blaise had wrought, they became visible, beautiful intricate webs of silver light that tightened and cut like wire into the bulging horror within.

'Lord, protect us,' Blaise whispered.

Thunder broke directly above. Gilla, thought Straccan. Janiva. He fought the deadly weakness and the throbbing in his head, and got up drawing his sword, for all the good it might do. Lightning tore the darkness apart, illuminating the lightless impossibility straining to escape. Straccan's legs gave way, but as he toppled forward he hurled his sword into the middle of the creature and thought he saw lightning streak along blade and hilt as it flew, a long glowing cross, to split the shadow through.

There was a hideous braying roar. With a great thump the ground heaved, as if earth's vast heart had beaten once. Lightning ran down the sides of the stones into the ground, sizzling. The wet grass steamed, and there was a metallic stink of burning.

The demon was gone. The air within the Nine Stane Rig had a scent of wet grass and wild thyme. A damp west wind, gathering force as it came, flung down a faceful of rain and shouldered the clouds aside to liberate the moon, which now swam out amidst a shoal of stars.

Together, Straccan and Miles half-dragged half-carried the old man out of the circle. In the moonlight Blaise looked bleached, skull-like, dead, but the thready stumbling pulse still beat.

From below came a shout. 'Sir Miles! You there?'

'Larktwist,' Miles yelled back. 'Up here!'

The spy came panting up. 'Bane sent me, he said something was up. Christ, what happened? Is the old man dead?'

Tears and rain mingled on Miles's face. 'He's still alive,' he said. 'Straccan's in a bad way too. We must get them back to Skelrig.'

From the direction of the tower there was a bawling beast-like noise, which rose and fell, growing ever louder. The din resolved itself into a continuous baying, and presently folk could be seen running towards the Nine Stone Rig, dozens of them, with torches.

'What's going on?' Miles panted.

'They've got Soulis,' said Larktwist. 'Where are your horses? Mine ran away.'

'In that clump of rowans by the stream. There!'

They packed Blaise, unconscious, over his own saddle, and Miles managed to get Straccan astride the other horse. 'You lead that one; I'll take this,' he said. 'Let's keep out of their sight. I think they're pretty well occupied.'

The night was getting warmer.

They dragged him on a hurdle, a strange stiff bundle that howled and screamed but could not struggle because they had wrapped him in lead, a sheet of the lead for the new cisterns which had been stacked in the yard. They had bound and laid him on it, folding the lead round him like a cloak, pressing it down over his shoulders and in below his knees. His screaming head stuck out at one end, his flapping feet at the other.

Everything they needed they had brought from Skelrig. A cart was piled with logs and brushwood, and atop the logs was tied a great iron cauldron, swaying and lurching over the rough ground like a monstrous humped beast. Some men carried long poles and a length of chain.

They made a great pyre in the centre of the Nine Stane Rig and lashed the poles over it as a tripod from which the cauldron hung.

They were silent now, the only sound the mad screaming of their prisoner, so continuous it seemed he could not be drawing breath. They looped a chain round his ankles and suspended him head down in the cauldron. Someone thrust a torch into the pyre, and the flames, encouraged by jugs of oil and bowls of grease, leaped to envelop the pot and its dreadful contents. The screaming was followed by prolonged howling as he called on his devils and, at the last, on God.

The molten lead engulfed his head and his crumpling body. Then there was just the crackling of the fire and the soughing of the wind.

Chapter 38

Servants fetched an improvised litter for Blaise, and between them, Miles and Larktwist got Straccan up to the hall.

'Whoops,' said Bane, catching him as he pitched forward, and heaving him on to a bench. 'Come on, ups-a-daisy, let's get you to bed.' He propped Straccan along to a small mural room, away from the noise of the hall, and having got him undressed and between blankets, went to find the children, who had gravitated to the kitchen.

'Sir Blaise is very ill, and your dad's poorly too,' he said, swinging Gilla up in his arms. 'Can you help look after them?'

'Of course I can. What shall I do?'

Bane felt a tug at his tunic and found Hob at his side.

'Hob too,' said Gilla.

'Good boy. The old man just needs rest, I think; there's nothing else we can do for him. But your dad will need a tub of clean water, to wipe him down when he gets hot. Will you get that. Hob? And clean straw; what he's lying on will get wet.' Hob nodded and made for the door. 'And Gilla, somewhere in your Dad's baggage there's a bag full of bits of willow bark. Will you look for it? We have to brew medicine with it, and keep getting it down him.'

The child ran out of the kitchen. Bane looked out of the arrow loop in the direction of the Nine Stane Rig and saw the flickering glow of fire. 'Let em get on with it,' he muttered, crossing himself. 'Good riddance!'

Straccan could hear screaming, faint and far off. 'What?' he mouthed, but though his dry lips moved, no sound came from them. Gilla rinsed another towel in the bucket of water and laid it on his burning forehead. She could feel the heat radiating from his skin before she touched him, and when the towel baked dry, she soaked it again and replaced it.

Hob stood on a stool at the arrow loop, looking out towards the hills. He'd seen the people leave with their prisoner and he could hear the distant shouting and cheering.

'What is it?' Gilla asked, touching his hand. He shook his head and shrugged. She gave him a quick bright smile and went back to the bedside. 'Hob, this water's got warm.' He nodded and picked up the bucket.

They put the invalids in one room, the better to care for them. They lay oblivious to everything, one tossing and muttering as fever waxed and waned, the other corpse-like but for the faint rise and fall of his chest under the blankets. Now Hob came into his own, tending the sick men with a gentle competence that gave him new authority. His demands, filtered through Gilla, for medicines and comforts for his patients were met with alacrity.

'That boy's a born doctor,' Miles observed, obediently warming a blanket by the fire for Hob to wrap round Sir Blaise after he sponged him down. The full tale of Hob's rescue of Gilla from the Nine Stane Rig had emerged, and when, with vividly descriptive mime, he described how he had felled the witch, all those in the hall had clapped and stamped their applause.

Hob was master of the sickroom but Miles and Bane helped lift and turn the men who were too heavy for him alone. Like errand boys, they took it in turns to fetch hot stones, warmed in relays in the kitchen ovens, to pack in towels round Sir Blaise night and day, and round Straccan too when the shivering fit was on him.

'What's the matter with Sir Blaise?' Gilla asked.

Hob banged himself over the heart region and wagged his fingers several times to indicate something amiss with the heartbeat.

'Will he die?'

Hob shook his head fiercely. Not if he could help it. But he kept up a perpetual barrage of half-threatening prayer to God-and-

Mary. Make him better, make them both well, or I'll never go to church again. I'll never dust you, I won't bring you any more flowers. One of his self-imposed duties at the tower had been to keep the chapel clean and occasionally wash the statue, an ancient squat almost featureless Virgin holding a shapeless lump that bore no resemblance to a baby. I know you can do it, Hob nagged silently. You can do anything. So come on! That's what you're for! Father Kenneth would not have agreed with him but Father Kenneth wasn't there, and Hob followed the constant-water-weareth-away-stone school of faith.

On the third morning, the old knight opened his eyes. Hob sent Gilla running for Sir Miles. By the time Miles reached his bedside Sir Blaise was asleep again, but Miles sat patiently until, hours later, the old man's eyes opened once more and his pale gaze found Miles.

'Told you ...' he said, his voice not much more than a thread. 'Not to go there ... disobeyed me.'

'Forgive me,' said Miles, wretchedly. 'How could I let you go alone?' He bowed his head, and his tears fell, surprisingly hot, on the old man's cold waxen hand. Sir Blaise seemed asleep again, and presently Hob chivvied Miles away. Bane found him later, sitting by the fire in the hall, and put a cup of mulled wine in his hand.

'What happened up there?' he asked at last, having nearly burst with the effort not to probe too soon.

Miles frowned. 'It's queer. I know I saw *something*, and I know it was ... oh, Christ, terrible. But I can't seem to remember what it was. I followed Sir Blaise. He didn't know I was there. I hid outside the ring. He told me not to go but I feared for him; he was pretty groggy but he wouldn't admit it. I saw him doing something, he sort of *drew* in the air with his hands and he was chanting in some foreign lingo. I thought, when his hands moved they left marks, like lines of light hanging in the air. But they faded, and I couldn't see them any more. It took a lot out of him; he was pretty wobbly. That star-thing he wore round his neck, he buried that too, beside that big fallen stone.

'All the time, he was chanting and getting more and more breathless, and then he just sighed and gasped and fell down.

'That's when I went in. And that's where it gets all blurred. I had a real job to get to him. God knows why, but it was hard to move in there. And my ears hurt. And it got harder and harder to breathe. But I got to him, and he gave me that string of relics and told me what to do. It felt as if a strong man was hanging on to both my arms, to try and hold me. It sounds daft, but it was the hardest thing I've ever done.

'I thought I saw – I don't know, it was so dark and I couldn't look at it – something struggling in a silver net. Something terrible.' Miles's cheerful young face was twisted with distress and his eyes had a faraway haunted look. 'Suddenly Richard was there, then I thought the lightning had hit us all; there was a God-awful noise and then nothing.'

'Drink your wine before it gets cold,' said Bane.

'What about Soulis?'

'What about him?'

'Will there be trouble, them killing him?'

'God knows! Perhaps not. Though, whatever he was, it was murder.'

It was a week altogether before Sir Blaise could travel and by then Straccan had been on his feet for three days. Although the old knight tired quickly and had not yet recovered his full strength, he was able to sit a horse. It was the last day of June.

The bustle of their departure filled the bailey. The sergeant-at-arms was left in charge pending the arrival of a new lord, and Julitta's servants had elected to remain until then, with a reasonable anticipation of being taken on the strength when the new lord came.

Farewells were said with promises to meet again. Straccan had shared Soulis's letters with Blaise who, taking the journey in easy stages, was riding with an escort of two men for Roxburgh and King William. Sir Miles would return to Durham. Straccan, Bane and Gilla would journey home by the Great North Road, and once Gilla was safe, Straccan would find King John.

They had put their heads together about Hob who stood forlornly by the kitchen door, watching the comings and goings the loading of pack pony and mule. Blaise, not yet mounted, called to him.

'We all have good cause to thank you, Hob. And none of us wants to leave you. What do you want to do? Listen, and tell me. You can stay here and live with your grandsire, if that is your wish. In any event I will see he is paid a pension; he will not go cold or hungry ever again. Or you can go to Sir Richard's home in England, and he will treat you as a son. Or, would you like to come with me? I will take you, after I've seen the king, to the priory at Coldinghame, where you can learn the healing arts from Brother Alan. He'll welcome a young helper. They are gentle folk at the priory. But the work won't be easy. It will take years to learn.'

Hob was smiling and crying all at once; tears ran down his face and dripped off his chin and he was nodding so hard he sprayed tears in all directions. He seized Sir Blaise's hand and kissed it.

'Well,' Bane said, 'that seems settled.'

Gilla was crying too, and she hugged Hob. 'I'll miss you,' she said. 'I won't forget you. I love you, Hob.'

Straccan put his hands on the boy's shoulders. Hob had grown, surely, in just this past week: he was taller and broader. 'I owe you my daughter's life. I could never thank you enough if I spent all my days trying. My home is yours whenever you want it, and I am your servant if ever you need me.'

'Where's Sir Miles?' Larktwist asked. He was to accompany the young knight on his journey south, until his calling waylaid him. Just then Miles emerged from the hall and stood on the steps above them, looking down.

'Sir Blaise,' he called. The old man looked questioningly at him. Miles ran down the steps and across the yard to Sir Blaise's stirrup. 'Sir,' he said, all in a rush, for he'd rehearsed it and must get it out before his nerve failed. 'Sir. Master, you spoke of your nephew who died, he that was your pupil. You said there was no one now to whom you could pass on your learning.' Miles stared at the foot in the stirrup, not daring to raise his eyes. 'Sir,' he said again, gathering courage, 'I have no parents, no kin save my Uncle Hoby your friend, no holding, no wife or sweetheart. What I mean is, Sir, if you need another student, well, will I do? I will serve you with all my heart and learn to ... to watch and guard, if you will teach me.'

Blaise leaned down and embraced him. 'I won't ask if you've thought this over,' he said. 'I see that you have. You must go and tell your uncle – you can ride that far with Sir Richard – and then, when you're ready, join me at Coldinghame. God be with you, boy.' Blaise, his escort and his baggage, and Hob, nervous but proud on a Skelrig pony, rode out of the gate and took the Roxburgh road.

A stable man brought Straccan's party their horses. Now, at last, they turned their heads towards home.

Chapter 39

A few fishing boats and two bigger trading vessels moved sluggishly at anchor on the ebbing tide. Crewmen lounged on decks for none could sail as long as the onshore wind pinned them there. Gulls wheeled and screamed above, smoke streamed westward from the chimneys ashore, and more gulls picked along the smelly tideline of weed and dead shellfish.

On the shore sat a few ragged abjurers, criminals condemned to exile but unable to afford a passage oversea, out of reach of justice. Slowly starving, they picked the shoreline as eagerly as the gulls, and ate them too, when they could catch any. From time to time one or more would wade into the water, skinny arms raised in pleading, to wail in vain at the men aboard the trading vessels. Those who could pay bought passage to France, Flanders or Holland; but these penniless leftovers had no hope of safe exile; they must stay on the beach between land and sea until they starved to death, and good riddance.

The hulk *Mary Maid* was old and small, and looked every inch the smuggler she was. Her crew hadn't expected to put to sea today, or tomorrow either, not with this relentless south-easter. When the woman came aboard seeking passage to France the skipper eyed her up and down, not that he could see much of her in that all-enveloping cloak; she might be young or old, but she was certainly female and therefore bad luck. He spat contemptuously over the side and refused to take her, until she put a purse in his hand. Then he peered inside and changed his mind. His crew began to argue, but he was the skipper.

While they argued, the wind changed.

A howl rose from the abjurers, seeing vessels suddenly preparing to sail. They surged into the sea, screeching and praying; one even grabbed at a dangling rope that had no business to be there and tried to haul himself aboard the *Mary Maid*. It took several blows with a boat-hook to knock him back into the water, where he floated face down and bleeding. His fellows in adversity took no notice of him. It was every man for himself.

The *Mary Maid* headed southward, sail taut.

There was a tiny shelter on deck, made of hides tacked on a wooden framework, and the skipper ushered the woman inside, out of sight. His men stared enviously at his disappearing back and grinned at one another, but after a few moments he backed out again, pale and cursing, and laid about him with a rope's knotted end to make them pay for his embarrassment.

Inside the shelter the woman sat still as an image, but her lips moved silently as if she was praying.

The water ran murmuring along the sides, and the wind blew the *Mary Maid* steadily down to where the Tweed joined the true sea, and the heaving swell grew strong.

Through a gap in the hides, sunlight struck into the shelter. The woman stirred, drew from her belt pouch a flattish piece of grey translucent quartz and angled it towards the light. Shaking back the hood of her mantle, she stared intently into the crystal, seeking her enemy.

Kneeling at the streamside, sunlight hot on her back, Janiva was washing her shift, turning it in the water and beating at a stain with a flat stick. Smooth multicoloured pebbles seemed mere inches below the surface, but here at this deep pool her arm's full length could only just reach them. She sat back on her heels, wringing the water out of the garment. The blue-jewelled flash of a kingfisher caught her eye as it rose from the water clasping a tiny silver fish in its orange beak.

She felt suddenly cold. The light had changed – she looked up – the sun still shone but its disc was cold and white, dead as the full moon. The water, a moment before alive with sunlight, now looked grey, cold and hard. Like stone.

She leaned over the pool, curious, off-guard, reached out a hand to touch the grey gleaming surface – and was caught.

Julitta drew in her breath sharply, staring at the face, small and distinct, in the crystal's smoky heart. A woman, and young to have such power! There she was at last, the meddler: the low-born interfering trull who'd released that bone-pedlar Straccan from the spell which would have rid them of him and, worse, somehow warded his brat from the power of the master and thereby brought all their plans to ruin. Because of her, Arlen and many others would die. Because of her, Julitta had lost everything, all she had striven for, and must flee into exile to wait on King Philip's coffin-cold mercy.

In the crystal, Julitta looked into her enemy's eyes.

In the water, Janiva looked back at her, tranced.

'Mistress Janiva! Mistress!' The forester's worried face filled her vision. Janiva was lying at the pool's edge, soaked and cold as ice. She coughed, gasped, and turned to vomit water into the grass.

'Tostig,' she said weakly. 'What happened?'

'You fell in. Lucky I came by! I pulled you out. Are you all right?'

'I fell?' She sat up, shivering hard.

Tostig threw his cloak around her. 'Well, sort of. You were kneeling on the edge. I called to you, and you just seemed to lean forward and fall straight in. Did you faint, Mistress?'

She remembered looking into stone-cold grey water, into stone-cold green eyes that numbed her mind and will. Wanting to resist, not able to resist. What had happened? Tostig took her hands and pulled her to her feet.

'Faint? I suppose I must have,' she said, her voice as unsteady as her legs. 'Tostig, please help me home.'

Julitta closed her fist round the crystal, gripping it so tightly in her fury that its edge cut her flesh and blood oozed through her clenched fingers. The wind dropped and the sail hung limply for a few moments as her concentration shifted, then filled again.

'I've not done with you, slut,' she said softly. 'I almost had you. I know you now. Threefold I curse you. All that you are, all that you have, all that you love you shall lose!' She let her blood collect in her cupped palm, and in blood on the crystal wrote the rune of destruction.

Chapter 40

Larktwist left them at Alnwick. They were riding past the castle when a beggar-child snatched at Larktwist's reins and mouthed something at him, the others didn't hear what. He nodded, gave the child a coin and turned to his companions. 'I must leave you here,' he said. 'I won't say it's been a pleasure exactly but it's certainly been interesting. No hard feelings, eh, Sir Miles? Sir Richard? Master Bane, here's the dice I promised you.' He handed Bane a small wood-shaving box. 'Perhaps we'll run into one another again, one of these days. God be with you all!' And he was gone, into the crowd at the castle gate, round a corner, out of sight.

Miles said, 'I suppose he's gone to report on our business to whoever's paying for the information.'

'It's a living,' said Bane, tolerantly. The little box was in his pocket, and he patted it affectionately.

They parted with Miles at Durham, where they stayed for two nights as guests of Sir William Hoby before setting off again.

'Miles, brother,' said Straccan, 'you have my love and gratitude all life long, for your help and your company. We wouldn't have got through without you. You know where I live; come whenever you will. My home is yours. God's blessing go with you.'

Shawl was not on their road home, but that's where they went next. Straccan's horse lasted just long enough to reach the manor before it went lame. He led it, limping, into Sir Guy's stable to be left until called for. Sir Guy and Lady Alienor, who had never met him, greeted him cheerfully and offered their hospitality. Visitors, with their news and gossip, were a breath of life and their welcome was assured.

'Thank you, Sir Guy, My Lady, you are very good. We will be glad to sleep under your roof tonight, but first I have to see a friend.'

As he left with Gilla, Alienor nudged her husband. 'He's going to see Janiva,' she hissed.

'Is he? How on earth do you know that? Still, seems a nice enough fella.' Sir Guy tugged thoughtfully at his earlobe. 'Old Duffy St Obin was a friend of his father.'

'He was?' Lady Alienor's eyes were bright with interest. 'Tell me about him, this Straccan.'

Sir Guy settled back comfortably. He prided himself on genealogy. Knights and barons knew all about one another's antecedents, good and bad. Most of them were related to some degree, by marriage or blood, and reckoning kinships was a popular pastime during winter evenings. 'Well, let me see. His father was William Straccan; he was killed on crusade – didn't have any property – *his* father Draco supported King Stephen and lost everything, of course, when FitzEmpress took over. Draco's name was FitzEstraccan; goes back to some Breton fella called Estraccan de Something who won lands serving Rufus. *This* Straccan's father dropped the Fitz bit and just called himself Straccan.'

'Yes, yes,' said Lady Alienor impatiently, 'but who *is* he? Has he any property?'

'Oh, he's rich enough. Went on crusade. Came back with money. Bought property from the abbey near ... where is it?' He drummed his fingers on the arm of his chair and screwed up his face with the effort of memory. 'Dieulacresse! That's it.'

'Is he married?'

'Was. She's dead. Odd chap. Does some sort of trade nowadays. Relics. Funny business really.'

'He'd be a good match for Janiva,' said Lady Alienor.

'Match? *Janiva*? But he's a knight!'

'All the better. He's already wealthy, he can choose to marry where he likes. I'll have to talk to her.'

'Alienor,' said her husband warningly, 'don't meddle!'

'Meddle? Sir Guy! How could you say such a thing? I *never* meddle!'

'Not much,' muttered her lord to his lady's retreating back.

'What did you say?' She looked back at him over her shoulder, chin high, very pink.

'Nothing. Nothing, sweetheart. Nothing at all!'

She was smaller than he remembered, and more beautiful.

To Straccan's surprise, when he lifted Gilla off her pony she went straight to Janiva as if they knew each other and knelt on one knee at her feet, kissing her hand as if she was an abbess. Janiva put her arm round the girl, and they stood together, smiling.

'Mistress Janiva,' said Straccan, pulling off his cap.

'Sir Richard, and Gilla, I am so glad, so very glad to see you well.'

Later, when Gilla began yawning, Janiva put her to bed and rejoined Straccan outside in the sweet warm summer evening. Subdued birdsong surrounded them, and there was a scent of roses and mint. They sat on a bench among the herbs, Janiva with her spindle, Straccan shredding a sprig of thyme.

'Sir Richard, may I ask ... do you mean to place Gilla in the convent again?'

'I've been wondering about it. I'm away so much, it seemed wise, and she was happy there. But now ...'

'I have a suggestion,' she said, hesitantly.

'Tell me.'

'Keep her with you when you can. Let her visit the convent, spend a few days there from time to time. It would look strange else. But when you must go away and will be away some time, send her here to me. No –' as he made to speak '– wait, let me finish. So much has happened to her, such strange things, she is changed from the child she was. To me, if she needs to, she can talk about it; but if she talks at the convent of things she has seen and done the good sisters won't know what to make of it, or of her. She won't fit in.'

'Misfits,' said Straccan, frowning.

'What?'

'Soulis said I had roamed about the country collecting misfits. Is that what my daughter is now?'

'No more than I am! But that is why I ask you to let her come to me where she can talk, and be understood and safe, and loved.'

'If she becomes a woman such as you are,' Straccan said, 'I will be well pleased.' He took the spindle from her and laid it on the bench between them, then took her hands in his. They were well shaped, fine but strong, not the pale delicate hands of a fine lady but capable, loving hands, skilled in many crafts. He kissed them.

'Janiva—'

There was the sound of a horse coming fast, and Bane burst over the fence and flung himself from the saddle. 'King's men,' he gasped. 'At the manor. Asking for you. Coming here.'

And as Straccan got to his feet, sending the spindle flying, there they were – half a dozen mounted archers in the king's livery, with their captain – neat, efficient, polite, implacable.

'Sir Richard Straccan?'

'Yes.'

'The lord king summons you to attend him at Nottingham, Sir. I am to escort you.'

'What for?'

'I'm not privy to the king's mind, Sir Richard. I just do as he tells me. And he told me to fetch you.'

'Janiva . . .' He turned to her. 'Gilla . . .'

'It's all right,' she said quickly. 'I'll take care of her. She needs rest. Don't worry about her; she's safe now.'

Straccan turned back to the captain. 'What about my man Bane?'

'I've no orders concerning him, Sir. He may go or stay as you please.'

He unbuckled his purse. 'Hawkan, take this to Saint Mark's Priory. It's somewhere near Christchurch. Give it to the prior. Tell him all about it. Tell him how we met Brother Celestius, and that this gift is in gratitude for your life. Go *now*.' Before anything happens to stop you, his eyes added. Bane put the purse inside his shirt. 'When you've done that,' said Straccan, 'come back here and escort Mistress Janiva and my daughter home to Stirrup. I'll see you there, when the king's finished with me.'

He fastened his jerkin, feeling the crackle of the letters inside against his shirt. The sound of the grey's hooves receded fast as Bane left on his errand. Straccan's sword and harness hung by the door; he reached for them, then drew his hand back. 'You will want my sword?' he asked the captain.

'I have no orders concerning your weapons, Sir,' said the young man looking surprised. 'You are not my prisoner. I am to take you safely to the king.'

'Ah! Do you have a spare mount?'

'Er ... no, Sir.'

'Well, I have no horse.'

The captain rose to the challenge. 'Simon!' One of his company nudged his horse forward. 'Sir Richard will take your horse. Double up with Tom.'

'Then I am ready,' Straccan said. He went into the house, bent over the bed and saw his daughter's eyes were open. 'It's all right, sweetheart,' he said quickly. 'I have to take those letters to the king, that's all.'

'Can't someone else take them?'

'No, there are things I must tell him. I shan't be long. Mistress Janiva will look after you, and Bane will bring you both home when I get back.' He kissed her and stroked her hair. Then he took Janiva in his arms, held her close, smelled the perfume of rosemary that scented her hair and clothes. Spurs and harness jingled outside. Buckling his sword belt, he walked out and mounted the horse held ready for him.

When they were out of sight, Janiva turned back to the fragrant little room and saw that her cat had crept under the blanket and was purring happily, tucked against Gilla's shoulder.

Chapter 41

He had been killing time in Nottingham Castle for three days before he saw the king. It was a relief to find that he was, in no sense, a prisoner; he could come and go about the town as he pleased. And Straccan told himself he should not really be surprised that the king had come to Nottingham on his way to the Scottish border, stopping also at York and Durham to gather men and supplies for his expedition. If spies were set to watch men as politically insignificant as himself, of course they would be watching the great ones. King William's designs on the north lands would be no news to King John.

On the morning of the fourth day the king sent for him. They had not met before, though he'd seen the king at a distance a few times. Now he remembered everything he had ever heard about John: murderous, perverse and deceitful, suspicious, ungodly, touchy – and the other side of the Angevin coin – generous, genial, brave, indulgent, dangerously intelligent.

'Sir Richard! How good of you to come!' The king put a friendly arm round Straccan's shoulders and walked up and down in the castle garden with him. 'This isn't anything like it was in my mother's day,' said John, jerking a disparaging thumb at the shrivelled roses. 'Greenfly! See?' He pinched one off a bud and squashed it. 'The gardener tries everything, but nothing works. Do you know anything about roses. Sir Richard?'

'No, My Lord. I've not had much to do with gardens.'

'Nor me, nor me. I knew she was a witch, of course.'

The abrupt change of subject made Straccan blink. 'The Lady Julitta, My Lord?'

'Julitta, yes, who else? Haven't run into any other witches recently, have you? Christ, I hope not! Pity she got away. Not that I blame you. You have letters for me.'

'Yes, Sire.' Straccan proffered the packet, and the king leafed through them.

'De Vesci,' he murmured. 'Well, well, *what* a surprise! And that little sod Mowbray, after all I've done for him. Percy, too, another ingrate. Grellay, he owes me a thousand marks, FitzWalter, de Lacy – all of em northerners. Must be the climate.' He handed the letters to the clerk who followed him about, writing desk hung round his neck, pen and inkhorn always ready. 'This the lot?'

'No, My Lord. We divided them, these for Your Grace, the others for the King of Scots.'

'I'm on my way north, as it happens, for a few words with my brother of Scotland,' John said ominously. 'Didn't meet him yourself, did you? No? I don't suppose he calls me his brother of England,' he added morosely, kicking at a faint-hearted clump of pinks. 'I wouldn't like to think what he calls me. He'll have to be brought to heel again; it's getting to be a habit. What were you doing in Pontigny, by the way?'

It seemed an age ago. 'It's rather a long story, Lord King,' said Straccan.

'Good,' said John, bending and pulling up a wilted something. 'Look at that! Shocking!' He threw it disgustedly down among the sorry-looking roses. 'Carry on, Sir Richard. I like a good story.'

Straccan told him about the icon, and how it led him to Julitta. About Soulis's order for the finger of Saint Thomas. 'That's why I went to see the archbishop,' he said. 'I didn't expect to get anywhere, but I had to try.'

'He's no archbishop of mine,' growled the king.

Whoops, thought Straccan, and said, 'No, My Lord. Your pardon.'

'A figure of speech, I know, I know,' said John. 'Let's go back inside.' On the doorstep he half-turned and shouted, apparently to nobody, 'Get these things *watered*; they're probably dying of thirst. I know I am,' he added to Straccan. 'Come in, come in, I'm expecting someone, and I *do* want to be in when he arrives. How did you get Langton to let you have the relic?' He held out a hand, and a servant placed a cup of wine in it.

'It turned out that he felt himself under some obligation to me. I had done a service to his nephew, years ago, in the Holy Land.'

'Ah,' said John. 'How fortunate! You seem to be a lucky man, Sir Richard. Luck's a strange thing, so unaccountable. Your horse was killed, I'm told.'

Straccan was surprised. If the king's uncanny knowledge of such minutiae was due to Larktwist's report and Larktwist only one of many wandering spies, then John's espionage system must be the envy of Europe. 'Yes, Lord King,' he said. 'By the man-eaters.'

'Well, well,' said the king thoughtfully. 'Pity to lose a good horse. Had him long?'

'Eleven years, My Lord.'

The door opened, admitting a sergeant and two men-at-arms roughly pushing another man before them. 'Ah,' said the king, beaming. 'Sir Gilbert. Feeling better, now, are you?' The man reddened, gazed at the floor like a naughty child and said nothing.

'Gilbert was very sick when first I sent for him,' John told the smirking company in general. 'But it seems my second summons found him recovered. A minor miracle, perhaps? It's been a good year so far for miracles. Why, only this summer a band of white monks from Altraham took their skull of Saint Joseph on the road to raise money, and by God's Grace the rest of the saint's body grew back! They ended up with the whole thing, bar a few toes. Isn't that a marvel? I wonder what happened to the toes.' He looked slyly at Straccan. Oh Christ, thought Straccan, those silly sods, no idea where to stop! And pox take that Larktwist and his big accurate mouth! But he met the royal gaze innocently, and the king smiled.

'Well Gilbert, speak up,' said John cheerfully. 'Cat got your tongue, has it?' He put a handful of grapes in his mouth and began chewing.

'Yes, My Lord, I mean no, My Lord.'

A royal-liveried man appearing in the doorway caught the

king's eye, was beckoned forward, and whispered for a few moments into the royal ear. John nodded, his bright eyes on Sir Gilbert. When the messenger had done, the king snapped his fingers, and a servant popped out of the crowd to give the man a few coins.

'Now,' said John. 'Sir Gilbert. About this business of yours. Do you still maintain that the wreck of the *Sleipnir* is yours to use as you please?'

'I was badly advised, My Lord.'

'God's teeth, I'll say you were!' The king spat a mouthful of grape seeds. 'Oh, sorry, did they land on your sleeve? Never mind, it's a bit behind the fashion, don't you think? You can visit a good tailor while you're here. Now then, you've had the wreck, the crew and the entire bloody cargo, and you thought I'd either not find out or couldn't be bothered to do anything about it, what with all my other troubles, that right? Nice try, Gilbert, but that's *my* money you've been spending; and that's naughty. Oh, don't look so worried! I'm a reasonable man. You can choose.'

'Choose, Sire?'

'Yes. Whether to have my goodwill or not. Up to you.'

'Sire.' Sir Gilbert ran a nervous finger round the sweat-wilted neck of his fine shirt. 'My Lord, it would grieve me to lose your goodwill.' To say nothing of being the end of me, he thought miserably. He'd been a fool to try and keep the wretched wreck a secret. Everyone said there was nothing the king didn't know, and it was true.

The king hummed a snatch of tune and scratched his backside. 'So if you'll just have the cargo sent here as soon as you get home.'

'Of course, Sire.'

'Oh, and I understand there was a passenger, now enjoying your hospitality?'

Oh God, thought Gilbert, he even knows about the woman! 'There were two passengers aboard, Sire: a man and his wife, but he drowned.'

'With a bit of help, was it? Good of you to care for his widow; charity begins at home, that's what I always say. But you can send

253

her along as well, together with her belongings, of course. Clothes, *trinkets* ...' His voice crunched on 'trinkets' and Sir Gilbert winced and failed to meet the hard gooseberry stare. The king knew about the jewellery too. What Gilbert's wife would say when she had to give up that magnificent set of Byzantine bracelets and the rubies, God only knew. Gilbert thought a small pilgrimage would probably be a good idea, to get himself safely away from her tongue for a few months. Not that she'd have run out of things to say even then. Or ever.

'So, Gilbert.' John beamed. 'You admit your fault humbly and wish to make it up to me.'

'Oh yes, Sire.' Fervently.

'After all, just who is king of the English, Gilbert? You, or me?'

'You, Sire.' Squirming.

'Oh *good*,' said John. 'I'm glad that's settled. No need for any of these little misunderstandings at all, really, if you'd *all*' – his stare swept everyone in the room – 'just bear that in mind. And shall we say five hundred marks, Gilbert? As an indication of your remorse? That sound about right?'

'Yes, My Lord.'

'And you might throw in a little sweetener,' the king suggested brightly.

'Sweetener, Sire?'

'Ye-es. To have my goodwill in full measure. No point in half measures, really, is there, when you think about it? What about that big bay horse your son was slopping about on when you arrived?'

'The horse, Sire? Certainly, Sire.'

'Oh thank you, how kind!' The king turned to Straccan. 'Well, there you are, Sir Richard.'

'Pardon, My Lord?'

'Don't say I never did anything for you. The *horse*, man.' He grinned, seeing Straccan's blank face. 'The horse! You can pick it up when you leave. See to it!' He snapped his fingers in the general direction of the gaggle of underlings. Two boys detached themselves from the cluster and rushed to the door together, where one blocked the other's way, kicking him sharply on the shin. The loser let out a yip of pain, yielded the errand to his rival and limped back, scowling.

'Thank you, Sire.' Straccan was truly grateful. He missed Zingiber sadly, and such an animal was a princely gift.

'Quite an adventure you had,' said the king. 'Interesting. What became of the icon, after all? Lose it, did you, in the heat of things?'

'No, Sire,' said Straccan with an inner sigh. He hadn't expected to get away with it, not really. 'In fact, I have it here, My Lord.' He took the icon, in its new wooden case, from his pouch and offered it to the king.

John unrolled the picture and stared at it for some time. Then he rolled it up and slid it back in the case. 'Remarkable,' he said. 'Thank you, Sir Richard.' He pulled on his gloves and made for the door.

'Are you going straight to Durham, Sire?' quavered Sir Gilbert.

'I might,' said the king.

'Only the bridge—'

'Is washed out. I know.'

'There is a back way . . .'

'I *know*,' said John. 'I know the back way to every town in my kingdom.' The door banged behind him.

'I just *bet* he does,' hissed Sir Gilbert, sinking heavily on to the nearest stool. 'Five hundred marks, oh God, and the horse too! *And* the bloody jewellery! My wife will kill me!'

The king put his head round the door. 'Oh, and Gilbert!'

'Oh Jesus! Yes, Sire?'

'The saddle goes with the horse, naturally.'

'Oh, naturally, Lord King!'

Chapter 42

The stallion was a splendid animal, three years old and well trained, and after toying with several possible names Straccan fell back on Zingiber, which really seemed to him the only name for a ginger horse. It was a joy to ride, and the fine saddle fitted man and beast perfectly. Poor Sir Gilbert!

He saw from a long way off the lookout on the watchtower at Stirrup, and heard the warning tocsin begin its familiar cracked clanking. His people were milling about in the open gateway: Adeliza in her best gown, his clerk Peter, Cammo his steward, and the rest. Home! His loving eye noted the crops doing well, the vegetables looking fresh and well tended; his sheep, newly-shorn and skinny-looking, with new lambs at heel – surely that one had twins? Yes! His cattle, heads down and tearing at the grass. Everything in good order.

For the next few days he was fully occupied. There was a backlog of business for him and Peter to deal with, as well as the farm. Cammo managed well, but the master's decision was necessary in some matters: whether or not to buy a bull, whether to sell this year's clip to Walter Durnford as usual or perhaps take it to Lincoln or Nottingham for a better price, whether or not to sell the colt foal born at the new year.

Several times a day he climbed the ladder to the watchtower and spent some time staring at the road where it met the northern horizon, hoping to see three riders. His heart beat faster whenever a cloud of dust appeared and sank when it resolved itself into merchants, pedlars and other travellers. He kept reckoning up the days: the least and most it should take Bane to reach Christchurch and return to Shawl, and then the time to travel from there to here. He was too impatient; they could hardly be looked for yet. Another week, at least ...

But that evening and next morning he was on the watchtower again.

The clanking of the tocsin brought him from the stable at a run but it was only a delivery of wine. Later in the day it clanked again to announce the arrival of a pedlar with his gossip and rubbishy goods. Next day when it clanked to herald yet another nonentity, he lost his temper and bellowed up at the startled watchman. 'Don't ring that bloody thing again! Not until Gilla's coming!' Then he went into his office and worried Peter until he made a mistake in his subtraction and a blot on his page. He wandered into the kitchen where he pried into the cook-pots, picked at a piecrust, knocked over a pitcher of milk and trod on the cat, until a harried Adeliza shooed him out.

Eventually he took an axe and began splitting logs, keeping at it for hours while swallows flicked around him, in and out of the woodshed where they'd built their nests. 'Messy things, shall I clear em out?' Cammo had said years ago. 'Let them be,' Straccan replied. 'I wouldn't like to do all that work for nothing, would you?'

So many days to the south coast, to Christchurch, barring accident or incident; so many days back to Shawl; so many days from Shawl to— And what the hell was that noise? The tocsin was clanking. He dropped the axe, leaped over the logs and ran.

'You look as if you've seen a ghost,' Straccan said. Bane followed him into the office. On the table was the prior's thank-you letter and a bottle of wine. Gilla and Janiva were happily occupied watching the new lambs.

'I have,' said Bane. 'And so have you, so did all of us. We all saw them.' His eyes seemed to gaze through Straccan into the distance.

'What is it? Are you all right?'

'Listen. Sit down and listen,' Bane said. He paced back and forth as he talked. 'I went to the priory. I gave the money to Prior

Ranulf. I told him how I'd met Brother Celestius at Altarwell, and how he turned up again in Scotland and healed me when I was dying. I *was* dying, wasn't I?'

'Oh yes.'

'He asked me, the prior did, when it happened, what day I was healed. The sixth day of June, I told him. Were there witnesses? Oh yes, I said. Were they reliable people? Three knights, I said, and one spy. Can't get much more reliable than that.'

'There have to be witnesses if they want to prove a miracle.'

'I know. He asked me, was I certain of the day? A little scribe chap was writing it all down, and the sub-prior and the sacristan were there, staring at me as if I had two heads. I said yes, it was the sixth day of June without any doubt, Saint Gudwal's day. And then they told me.' Bane picked up his cup; it was empty. He put it down and Straccan refilled it.

'Brother Celestius,' Bane said, 'and all his poor dear loonies were killed in a fire at a hospice near York, on the eve of Saint Pamphilus, seven days before the sixth of June.'

'I don't understand,' said Straccan after a while.

'It was an old wooden building. The pilgrims slept upstairs, and there were fleeces stored below. Somehow they caught fire and went up like thistle down. All the pilgrims were asleep and none of them got out. Fourteen bodies, they found.'

Straccan was silent for some time and then said, 'When you were dying, Blaise and I, and Miles, we wondered ... We thought he might be a saint. Christ, Hawkan, he was a bloody *vision*!'

'That prior is going to get him canonised no matter what it costs. He's already mortgaged most of the priory's lands and sold what he can. They'll be famous. Rich.'

'He wouldn't take any money,' Straccan recalled. 'After he healed you, when he was leaving, we tried to give him some money and he wouldn't take it. Funny ... He took your raisins.'

'I wonder what happened to them? Visions can't eat, can they?' Bane yawned hugely. 'I've got to get to bed for a while. I've never been so tired in my life. How'd you get on with the king?'

'He was very affable,' said Straccan. 'He gave me a horse.'

'Watch out he don't send you the bill for it.' On the bottom step up to the bedchamber, Bane paused. 'Remember the dice that spy gave me?'

'Yes.'

'I got them out, just for a friendly game with a couple of lay brothers at the priory. I opened the box and tipped it on to the board. They leaped up and started yelling. Know what? That little sod had given me his bloody box of maggots instead!'

Straccan laughed. 'I expect it was a mistake,' he said, wiping his eyes.

'Mistake my arse! I hope we meet again, I'll give him bloody maggots!'

The tocsin was clanking. Straccan, about to farewell a knightly client who'd taken the unusual step of coming in person to pay his account, thought – not for the first time – that he really ought to get a decent little bell. He could hear Gilla calling excitedly from the watchtower. 'Father! Father! It's Sir Miles!'

'Excuse me, Sir Walter. A friend is arriving. Won't you stay and meet him?'

'Well, just to say hallo, you know,' said the client, eyes alight with curiosity. 'Must be off soon, though. Promised to pick up the wife from her cousin's; she gets ratty if I'm late.'

Straccan and Miles hugged each other, beaming and both talking at once, as if it was a year since they'd parted and not just a few weeks.

'Nice little place you've got here,' said Miles, admiring in one sweeping glance the lambs, the cabbages, the steaming dung heap, the kitchen cat and Gilla's new blue dress. 'Thank you,' to Adeliza as she offered him a cup of ale. 'That's just what I need, I'm full of dust. Gilla, you've grown. Master Bane, I am glad to see you well. Your servant, Lady,' with an elegant bow to Janiva. 'Richard, I have a message from my uncle.'

'Come into the office,' said Straccan. 'Sir Walter Covelin is there, but he's just leaving. Let me see him off, then we can talk.'

Sir Walter was nosy. He knew Miles's uncle, and assumed the

young knight was either coming from, or going to, some tournament or petty war. What else were knights for, after all?

'No,' said Miles. 'I'm on my way to Scotland, to take service with a friend.' Sir Walter wanted to know who. 'He is old and lives in retirement,' said Miles, not choosing to tell him. 'I shall take care of things for him for a while.'

'Humph.' Sir Walter disapproved. 'Young fella like you should be fightin, not lookin after elderly friends! There's a nice little war comin up in Poitou. That's where I'm goin. Action, that's the stuff! A good fight, and then all the customary rewards of victory. Eh?' He nudged Miles with a bony elbow.

'Rape and pillage,' said Miles.

Sir Walter looked shocked. 'Oh, come now! Nothin like that! We're gentlemen, ain't we?'

'What, then?'

'Well, bit of leg-over, souvenir or two. Not a lot of point otherwise. Eh?'

'See what I mean?' Miles banged his cup down, splashing Sir Walter, who presently took a rather frosty leave of them.

'Come to the bathhouse,' said Straccan. 'We can talk while you bathe and have a change of clothes.'

Miles was in the tub, squeezing the soap bag over his head and shoulders, when Straccan came in with a tunic and hose and house-gown. 'I hope these won't be too tight; you're a bit wider across the back than me, I think. When are you off to Scotland?'

'When I leave here. Uncle William asked me to come. He put the word round to Templars everywhere, asking for news of Julitta and her husband. Arlen was caught trying to find a boat to carry him to Normandy. He had a satchel full of those queer gold coins. The king ordered him put to death.'

Straccan shrugged. That was the price of treason. 'So he's dead.'

'They took the coins and put them in a crucible,' said Miles grimly. 'They tied him down while they melted. Then they poured his Judas gold down his throat.'

Straccan took a deep breath. 'Quite an object lesson.'

'Yes. As for Julitta, she got to France. King Philip is paying her charges but he won't receive her at his court, in case his noble image gets tarnished. The Holy Father's blue-eyed boy can't afford to have his name linked with a witch.'

'And the Arab; what news of him?'

'No sign of him, nor the men that fled with him.'

'How long can you stay with us, Brother?'

'Until Friday. I've arranged to join a company of merchants and pilgrims as far as Durham. I'm to frighten away any robbers!'

'They'll run a mile soon as look at you,' said Straccan.

'How did you get on with the king?' Miles pulled on the tunic and hose and put on the house-robe.

'Very well.' Straccan laughed. 'He gave me a horse and helped himself to the icon.'

'Ah.'

Straccan handed him a towel to rub his hair. There was a soft knock at the door and Gilla put her head round. 'Father? May I speak to Sir Miles?'

'Come, pigeon.'

She smiled happily. 'Sir Miles, you'll be going to the place where Hob is, won't you?'

'To Coldinghame. Yes.'

'Will you take a message from me?'

'Gladly.'

'Just say that I send my love to him always.'

When she left, Miles said, 'How is it with her?'

Straccan frowned. 'Mercifully, she seems to remember little. But she said a strange thing. She said she saw her mother; that Marian was there, and took care of her.'

Between Wednesday and Friday Straccan was never able to find Janiva alone. Sometimes she was with Gilla – he was overjoyed by the love that had sprung up between them – or they were both with Miles, or she was in the kitchen exchanging recipes with Adeliza, or they were riding or playing Hoodman Blind, or Janiva was teaching Gilla a new dance, or Miles was entertaining everyone with an astonishing repertoire of ballads. Still, there would be time later to talk. And before long, they would be married.

When Miles left, all the household turned out to see him off. Gilla hugged and kissed him and cried.

'I'm not going away for ever, sweet,' he said. 'I'll come back and see you again.'

'Promise?'

'Of course I promise. Nothing can stop me. Besides, Adeliza makes the best ale in all England. But where's Mistress Janiva this morning? I hoped she'd wish me God speed.'

'I don't know,' Gilla said. 'She was up before me. Yesterday she said something about the herbs in the water-meadow. Perhaps she's gone there.'

'See if you can find her, poppet,' said Straccan. 'She'll be sorry to miss Miles leaving.'

But Janiva was nowhere about, and at last they waved Miles off. Gilla ran up the tower steps, to watch him until he disappeared in the distance. She leaned her head against Straccan's hip. 'I hate goodbyes.'

'Well, honey, if there were no goodbyes there would be no happy returns, now would there?' He swung her up and carried her, laughing, down the steps.

Somehow the place didn't feel quite the same, as if it missed the young knight with his singing and laughter. If places could miss people, Straccan thought, Stirrup was missing someone.

He began to feel uneasy. She'd not have forgotten Miles's departure. Perhaps she had hurt herself in the water-meadow. It was a long way from the house. The certainty of something wrong grew fast.

'Adeliza, did Mistress Janiva say where she was going?'

'I haven't seen her this morning, Sir.'

'She said something about picking herbs in the water-meadow.'

'Oh no, I don't think so. She hasn't taken the basket or the shears. She always takes them when she's—'

He went up the stairs to the bedchamber three at a time. The bed she'd shared with Gilla was tidy and smooth. The pegs where her mantle and travelling cloak had hung were bare. The leather satchel she'd brought with her, which had been at the foot of the bed, was not there now.

He made for the stable at a run. Her palfrey was gone.

He flung a saddle on Zingiber and spurred out of the gate. North, she'd have to go north; she could only be going home, but why? Why run away? He wanted to marry her, wanted her here, safe with himself and Gilla. Here to say goodbye to when he went away, to be waiting when he came back. At his table. In his bed. His wife.

She had only gone half a league when he came up with her. Hearing hoofs, she looked back and saw him, and stopped. When he reached her he saw tears on her face and lashes. He dismounted and lifted her down. He could feel her trembling.

'Why?' he said. 'Why run away from me?'

'Richard—'

'I want you to stay. We'll be married.'

'No!' she cried. 'That's why I left. You're right, I ran away, and I'm sorry, but I knew you would ask me. We *can't* marry, Richard!'

'Why not?'

'It wouldn't work.' She turned her face away, wiping at her tears with the back of her hand.

'Why not? What's wrong? I know you love me.'

'That's got nothing to do with it.'

'Then explain it to me!'

She sighed. 'You are a knight,' she said. 'My mother was villein. Knights don't marry freedwomen.'

'More fool them,' said Straccan. 'Knights can bloody well please themselves! I don't believe that's all that's worrying you.'

'No. Richard, it would do you no good – it could do you much harm – to have people say your wife is a witch.'

'A witch?'

She stared at his stunned face and laughed. 'Oh, Richard, didn't you realise? That's what they call women like me.'

'No, he protested. 'A witch? Julitta is a witch, not you!'

'Yes, me! She chose a dark path, because it promised to lead her to power. But to begin with we would have been much alike. She hurts, I heal. I love, she hates. Two faces of one coin, Richard, but both are called witch.'

He said nothing but stared at the trees and the sky, unseeing, trying to find the right words to shake her argument. After a while she walked away from him and sat on the grass under an oak tree. She had not mentioned the strange experience by the stream and the unease that had troubled her ever since. She would not involve him, or Gilla, in that. It was for her to deal with. Her palfrey whickered softly. She closed her eyes and leaned back against the warm rough trunk. The sun shone on her face, and then his shadow darkened her closed eyelids.

'It doesn't make any difference,' he said.

'Richard—'

'No, listen. Freedwoman, witch, whatever you are, I want to marry you. Because I love you, Janiva. Understand? If you want to go home now I'll take you, but I'll keep coming back until you see sense.'

'See it your way, you mean,' she said, but he had turned to catch Zingiber's reins and didn't hear her.

He'd take her home. She needed time to think about it. When she'd thought about it, she'd see she was wrong.

She loved him. He knew she did. He'd bring her round.

Prologue

Mid-winter, and the wind still came scything from the east, its howl drowning the chanting of monks and nuns shivering in the church. Candle flames dipped and swayed, flaring in the draught and casting strange shadows. If only it would snow, said the farmers and thralls huddled round their fires – snow would dull the bitter edge; but although the clouds massed heavy and dirty yellow, the snow that should have fallen still held back, and nothing softened the stone-hard ground or the sharp vicious outlines of leafless trees.

Mid-winter, and day by day for weeks the ice had spread and thickened until now the island of Avallon was an island no more; folk could walk dryshod instead of poling their flat boats to the convent's jetty.

Mid-winter, in the year of Our Lord five hundred and sixty-five, and in her stone cell on a narrow bed lay an old woman, dying hard. For thirty years she had lived within these walls and the world outside had forgotten all but her name, which men would remember for ever. Her confessor prayed, a tall dark rook of a man; and two nuns tended her, wiping the death sweat from her face and chafing her cold hands.

She was not aware of them. Behind her flickering eyelids she was young again, bride of Arthur, the warlord who called himself king. He was in her dream, seated in his hall with his captains. There they were, Bedwyr, Cei, Drustan, Gawain; she could see them, she could even smell them – leather, iron, sweat, and blood.

She woke, heart hammering, fearful eyes staring past pools of candlelight into the shifting shadows. Her fingers plucked at the coarse blanket and her cracked lips moved.

'Who's there?'

'Dear Mother,' said Sister Berenice tenderly. 'Be at peace. We are here and God is here.'

Of course He was. God was everywhere, even in Camlodd . . . Camlodd! Sinking back into the dream she rode again through muddy vennels between traders' stalls, where little brown pigs rootled, grunting around folks' legs. She could smell the throat-catching reek of dung, tanning, brewing, rancid fat, sour milk and smoke, and heard again the sounds of battle, horses neighing, men shouting, women screaming and the shrill cries of children.

But the stronghold of Camlodd was gone, laid waste long ago, destroyed so thoroughly that no one was even sure where it once stood, or could say, 'Here was Arthur's hall, here Guinevere's bower.' It had become legend: Camlodd, that had been no more than a squalid huddle of huts and stables around Arthur's hall, with the heads of enemies stuck on the stockade posts, stinking and shrivelling until at last the skulls of kings and warriors fell to the ground to be kicked about by little boys.

Camlodd was gone, Arthur too, and his captains. Gone, Cei and Bedwyr, Gawain and Gwalchmai, and – so they said but Guinevere knew better – Medrawt. Sometimes, when her shields of prayer and penance were lowered in the unguarded moments when sleep took her, or as she woke, she heard his bodiless voice calling her name.

For thirty years she had mortified the guilty flesh that had yearned for Medrawt, lacerating her skin with the lash, tormenting it with a hair shirt, ulcerating her knees to the bone on cold stones, praying for the souls of those who had died because of her lust; all but one. She did not pray for Medrawt.

Something touched her face. Warm, wet. Tears. Sister Gruach was weeping. Guinevere touched the young nun's hand. 'My daughter . . .'

These were her only children, no child had been born of her body. If she had given Arthur a son, would men still have turned from him to Medrawt? Thousands might have lived; Camlodd itself might still stand had she not been barren. But she was not to blame.

Virgin she had gone as bride to Arthur's bed, and ten years later, virgin to Medrawt.

Medrawt . . .

'*Still here, old woman? Not dead yet? I am waiting for you.*'

'Lord Jesus, protect me . . .'

Father Magnus bent, his ear to her lips to catch the faint breath. 'The Banner,' she whispered. 'Bring it to me.'

He fetched it from the altar, Avallon's treasure, in its precious case of garnet-crusted gold, the dragon-blazoned war banner of Arthur; and more precious still, stitched between its doubled layers of heavy silk, a relic beyond all price: a linen cloth stained with the blood of Christ.

Reverently Magnus placed the reliquary in Guinevere's hands. She fumbled with the clasp, and as he bent to help her the distant chanting stopped and the screaming began. There was a clash of weapons. Nuns and priest stared at one another in sudden terror. They knew what it was, they had all heard it at some time in their lives.

'Raiders!'

'God have mercy on us!'

Berenice slammed the door and leaned against it – there was no bar. Magnus bent over the dying woman, touching her eyelids and lips with his crucifix and holy oil.

There were shouts and rushing feet in the passage. An axe blade split the door which fell inward under blows that burst its hinges, crushing Berenice beneath. The raiders pushed into the room, a nightmare of helmets and grinning teeth, brandishing swords and axes oily with blood.

'Don't hurt her,' Magnus cried, standing between death and the dying with arms outspread. 'She is a most holy lady, and was a great queen!'

But in seconds the cell was a shambles, the priest speared to the wall, the old nun's worthless carcass hacked, kicked aside and trodden underfoot. Gruach flung herself across Guinevere's body, but was seized and stripped, her value as slave or bedmate expertly, brutally assessed: young, fair, virgin – worth keeping.

The chief of the raiders snatched the reliquary from the dying woman's hands, laughing with pleasure at its weight and richness. The plain silver ring on her swollen finger was a paltry thing, but Borri let nothing pass, not even a trifle such as this. He cut off the finger.

Guinevere died.

Borri opened the reliquary, discovering the fabric rolled within. 'What's this?'

'That's a treasure of the Cross-God,' said a thrall, one of the convent's kitchen slaves and fellow-countryman of the raiders whom he had let in at the back door. 'They keep it on the altar. A mighty talisman. Very magical.'

'Magic?' Borri shook out the heavy silk, and the scarlet embroidered dragon quivered as if it breathed. 'What does it do?'

The thrall questioned Gruach and turned triumphantly to Borri. 'Long ago,' he said, 'their god was murdered. The night before he died he was in a garden. He was afraid, she says,' he added disgustedly, 'and the sweat of his terror turned to blood.'

'Gods fear nothing,' said Borri. 'But I have heard this Cross-God is a womanish thing that fears blood and battle and the business of men.'

The thrall nodded. 'True, master. One of the god's servants, *Yosif* by name, mopped up the blood with a linen clout. Christians value such stuff. That,' pointing at the pennant, 'has a bit of the cloth sewn inside it.' He jabbered at the nun again, heard her reply and continued. '*Yosif* came to this land, and that talisman brought him great wealth while he lived. That was long ago, but later Arthur Pendragon, the one called the Bear, had it sewn into this pennant to give him victory in battle.'

Borri snorted. 'He was defeated.'

'That was because he lost the talisman and his luck with it. His sister's son Medrawt stole it. There was a battle where each slew the other. After that the talisman was brought here. It has great powers, this woman says.'

'I'll keep it,' said Borri after some thought. 'Let it bring wealth to me, my kin and my friends.'

Gruach snatched at his arm mouthing nonsense. He shook her off, looking at the slave for translation.

'She wants someone to bury the old woman. She says she was once queen of this country.'

'Torch the place,' said Borri. 'We dig no holes for their carrion.'

'She says the old one was Arthur's queen.'

At that there was an uneasy silence. Arthur had been dead for thirty years but his fame was very great.

Borri frowned. 'It would not be wise to offend such a ghost as his. We will bury his old woman.'

They buried her in the leafless winter-bitten orchard and heaved the great altar slab off its base to lie over her grave. They fired the convent, took their captives and plunder and moved quickly onto the next settlement, the next rich church.

A trail of bloody destruction led back to their ships in the river called Sabrina. Two nights ago they had landed there and marched inland to Avallon, leaving a smoking spoor of crows and corpses. They met no defence for in winter no one feared sea raiders; like everyone else, they stayed at home by their firesides. But a spae-wife had told Borri to fare forth over sea and win great fortune. She gave true rede. When at last they turned back, their plunder filled three long carts.

Two ships foundered on the way back, but Borri's, carrying the talisman, was spared. At home, he set it in the place of honour, but was careful to placate Odin with a blood offering.

A man needed all the gods he could get on his side.

Chapter 1

It began like any other Showing Day. Who could have foreseen it would end in the abbey's ruin?

Pilgrims had been turning up since dawn. Laughing, chattering, singing and cheering, some drunk, some weeping, some propping along others in worse case than themselves. By midday the queue had grown quite long, a hundred or so. Some brought food, others fasted. A few of them seemed whole, but mostly they were a collection of the afflicted – harelipped, wry-necked, club-footed, goitrous, pocked, scrofulous, limbless, blind, deaf, mute, palsied, tubercular, deformed and insane. Some walked, some limped, some crutched and some crawled. Some were self-propelled on little trolleys, paddled along by the hands, or else levered themselves forward on hand-trestles. Others were led, pushed, dragged or carried; the hopeful, the hopeless, young and old, the living, the dying and occasionally – carried by friends or relatives – the already dead.

The great doors of the church opened and the queue began to shuffle forward. They were let in a few at a time and looked over, shut up, exhorted, and suitably intimidated by the sacristan, Brother Harold, whose skull-faced severity put the fear of God into the most obstinately cheerful spirit. The senior brethren had seen the uninhibited goings-on at many another shrine and they weren't having any of that *here*, thank you very much! Pilgrims the worse for drink were weeded out at the door, and any misbehaving once inside were collared and hauled away by burly Brother Simon.

By the time the hopefuls had been inspected, sorted, preached at, rebuked, dusted and tweaked into tidier presentability, most of them were quite deflated. Then they were made to kneel and only managed a timid cheer when the relic, the hand of Saint Derfel, was held up to their eager eyes; creeping out afterwards like chastened children while the next bunch was admitted.

The hand had a notable history of miracles in the past but in recent years its reputation had fallen off. Fashions come and go, in saints as in garments, and Derfel was no longer popular. Like many other shrines throughout the realm this one had lost out to Becket. Fifty years ago there would have been a thousand or more pilgrims here. The flood had become a trickle. Nevertheless, twice a year on the Showing Days some pilgrims still came, and from midday to dusk the relic lay in full view on the altar.

It was not imposing. Its original reliquary, a jewelled silver gilt casket in the shape of a hand, had been sold, for with the decline of offerings the priory was feeling the pinch. Now, when not on show, the hand was kept in a plain wooden box. The priory had grown disenchanted with its relic; instead of locking it carefully away with the prescribed ritual and prayers at dusk the brethren more often scurried off to their suppers and left the hand lying on the altar, sometimes all through the night until Prime.

There it lay, claw-like, mummified, brown. Most pilgrims were permitted merely to touch the faded purple silk bands tied round the stump of the wrist; these hung down over the edge of the altar for that purpose, their ends blackened and frayed from innumerable fingers, kisses and tears. The more pitiable, however, were privileged to be touched with it.

Outside, a fashionably dressed man had been watching the queue. Fine clothes strained around his broad belly, and the brimmed and feathered cap pulled well down over his eyebrows and shadowing his fat face couldn't hide the ugly red pits and furrows left by smallpox. Not until evening did he join the queue. By then the crowd was thinning and drifting away, locals heading for home and travellers for the Maison Dieu or more interesting places to spend the night. Small parties had set off already to reach other towns before nightfall.

The dandy tipped a boy to hold his horse, and tacked on at the end.

It was damp and perishing cold inside the church. The candles had burned low and the fiery sinking sun shone through small panes of precious coloured glass in the centre of the western window, splashing rainbows over the stone floor. As the pilgrims shuffled, some on their knees, towards the altar, their flesh and garments were tinted violet and emerald, ruby and amber. A child crouched, patting the coloured flagstones, smiling at the play of colours over his small scabby hands. His mother yanked him to his feet, whispering loudly, 'Don't let them bloody monks see you muckin about!' Harold scowled at her. The child's upturned snotty face, lit red and green, was marred by a harelip.

This was the last group and the guardian monks, chilled through, were stamping their cold feet, yawning, scratching and huffing warm breath on their fingers, their minds on supper. The pilgrims were relieved of their offerings, mere fourthings and half-pence for the most part, before they trooped out. The dandy came last.

As he bent his knee at the altar he glanced back over his shoulder; the monks were already vanishing through the door into the slype, which led to cloister, wash house and refectory. The door squeaked shut behind them and the dandy heard the key turned in the outside lock.

Now only one monk remained in the church to herd the pilgrims out, the dandy coming last with the gaunt figure of Brother Harold right behind him, ready to close and lock the great doors.

The dandy unhooked a flask from his belt and handed it with a coin to the boy waiting with his horse. He made a shivering noise with his lips.

'Brrr! Is cold, no? Get this filled. Wine, not ale, and urry!'

A Frog, thought Brother Harold with instant Saxon dislike. The boy handed the Frog his reins and ran to the nearest pothouse. The Frog gave Harold, who was hoping for more, two pennies, then clapped a hand to his belt for his gloves and found them missing. He turned back to the doors which Harold, coming forward to take the pennies, had left ajar.

'*Sangdieu! Mes gants!* I ave forget ze gloves. Old ze orse!'

Before the monk could object the Frog had shoved the reins into his hands and darted back inside. The horse shifted its feet, stamped, sidled and snorted. Harold eyed it with irritation and clung on. After only a few moments the Frog emerged, pulling on one elaborately embroidered and tasselled glove and carrying the other.

'*Merci, mon frère.*' Heaving himself into the saddle, he trotted towards the Maison Dieu where the boy, coming with his flask, met him.

When he had closed and locked the doors Brother Harold, blissfully unaware that he'd be kicking himself for ever more, hurried around the side of the church to the warming house.

Tuppence, he thought disgustedly. *The fat Frog was a miserly sod.*

The fat Frog trotted sedately southward. After he'd gone a mile or so, he hooked the uncomfortable wax plumpers from inside his cheeks and tossed them aside into the bushes. Under his padded garments he was neither fat nor French but English: Sir Richard Straccan, former crusader but now buyer and seller – and not for the first time stealer – of precious relics.

Five miles from Cheringham he turned off the road, urging his hired nag to an unwilling gallop over rough country to Belmarie Wood. Dismounting, he led the horse in among the trees along ever narrower paths until he came to the clearing where his servant, Hawkan Bane, sat comfortably cooking sausages over a small bright fire. Two hobbled horses whickered softly in greeting as Bane scrambled to his feet.

'You're late,' he said. 'Any longer and I'd have scoffed the lot. How'd it go?'

'Give me a sausage, for God's sake,' said Straccan. 'Here.' He passed the relic to Bane and seized the skewer of sausages from the flames.

'Mind,' said Bane. 'They're – '

'Ow!'

' – hot. Any trouble?'

'Not so far, but we'd best put a few more miles behind us while the moon shines, and get rid of this nag. Someone might recognise it.'

No one was likely to recognise him. He peeled the lurid flour-and-paint scars from his face and wolfed six sausages before shedding the Frog's garb and donning his own breeks, shirt and jerkin. Wadding the discarded hat, gloves and padded clothes into a tight bundle he shoved them well down into the middle of a tangle of brambles.

Wrapping the relic with great care, first in a piece of silk and then in sheep's wool, Bane stowed it in a leather satchel which Straccan buckled to his belt. They packed up the small camp and put the fire out, careful to cover all traces.

The moon was right overhead when they struck on the worn and muddy line of Watling Street. Barring accidents they expected to reach Bromfield the day after tomorrow.

Prior and community at Bromfield would be well pleased and not a little astonished. The relic had been stolen from them – they said – seventy years ago, when the Empress Maud's army sacked the priory and burned the church. Some years later, the thief, dying, had bestowed his looted treasure upon the abbey at Cheringham, hoping to bluff his way past Saint Peter with the aid of the monks' prayers. Civilised requests over the years from Bromfield's Benedictines for the relic's return had been met with scorn, insults and even blows from Cheringham's Praemonstratensians. Hiring Straccan to steal it back had been a final act of desperation; the brethren of Bromfield never really expected to see the holy hand again.

That wouldn't stop them trying to screw the price down!